FAE'S CAPTIVE

TAYLOR & LEANDER

LILY ARCHER

FAE'S CAPTIVE

TAYLOR & LEANDER

Lily Archer
Copyright © 2019 Lily Archer

Cover Art by Deranged Doctor Designs

Copy Editing by Spell Bound

FAE'S CAPTIVE

1

TAYLOR

*M*y roommate is a terror. Stumbling in at all hours of the night with strange men in tow, raiding the mini-fridge and devouring my food, leaving her clothes all over our dorm room, rarely going to class, and refusing to clean a single thing.

"Why did you even decide to go to college?" I grumble under my breath as I scoop up her clothes from yesterday and dump them into the hamper.

"Not my idea."

I jump as she strides in and slams the door behind her.

"My dad insisted." She yawns and falls into her bed fully clothed, her stiletto heels from last night still strapped to her feet. Her long blonde hair fans out over her pillow and she drapes one willowy arm across her eyes. "Keep it down, will you? I'm tired."

"It's noon." I stare at her. "I have a study partner coming over. And have you seen my black jacket with the Gryffindor patch on the front? I can't find—"

A heavy snore rises from her delicate nose.

I run a hand through my light brown hair and yank at the strands. When I agreed to her as a roommate, it was out of desperation. I couldn't afford a single room, and Cecile looked great on paper—a fellow junior who shared many of my same interests. So, I chose her as my roomie. Mistake. It didn't take long to figure out that her entire roommate questionnaire had been copied from someone else—someone who *should have* been my roommate. Instead, I got Cecile, replete with her spoiled ways, her utter disdain for me, and her weird quirks.

"Hey."

I startle as she opens one eye and stares at me.

"Yeah?"

"What's today?"

"Tuesday."

The one eye rolls. "No, dummy. I mean what's the date."

"Don't call me names." I grind my teeth, but answer her, "October 27."

The eye opens wide. "Already?"

What was I supposed to say to that?

"That was quick." She sits up, her slinky red dress stained with something dark along the front. Wine I'd guess, from the smell of her.

"Yeah, that's sort of how time works." I toss a Hot Pocket wrapper—it was my last one, devoured by Cecile, of course—into the garbage. "It passes."

"Hey." She smiles. She never smiles at me. "What are you doing tonight?"

"What? I'm busy." I back up a step and grab my

phone to cancel with my study partner. No way I'd force Cecile on another victim.

"Let's go out." Her eyes brighten, the hangover suddenly gone.

I cock my head at her, not sure if my hearing was shot. "Go out?"

"Yeah." Her smile widens. "We should party."

I don't party. I study. I work at the student union. I tutor in what little free time I have. Everything I do is designed to either get good grades or make money so I can eat. Partying isn't in my repertoire, and Cecile knows that. "No thanks."

"Oh, come on." She rubs her hands together. "It'll be fun. We can pregame here and then hit the frat houses."

"It's *Tuesday*." I grab my worn gray backpack from my bed.

"So?" She sits up, her big gray eyes focusing on me for the first time in months. "We can still have a good time."

"No, but thanks." I grip the door handle.

Her tone changes, going colder. "I'll pay you."

"What?" I turn to look at her.

"I'll pay you." Her voice lightens in an ugly, forced way. "To be my designated driver."

"Since when do you care about driving drunk?" Half the time I had no idea how she made it back to the dorm room. The other half, her red sports car would be triple parked in front of the building.

"Since tonight. Safety first from now on. And like I said, I'll pay you." She twirls a lock of her blonde hair around a thin finger. "I'll give you a hundred bucks just to drive me to the parties and then back here."

I want to turn the handle and walk out of the room. But money is money. It would take four tutoring appointments to make that much cash, or I could take it from Cecile while sitting in her car and doing homework as she got shitfaced at the frat houses.

"Let's make it two hundred." She grabs her little crystal-encrusted crossbody and opens it, thumbing through several bills before pulling some out. "And I'll pay half up front."

I can't turn it down, and she knows it. Cecile may be a reprobate, but she's shrewd. I've noticed that about her —those light gray eyes don't miss much, even when they're bloodshot.

With a sigh, I walk over to her and reach for the money.

She pulls it away. "Meet me out front at nine."

"Fine." I hold out my hand.

She smiles, her teeth perfectly even and white. "Then we have a deal."

When I take the money, a shiver runs down my spine. She's eerily perfect up close.

Cecile lies back on her bed and flings her arm back into place, and I back away.

"Taylor," she calls, her voice already fading into sleep.

"What?" I open the door.

"Don't forget. Nine o'clock. Where I come from, if you break a deal, the punishment isn't pretty."

"You come from Long Island." I shake my head and shoulder my backpack. "And I'll be there."

Her freight train of a snore follows me down the hall.

"Let's go." Cecile is wearing a red tank top and a black miniskirt. And nothing else. Even though fall arrived with a vengeance the week before, Cecile doesn't seem to mind the cold.

"I thought I was driving," I protest as she strides to the driver's side.

"You are, but not until after the parties." She opens the door. "Get in."

I yank my door open and toss my heavy backpack between the seats.

She starts the car, the foreign machinery purring to life. I think the engine is actually in the trunk. "You sure you don't want any?" She pulls a silver flask from the center console, takes a long swig, then offers it to me.

I gawk. "You're *driving*."

"It'll be fine." She shrugs and puts the car in reverse, tires squealing as she backs up.

I grip the door handle.

"Scared?" She smiles, and it's a real one. I can tell because there's no warmth in it.

"Let's get to the party in one piece, okay?"

"Sure thing." She guns it out of the dorm parking lot and hits Campus Drive too hard, the car bottoming out on the pavement for a second, then lurching forward.

"Jesus!" I grip my seatbelt with one hand and the door handle with the other.

"Don't worry. I need you alive."

I snap my gaze to her. "What?"

"Nothing." She laughs. "I just mean I need you alive to drive me home."

My fingers wander to my necklace, touching the opal stone that is the only permanent thing in my life.

"Clutching your throat again?" She turns to look at me even though she's speeding through campus, her hand shifting the car's gears effortlessly. "You must be nervous."

I drop my hand back to the seatbelt. "You drive like a maniac. Of course I'm nervous."

Her high laugh causes goosebumps to rise along my arms. "Don't worry. We're almost there."

She's right, the row of Georgian mansions appears to our left, each frat house decorated with a large insignia of Greek letters. Though it's a Tuesday night, loud music wafts from every other building, and plenty of students mill around with red Solo cups in hand.

She double parks in front of Omega Nu and kills the engine. "Be a good little virgin and wait here, okay?" She smirks. I want to deny it, but there's no point. It's one of her favorite barbs, and my reaction gives away the truth every time she levels that word at me.

Reaching behind her seat, she pulls out an unopened bottle of water. "Here, I got this for you."

I take it, my eyebrows hitting my hairline. Cecile never did anything for anyone other than herself.

"Stay hydrated. I'll need you on top of things tonight." She checks her face in the mirror, her red lips still perfect. "Be back in a bit."

I stow the water in the cupholder as she gets out. Once her door slams, I pull my backpack up front and drag out my chemistry book along with my laptop. The tight interior of the sports car isn't the best for doing homework, but I'd rather be in here than the frat house or outside in the cold. So, I get to work.

After about an hour of sketching molecules, I yawn and look up. The Omega Nu house is hopping, all the lights on and the front door wide open. Rap music muscles its way into the night, and more people have arrived, the front porch littered with chatty couples and smokers.

I sigh and reach for the water. For some reason, I stare at the cap and make sure it's factory sealed. It's stuck tight to the little plastic ring. Maybe Cecile isn't going to poison me after all. I unscrew it and take a big drink, then another.

Returning to my drawing, I sketch an octagon, then peer at the combination of chemicals I'm supposed to be rendering. Something warm blooms in my stomach. I blink, my eyes tearing up.

"What the..." I drop my pencil, and my laptop lists to the right.

I get even warmer, sweat breaking out across my forehead as my vision goes wavy. Something's wrong. Bad wrong. I paw at the door handle. If I can get out, I can get the people on the porch to help me. But I can't get a grip. The handle seems to be covered in butter.

Without warning, the door opens.

Cecile drops down to her haunches, her face a blur. "About time."

"What took so long?" Another girl, her image shadowy, prowls around behind Cecile. Her voice is familiar.

"What did you do?" My words slur.

"It's time." Cecile tweaks my nose. "For you to go."

"Go where?" My body slumps back, my muscles going lax.

"Let's get this done." The other girl. The too-familiar voice. She moves closer, a faintly curious look on her face. On *my* face.

Chills shoot through me, fighting with the heat that seems to be burning me from the inside out. She has my face! She's even wearing my clothes, the black jacket with the Gryffindor logo that I thought I'd lost. This is a hallucination. I must have fallen asleep in the car. *Wake up. Wake up. Wake the fuck up!*

"You sure cut it close. The ley line wouldn't have lasted another day," I said. But it wasn't *me*. It was the one with my face and favorite jacket.

Cecile shrugged. "I'm getting it done."

"What is going on, Ceci—" My voice fails, my eyelids closing despite all my effort to keep them open.

"You'll see." With a gleeful laugh, she slams the door.

Everything goes black.

2

LEANDER

The assassin writhes as I press my iron blade into his shoulder.

"Tell me who sent you, and all this will be over." I walk around the male, his silver eyes fixed on me as he bares his fangs.

"The king beyond the mountain," he grits out.

"Funny." I pull another iron blade from my pack, the metal sizzling against my palm. "You're the third would-be assassin I've caught and also the third to say that." I dig the blade into his thigh, twisting as I go.

This time he groans, his face contorting with pain. Good.

"There is no realm beyond the Gray Mountains. No king. Not even any fae. So who are you talking about?" I turn the knife a little more.

"The king beyond the mountain." He pins me with an icy glare. "One day soon, you will kneel at his feet before he takes your head."

"He's your king, then?" I cross my arms and stare down at him.

He doesn't respond.

"This king you speak of, he's responsible for the disappearances of lesser fae such as yourself?"

"Not *lesser*. Not in his kingdom!" He snaps his teeth at me. "You are no king, not of me or any of my brethren. The winter realm will fall and you with it."

That was new information. Whoever this king was, he had an agenda beyond taking my head. He wanted much, much more. I'd suspected as much, though he seemed fixated on my realm. I'd had no reports of attempts on other rulers.

"Whatever he's promised you and your kind, it's a lie." I pull my finishing blade from my pack.

"You're the lie. You and all the rest. When he comes, he will burn all, cleanse all, and destroy the realms."

"Seems like he's got a lot on his plate." I flip the iron blade in the air and catch it. "So I'll give him a hand and take care of his talkative assassin."

"My king will reign!" His yell is cut off by my blade, but not before a knock sounds at my door.

I throw up a cloaking spell around the male as his soul departs to the Spires, then approach the door.

"Yes?"

"My lord." A representative of the summer realm bows low, but not low enough. "The guards suggested there might be an issue? There have been ... noises." He peers at me.

I throw my shoulders back, highlighting the grave

differences in our statures. "You disturb me based on idle prattle from your guards?"

"Problem?" Gareth strides up, his lanky frame dwarfing the guards posted outside.

"Ah—" The courtier swallows hard as he stares at both of us—two battle-hardened fae from the winter realm. "No. No problem. Apologies, my lord." The courtier bows and backs up, his jeweled sash glittering in the light and his perfectly-coifed white hair wisping slightly. "We simply want to make sure your stay in the summer realm is to your liking."

"Sweltering heat, simpering courtiers, and a postponed meeting about the ongoing disappearances? No, it's not to my liking." I glower.

Gareth walks into my room and heads to where my cloaking spell lingers. My second-in-command snorts with amusement but says nothing.

"Tonight, my lord. The conclave is set for this evening." The courtier stumbles over his words and backs away slowly. "It will go off as planned, I can assure you. Queen Aurentia is just as concerned as you are."

I doubt that, given that the vast majority of disappearances have been from the winter realm, *my* realm. The perfumed peacocks of the summer court care only for themselves. I was a fool to come here, but I will do anything I can to help my people. They deserve nothing less from their king.

"It had better be tonight." I glower at the bejeweled buffoon. "For your sake." I back up and slam the door.

"Who's the stiff?" Gareth hitches his thumb at the dead assassin.

"Another one from the king beyond the mountain." I stare at the brand on the assassin's neck, a twisted black tree, the same mark the others bore.

"You should have sent for me." He pulls his silver knife from his belt and twirls it in his palm. The jagged scar on the right side of his face looks particularly stark here in the summer realm, where flowers and greenery seem to soften every rough edge except ours.

I shrug. "I handled it."

"I'm here to watch your back."

"You do that just fine." I stride to him and peruse the bloody mess.

He shakes his head. "You're king now, Leander. You can't put yourself at risk. This isn't the same as when we were on the battlefield. I need to know when there's any sort of threat. You can't just handle things on your own. You know that. If we want to maintain the peace we fought so hard for, you have to put aside the warrior and live as the king. Find your mate and—"

"I can't force my mate to appear, Gareth." I try to run a hand through my hair, but my silver crown stops me. How many times had I wished for my mate? Only the ancestors knew. But no winter realm high fae have felt the mate bond in 150 years, not since I defeated the necromancer and won the throne. Some dark magic took hold as I twisted my blade through his black heart, and none have been able to break it since.

"I know you can't will it. But she will come, and then with an heir, we will finally be past the dark days. The necromancer's curse can't last forever. I won't give up on finding my mate, and neither should you." He squeezes my shoulder just like he'd done so many times when we were soldiers, before I was king.

He's right of course, and that fact grates at me. The winter realm is mine to rule, but my throne was hard-won over centuries of bloodshed. The winter fae are a harsh people, wily and dark. But with the establishment of my reign, we finally have a tenuous peace amongst the high fae, lesser fae, and the summer realm. It is up to me to preserve it.

Gareth lets out a long-suffering sigh, then kicks the dead fae's chair. "He tell you anything?"

"More of the same. But he did add that the mountain king doesn't just want me dead, apparently. He's after the realms. All of them."

"Him and what army?" Gareth pulls my blades free and wipes them on the assassin's tunic.

A streak of foreboding careens through me. "That's what we need to find out."

3

TAYLOR

*S*omething tickles my nose. I swat at it, but it doesn't go away. My eyes open slowly, achingly. What's wrong with me?

A flash of memory darts across my mind—a nightmare of myself standing next to Cecile in a dark parking lot. I sit up and knock my head on something hard and unyielding.

"Ow!" Putting a hand to my head, I fall back onto a bed of scratchy hay, some of it once again tickling my nose.

"Shh." A harsh whisper nearby.

"Who's there?" I press one palm to my aching forehead and turn to look into the gloom.

"Shh!" This one is even more urgent.

I can't make out much, just some sort of room with hay on the floor and—wait, are those bars? My breath leaves in a whoosh, and I scoot sideways until the air above me is clear. I'd been lying on the bottom level of a crude sort of bunkbed carved into a stone wall. My jeans and t-shirt are gone, replaced with a crude shift dress, the material rough against my skin. I press my hand to my neck, a hint of relief blooming in my mind when I feel the necklace.

My eyes aren't accustomed to the dark as I move toward the bars, but I keep staring hard, trying to find the source of the shushing voice. All I see is hay and gray walls.

"Hello?" I whisper.

"Do you want a bloodletting?" The hay to my left shifts, and a pair of eyes peer at me.

"Where are—"

A clanging noise shatters the stillness. I jump as heavy footsteps approach, the sound paired with what sounds like sharp nails raking against stone.

I scurry back beneath the stone bunkbed and press myself against the wall. My head throbs from where I knocked it earlier, and my pounding heartbeat doesn't help.

"Great. Just great." The eyes disappear, the hay settling.

A hissing voice, one that slithers up my spine, echoes off the walls. It's heavily accented and speaks a foreign language. A rhythmic rustling noise grows louder with each second.

The instinct to hide, to somehow melt into the stone behind me, rushes through me. But there is nowhere to go. The one spot where the hay is thickest is already taken.

The voice is closer now, and I stare into the darkness outside the bars.

I press my palm to my mouth to stop any noise from escaping. But my body shakes, everything inside me freezing up and rattling.

Movement catches my eye, and a monstrous, clawed hand appears just outside the bars.

A scream wants to pull free from my lungs, but I swallow it down. Too afraid to look away, I don't blink as the rest of the creature comes into view. My mind can't seem to grasp the horror of what my eyes are seeing. A huge snake body propels the torso of a man, the rhythmic hissing sound coming from the scales as they slide along the floor.

It says something I can't understand. Pointing at me, it presses its face to the bars, its slitted eyes taking me in. It's almost a man's face, but it's grimmer, and when his forked tongue darts out, I make a keening sound that I can't hold back.

"No. Please leave me alone." I shake my head.

It grins, showing curved fangs. "Noisy little changeling. And speaking the slave language, too. Naughty little thing." It says it in English, the words thick and misshapen from its lips.

I shake my head, and put a hand firmly over my mouth.

"Pretty thing. So pretty." It blinks slowly. "One more sound, and I'll have to discipline you." The tongue shoots out. "I'd enjoy it, but you wouldn't."

I can't close my eyes, can't breathe, can't think.

The sound of a door hinge squeaking pulls the monster's attention away, and a voice down the corridor says something in the unintelligible language. The thing in front of me hisses its reply and gives me one more look before sliding back the way it came.

I lie there shivering for a long time, my mind racing, stumbling, careening. I was in Cecile's car doing my homework. And then I had to have fallen asleep. Because everything that happened after that doesn't make sense.

Asleep. I'm asleep. There's no way I saw a woman who looked exactly like me, no way I'm in some sort of prison, and no way that a half-snake, half-man creature just came and threatened me. My breathing quickens and spots float in my vision. Hyperventilating. Can you hyperventilate in a dream? *Wake up.* I pinch my arm hard. Pain that matches the ache in my head blooms along my skin. I pinch again. But I don't wake up. This can't be. None of this makes sense. But the more my body aches and the chill air seeps into my bones, the more panicked I become. *This is real.*

"Whisper, dumbass. You can only whisper in here. If Zaul hears you again, it won't be pretty." The hay shifts, and a woman appears, her face dirty and her hair in bedraggled waves.

I nod, afraid to use my voice. My breathing is still too fast. I curl into the fetal position and press my forehead to my knees but keep the stranger in my peripheral vision.

She eases closer, and I notice she's wearing the same potato sack I am, though she's much thinner, her cheeks gaunt. "What did you do to land in here?"

"I didn't do anything." My voice is barely a sound. "I don't know how I got here."

She smirks, and I can't tell if she's twenty or fifty. "I refused to let my master's vampire hound feed from me."

She rolls up her baggy sleeve and shows me her arm. Even through the filth, I can see dozens—maybe hundreds—of scars, puncture wounds that come in pairs. "I'd rather die than serve as a meal for that dog one more time."

I push aside the horror that threatens to swallow me whole. "Where are we?"

"*Byrn Varyndr's* dungeon, obviously." She lays on her side and props her head on her hand. "Where they put bad girls."

"Why?"

"Why what? Why are you here?" She wrinkles her nose. "How would I know?"

I press one hand to my face. "This doesn't make sense."

"You speak the old tongue really well." She sucks on her teeth. "I'm surprised I even remember it, it's been so long since I've heard or spoken it. I was exchanged when I was five, so I remember a little from that. And the older changelings still speak and teach it to each other. There are other tongues, too, but everyone seems to stick to this one."

"You mean English?"

"Yeah." She shrugs. "Here, we're only supposed to speak *their* language. English is forbidden. Mainly because most of them don't know it. Only the lesser fae who work alongside us learn it. Some of the older high fae know it, too. But that's rare. They usually don't bother with us."

"They?"

She lowers her brows. "You must have knocked your

head a good one. *They*—the fae. Our supposedly benevo-
lent masters." She laughs low. "They say the summer
realm is the kindest of all. But the fae here are just like all
the others."

"Fae? What's a fae?" I glance at the bars. Was that
snake monster a fae?

She says something in that strange language, though
it's beautiful as it lilts from her tongue.

I shake my head. "What did you say?"

Her eyes narrow. "I said you need to see a healer
since you can't even remember how to speak fae."

"I'm not supposed to be here." My breathing begins
speeding up again, dread constricting my throat. "I was at
school. That's where I'm supposed to be—"

"School?" She tsks. "We aren't allowed to learn. You
know that."

"This isn't real." I rock a little, the hard floor grinding
into my hip. "None of this is real."

She taps her fingers on the cold, grubby stone.
"What's your name?"

"T-Taylor."

"Taylor of?" She gestures for me to go on.

"What do you mean?"

"I'm Lenetia of Granthos. You are Taylor of your
master. So, who's your master?"

"I don't have a master."

"Of course you do," she coaxes. "Give me a name.
Maybe I can talk to the guard and tell him you need to
see a healer. If your master is high up enough, it may even
work."

"I don't have a master." My voice begins to rise, panic

infecting me. "I'm a college student. I'm majoring in chemical engineering. I don't know how I got here, or where *here* even is!" I run my fingers over the lump on my forehead. It feels like a golf ball.

"Shh!" She scurries back toward her hiding place.

"This isn't real." I edge out from beneath my shelter and stand. "None of this is real. So that thing can't hurt me. It's just a dream." I grip the frigid metal bars. "Hey, ugly! Let me out!"

"Stop, for your own good." She buries herself under the moldy hay.

A metallic clang shoots down the dark corridor, and then that rhythmic rustling sounds again.

"Get down," Lenetia hisses. "By the Spires, stop courting pain and death."

"Open this cage!" I yank on the bars. They don't move.

"I'm trying to help you, girl." She peers out from her hiding place. "Changelings should stick together. Now come hide with me before he—" Her words end in a horrified squeak.

The creature appears. I back up involuntarily. Even if it's a dream, it's a terrifying one.

Fangs bared, it pulls a ring of keys from the side of its tunic.

"Oh no, no, no," Lenetia whispers from her hiding spot.

The monster says something in that foreign language as he swings the bars open, but he doesn't come in to get me. Maybe it worked. Maybe I'm on my way out of this nightmare. I just need to wake up.

It hisses again and motions for me to come out, then speaks again in an unintelligible rant.

"Go, girl. He says your master Tyrios has come to free you," Lenetia's urgent whispers catch the monster's attention. "Tyrios is a powerful noble."

The creature glowers and moves to enter the cell. The stranger squeals, the hay rippling as she scurries back.

"I'm coming." I step out quickly, cutting the monster off and bringing its attention back to me.

"Too bad we didn't get to play." He reaches toward my face with a dirty claw.

"I'd like to wake up now."

He cocks his head to the side and lets out a rusty laugh. "Wake up?" Slamming the cell door shut, he grabs my arm, his grip cold and unforgiving.

"I'm going to wake up!" I cry as he drags me down the dank hallway toward another barred door. "Wake up, wake up, wake up!" I shake my head hard, but nothing happens. Everything feels too real—the hard stone, the chill in the air, the rough hand holding me too tightly. No, no, no.

The beast shoves me through the door and into what must be a guard room. Two other creatures—one feathered like a bird but with the body of a man and what can only be described as a scorpion with a beautiful woman's face—play cards in the corner near a small fireplace. They don't even look up as the creature drags me through the room, down another hall, and finally into a room with high windows that show an impossibly starlit sky.

The snake-like monster throws me at the feet of a tall,

blond man with silver eyes and speaks to him in the fae language, though its tone is markedly more respectful than it ever was with me. The man's face turns cross, and he gestures at the lump on my head as he talks.

I climb to my feet and try to find an exit, an escape. But there are only two doors in this stone hall, the one at my back and the one behind the tall blond man.

After a harsh flurry of words, the blond man takes my arm—not gentle, but not as hard as the beast—and pulls me toward the other door. I resist, yanking back against him. With a move so swift I almost miss the movement, he backhands me across the face.

When I taste blood, I know it's real. All of it. And it's not a dream. It's a nightmare.

A scent lingers in the air, something I can't quite place. I didn't smell it before. Only now. Only when I'm walking through the summer palace with my ancestral sword at my side and Gareth at my back.

I turn toward him slightly. "What is that?"

"What?"

"You don't scent something?"

He lifts his nose. "Nothing except the usual floral nonsense that coats this realm like a plague."

I turn back, regaining my stride as we approach the main wing of the castle where the meeting is to take place. It's not cloying floral. It's something else, something pleasant. Like a warm fire, but it isn't a smoky smell.

Whatever it is, I have to get it out of my mind. This conclave could very well determine the future of the realms. My peace with the summer fae is contingent on mutual respect of borders and customs. If I were to discover that they were responsible for the rash of disappearances or in league with those who were, it would be war all over again. A return to the days of the necromancer Shathinor, the brutal former ruler of the winter realm who killed every summer fae he could get his hands on.

So, in the name of peace, I continue down the corridors with walls of ivy and night-blooming jasmine, fairy lights twinkling overhead. The guards we pass tilt their heads in recognition, but their eyes remain wary. After all, summer and winter were enemies not that long ago.

"My lord." The courtier from earlier greets us as we enter the main hall. It's already filled with the clatter of summer realm nobles, many of them turning to stare as I march in. I smirk. The winter realm fae don't douse themselves in jewels and overdone finery like these peacocks. I wear the customary black tunic and pants, my silver crown atop my head and my sword at my side. An array of knives are concealed all over my person, and Gareth is practically a walking armory. At home, we would have fewer weapons but more clothes—furs from our kills or soft leather draped over us as we talk around a roaring fire. But here, where the weather is oppressively pleasant at all times, we have to adjust. Even so, we stick out. Our dark eyes, black hair, and large size all reveal us as males from the winter realm. More than that, our weapons and battle-hardened features mark us as warriors, not the pampered courtiers that surround us as we pass.

"The queen will be with us shortly. Dinner will be served during the conclave." The courtier, Pilantin is his name, practically prances ahead of us as the socializing nobles give me deferential nods. It isn't lost on me that many of them whisper amongst themselves or cut their eyes at me. In the summer realm, the rulers are all chosen via a bloodline that goes back for millennia. They believe that makes them above reproach—and also immune to rebellion. The winter realm is ruled by might alone. Any high fae with the strength to take the throne can have it. One-on-one combat is the only way, and it's how I became king. I haven't been challenged yet, but I look forward to a day when a fae seeks to prove their mettle against me.

We pass out of view of the gawking nobles and into an ornate dining room. The table is decorated with bejeweled centerpieces and golden plates. The chandeliers overhead sparkle from a million facets, and I have no doubt they are made from precious diamonds.

"I see they've set out the good dishes for us." Gareth snorts and swaggers along behind me.

"Only the best for our guests." Pilantin misses the sarcasm and beams at me. "I hope it's to your liking."

"It's fine." That scent wafts past my nose again, and I take a sampling breath. Perhaps it is one of the foods to be served? Whatever it is makes my blood pump faster and the tips of my pointed ears tingle. It also makes something stir below my belt, an odd reaction to nothing more than a scent. I pause and try to place that sweet aroma.

"What?" Gareth tenses, his voice lowering. "What's wrong?"

"Nothing." I can't discern where it's coming from.

"My lord." A servant pulls a golden chair out for me near the head of the table.

I try not to glare at him. Do the summer realm prisses really need a servant just to help them take a seat? I sit, the chair groaning beneath my weight. Everything here is delicate and fine, crafted for the high fae that have never known the bite of winter or the ache of hunger. They pretend they are more civilized because of it, but their darkness is simply hidden beneath a thin layer of gold. Gilded, not pure.

A handful of nobles have followed us into the dining room and take seats farther down the table.

Gareth sits to my left, his gaze always scanning the room, looking for trouble. "I thought this was just supposed to be between us, the queen, and a few of her trusted advisors," he grumbles.

"I suppose this is what 'a few' means in the summer realm." I have a small inner circle of trusted warriors—the Phalanx as they are known in my realm. But it seems Queen Aurentia has about two-dozen nobles she trusts to overhear this high-level discussion.

Once the table is full except for the sparkling seat at the head, Pilantin claps his hands. "The queen would like us to start without her, but she will be here shortly."

The side doors open, and Gareth's hand goes to the blade in his belt.

"Easy." I force my face into what I hope is a neutral expression.

Servers enter the room, each of them carrying wide platters full of meat and vegetables. The summer realm wants for nothing, their existence easy.

Gareth drops his hand but keeps an eye on each servant that comes near me. Most are lesser fae though a smattering of changelings hurry around, struggling to keep up.

The mysterious scent is stronger now. I peer around the table, catching the gazes of the few nobles who have the fortitude to meet my eye. Nothing strikes me, and I can't exactly walk around the table and sniff out each of them.

"What?" Gareth is drawn tight amongst all these former enemies.

"Nothing."

"Why do you keep going still?" He stabs a piece of meat and stuffs it in his mouth unceremoniously. "It's making me jumpy."

I grunt in response and try the root vegetables.

The rest of the table begins to eat once I've taken my first bite. They were waiting on me. Summer realm manners are stiffer than my cock, which is saying something, because it is acting up at the moment. Glad I'm sitting down. I don't know how I know, but that strange scent is causing it. Has to be. Is this some sort of sorcery?

I continue eating, mainly to keep Gareth from accidentally stabbing one of the summer realm nobles. They whisper amongst themselves, shooting me glances in between their gossip.

"My lord, how do you find the summer castle?" one noble, his nose almost as pointy as his ears and his hair long and white, asks.

Stuffy, hot, and overdone. I don't offer my most honest assessment. Instead, I say, "Adequate for my purposes."

His silver eyes narrow. "Your purposes?"

"I'm here to meet with the queen and discuss the

troubles along our borders." I wave my steak knife at the golden walls and diamond chandeliers. "This room will do just fine."

Conversation stops for an awkward moment—awkward for them, anyway. I have no inclination to flatter them or crow about their lavish tastes. I'm here to stop the abductions of my people and strengthen the tie between myself and Queen Aurentia.

The meal continues, the sweet scent bothering me the entire time, until Queen Aurentia finally deigns to make her appearance. We all stand as she enters, her gown of sky blue cinched tight around her small waist, and her silver eyes wide and seemingly guileless. But her beauty hides a cunning that cannot be underestimated.

Guards trail behind her and take up positions around the room, some of them watching me with open menace.

She stops at my chair and offers her hand. I take it and kiss the back, her skin cold and pale. Gareth doesn't make a sound, but I can sense his laughter as if he were guffawing loudly at the summer realm's etiquette.

"Thank you for coming this evening." She pulls her long fingers back.

"Of course." I've been pressing for this meeting for years, ever since the first sign of trouble. She's put me off, though. Probably unworried about winter realm disappearances. But now some of her people are missing as well.

She glides to her seat and settles, the rest of the table following suit. "Where is Lord Tyrios?" She asks no one in particular and glances to the empty seat at her right hand.

"He had some business in the dungeon. Runaway changeling, apparently. Nasty business. But he will be—"

The doors at the end of the room open and a high fae strides in, his gait unhurried despite his lateness.

"Speak and he appears." The queen smiles.

"My deepest apologies." He bows to her before taking his seat. "Changeling trouble."

"They can be so difficult." She tsks and motions for everyone to continue their meal.

She says a few more things to Tyrios, but I'm not listening. The scent. He's covered in it. I stare at him, trying to place it, trying to figure out what it is and why it's sending my mind into a tumult of confusion.

He catches my gaze, and a hint of fear passes across his face. I suppose it's not every day that a winter realm warlord examines you with such focus.

"Shall we get down to business?" The queen waves away her plate. "I have no appetite for anything other than a solution to this pressing problem of disappearing summer fae." She nods toward me. "And winter fae, as well, of course."

Of course.

"The disappearances began in the winter realm, did they not?" A noble toward the end of the table pipes up.

"They did." I push back from the table and stand. "We have been working to solve the situation for nearly a decade."

"And you have no leads?" Tyrios arches a white brow.

"No. I've sent my most trusted soldiers to the border areas where the lesser fae are going missing. No one knows anything. The only thread we've found that runs through each disappearance is a certain melancholy feeling settling on the missing fae within the months prior."

"But this only affects lesser fae." A female in a ruby gown tips her nose into the air.

One of the servants—a lesser fae—pauses, his eyes widening, then continues with his duties. Surely he's accustomed to these preening dandies not giving a damn about him?

"If it only affects others, what cause do we have to worry?" she asks.

I force myself to keep my composure, even though her words rake across my skull like icy fingers. "Lesser fae are members of our realms. They have families, businesses, entire communities. More than that, they are a part of our world. We can't turn our backs on them. High and lesser fae live and work together. Before the curse, some high and lesser fae were mated in the winter realm—"

Lord Tyrios snorts. "Perhaps that is considered appropriate in the winter realm, but we do not allow high and lesser fae to mingle in such a demeaning fashion."

Gareth tenses. I remember attending his sister's wedding to a lesser fae, the groom's ancestry a mix of fae and water sprite. This conversation is already getting out of hand.

Tyrios continues, "But, then again, Queen Aurentia's line has long forbidden dirtying the high fae bloodlines with—"

"Dirtying?" Gareth leans forward, his voice a gravelly threat.

Tyrios blanches.

"You sit here with your jewels and finery—all of it given to you by your lesser fae slaves in the southern mines or the silk factories of the east—and dare to impugn our king for—"

"Gareth." I grip his shoulder.

He goes silent and sits back, but I can feel the anger roiling inside him.

Tyrios swallows hard.

"King Gladion is correct." Queen Aurentia holds my gaze. "Lesser fae are members of our realms and deserve our protection. To that end, I believe winter and summer should work together to find whoever is behind it. I've already sent my spies to the affected towns along our western border, but they've yet to find any clues. Perhaps if we work together, we'll have better luck. Lord Tyrios, do you have the letters of cooperation I asked you to draft?"

"Of course, my queen." He snaps his fingers.

I mask my surprise as I re-take my seat. If she already has letters drawn up, she intended to agree to my request before we even met this evening. Perhaps she is more worried about the disappearances—and the so-called king beyond the mountain—than she's been letting on?

Tyrios snaps his fingers again, his lips twisting into a glower. "My changeling has been acting odd. She used to belong to my daughter, who went and spoiled her. Now she's practically useless. So hard to find a decent servant from human stock."

A lesser fae hurries out of the dining room as the rest offer dessert to the nobles. After a moment, a slight scuffle sounds from an adjacent room before a changeling is pushed through it, a sheaf of papers in her hands.

The world goes silent except for her. All I can hear is her thundering heartbeat. All I can see is the fear in her eyes, the painful marks along her face. Her scent hits me full force, and something inside me unfurls like dark wings. She is mine. I can feel it, an unbreakable tether linking me to her.

I rise to my feet, staring at her as she shuffles forward and hands the papers to Tyrios. Her hair is light brown, and I know it will feel soft under my rough fingers. Though her eyes are downcast, I can tell they are a light blue, like the sky at first light on a snowy morning. Her stained shift covers the rest of her, and the need to rip it away and see her has me practically humming with tension. She doesn't look up, doesn't sense her mate—but that doesn't matter. I've sensed her. Her fate is sealed.

"All my papers are wrinkled and covered with your filthy changeling fingerprints." He snarls and raises his hand to strike her.

I'm across the table with my hand around his throat before he can blink.

he huge man lunges across the table, food and cutlery flying. I stumble backwards as he grabs my master's throat. His dark eyes pin me to the spot as the soldiers stationed around the room rush forward. I drop the papers and try to back away, only to bump into one of the guards, several of them forming a wall behind me.

The gigantic man with the crown and the black hair snarls at them, and my master lets out a quaking whimper. The guards advance, their swords all around me, as if I'm not even standing here. They'd cut right through me without a thought. The crowned man points at me, the fierceness in his eyes like a knife through my heart.

Oh god, he is going to kill me. I can't breathe.

My knees weaken, and under the harshness of the ferocious man's stare, my bladder lets go. I'm going to die here. And I don't even know where here is.

Another dark-haired man stands and yells something,

blades in his hands as he stands in a defensive posture. The guards continue advancing.

The beautiful woman at the head of the table says something in a tone that seems to slice through the air. Everyone stops. Everyone except the man with the death grip on my master's throat.

She addresses him directly, and he responds, his voice low and gruff in that odd tongue.

Her white eyebrows rise, and she flicks her gaze to me, catching me like a deer in headlights.

Footsteps echo inside my mind, and a voice whispers like a tickle against my skull. *"Strange changeling."* It's the woman's voice. *"I suspect there's more to you than I can presently see."*

"Let me go." I think, wondering if she can hear it. *"I don't belong here. I want to go back."*

"I'm afraid there's no going back." She flicks her gaze to the deadly warrior who even now stares at me. *"Not now. Not ever."* Her presence fades, and I blink, unsure if I'm losing my mind.

She flicks a hand at the black-haired man and speaks in the strange tongue. Finally, he releases my master, who stands and backs away sputtering. I take some joy in seeing him afraid, but it's short-lived. The black-haired man advances on me with his hand out, as if to grab me.

I scream and try to escape, but the men at my back don't move. I'm trapped.

The black-haired man speaks to me, his voice still dark and gravelly but somehow coaxing, as if he's speaking to a skittish kitten. I shake my head as he slowly comes closer, his hand still out.

"Don't." My eyes well and I wrap my arms around myself. "Please."

He keeps talking and advancing.

I want to scream again, to run. But there's no use. The fae at the table just watch, some of them with their mouths hanging open. The other black-haired man has stowed his blades, but he observes warily.

"Let me go." I tremble and blink the tears away. Sending an imploring look to the beautiful woman who spoke in my mind, I find her whispering with another fae and paying no attention to me.

The black-haired man reaches me. I fold in on myself, my head down, my heart floundering. I'm going to be punished, killed, or worse. My master is a nightmare, but this man is an enormous brute. I can't catch my breath, my chest heaving.

I scream when he touches me, his large palm grasping my upper arm.

He pulls me toward him.

I fight his grip, but he's a wall of steel.

"No!" I can't breathe.

He pulls me against him, his arms like iron bars across my back. I can't escape. There's no air, no light. My vision goes black, and I fall. The last thing I sense is his strong arms scooping me up.

Low voices rouse me. Cecile must have brought home her newest boytoy last night. Odd for him to still be here in the morning, though. They usually get the boot as soon as she's done riding them. I stretch and bury my face in my pillow. It smells heavenly, like leather and wood smoke and some sort of tall tree with snow on the boughs.

The voices have stopped. I reach up and touch my forehead. A spot there aches. I freeze and remember, the last twenty-four hours crashing down on me like a tidal wave. A strangled sound sticks in my throat as I roll over and sit up. My scratchy shift is gone, and I'm draped in some sort of fur despite the warmth. It slides off to reveal a simple black tunic that swallows me. Somehow, I'm clean, even though I distinctly remember peeing all over myself when I was certain I was about to die. I'm in a huge bed with a canopy of white gauzy material overhead.

My head pounds, and I'm parched as I peer around the room. I yelp when I find the brute from earlier staring at me from only a few paces away. The other dark-haired man says a few words to him before leaving, the heavy wood door clicking shut behind him as I'm left alone with the terrifying brute.

I yank the fur up to my chin and backpedal until I hit the headboard. "Leave me alone." My voice shakes, and I'm weak, but I'll fight till my last breath.

He holds his hands out, palms toward me and eases to the edge of the bed. "Taylor." He says my name almost reverently in his heavy accent.

I clutch the dark fur so hard my fingers ache. "Please, just let me go."

He presses one hand to his chest. "Leander."

"Your name's Leander?"

When I say it, he closes his eyes as if he's heard something unimaginably beautiful. He nods. In the soft light that filters through the high windows, he looks out of place here. He's a dark slash on the white stone of the walls and the pastel décor. His black hair falls to his shoulders, and he wears a gray shirt and black leathery pants. His skin is tan, and his eyes aren't just dark, they're like onyx. With an angular face, sharp nose, and hulking body, he's easily the most striking man I've ever seen. But, he's not a man. The ears pointing out of his hair attest to that.

"I want to go home." My eyes water. "Please."

He speaks in the foreign language I can't follow.

I shake my head. "I don't understand you."

He stops, his dark brows drawing together. "Changeling language?" he asks, the words so heavily accented I almost can't catch them.

"Yes. I don't speak fae."

"Taylor." He says my name with a rolling r, something like a purr. It's almost ... soothing. But then he puts a knee on the bed.

I open my mouth to scream, and he backs off, his hands out in front of him again.

"Just let me go home." I sniffle.

His eyes soften, and he presses his palm to his chest. "Home."

He must not understand what I'm saying. I glance toward the door. Maybe I could escape? But even if I did, where would I go? I don't know how to get home.

A low growl sends goosebumps shooting up my arms, and I yank my gaze back to him.

He pats his chest again. "Home."

"Sure, fine, whatever." I shrug. He clearly doesn't know what he's saying.

His dark brows pull together again, but he seems to accept my response. Turning, he strides to a table near one of the high windows and returns to the bed with a tray of food. I don't recognize the fruit—the strange purple and red berries glisten faintly. But I know bread when I see it. And butter.

My stomach rumbles. I haven't eaten since ... I can't remember. Not since I've been in this place, at least.

A smile quirks up one side of his lips, and the goose-bumps spread down my back. He's handsome in a brutish, alien sort of way. But definitely more scary than anything else. Those dark eyes hide traps and barbs, I'm certain of it.

He edges closer and rests the tray next to me.

My stomach growls again, and I can't take my eyes off the food. But should I eat it?

With a nudge, he pushes the tray even closer. I can smell the sweetness of the fruit and the doughy bread. Food is food, right? But what if it's poisoned?

He says something, one word. Maybe it's 'eat', since he gestures toward the tray with one of his bear paws.

My stomach makes the decision for me as it complains loudly and a hunger pang shoots through me. I reach for the bread and take a small piece, then put it in my mouth, testing it. Sweeter than the breads I'm used to, it melts on my tongue.

He nods, his dark eyes glinting, and he says the word again. It sounds like "brantath" to me. I form the word as best I can and repeat it back to him. His face lightens, and he tears another piece of bread from the round loaf and gives it to me.

I take it, swallowing it just as fast as the first. "So *brantath* means eat." My stomach seems to rumble even more. "Or maybe it means bread?"

When he sits on the bed, I yank the fur up and pull my knees to my chest. The entire mattress shifts under his weight as he leans over and butters a bigger piece of bread and offers it to me.

"*Brantath.*" He leans closer. The scent from the fur and the shirt I'm wearing is the same one that wafts from him. It's the promise of a cold winter's night spent next to a roaring fire.

I take the bread, my fingers gently brushing against his. A low growl in his throat has me pulling back. It stops, but he gives me a predatory look, one that frightens me and sends heat blasting through me at the same time. Something's wrong with me, but I'm too happy about the food to care.

I devour the bread, the butter creamy and delicious. He rises, the bed groaning with relief as he grabs a pitcher and pours water into a crystal cup, then hands it to me. I sniff it. No smell. But it's not like I'm an expert poison sniffer or anything. I drink, mainly because I'm parched and don't know when I'll get my next chance at food or water.

He watches me swallow it down, then holds his hand out for the empty glass. When I reach out to give it to him, he stills, his eyes narrowing. Ferocious. That's the only word for the look on his face. I clutch the fur and scoot away from him.

With fluid fury he reaches to the table behind him and draws an enormous silver sword.

A choked sound catches in my throat as he raises it. *I'm going to die.*

"Please, don't." It's the only words I can get out as he lunges toward me.

LEANDER

*D*ashing across the bed, I put myself between my mate and the threat. The faint shadow darts to the left as I swing hard enough to cut down any foe, but it's too fast.

My mate whimpers, and her fear makes rage bubble through my veins. I will slay anything that dares to hurt her.

The shadow oozes along the wall toward the window. Not a chance. I rear back and thrust the blade into the seemingly empty space near the windowsill. A low grunt sounds, and the intruder's glamour fades as he slumps to the floor, his blade clattering on the stones.

Taylor gasps as the male comes into view, one hand gripping the wound in his stomach as he stares up at me with reptilian eyes.

"Let me guess, the king beyond the mountain sent you?" I note the twisted tree brand on the lesser fae's throat.

"He will rule." His eyes flicker to Taylor, and he

tastes the air with his tongue. "The prophecy is already coming true."

"What prophecy?" I press the tip of my sword to the mark on his throat.

Blood oozes between his scaled fingers. "You will burn, false king."

"Not today." I raise my sword.

His eyes return to my mate. "He is waiting." The words are a threat.

Fury pulses through me, and a phantom wind rustles the curtains. "Don't look at her."

"Waiting." He gurgles blood, his slitted eyes never blinking.

I should keep him for questioning, turn him over to Gareth so we can both go to work on him. But the way he's looking at Taylor ... I can't let him live another second. With a hard swing, I separate his head from his neck.

Her scream cuts through the heart of me, ripping and tearing like a flaming blade. I rush to her and pull her into my arms. She struggles against me, her hands in fists as she tries to beat my chest with ineffectual blows. It would be adorable if I didn't know she was terrified.

"Calm down, little one." I keep my back to the blood spreading across the white stone floor. She doesn't need to see it.

She eventually stops struggling. But she starts crying, her tears like iron nails in my head.

I sit on the edge of the bed and rock her in my arms. Her sobs wrack her body, and she says something in the changeling language I can't understand.

"I will protect you with my life." I kiss the crown of her head, her light brown hair beautiful in the too-bright sun. "Nothing will harm you as long as I walk this world, and I will take my love for you to the glowing lands of the ancestors if my time is cut short. I will wait for you there. Just as I have waited for you here."

She sniffles, her tears wetting my tunic and says something. I can only figure out a few words: "language" and "beautiful."

I have so many questions for her. Chief among them is why she doesn't speak the fae language. As a changeling slave—my ire rises at the thought of my mate being enslaved, but I push it down—she should speak perfect fae. It's required in the summer realm.

These summer realm fae with all their finery and manners can't hide the brutality with which they treat their servants. The bruises on Taylor's forehead and the cut on her lip are my next questions. I want to flay the one who harmed her, no matter if it means war with the summer court.

She pulls back and looks me in the eye—her strange blue ones just as fascinating as when I first saw her. Changelings are rare in the winter realm. They often can't survive the brutal landscape. But even though I've seen plenty of changelings over my centuries, I've never seen one with such sparkling blue eyes.

When she wriggles in my lap a bit more, her ass grazes my erection, and she makes a small squeak noise and tries to scramble off me.

"No, my mate." I hold her in place. "I will not take you until you are ready, but you must know what you do to me." I graze her little rounded ear. "And I can scent that it isn't entirely unwelcome." I've wanted to bury my face between her thighs for every second I've had her alone—and some when I haven't. Her scent heightens like the color in her cheeks, and I know if I reached between her creamy thighs, I'd find her wet for me. My cock pulses at the thought.

She wriggles again. If I don't let her go, she'll push me over the edge. The need to claim her as mine builds with each moment I spend in her presence. She is a gift. The first mate the ancestors have granted since the defeat of the old king. And she's *mine*.

I nuzzle against her ear a bit more and enjoy the slight shiver that runs through her body. Not fear. Her scent tells me that little tremor came from desire. But she's also unsure about me. She doesn't feel the bond. Not yet. Perhaps because she is a changeling.

She leans away and shakes her head. "Leander."

My name on her lips is an answered prayer. "Say it again."

She cocks her head to the side, one eyebrow slightly arched.

"Leander. Say it again." I gesture toward her.

"Leander?"

"Yes." I stroke her hair.

She swats my hand away, and I let her stand. I've placed a cloaking spell over the assassin's body, but she seems to have forgotten about him. Instead, she keeps glancing at me and twisting her tiny hands together. My mate is small, fragile. I will feed her the richest meats and fruits until she is hardy enough for the winter realm. Not that I will ever let her feel the bite of the snow on her fair skin or the cut of the mountain wind against her. She is far too precious.

Noise in the hallway has me standing and pulling her behind my back.

"You will let me pass!" The haughty voice belongs to Lord Tyrios.

"Not happening." Gareth's tone is lethal. He's had enough of the summer realm. I don't blame him. In all of Arin, it's my least favorite.

Small hands grip the back of my shirt. I turn to look at Taylor, and she's pale, her body quaking. I hate the scent of her fear. Her gaze is fixed on the door as Lord Tyrios demands entry and is again denied.

She starts shaking her head, hurried words falling from her lips. Her eyes are turned up to mine, beseeching me as her tears well.

"Taylor is my servant. You can't keep her from me!" Tyrios complains.

I stroke my thumb across her soft cheek, wiping away a tear. "He will never touch you again, little one. You are mine. You are safe." I wrack my brain until I find the changeling word. "*Safe*," I take her hand and press it to my chest. "*Safe*."

Tears still sparkle in her beautiful eyes, but she gives me the slightest nod. It's all I need.

I pull her behind me and open the door. "She is mine."

Tyrios holds up an aged piece of parchment. "This document shows my ownership. She is mine. I inherited her from my former wife." He shakes the paper, as if it will matter. "Use her for your needs. But return her to me when you're finished with her."

His implication sends shards of ice floating through my veins. Is this how they "use" their changelings in the summer realm?

Gareth's hand rests on the hilt of his sword. He'd like nothing better than to hew this fool in half. I'm inclined to agree with him, but killing this idiot would destroy any chance we have at enlisting the queen's help to solve the disappearances. Sometimes, like now, I wish I could go back to the simplicity of open warfare with the summer realm. No diplomatic niceties, just simple bloodshed. But those are the thoughts of a soldier, not a king.

"She is no longer yours." I cross my arms over my chest and glare down at him. "She belongs to me. Leave here now or your blood will paint these stones." I gesture to the pale floor.

He sputters and backs up a step. "You can't threaten me! I'm a noble of the summer realm. Your kind doesn't belong here. The queen should have never granted you entry into these lands. Unseelie fae are cursed—"

Gareth's movement is faster than a Red Plains adder. He has the screeching Tyrios by the throat. "You dare speak that word? And in the presence of my *king*?"

"I speak only the truth." He pushes the words past Gareth's palm. "Filthy dark fae. *Unseelie.*" He spits the forbidden word, the one that used to brand winter realm fae with a black mark that went soul-deep. The distinction of Seelie and Unseelie has long since been abandoned. Good and bad reside in both the fairer fae of the summer rains and the darker fae of the winter winds.

Even so, Unseelie eventually became an insult that still stings those from the winter realm.

"Know this, Tyrios." I step toward him until I can see the beads of sweat on his pale brow. "Taylor is under my protection. You will never lay claim to her again."

Taylor's small hands clutch the back of my shirt again, her tremble telegraphing through me. She has nothing to fear, and certainly not from the imbecile before me.

"The queen will hear about this. You have no right to that changeling. I will take this to the high court and have her returned to me before the day is out. And when the queen hears you've threatened me, she'll—"

"Please escort Lord Tyrios to the main hall." I give him a smile that's colder than the tip of Sun's Bane Peak. "If I find you in this wing of the castle again, you will regret it."

Gareth drags the squawking noble away as I turn to Taylor and hoist her into my arms. Her gaze sticks to the retreating back of Tyrios, worry in her eyes.

"You have nothing to fear from him." I sit on the bed and keep her in my lap. "He's nothing. Just the ash from a long-dead fire, gray and cold."

Her chin trembles as she looks at me, and she says something I can't understand. But she seems relieved.

She calms slowly, the pinched look on her face almost gone until Gareth storms back through the door.

When she tenses, I press her close to me. I can't seem to stop touching her.

"Tyrios intends to get her back." Gareth walks to the

dead assassin, though I'd forgotten all about him. "Another?"

"He will be sorely disappointed." I growl and stroke my hand down Taylor's back. "And yes, another."

"Get any information from him?" Gareth hunches to his knees and inspects the brand on the fae's neck.

"He threatened to harm my mate." I shrug.

"So that's a no." Gareth nods and rises again. "It's not safe here. The summer realm allows all manner of inter-lopers to infiltrate their stronghold." He scratches his chin. "I'm beginning to suspect they *want* the assassins to get to you."

"Why would the queen want me dead? I'm the only thing preventing another war between the realms."

"Who knows." He shakes his head. "But one thing is certain, we have to leave. Now. Lord Tyrios isn't letting her go. I have enough understanding of their laws to know that his claim on her—if confirmed by that docu-ment he held—is absolute. He can—"

"I will *never* give her up." The mating bond wraps around my heart like an iron thread, each heartbeat drawing it tighter.

"Of course not." Gareth glances at her.

Even though I trust him with my life, I have the impulse to hide her, to keep her all to myself and away from any other males.

"I would sooner swear fealty to the summer realm than let the first winter realm mate in a century slip through our fingers. And *your* mate, at that." His lips quirk into a smile. "You've always been a lucky bastard."

Taylor points at the door and says something, the last word turning up in question.

Gareth responds in the changeling language. He speaks it far better than I do. I try to tamp down my jealousy that he's able to converse with her while I can't. It isn't easy. I'm desperate for any word from her lips.

When they finish talking, I raise my eyebrows at him.

"She wants to know where she is." His forehead wrinkles as he looks at her with open curiosity. "She says she's not from here. She's from the changeling world and just got here today."

"That's not possible." I shake my head. "Exchanges aren't allowed when changelings are this old." The fae have few universal tenets, but that is one of them. No fae can be exchanged for a human once the human reaches maturity. Too many questions would arise, and it would violate the ages-old treaty with the humans.

"I know. She said she woke up in the prison—"

"My mate in a *prison*?" My fangs lengthen, but I'm careful to close my mouth. If she truly is new to the fae world, she must be terrified. Fangs won't help. They retract slowly.

"She met another changeling there who helped her get her bearings. But otherwise, she has no idea what's going on."

I swallow hard, my mouth suddenly dry. "Does she know I'm her mate?"

Gareth darts his gaze away from mine. "She didn't say."

I force myself to stay calm, to ignore the sting. She may not know it yet, but she will when I claim her. "Who hit her?" I smooth my palm along her hairline where a dark bruise has risen.

Gareth asks her in her language.

She presses her fingers to her forehead and speaks to him, then touches her lip.

Gareth's face turns into a glower. "She hit her head by accident. But Tyrios split her lip."

Tyrios. And I'd just let him get away. I'll have his head for daring to harm my mate.

She whimpers. I realize my grip has tightened too much.

"I'm sorry little one." I press my lips to her forehead. Just that bit of contact sends a buzz through me that ends in my cock. The need to take her makes me dizzy.

"Two choices. Stay here and fight Tyrios, which would endanger the agreement with the queen. Or take your mate and flee. That option may leave a sour taste in the queen's mouth, but at least you won't have spilled one of her noble's blood."

"Tyrios will die by my hand." My words are a promise, one that will never be broken.

"I have no problem with that. But now is not the time." Gareth jerks his chin toward Taylor. "Getting her safely to the winter realm is the most important thing." His eyes light, as if hope set off a spark inside them. "A royal mate. Do you know what this could mean for the winter realm? For our future? Maybe this is the end of the curse for all of us."

I wasn't the only one who had wished for his mate during the dark years of the war and the ones that came after. Gareth is right. Tyrios can wait. I will strike, but it doesn't have to be now. My need to protect Taylor overwhelms even my desire for vengeance.

I peer at her—at my future—and almost burst with pride. She is mine, and I would lay down my life to keep her safe. Once we are surrounded by snow and ice, wind and cold—the chilled heart of the winter realm—I will breathe easier. "We leave at nightfall."

*B*eing cradled in the arms of the huge warrior should be terrifying. Instead, I'm oddly comforted. His scent of crisp winter wind and warm fires calms the worry that eats away at me. But I'm still on edge and trying to figure out how to get back to where I belong.

This strange place doesn't make sense to me—not the people, the weather, or the language. At least the other massive brute speaks English, though he hasn't given me much comfort.

"We're leaving tonight," the other one—Gareth is his name—says.

"Leaving? But how can I get back if we leave?" I shake my head. "I can't go. What if the only way back is here somewhere?"

Gareth ignores my questions and kneels in front of me.

Leander's grip tightens for a second, then relaxes.

Gareth holds my gaze and speaks in the fae tongue,

his tone lilting, the words almost a song as he stares up at me. When the near-song comes to a close, he lays his sword on the floor in front of Leander and me.

"What's going on?" I'm almost at eye level with the scarred fae, though he doesn't scare me. His eyes are warm, far warmer than Tyrios's or even the royal-looking woman's who could speak to me without saying a word.

"I have sworn my allegiance to you as my future queen."

"As your *what?*" I shake my head and push away from Leander's arms. He doesn't let me go far.

"More will become clear in time." Gareth bows his head. "It's customary for the queen of the winter realm to respond to the Winter's Oath with the phrase '*bladanon thronin.*' It means 'your pledge is honored' roughly."

"I'm not your queen. I don't belong to Tyrios or anyone else. I don't belong *here*. I just want to go home." I finally manage to scoot away from Leander's grip, though I realize it's only because he allows it. He's twice my size and made of pure muscle.

"I cannot rise unless you say the words or strike the head from my body." Gareth lowers his dark eyes to the floor.

"What?" My voice takes on an edge of panic. What is he talking about? If things didn't make sense before, now they were utterly bananas. Me? A queen? I'm a college student with Bs in literature and history and straight As in my science classes, a love of *Friends* reruns, and a penchant for eating an entire pint of Ben & Jerry's in one go. I'm not a queen. I don't even feel like an adult half the time. Hell, I can't even drink legally for another month!

"I'm sorry, my lady, but we are in grave danger here. We must leave for the winter realm. I have sworn to protect you with my life. If you deem me unworthy, and my pledge dishonorable, it is tradition for you to end me. And I would prefer death to living a life of shame."

"I'm not going to kill you. I just met you, for crying out loud!" I press my palm to my forehead. It's covered with a fine sheen of cold sweat.

Leander doesn't intervene, just stares at me with an intensity that seems to grow by the second.

"But I need to go home." I hate how helpless I sound.

"This is a step toward home." Gareth still doesn't rise.

I pinch the bridge of my nose. "So, if I say the words, we can get as far away from Tyrios as possible and find a way for me to go home?"

"Yes, we will be leaving Tyrios behind, and yes, you will be going home."

I narrow my eyes. "I'm pretty sure your definition of 'home' isn't quite the same as mine."

"Even so." He shrugs but doesn't move from the floor.

"What if the only way back is here somewhere? I mean, I woke up in the dungeon. Maybe that's the way to get back?" I chew my lip.

"Did you see any way out when you were there?" He still doesn't look up.

"Well, no." I search my memory. "There was just stone and bars and some hay. No other way in or out."

"Then you were likely brought here through magic. It's not specific to this place. Magic runs through all of Arin."

"Arin?"

"This world. There are many, but this is Arin."

"Arin. And magic." I swallow the disbelief that tries to overwhelm me. "So, I can go back with magic?"

He's silent for a beat too long, then says, "Perhaps. We have certain magic wielders in the winter realm who will know better than I can tell you. My magic is more of a ... destructive variety."

At least it sounds better than going back to the dungeon. "What are the words again?"

"*Bladanon thronin.*" I repeat the words and even wave my hand a little like the queen of England might.

Gareth's grin lights up his entire face, his black eyes glinting like jewels. He speaks to Leander, who rises and clasps forearms with him, both of them painted with happiness.

I run my fingers along the stone at my neck. At least I have this tiny piece of familiarity. Something to lead me back home.

Leander eyes the movement, his brows drawing together for a second before he turns back to Gareth. He doesn't like my opal?

"Gareth?"

"Yes, my queen?"

I shake my head. "I'm not a queen."

"Not yet. But soon."

I grind my teeth together. "Call me Taylor. That's my name."

"It's not customary. But I will do as you wish."

"Taylor it is." At least I can control that one little thing. It's the base. I can build on it until I either wake up from this bizarre dream or fight my way back to reality. "Can I ask you for one thing?"

"Anything, my que—Taylor."

Leander barks out a question, and Gareth responds. Maybe explaining our conversation in fae. Leander relaxes a hair and re-focuses on me.

"What is it you wish?" Gareth asks.

"There's a woman in the dungeon. She tried to help me. I can't just leave her there."

"A prisoner?"

"Yes. Her name was Lenetia of something-or-other. I can't remember her master's name. Is there any way you can free her before we go? She said her master was particularly cruel and she had these—" I gesture toward my arm. "Fang marks all over her. Anyway, she needs help. And she's a changeling like me." *Changelings stick together*, she had said.

He relays my words to Leander, who seems to weigh my request before giving Gareth a curt nod.

Gareth bows his head toward me for a moment. "I will free her."

"Be careful. There's a snake monster thing guarding her," I offer.

Leander stands and motions Gareth toward the door where they converse in low tones for a moment.

After that Gareth leaves in a rush.

"My queen." Leander takes my hands in his and kisses each of my palms.

"Did Gareth teach you that word?"

He smirks but doesn't answer.

"Okay, but I'm not really a queen." It finally occurs to

me that when I first saw him, he was wearing a crown. Am I supposed to be *his* queen? "Whoa." I pull my hands back. "You and I aren't a thing. I don't know you. I don't even speak your language." I stand, almost walk toward where the dead fae's body was, then change course toward the back of the room.

Strong hands on my shoulders stop me, and Leander turns me to face him. I have to crane my neck back just to meet his midnight eyes. He pats his chest again. "Home." Then he takes my hand and rests it over his heart. "Home, Taylor."

He's so gentle with me. But I need him to understand that I don't belong.

"My home is far away from here. I have to get back. I have finals coming up soon. And my roommate will miss me and ..." My words fade as I remember Cecile and the woman who looked just like me. *Cecile*—she did this, she's the reason I'm here. "My roommate. She sent me to this world somehow. Her *magic*. And there's another me. How is there another me?"

Leander smooths his rough fingers along my wrinkled brow and speaks to me low and soft, his voice like a warm blanket. I have no idea what he's saying, but it's clear he wants to comfort me.

"I think my brain is broken." I sigh.

He wraps his arm around me and pulls me tight.

This is the most contact I've had with another person in my life. My mother certainly isn't a hugger, and I never let anyone else get close to me. I'm too damaged for it. But this man with the pointy ears and muscles of steel doesn't know that. Doesn't know me.

"Hey." I grip his sides. "I don't know what you think this is, but I'm not your queen. I'm not even sure if this is real."

He tips my chin up. "Mine."

"Gareth teach you that one, too?"

The smirk reappears and sends warmth shooting to my every extremity.

"I'm not whatever you think I am, okay?"

"Mine." He repeats, his low voice vibrating through me.

"I'm not—"

The door opens, and Leander has me pushed behind him and his sword brandished before I can even look to see who it is.

Gareth hurries in, a large bag slung over his shoulder and another in one hand. He tosses the one from his shoulder onto the bed. It squeaks and moves until Lenetia's thin face appears.

"This female is descended from the spirits that shriek in the burning woods of Galendoon!"

"If that were true, I'd have burned you to ash already." She struggles out of the sack.

"She tried to take one of my eyes with her filthy fingernails." Gareth grumbles and pulls a dress and some other clothing from his bag.

Leander positions himself between Lenetia and me.

"It's okay." I pat his back, my hand comically small against his broad expanse. "She's a friend."

"Am I?" She looks around. "This oaf pulled me from the dungeon, but they'll send the Catcher for me, I'll be recaptured, then fed to my master's vampire hounds. Thanks for nothing."

I try to sidestep Leander, but he isn't having it. I have to talk around him. "We're leaving this place. You can come with us."

"No." Gareth frowns and shakes his head. "No way this guttersnipe is coming with us. She'd knife us in the back as soon as she could."

"Just you," she simpers sweetly.

Gareth growls and points to a dress he's laid on the bed. "For you, Taylor." He says my name as if it tangles on his tongue.

I try to peek around Leander to catch Lenetia's eye. "You can come with us."

Gareth sours. "We shouldn't—"

"Didn't you just swear an oath to me?" I don't recognize the sharpness in my voice, but it pulls Gareth up short, so I go with it. "Well?"

"Yes." His long sigh is paired with a cutting look at Lenetia, then he has a quick discussion with Leander. When Leander laughs, the low notes rumbling through the room, I lean a little closer.

Gareth says something I can only imagine is a curse in fae and turns to Lenetia. "Behave, female. One wrong step, and it will be your last."

She sticks her tongue out at him.

"You should change. This will help you fit in enough for us to get off the palace grounds once night falls." Gareth points at the dress he's laid out. It's a pale gray, simple yet nice.

"Thank you." I grab the dress and peer around the room. "Where can I change?"

"There's a bathing chamber at the back." Gareth jerks his head in the direction of a doorway.

I head towards it, then stop. Turning around, I address the hulking man at my heels. "I have to change."

He gestures to the bathing room and grabs my hand, leading me to it and stepping across the threshold.

"Alone," I say pointedly.

He cocks his head to the side as if he doesn't understand, but this time I'm almost certain he knows what I'm saying.

"Alone." I point to myself and then the bathing room, then hold one finger up. "Just me. Not you."

He crosses his arms over his chest, his thick biceps straining against his shirt, and says something in fae.

"I'm not changing in front of you." I mimic his stance, arms crossed. "I can wait all day. But I was under the impression we were in a hurry."

Lenetia snorts and speaks to him in fae.

He responds with a glower and a few words.

She shrugs and gives me a half smile. "He won't leave you alone."

"I've noticed. Tell him I'm just going to change and then I'll be right back out. Between you and me, I need to pee, too." I glance at him, the glower still pulling at his lips. "Tell him I need privacy."

"Alpha fae like him don't understand privacy. Especially not when it comes to their mate."

"How do you know they're mates?" Gareth rests his hand on the sword at his waist.

"Calm down." She leans over on her elbow, the picture of relaxation. "Anyone can see it. Just look at him. He's like a vampire hound on a scent. Can't take his eyes from her."

"That information is not to be tossed about, especially not while we're in enemy territory. If anyone learns that the king of the winter realm has found his mate—"

"Mate?" I nibble my lip. "Why do you keep calling me that?"

"You two are bonded." She puts a grubby fingernail between her teeth. "Or, you will be. You obviously don't feel the bond yet."

"What?" I can't even begin to put all my questions into words.

Gareth gives an exasperated huff and speaks to Leander.

"Grumpy Fae here is explaining that you want privacy." She cocks her shoulder toward Gareth.

After a litany of words, Leander steps away from the door, but not far. He leaves just enough room for me to shimmy past and gives me a look that seems both angry and concerned at the same time.

"This may be the last time you get to do anything without King Muscles over here," Lenetia calls. "So enjoy it."

I press the door closed and lean against it. *Mate?* As in the way animals pick a mate? Does that mean he expects to ... have *sex* with me? I bounce my head against the door. Surely not. We aren't even the same species. We don't know each other. That's ridiculous. But when I remember the way he holds me, the heat in some of his looks—I press my thighs together and try to banish those thoughts.

A low growl pulses through the door.

"Whatever you're thinking about in there, stop." Lenetia's laugh floats through the wood. "He can smell your—" She clears her throat. "He can smell if you're thinking about him, let's put it that way."

He can smell my—I glance down and then turn every shade of red.

"Quickly, Taylor. Night will be here soon," Gareth calls.

"Okay." I push away any thoughts of mates or what Leander can smell. "Jeez," I whisper to myself. With a tug, I pull the shirt off and lay it on the edge of a deep copper tub. The dress slides down my arms and into place. It falls to my ankles and hugs my breasts and hips. But it's made of a thicker material, so I don't feel too exposed. Bright daylight pours through an open window over the tub. The scent of flowers, so thick it's almost cloying, floats on a warm breeze.

I glance at myself in a floor-length mirror. Everything looks fine, I suppose, though my forehead still has an ugly bruise and my lip is puffy. I'm about to step back toward the door when a movement in the mirror catches my eye.

Before I can scream, Tyrios's hand claps over my mouth.

I can feel her distress before I hear the sounds of a scuffle. With a roar, I burst through the bathing room door.

Tyrios has my mate by the throat, a dagger in his other hand. The terrified look in her eyes will haunt me until I take my last breath.

"Release her."

"She belongs to my family, to *me!*"

Gareth is at my back, sword drawn. But I don't need him. I already know how this is going to go.

"I won't tell you again." I step closer, but when Tyrios raises his dagger to her side, I stop.

"I can kill her here and now. It is my right," he snarls. "This changeling is garbage, but she is *my* garbage."

"She is my mate. The queen of the winter realm."

He sputters, his silver eyes widening. "A changeling mate?" His surprise changes to amusement. "Typical that winter realm filth like you would find his mate in a human, baser even than the lowest fae."

"Release her now, and I will make your death quick."
I palm my silver blade, the metal smooth against my skin.

"Your mate is my slave." He grins. "You can't have
her. I won't allow her to be taken by some Unseelie
pretender who plays at being king when—" The
surprised look in his eyes is almost as sudden as the
gargling noise in his throat.

I pull Taylor from him and push her behind me.
Gareth whisks her away as I approach Tyrios and slide
my throwing blade from his neck.

"I was going to leave you here, unmolested." I knock
the knife from his palm as he sinks to the floor. I follow
him down, not letting him escape my gaze. "You would've
had more time, months, maybe even years, before I trav-
eled back to Byrn Varyndr to end you for touching her."

He presses a hand to the wound, but the blood is
pouring too swiftly.

I pry his fingers away, crimson coating my skin, and
lean even closer as the silver begins to darken in his eyes.
"I'm glad you came." I laugh, the sound echoing through
the bathing chamber and carrying with it the bite of the
winter wind. "Your corpse will be a warning to any who
seek to harm my mate."

His mouth moves, trying to form words, but only a
wet whisper escapes.

"This will not bode well for our alliance." Gareth
lurks in the doorway.

"No, it won't."

"Shall I finish him, my lord?" Gareth asks.

"No." I sit back on my haunches. "I offered him a
quick death. He refused." I want to sit here and watch his

eyes turn a dead gray, but my need to comfort Taylor transcends my ire.

"Watch him. When he's dead, we leave." I stand and brush past Gareth.

Taylor is huddled on the bed, the other female petting her hair and speaking to her in the changeling language. When I see tears in her eyes, it spurs me onward. I rush to her and elbow the tiny changeling away.

"I am sorry." I pull her to my chest, and she lets out a sob. "I swore to keep you safe. I will forever live with the stain of failing you like this." I kiss her forehead and rock her. "Tell her," I urge the other changeling.

She wrinkles her nose but translates my words.

Taylor mumbles something back to her.

"She says it's not your fault."

She's wrong, but I don't argue, just hold her tight as she shivers. When I think of Tyrios putting his hands on her, I want to kill him all over again.

Gareth strides from the bathing room. "He's gone to the ancestors, or more likely, straight to the Spires."

"Good." I rub Taylor's back as her crying lessens.

"Killing Tyrios." The changeling woman winces. "That's not going to go over well with the queen."

"We don't intend to address it." Gareth grabs the few things in the room that belong to us and stuffs them in his pack.

Taylor wipes her eyes and leans back. "Thank you."

I know what those words mean, at least. "Welcome," I say as best I can.

She nods and takes a deep breath.

"Are you ready to go, my little one?" I tip her chin up and meet those startling blue eyes.

The changeling translates.

Taylor nods again. "Ready."

My need to claim her thrums in my veins. When I caught her scent earlier, I was only a hairsbreadth away from breaking down the bathing room door and answering the mating call. Perhaps her mind hasn't awoken to the fact of our bond yet, but her body has. Even now, I can scent what remains of her arousal, and it makes my mouth water. One little taste couldn't hurt. *Take her. She belongs to you. She will thank you after you sink inside her and seal the bond. Take her now.* I shake my head. Those are the thoughts of a feral fae, of the beast that hides deep inside the heart of every timeless creature. But I would not listen to it. Not give in. No matter how I ache to feel every inch of her.

I set her on her feet. "Changeling—" I point at the waifish one. "Lenetia, is it? You will serve my lady. See to her needs, and teach her our language. Do this, and you will be welcomed in the winter realm."

"As a free changeling?" she counters.

"All are free in the winter realm." Gareth shoulders his pack. "Even changelings."

"We'll see what being free is worth when the summer realm finds out about Tyrios." She casts a glance to Taylor. "But lucky for you all, I rather like your naïve mate."

"So you accept?" I don't mention that if she doesn't, we'll have to take her with us anyway. She already knows too much about Taylor.

"I do. As long as you speak true about my freedom in the frozen wastes of the winter realm."

Gareth snorts. "'Frozen wastes,' eh? Good to see the summer realm propaganda machine is still going strong."

I strap my sword around my waist and pull one dagger from its hiding place along my side. Pressing it into Taylor's hand, I say, "Keep this hidden, but don't be afraid to use it."

Her eyes widen, but she tucks it into the pocket of her dress.

I hold out my hand for Taylor. She takes it with no hesitation, and the mating bond inside me snaps even tighter. I keep my other hand on the haft of my sword.

Gareth waits at the door, his stance like a drawn bow string, and glances at my stance. "You expecting trouble?"

I grin and squeeze Taylor's small hand. "Always."

𝒲e leave the large bedroom and enter a bright hall alight with blazing rays of sun. The heat verges on oppressive, and it doesn't help that I'm anxious and still disoriented. Leander doesn't seem to mind my sweaty palm as he leads me along with Gareth and Lenetia at our backs.

A pair of guards, their armor gleaming, peer at us as we pass, but say nothing.

Leander somehow manages a casual swagger, his head high. We get more than a few stares from passersby, but no one speaks to us.

"Keep cool," Lenetia whispers. "We're supposedly going to walk right out the front door." The skepticism in her tone isn't lost on me.

We make it to a cavernous hall with light pouring in from all angles. Fae in decorative dress stand around talking or walk with haughty importance. One in particular makes a beeline for us.

I tense, but Leander squeezes my hand. His touch

manages to calm me a little—perhaps because I know he's armed to the teeth and has already demonstrated he has no qualms killing to protect me. My stomach churns at the memory of Tyrios's hands on me, the surprise in his eyes, and the blood at his throat.

The fae stops in front of us and wrings his hands, his voice tipped with anxiety as he speaks to Leander.

I can't follow what's being said, but it definitely seems like this fae doesn't want us to leave. Eventually, Leander brushes past him and continues toward a huge set of wooden double doors that lead into a wide courtyard.

The nervous fae hurries away.

"He's going to rat us out." Lenetia quickens her pace along with the rest of us.

"Easy now. Just keep calm, and everything will be fine." Gareth's low voice doesn't hold any hints of worry, but I'd be willing to bet his hand is resting on some sort of weapon.

The whispers of the glittering fae around us intensify as we stride past. But we enter the courtyard without incident. Bushes and flowers bloom all around, and tiny white puffs swirl through the warm air. It's a fairyland all the way down to the moss between the walkway stones. Even so, I'm happy to leave it behind.

Worry eats away at me, and I hope I'm making the right choice. Leaving here could be a mistake—one I won't recover from. If this place is the only spot that will allow me to return home, then I'm foolish to go with the warrior king at my side. But if Gareth is telling the truth, then the only way for me to get back is to go with them to the winter realm. Like Dorothy, I can't go back the way I came, I can only follow the yellow brick road until I get to Oz. I touch the pendant at my throat, the stone cool against my warm fingers.

We continue our trek, Leander casual but alert, his gaze missing nothing as we exit the courtyard and enter a narrow lane with ivy climbing its sides. I glance up and find more guards, a few of them watching us, crossbows strapped across their chests.

"This is the portico to the palace. Once we're out of here, we'll reach the stables and ride north," Gareth says.

"Can't wait to be on the road with you lot," Lenetia grumbles.

Gareth bites off a few foreign words, the very sound of them unpleasant to my ears.

"Kiss your sister with that mouth?" Lenetia shoots back.

"Silence," Leander hisses as we approach a high gate, the bars separating us from what looks like a bustling village beyond. At least a dozen guards stand along the high stone walls, and several more are atop it, some of them holding their crossbows.

One of the soldiers steps forward, a question on his lips.

Leander responds, his tone conversational, as if we're all just out for a stroll, not escaping a murder scene.

The soldier's brow wrinkles, and he gives me a long look.

Leander bristles and steps in front of me, his voice turning cold. The two of them engage in an escalating flurry of words.

"Shit." Lenetia takes my arm. "We should go."

"Can we?" I can't see the guard past Leander's wide back, but I can hear him.

"Never hurts to try. He's more interested in why the king and Gareth are leaving than us." She pulls me gently toward her and we move to walk toward the open gate.

Two guards step from the shadows beneath the stone overhang, swords in their hands.

"Keep walking. Eyes down. Like changeling slaves." Lenetia links her arm through mine.

I follow her instructions and stare at the cobblestones beneath my feet. My chin tries to shake, but I clamp my teeth together. Leander's voice rises even louder behind me, the rumble of it like deep thunder.

We're almost through the gate when one of the guards steps in our path and says something sharply. Lenetia responds but keeps her gaze down. My stomach twists in a knot when he reaches out and tips her chin up so she has to look him in the eye.

I look, too, and find a handsome soldier with those odd silver eyes. He sneers as he speaks to Lenetia, and for once I'm glad I can't understand their language.

He lifts his gaze over her head and stares back toward the palace. And then I hear it—yells and a multitude of heavy footsteps, as if the entire castle guard is running out.

The guard pushes past us, and Leander's voice bristles. My stomach sinks as I realize he's in trouble.

"Run!" Lenetia pulls me with her.

"What's happening?" I follow her through the gate and out onto a busy street full of carts, horses, and fae. An entire city with stone buildings and wide roads fans out from the foot of the palace.

"They've found Tyrios!" She darts to the left. "They'll kill us if they catch us!"

"What about Leander and Gareth?" I glance behind me and almost freeze at the sight.

10

LEANDER

The soldier falls before me, my punch taking him by surprise. The rest of the guards rush toward us, and Gareth and I draw our swords. My mate runs with the other changeling, safely away from the fray, though her gaze rests on me, her eyes full of worry. I want to take that fear away, to pull her in my arms and whisper the secrets of my heart. But it's too late.

An alarm sounds from deep within the castle. We aren't getting away. Not now. But I won't go down without a fight. My mate deserves nothing less. I will fight till my last breath to give her a chance at escape.

"Well, this is a right mess." Gareth backs to my elbow as the guards encircle us.

"Reminds me of that time in the Freckarian Mines."

He laughs. "The goblins were a good bit shorter than these guards."

"They'll bleed the same." I raise my sword as one of the soldiers brandishes his blade.

"It's been an honor, Leander." Gareth takes his battle stance as the ranks increase.

The soldiers advance en masse, their weapons drawn, their intent clear. We won't survive. Not against these numbers. I send a prayer to the ancestors that my mate gets away and that the other changeling will serve her as promised.

The first attack comes in a whirl of speed. I parry and thrust, using every bit of warrior ability I possess. The soldiers come all at once, their silver gleaming in the too-bright sun as they attack. The ring of metal on metal sings through the warm air, and Gareth and I—no strangers to long odds and mortal danger—fight for our lives.

I parry and counter-strike, my instincts telling me where the next blow intends to land. The nearest soldier slashes at me, leaving his flank open. I swing to end him, but a flash blinds me and my sword hits stone.

"The queen!" A soldier yells. "Protect the queen!"

"Stand down!" She appears before me, her hand holding my blade. She's covered in a diamond sheen, her powerful magic on display.

"But, your majesty, these two have—"

"I said *stand down*." Her silver eyes glint deadly, and the soldiers obey, sheathing their weapons and backing away.

I lower my sword to my side but keep it ready.

"You slew Lord Tyrios." It's an emphatic statement, not a question.

"I did." I meet her silver eyes as her diamond spell shimmers and dissipates.

"Was there a reason?" She seems almost bored as she releases my sword.

"He threatened my—"

Gareth coughs into his hand.

I take the easy hint not to mention that Taylor is my mate. "He threatened to kill a changeling female."

"Oh?" A sly smile plays at the corners of her red lips. "Is it a special one perhaps?" Her gaze slides past me, as if she knows exactly where Taylor went. "Where is she, by the way?"

"She is mine." I bite the words out. "And no one will harm her. If they do, they will suffer the wrath of the winter wind." An icy breeze wraps around us, pushing at the summer heat. My magic is barely contained and wants to lash out as badly as I do. But with my emotions churning with the discovery of my mate, it would be like setting off a powerful bomb of snow and ice, destruction and death.

"Lord Tyrios was one of my top advisors and one of the oldest fae in my service." She levels me with a hard stare. "You've taken him from me at a time when we need all the counsel we can get to solve the growing threat along our borders. And you've turned the rest of my court against you with this rash act." She shakes her head gracefully. "Where we had grown a bond between our realms, now the fabric is torn."

"I drew blood in the summer realm, which is a stain upon our truce." I sheath my sword. "But I would do it again to one such as Lord Tyrios."

"That's not helping." She waves a hand, and the diamond barrier from before forms around the three of us, effectively cutting off her soldiers from hearing our conversation. "I understand why you did it. She is your mate."

I tense, but I can't deny it. I will never deny Taylor.

Her shrewd gaze lightens a bit, but her brow remains troubled. "This has created another wrinkle between us. And, though I realize you don't agree, Tyrios *did* have a legal claim to the changeling. My nobles call for winter realm blood in retaliation."

"Then take mine." Gareth steps forward. "I have plenty to spare."

"It's not that simple." She eyes him. "Though your bravery does you credit."

"Do you seek blood, as well?" I ask.

She sighs. "I've lived for far too long to play the short game. Tyrios's blood is still warm, but his line will continue without him. The summer realm will quickly bury his memory and focus on new scandals or trivialities. At least, that's my hope." She turns and gazes toward the west, as if she can see beyond the garrison wall. "Keeping them steeped in gossip and spats means we don't have any true enemies knocking at our doors. When they get quiet and pay attention, that's when I worry. But the disappearances, they trouble me. And solving them is more important than Tyrios at the moment."

She's more level-headed than I ever gave her credit for. Beneath the summer realm glitz, she has the mind of a tactician and a cunning sort of foresight.

"What do you suggest?" I eye the soldiers who wait with caged aggression beyond the wall of diamond.

"I will call off my guard so you can escape, but I can't

promise my nobles won't give chase. Some of them are so old that their insides are twisted with malice and hate."

"Like Tyrios?" Gareth spits.

"Worse. Far worse. And he had plenty of allies who will feel the sting of his loss. I wouldn't be surprised if assassins have already been dispatched for you. Make haste from the summer realm." She holds a hand out toward the diamond encasement but pauses and meets my eye again. "Your mate. She's different. There's something about her I can't place. Be wary." With a snap of her fingers, the barrier fades, and she orders her soldiers to return to the castle and their posts.

They stare for a moment, disbelief flitting across some of their faces, then disband under the calm stare of their queen.

The pull to Taylor is strong, and she's been out of my sight for far too long. I motion to Gareth. With a brief nod to the queen, I turn and dash away from the gate. Gareth guards my back as we barrel into the busy city street.

"Where did they go?" I peer past the gawking city fae, searching the sidewalks for her.

A male approaches from the right with another behind him. My hackles rise, my fangs lengthening. They push changelings and lesser fae out of their way as they stalk toward us.

"Leander." Gareth draws his knives.

"I see them."

"That changeling from the dungeon. She's clever. Would have made for the stables when things got hairy." He sidesteps me and shoots out a hand, swiping a throwing blade from the air just before it makes contact with my skull.

"I would've caught that," I say as the metal clangs to the ground, and the assassin who threw it palms another.

Gareth grins and twirls his knives. "Go, I've got these two."

"You can't—"

"You're the hope for our future—you and your mate." He darts toward the two fae as the crowd senses the danger and parts for him. "Go. I'll catch up!"

I hate to leave him, but he can take care of himself. Taylor is the one who needs my protection. Turning, I hurry down the lane, the crowd dwindling as danger coils through the air. I'm almost to the road leading to the stables when a silver blade pierces my shoulder.

"*H*ere!" Lenetia yanks me into a muddy yard in front of a long gray building.

The street is clearing quickly, fae running into nearby businesses and narrow alleyways as the sound of fighting rings out behind us.

A fae stands at the entrance to the building, his arms crossed over his chest and his gaze trained on us. He asks a question.

Lenetia does the subservient thing again, staring at the muddy hay on the ground, and responds.

He spits, his gaze narrowing. Whatever she said, he clearly doesn't believe her.

"What's going on?" I edge closer to her.

"He won't give us the horses."

"I certainly won't." He speaks English. "There's no way the lord of winter sent you two changeling wastrels for his fine horses." He steps closer and reaches for us. "In the summer realm, horse thieves like you two get the lash.

Or maybe I should call the Catcher, see if he's on the hunt for escaped slaves."

We try to back away, but he's too fast, his meaty hands gripping our arms and dragging us forward.

"Get your hands off!" I try to pry his fingers loose, but it's like trying to bend iron, and he drags both of us into the stables.

"When the king hears of this, he'll—"

"Shut up." He slaps Lenetia, and she drops onto a bale of hay, one hand at her mouth.

My hand goes to the pocket of my dress, and my skin meets cold metal. I grip the dagger's hilt.

"And you, slave." He yanks me so close I can smell some sort of alcohol on his breath. "You'll need a proper lashing. Leather on your bare skin." He licks his lips, then snatches at the front of my gown.

I scream and fight him, but he's too strong, and the fabric gives a little at the seam along my side.

Lenetia stands and rushes him. He shoves her back so hard her head cracks on the wall, and she goes limp.

"Lenetia!" I struggle to get to her, but he wraps his arm around my waist and wrenches me away.

A horse whinnies deeper in the stables as someone screams in the street outside.

"Brought some trouble with you, eh? Let's see what's up under here, little changeling."

I swing wildly at him, but he grabs a handful of my hair, pulling so hard my scalp burns.

Terror wells up in me, the fear so tangible that my vision darkens and black spots swim in front of me. I take a deep breath and strike at him with the blade.

He roars and shakes me. "Filthy wench. I'm going to —" His grip on my hair slackens. "What did you ..." He lets me go entirely and stumbles back.

My vision clears, and I watch as he presses a hand to his chest, his eyes going wide.

"Taylor." Lenetia stirs and tries to stand.

I rush to her and examine her head.

"It's fine," she slurs.

Blood seeps from a cut along her hairline, but it's not too deep. At least, I think it's not.

"What?" She points at the fae who's still clutching his chest. Spidery black veins shoot from under his shirt and crawl up his neck. "What happened? Why is it black?"

"I don't know." I look at the knife in my hand. "There must have been something on the blade. Some sort of poison?"

"These northern realm fae aren't playing around," she says appreciatively.

The fae staggers toward us, then drops to his knees, the blackness spreading up to his chin.

"Get away from him." Lenetia shrinks back against me.

Another whinny brings my attention to the horses in the stalls along the back wall. Two large black stallions watch us, their eyes like liquid midnight. I have no doubt who they belong to.

"Come on." I help Lenetia up and half carry her down the row, the scents of manure, leather, and hay tickling my nose.

When we reach the large horses, they don't move, just look at us with what seems like a superior expression.

"Hi?" I've never ridden a horse, and these don't seem particularly friendly.

"Uppity horses. Typical fae rudeness." Lenetia laughs, but the sound is weak.

"Will they let us ride them?"

"Only one way to find out." She lifts the latch on the nearest stall and swings the door open.

The great beast doesn't move, just gives us that same stare. I glance at the fae. He's fallen onto his back, his eyes closed, but the blackness seems to have stopped spreading. I handle the blade gently as I slide it back into my pocket.

Lenetia speaks to the horse in fae. The horse breathes out hard and lifts its head, ignoring us. She grabs its bridle and pulls. It doesn't move, and she gives up, sagging against me.

"Stuck up bastard of a horse," she grouses.

"You need to use a gentle touch." Gareth strides up.

I jump and turn to find Leander behind me. He reaches for me, and I fall into his arms with an ease that should give me pause. Instead, I take his warmth and let him hold me.

"Is that blood?" I lean back and stare at his shoulder.

He makes an unconcerned face and shrugs, then casts a glance at the stable fae and raises his eyebrows in question. I hold up the blade. He grins, pride in his eyes. Heat bursts along my skin, and I'm certain my cheeks turn rosy under his adoring stare.

Gareth speaks to the two black horses. They huff, but walk out of their stalls. They tower over me, and Leander gives the haughtiest one a familiar pat on the nose. Not wasting a second, Leander lifts me onto the beast and then climbs up behind me.

"She's hurt." I reach for Lenetia, but Gareth scoops her up and onto his horse.

"I'm fine." Her eyelids flutter.

"Don't let her fall asleep," I warn, then yelp as the horse takes off toward the stable door.

Leander speaks to it in fae, and the beast jets out onto the cobblestone street and starts a thundering pace, scattering everyone in its path. The warm wind rushes by, creating a humming in my ears as the furious clip-clop of hooves echoes along the buildings ahead of us. The city is beautiful, flowering vines growing along the buildings and towering trees on every street corner. The buildings are made of the same pale stone as the castle. After a long while, we pass over a wide bay, its waters a bright Caribbean blue, and fly across the bridge and up the slight hill on the other side. The city is on an island, the water surrounding it like a vibrant, sparkling moat. But I'm not fooled by the beauty. Not after Tyrios and the fae in the stables.

Leander keeps one arm firmly around my waist as we hurtle down the road. The buildings eventually thin out, giving way to fields of unfamiliar crops and rows upon rows of flowers. Heat reflects from the blades of grass and hard dirt beneath the horses' hooves. Everything is too warm, too beautiful. I let Leander hold me closer, his chest a comfortable wall at my back. The miles fly away under the horses' steady gait. Deeper into the countryside we roam, the sun finally beginning to fade into a dusky twilight. I wonder again and again if this is just part of the odd dream that I must be having as I lie in the twin bed of my dorm room. But the jostling of the horse, the ache in my butt from the hard saddle, and the frequent kisses on the crown of my head from Leander tell me it's all real.

"Is she okay?" I peek over at Lenetia.

"She's awake." Gareth frowns. "She's been telling stories that would make a siren blush."

"You love them." Lenetia winks at me, though her face is pale. How long had she been in the dungeon when I landed there?

The horses slow somewhat as we crest a hill far outside the city that sparkles like a mirage. A deep wood sprouts up before us, the huge trees dappling the greenery beneath them with emerald light. It's a forest from a fairy story, but does that mean there's a wolf or worse inside?

Leander and Gareth kick off a long conversation as my eyelids finally begin to droop, the adrenaline of our escape wearing off. Leander rubs his thumb along my side in a circle. Round and round he's been going for a few moments, the touch soft and sweet. I inhale his winter snow and roaring fires and relax against him as his voice rumbles in that oddly beautiful tongue. I'm in a strange land with an even stranger man—fae—who's staked a claim on me.

We resume a gentler pace, heading for the forest.

"We'll make camp in the Greenvelde Wood for the night," Gareth says. "Then we'll ride at dawn. It will be three weeks before we reach the border of the winter realm. Then another three to reach the High Mountain, our home."

"Six weeks?" I clamp my eyes shut when the bridge of my nose begins to sting. "I have classes, and an exam, and my mom will eventually start looking for me and—" My breath catches in my chest as my voice rises. "And I don't belong here."

Leander wraps both arms around me and pulls me tight to him, his lips in my hair as he speaks low, foreign words. A tear slips down my cheek. I don't know how he sees it, but he does, because he wipes it away.

The horses move forward again, carrying me toward the darkening forest and an uncertain fate.

*C*laim her, claim her, claim her, CLAIM HER. My blood thrums insistently as I settle down on my bedroll and pat the furs beside me.

Taylor has spent the past hour fretting over the other changeling, seeing to her wound, and going over a few basic fae words. I've been grilling Gareth for more phrases from the changeling language. More of it's coming back to me, but I'm far from proficient.

I peer into the shadowy woods. Tiny fairies fly between the trees, chasing each other and stopping only to give us curious glances. They are far fairer than their winter realm brethren, but seem to be imbued with the same amount of mischief. We've already discovered some of our apples and briarberries are missing. We still managed a decent meal, though Taylor seemed unsure as I served her only the finest items from our provisions.

Gareth had laughed. "She says she can feed herself just fine."

I'd kept on, ensuring she ate until she was full, and

then tried to give her a little more. My mate would be well cared for, spoiled even. I smile at the thought and pat the furs again as Taylor rises from her spot next to the fire.

"Sleep," I say in her language.

She points to Lenetia and says something to the effect that she'd prefer to sleep with the other changeling. A growl vibrates under my ribs.

Lenetia shoos Taylor away. "No way I'm getting between a fae and his mate. I like my head attached, thank you very much." She says it again in English for Taylor's benefit, then turns her back to us.

Taylor bites her lip and looks down at me, her eyes tracing my chest. I'm still wearing my tunic, even though I prefer to sleep nude. I don't want to frighten her.

Gareth creeps around the edge of our camp, his steps silent to anyone else. My glamour camouflages our location, but it will dissipate if I fall asleep. Though, with my mate beside me, I don't see how I can slumber.

She edges closer and babbles in the changeling language while still pointing at Lenetia. Her nerves are adorable.

"Sleep," I tell her again, then hold my hands up, palms out. "Only sleep." I want far more than just a night of rest with her. I'd happily claim her in front of Gareth and the changeling, such is the nature of my need for her. But she's far too skittish for an open display.

"Just sleep?" She eyes the soft furs.

I nod.

She sighs, the fatigue evident in her movements. Keeping an eye on me, she sinks down beside me and lies on her back. The swell of her breasts makes my mouth water, and the moonlight shows her hardening nipples in sharp relief. Does she have any idea what she's doing to me? I have to shift my hips to hide my stiff cock.

"Just sleep," she repeats and looks at me, one eyebrow raised.

"Yes." I reach over and pull her to me.

She yelps and says something.

Lenetia pipes up from her spot by the fire with words like "mate" and "bond" and some other things I can't understand.

"Shh." I lie on my side so Taylor can rest her head on my arm.

She turns her head and peers at my shoulder. "The wound?"

"Heal fast." I say as best I can in her tongue. I intend to access my memories of the changeling language while I dream.

She says something like "not possible" and a few more things I can't catch, then she glances at the orbs floating through the forest, the fairies at play under the moonlight. She repeats "not possible" and sighs.

"Possible." I take her hand and press it to where the wound was. "Real."

Her skin is so warm against mine, and I can't imagine how good it will feel to have her hands all over me.

She swallows hard and crosses her arms over her stomach. Her small body is perfect next to mine, though I can't believe the ancestors have gifted me with such a fragile mate. Not fae, not from the winter realm—she's not one I would have ever thought was meant for me. But

just being close to her calms every bit of the raging winter
wind that has always swirled inside me.

She clears her throat, her eyes still wide open.

"You can't sleep like this. You must relax." I run my
hand over hers. The cursedly warm air prevents me from
soothing her beneath luxuriant furs, but all that will
change soon. Soon, she will be moaning for me as I taste
her sweet honey and take my time with her delicious
body.

"She can't relax with you pawing at her," Lenetia
calls.

Pawing? I would scoff, but I'm too attuned to my
mate's worry. "Tell her she's safe with me. Tell her I'd
never harm her or take anything from her without her
consent."

The changeling grumbles but translates. The words
seem to calm my mate, the tension falling away from her.

She looks up at me, her stunning eyes sparkling. My
heart beats for her, if only she could hear its song. Her
tongue darts out and wets her lips. My blood howls
through my veins, calling her name. The sweet scent rises
from between her legs, and her breaths come a little
faster. She feels the same need, the desire to be one with
me, she's just too scared to give in to it.

I settle next to her and whisper. "When I claim you
as mine, you will come more exquisitely than you ever
have in your life, little one."

A shiver courses through her, as if she understands
my words.

I hide my smile in her fragrant hair and hold her as
she eventually drifts into a peaceful sleep.

13

*L*eander cradles me all night, and I wake from dreams of crisp snow and icy lakes under a stunning blue sky. He was in them, too, but I push those memories aside.

His dark eyes meet mine, a hint of a smile on his angular face. "Sleep wet?" he asks.

"Um, what?" I scoot away, mortification turning my insides to lava. Was I so obvious? How could he tell what I'd been dreaming about? Oh my god. I press my thighs together. Can he *smell* me again?

"Well," Lenetia calls as she stirs a pot over the fire. "You meant 'sleep *well*.'"

"Well." His smile grows. "Sleep well?"

I run my hand across my forehead. Sheesh. "Yes. You?"

"Well." His hungry gaze strays down my body before catching my eyes again.

I swallow audibly and scramble up from the furs. My muscles ache from the night on the ground, and I try to stretch away the soreness as I walk to Lenetia. Leander rises and folds up the bedroll.

"You really let me down." Lenetia stirs what looks like a bubbling stew that smells of vegetables and herbs.

My mouth waters. "Let you down?"

"I thought I was going to see some hot mating fuckery last night. All I saw was awkwardness and then sleeping."

My cheeks turn about twenty shades of crimson. "I'm not *mating*."

"You will be." She scoops a ladle full of the stew into a wooden bowl and hands it to me. "You'll be riding that king over there like he's one of those stallions in no time."

"That's not—"

Leander walks past, a satisfied smile on his face, and straps the bedroll to his horse, Kyrin. I'm beginning to suspect he understands more English than he's been letting on.

I lower my voice. "I'm not having sex with him, okay? I'm just trying to get back home."

She snorts, the dirt along her cheeks cracking a little as she laughs. "Sure."

"I'm serious."

"So am I." She plops a wooden spoon into my bowl. "Eat up. Long day's ride ahead."

"I've never even done that before, so there's no way—"

"Never what?" She licks an errant drop of stew from her thumb and pours herself a bowl.

"Never, *you know*." I wish I hadn't said anything.

"Never been with a male?" She plops down next to me on the fallen leaves that blanket the forest floor.

"No." I take a bite of the stew and singe my tongue. Damn.

"Hmm." She shrugs. "Well, you're about to learn, queenie. So don't fret."

"You aren't listening." The food is delicious, despite the fact my tongue is in need of a burn unit. "I'm going to the winter realm so I can get back home. Not so I can be some queen or get with Leander—" I glance at him. He's hefting the saddle onto the other horse, and his broad back muscles stretch the fabric of his dark shirt. That little tingle between my legs begins anew, and I have to start again, "So, as I was saying, this is about me getting out of here."

"Right." She shrugs.

"And what about you?" I pull my gaze away from Leander before he catches me ogling him.

"Me?" She scratches her nose and examines her dirty fingernails. "What about me?"

"Don't you want to go home?"

"Home?"

"Yeah, back to the human world."

"That's not my home." She slurps her soup, apparently immune to the burn.

"But it's where you're from. Won't your parents want to have you back? Siblings? Friends?"

"You don't understand." She sighs.

"What don't I understand?"

"Changelings can't go back."

"Why not?"

Gareth strides up and serves himself some stew. "Morning."

"Morning." I hand him a spoon.

Lenetia ignores him. "I can't go back because some-one's taken my place."

"What?"

"When humans are exchanged, a fae takes their place in the human world. The parents don't know the differ-ence." Gareth blows on the steaming stew. "So there's nothing to go back to. As far as Lenetia's parents are concerned, she's still in the human world."

"Beth," she says quietly.

"What?" Gareth squints at her.

"My human name was—is—Beth. I think it was short for something, but I can't remember—"

"Elizabeth?" I guess.

She smiles, and I realize she's probably only a little older than I am. The dirt, bedraggled clothes, and tough personality all work together to hide her youth. Knowing that she was brought here against her will and forced to work as a slave while her parents believed she was safe and sound at home makes me hurt in ways I never have before. I reach over and squeeze her hand.

"Elizabeth. I think that was it. Yes." She hides her sorrow by downing her soup, but I saw the wetness in her eyes.

"Why do you take human children?" I ask Gareth.

"*I* don't take them." He meets my eyes. "It's an old tradition going back thousands of years. Sometimes, when a changeling babe becomes ill, its mother will choose to exchange it for a human. The human world is far more hospitable than many of the realms here in our world, and gives the fae child a chance at life. The fae child is given a permanent glamor to look like the human child and is sent to earth and exchanged. It's forbidden to do an exchange past childhood, because it's far too obvious that the switch has taken place. Children's memories fade, and humans are more likely to accept the child when it's young."

"But the fae parents don't treat the human child as their own."

He takes a careful bite of stew. "No."

"Definitely not," Beth grumbles.

"They use them as slaves." I can't hide the indignation in my tone.

He sighs. "Yes, much of the time."

"That's horrible!"

"I don't disagree." He takes another spoonful. "And that's why I've never had a changeling slave. Then again, I've never had children. If I had a babe that could survive in the human realm but not here, I don't know what I'd do." He holds up a hand. "But I'd never treat the changeling as less than my own."

"Why can't you just take your child to the human world without snatching someone else's?"

"The less the humans know about the other worlds, the better." His tone darkens. "Humans are both fragile and too clever for their own good. It's for their safety and ours. Swapping the child keeps everything in balance, and the humans are none the wiser."

"It's wrong."

"It may be wrong, but that doesn't mean it will stop." He stands. "We don't allow changeling slaves in the winter realm, but we do allow the exchange if a babe begins to fade."

I hand my half-full bowl to Lenetia, who gobbles it down. My appetite seems to have dried up with each explanation from Gareth, especially since I was exchanged and enslaved for no apparent reason. "Why was I swapped? The fae with my face didn't seem ill, and I'm far older than the allowed exchange age."

His brows furrow. "I don't know. That's something that we'll have to suss out once we reach the safety of the winter realm." He turns his head quickly, peering into the trees at our backs.

Lenetia tenses. "What? What is it?"

Gareth remains impossibly still, everything about him attuned to whatever he sensed in the woods. A tremor rolls up my spine, but I don't move, barely breathe.

After a long moment, he relaxes and turns back to the fire.

"What's out there?"

He rolls his shoulders. "Maybe nothing."

"But maybe something?" Lenetia spits on the ground.

"I don't know. For a moment, I thought I felt ..." He glances at me. "Doesn't matter. We're riding out as soon as we break camp, and then we're keeping a quick pace."

Leander strides up and has a quick talk with Gareth before sitting next to me.

"Food good?" He takes the proffered bowl from Beth.

"Yes." I'm still stewing over the changelings and apprehensive of whatever Gareth may have seen in the trees.

Leander must notice because he puts his arm around me gently. "Problem?"

"I could explain it, but you wouldn't understand me." I rub my eyes.

"Try me." He squeezes me gently.

"I'm going to clean up." Beth grabs the stew pot and heads toward the nearby stream.

"'Try me?'" I eye him. "You learn English overnight?"

"I knew the changeling language long ago, but I—" he screws his lips up on one side "—become rusted?"

"Rusty." I nod.

"Yes. I'm trying to renumber."

God, he's somehow cute when he says it wrong. This huge, brute of a man—male?—with the dark eyes and warrior's body is making me want to giggle. "Remember. You meant 'remember.'"

"Remember." He smiles. "My dreams help."

I don't know what to make of that statement. Dreams help? I'd ask for an explanation, but everything in me almost buzzes, as if there's some slight electrical current between us whenever we get too close. I try not to look at his mouth, the sinful curve of his lips, but I do, and I swear my heart trips and falls all over itself. To cover, I launch into an anti-exchange tirade that sums up my conversation with Gareth and my many objections to the practice.

He listens intently, then goes tense and still when I recount how I was exchanged.

"Two days here only?" His brow furrows.

"Right." I shrug. "That's what I've been trying to tell you. I don't belong here. I'm in college. I have classes.

And exams. And bills to pay. And *Friends* reruns to watch. And a roommate to strangle."

"Roommate." He scrunches his dark brows together and says something in fae that sounds like a curse "—fae?"

"No." Then I shake my head. "Well, then again, I really don't know. Maybe? She could have been a—"

A low, sharp whistle cuts through the air.

Leander is on his feet in an instant, pulling me up with him. Beth is rushing toward us from the stream, the pot left behind, as Leander throws me over his shoulder and runs to the horses.

*G*areth's warning whistle sets my teeth on edge, and I grab my mate and hurry to the horses. Once Taylor is secure, I climb up behind her and guide Kyrin deeper into the wood. The forest is still. Too still. No squirrels play amongst the leaves, and the fairies have all taken shelter in hollowed-out trees or drooping flower petals.

"What is it?" Taylor asks.

The answer to her question is 'danger,' but I don't want to say it. Instead, I grip her tightly and urge Kyrin to move faster through the trees.

"Curse the summer realm." Gareth and the changeling ride up behind us. "There's a witch trailing us."

"What sort?"

"From the scent of brimstone I caught, she's an Obsidian."

I clench my eyes shut for only a moment. "Can we outrun her?"

"We can try." He sighs.

The trees whisper around us, warning vibrating through the leaves and into the muggy air. A creature of pure evil, an Obsidian witch would be a foe that even Gareth and I might not be able to defeat. Who would have sent her after us?

"No nobles in the summer realm could command one such as this." Gareth seems to read my mind.

"Either she has a score of her own to settle or she was sent by the king beyond the mountain." I grit my teeth as clouds pass across the sun, turning the woods sullen and gloomy.

"What is going on?" Taylor turns and meets my gaze, her peculiar blue eyes open wide.

"We're about to get flayed to the bone while still alive, and then have our marrow sucked out." The other changeling shivers.

"What?" Taylor shakes her head.

"An Obsidian witch hunts us." Lenetia hugs herself. "We're dead."

"Leander?" Taylor says my name, uncertainty in her tone, and I know that I will die to save her should it come to that.

"She will not harm you." I stroke her soft hair, then pull her even tighter against me. "Kyrin, run as if the master of the twelve dark Spires chases us."

The beast snorts, his body going taut as a faint cackle floats through the darkening trees. With a slight rearing back, he takes off over the moss-strewn ground and plunges ahead. I hold on to Taylor and the saddle, pushing her forward so that she is bent over his mane and safe from the stray branches.

Even Kyrin's thundering hooves can't cover the sound of her heartbeat. A wild thing, it rampages against her ribs as we tear through the greenery and flowers.

I throw up a barrier behind us, one that camouflages our sight and sound, but I'm not foolish enough to believe that an Obsidian wouldn't be able to see through it. The last one I fought almost took me with her to the Spires, but I killed her with the help of Gareth and the fighters that would become my honor guard in the northern realm. Even now, members of the Phalanx wait for us at the border, but if the Obsidian catches us, we may never make it. The thought of what the creature would do to Taylor turns my insides into an inferno of aggression, but stopping to fight now would only put her in more danger.

So, we run. We run until Kyrin begins to flag, his jumps barely clearing fallen trees and low-lying brush, his breathing coming in too-fast bursts.

"Slower, my friend." I lean back, pulling Taylor to an upright position as Kyrin eases off somewhat.

The dreariness of the witch's presence is gone, the woods back to their dreamlike perfection. But the hair on the back of my neck still stands on end. She's on our trail, and an Obsidian will not stop until she draws blood.

"We can't delay." Gareth's horse Sabre is huffing out hard breaths, his fatigue matching Kyrin's.

"We can't keep running them like this either." I pat Kyrin.

"I know, and this waif is already exhausted just from

hanging on." He scowls at the changeling, but I notice he grips her tightly to him.

"She needs a break." Taylor reaches toward the changeling. "Beth, are you okay?"

"Fine," she mumbles.

"We can't stop now. Not with the witch at our backs." Gareth shakes his head.

"We have to. Beth can't take much more. She was far worse off in the dungeon than I was." Taylor puts her small hand over mine. "Please? Can we just stop for a minute so I can check on her?"

"Of course." I am powerless to deny her anything, especially when she shares her touch with me. She deserves safety and happiness as my queen, not danger from all corners.

Gareth frowns. "This is a bad idea."

"I hear a stream up ahead. The horses need a drink and a little rest. I'll keep my glamour up while we stop, and we'll be moving again before the sun begins its descent."

"I don't like it." He casts a glance behind us.

"I don't like it, either, but we can't let the horses get past the point of usefulness. And Taylor is right, your changeling is pale."

"She's not *mine*," Gareth grumbles but relents with a sigh. "Just for a moment, then." He pulls up next to the glistening stream and climbs down, then gently hoists Lenetia to the ground.

"Thank you." Taylor squeezes my hand, and the bond between us snaps even tighter. My everything, my entire future is right in front of me.

The witch wants to sever that link, but she'll have a hell of a fight on her hands before she can even come close. I've killed her kind once before. I can do it again.

*T*he bed roll isn't as warm without Leander in it. But he and Gareth prowl the edges of the camp, their weapons strapped tightly to their bodies.

"Isn't this fun?" Beth rolls onto her back and throws one arm over her eyes. "I doubt we'll survive the night."

We'd stopped only briefly at midday so I could tend to Beth and the horses could have a rest. Then we rode again, so far and so fast that I wondered if my ass would ever stop aching. The answer, I find, is no. No, it won't.

I roll over and face Beth. "What's an Obsidian witch? When I asked Leander, he pretended he didn't know the English words to tell me."

Though her color is better, and I managed to give her an extra helping of some strange vegetables, she still sounds weak. Whatever her master did to her isn't something that will fade quickly. She needs rest.

Her teeth chatter. "Obsidian. Ugh."

"That bad?"

"Kind of the worst creature in all of Arin." She

bobbles her head a little back and forth. "Well, no, the worst of all is a necromancer. But an Obsidian witch is up there."

"Why?"

She sighs. "Imagine a creature spawned from the Spires that—"

"What are the Spires?"

"You really *are* a brand new exchange."

I shrug, though she can't see it.

"The Spires are like, like ... hmmm. On earth there was talk of a place called hell, right?"

"Yeah."

"They are hell, but a real place with real evil and sometimes the evil manages to crawl out of it and torment the rest of us. That's where the Obsidian witches come from."

"Demons?"

"Sure." She splays her fingers and counts off on one hand. "Demon, succubus, child-eating, spell-casting, death-bringing harlots from the Spires. They're more powerful than most fae can ever dream of. Can even bend reality, so they say. And now one of them hunts us. Perfect."

Though the air is still warm, I pull a fur over my shoulders. "But Gareth and Leander can defeat it, right?"

She snorts. "I sure hope so. Otherwise, you're going to learn pretty quickly all the things the Obsidian is capable of. And I have no doubt you'll be a fine meal for her."

"You said they eat children."

She turns and peers at me with one eye. "They'll eat whatever flesh they can find. Yours and mine included."

"Jesus." I pull the fur tighter and try to find Leander through the trees. I can't see him. Panic rises in my gut, but I tamp it down and scoot a little closer to Beth. She needs a bath even worse than I do, but having her near is still a comfort.

"If she attacks, maybe these two can slow her down while we escape."

Leave Leander behind? I rub my chest, something like heartburn setting in there.

She laughs, though it's more of a gallows sound. "Calm down. I'm certain he would never leave you unless absolutely necessary."

"It's not that."

"It is. You're his mate. Somewhere inside you, you can feel the pull."

"How do you know all this?"

"I've been around enough mated fae."

"But I'm not fae."

"No. But you *are* mated. I can't imagine it's much different for a human. Besides, I see the way you look at him."

I feel my cheeks heating, but I can't deny what she's said. Leander is still a mystery to me, but I've found a safety in his arms that seemed impossible when I first woke in the dungeon.

"Don't worry about it." She settles in with a large yawn. "We'll probably all be dead soon anyway."

"Thanks." I turn to say more, but she's already snoring. Apparently, mortal danger doesn't faze her.

I'm not so lucky. I toss and turn, each sound in the trees drawing my attention as my imagination runs wild. By the time I finally close my eyes, the fire is burning low and it's been hours since I've seen Gareth or Leander.

I fall into an uneasy sleep, my mind refusing to shut down entirely. But when it does, I try to shake myself awake. It doesn't work. In my dream, I'm rising from my bedroll and walking into the dark woods. I know I shouldn't leave the safety of the camp, but I can't stop.

My footfalls are silent, and I can't scream, can't make a sound. It's as if I'm being pulled forward by a rope around my middle while an ice-cold hand clamps down on my mouth. I struggle against its hold and try to shake my head, to do anything that would wake me.

Onward I walk, stumbling over underbrush, tree branches scratching at my face.

"Leander!" I call his name over and over in my mind, but he doesn't appear. There are only trees and the growing darkness that seems to muffle every bit of faint starlight through the leaves.

A shadow flits through the trees and comes ever closer. It says something in fae, but I can't understand. A hot, streaking pain cuts through my mind, so much pain that tears well in my eyes.

"I said, 'He can't hear you, dearie.'" A low snort. "But I've fixed you so we can talk."

"Let me go." I ... I just spoke fae. How did I speak fae, *in my mind*?

"Because I taught you. Can't have a conversation unless you speak the same language, eh? And my changeling hasn't been worth two drops of fairy blood in ages."

The fae words come easily to my mind, but I'm too preoccupied with the situation to linger on my newfound language. "Please just let me go."

The shadow darts around me. "I would, but I'm hungry, you see."

I enter a clearing, the darkness whirling like a midnight tornado in the center. "Leander!" I try again in vain.

"Shh now, changeling." A form materializes from the darkness. A young woman, her skin crackled and black, as if she's made of dark glass that someone shattered and reformed. Obsidian. Her movements are fluid, her black eyes focused on me as her feet barely touch the ground. Her hair and eyebrows are a shocking white, impossible against her black skin.

My stomach churns, and my bladder feels uncomfortably full and on the verge of release.

Her forked tongue darts out, and she smiles, her lips crackling against each other. "Delicious." She sniffs the air hard, her sharp black teeth clacking as she exhales and comes nearer, so close I can feel her breath on my neck. "So tasty, fresh, and new." When her tongue slithers across my cheek, I scream.

"I like the sound of your fear." Her fingers dig into my sides, the tips like claws. "I will make a stew of you. Chew your marrow and pick my teeth with your bones. Taste like boar, you will. Rich and roasted and oh, how tasty you will be once you've rotted a while. Your bits under my nails, I'll lick them out slowly, savoring."

I scream again as she presses one claw to my face and draws blood.

Blood. My blood. This isn't a dream. Ice trickles down my spine. *This isn't a dream.*

Pulling back, she licks her finger. Her white eyebrows draw together, and her eyes flick back to my face. "Tasty, but ... But not quite right." She cocks her head to the side. "And what's this?" She points to the necklace I still wear.

"I don't know. Let me go."

She eases closer, the scent of fire and sulphur leaching from her into the air. "By the Spires, it can't be. But it is." Her cackle shatters my mind, the notes harsh and unrelenting.

I press my hands to my ears but don't dare close my eyes.

"Calm now, child. Calm." She presses one cold finger under my chin and forces me to meet her bottomless gaze. "You were foretold."

"I'm not supposed to be here."

"Yes, you are." She taps her finger to the side of her nose.

"If you let me go, I'll leave this place and never return. I just want to get back home to—"

"You *are* home." She reaches for my necklace but can't seem to grasp it, as if there's a barrier around it. "Home, home, home." Her cackle breaks through again, and I think my ears might truly be bleeding. "Sit, young one." The rope pulls me toward the murky tornado, which dissipates until only black flames in a cauldron remain. The unseen force makes me plop down on a log next to the fire as the witch peers into the iron pot.

"Are you going to kill me?" I speak past the knot in my throat.

She clicks her nails against her black teeth and gives me an appraising look. "Maybe." Her predatory stare doesn't ease.

I tell myself 'maybe' is better than 'yes' and continue, "Why are you following us?"

She spits into the cauldron, which sends a plume of black shooting high above us. "Compelled." Gnashing her teeth, she focuses on the cauldron. "Compelled to find the king of the winter realm. Treated like a slave, summoned from my cave, away from my lovely pile of bones and rotting flesh, *compelled*."

I push aside the visual of her crouching over putrefied remains. "By who? Who compelled you?"

"King beyond the mountain he calls himself." She spits again. "Compelled. Like a dog. Like a slave. I am Obsidian. I do not break! Not for anyone. But this king beyond the mountain. His magic." She shakes her head. "Pulled me from my cave, he did. Sent me to this horrid place. I must find the king of the winter realm."

"Why?"

She holds her hands up, and her black claws elongate, the edges sharper than the finest razor. "To kill him. To take his handsome head to the king beyond the mountain. I can have the rest of him. I can keep all those other parts, let them rot until they are gloriously foul." She smacks her hard lips. "He will taste even better then."

"Can I convince you to let us go?" I try not to sniffle.

She turns her head sharply like an owl. No one's head should be able to turn that far. "What can you give me?"

"I ... What do you want?"

"Making a deal in the realms isn't a good idea, young one. Promises here mean more, cost more, last longer. Forever." She turns back to her cauldron.

Her words raise something in my memory, something I can't quite see or recall.

"I asked you what you want."

"Compelled, young one." She pulls at her white hair. "*Compelled*. No bargaining. Nothing can stop the king beyond the mountain. I will kill the king of the winter realm. And then, young one, I may kill you, too. You were foretold, but I have no use for prophecy." She waves a black hand. "Not in my cave, in the dark, with all my lovely, lovely bones. Yours would look lovely in there, too."

A shudder wracks my body as I struggle to find something, anything to bargain with. "What do you mean I was foretold?"

"Doesn't matter. Kill the king, kill the king," she says in a sing-song. "Kill the—" Her head turns almost completely around as she stares at some spot in the woods behind me, and a vicious smile spreads across her face. "And here he is at my doorstep." Her sharp teeth snap.

"Taylor!" Leander yells for me, concern vibrating through the notes.

"Leander, run!" I scream until that cold hand slaps over my mouth once more.

The witch disappears in a plume of black, and seconds later I hear Leander's agonizing yell. It rakes down the sides of my soul, drawing blood from a place inside me I didn't know existed. I have to get to him, to help him somehow.

But I'm trapped by the witch, my body unable to heed my commands to move, to run.

Another roar rips through the silent woods, and I know—somehow I *know*—that he is badly injured. Tears roll down my cheeks as I try to free myself, but all I can feel is the witch's cold hands holding me still as she cackles in the dark.

ROAD TO WINTER

FAE'S CAPTIVE BOOK 2

1

LEANDER

*F*ire scorches across my back as I twist away from the witch's claws. Her venom is particularly potent, slowing my reactions and dimming my vision.

"On your right!" Gareth leaps for her, sword swinging, but she disappears in a black plume and cackles with glee.

"You taste like power, winter king." Her voice whistles through the trees. "Old, strong roots. Cold wind and the delicious bite of fresh snow."

I stumble forward, staying upright as I follow my mate's scent. Her fear is acrid in my nostrils. The vile witch took her as she slept, slipping her past my defenses with powerful dark magic straight from the Spires. I only realized Taylor was gone when the other changeling began to yell.

Gareth keeps close to my back, just like old times. We're at war again, but now the stakes are even higher. I can't lose Taylor.

"So sweet to try and save your poor, poor mate." The voice comes from everywhere and nowhere.

"If you've harmed her, I will—"

"No." A shadow whips to my right. "I won't harm that one. That wouldn't do. Don't you know what she is?"

I sense the attack coming and spin, lashing out with my blade. Contact, but my sword glances off her obsidian skin, the blow jarring up my arm.

"She's a changeling, foul witch," Gareth growls and throws out his hand, sending a wild blue fireball crashing into her.

But she's an Obsidian. Fire cannot harm her. She opens her mouth wide and inhales, swallowing the flames before disappearing again.

Her cackle sounds from behind the next tree. I rush forward and stab the spot, finding only air. Another slash of fire opens across my back, and I whirl as the dark creature dances back, her feet not touching the ground. Gareth rushes her, swinging for her face, but she vanishes before he lands the blow.

"A changeling?" The cackle grows to a cacophony that echoes around us. "Fools."

There's only one way to destroy an Obsidian witch, and it almost killed me the last time. But to save my mate, I will fight until my last breath. This sacrifice will be worth it.

"Draw her ahead of us." I back up to stand next to Gareth. Blood drips down a nasty gash on his face. If he's not careful, he'll have another wound to match the jagged scar on his right cheek.

"This one gives even better than the last one we

killed." He spits blood. "It will take all you have. Can you do it?"

"I have to. Be ready."

He grimaces. "You shouldn't—"

"Secrets make enemies, my lords." Her voice whispers right beside me, but when I strike out, nothing is there.

Gareth limps ahead of me, his sword down. He's exposed. The witch won't be able to resist. Dirty fighters, they take their prey however they can get it.

Her sharp claws click, each tap like a crack of lightning. Gareth drops his sword and trips, falling onto his knees.

The darkness grows around him.

I close my eyes and breathe in the strange warm air, the hint of brimstone, the flowery scent that pervades these woods. But when I open my eyes, I breathe out winter, snow, and ice. The ground freezes beneath me, shooting out in a ring of frost as I focus on the darkness that circles my second in command.

"Sleep now, warrior. Sleep and know I will take you with me. Back to my cave. You will join my beautiful bones. Your flesh will wilt until I'm ready to feast." She comes into view, standing behind him, her claws drawn back.

I focus on her as everything inside me unbinds itself, the magic flowing through me in a rush that almost knocks me off my feet. We only have one shot at this, one chance to destroy her before she kills all of us.

She slashes downward, her black claws glinting, and I

push my magic to her, unleashing the icy bite of the winter realm in all its beautiful terror.

The witch screeches, but the ice does its work, freezing her stone skin and locking her into a prison of frost. I keep my magic flowing as she fights against the winter's hold. Beads of sweat coat my body, and my wounds bleed like a mortal's. I can't heal myself, not when all my magic is spent to cage the witch. Her struggles slow, her body freezing into a mass of rage and fear. When the ice is thick around her, I hold my magic steady, pulling it deep from within and focusing all of it on her. Just like any stone, freezing makes obsidian brittle, prone to crack and shatter. Her skin provides the perfect armor ... until it's chilled by the heart of the winter realm.

Gareth grabs his sword and rises. "Almost there." Pulling back, he aims to shatter her.

"I relent!" she screams through frozen lips. "I relent and shall not harm any of your party!"

Gareth pauses and glances at me. I'm fading, my magic stores burning away. My radius of ice blasts outward, coating every tree and flower in sight with frost. I must freeze all the way through to her rotted heart before he can strike. I'm almost there, my ice diving into every dark nook and putrid cranny of her being.

"A boon in exchange for my life." Her voice is a wail, her black form frozen in a sea of white ice. "Please, my lords. A boon for your mate! Spare my life."

"Leander?" Gareth still holds his sword high, ready to splinter her into nothing more than shards of black glass. It's the only way to kill her.

If he doesn't strike now, we won't have another

chance. I can't let her go, not when my mate's life is on the line.

"A boon for your mate! I swear on the Spires!" Thunder cracks through the trees.

A promise like that cannot be broken, not in this world or any other.

"My lord?" Gareth vibrates with aggression, ready to strike the final blow.

"No." I release my magic. Or at least I try to. When I've drained it like this, it holds onto me like a tether, tugging me away from myself and into the otherworld. I fight its pull, but the effort takes me to my knees. This is the danger, the thorn on the rose of magic.

I glare at the witch. "One wrong move, foul one, and I swear to the Ancestors I'll find some other way to end your miserable life."

"I gave my word." She shakes off the outer layer of ice but doesn't dare move too much. "My word is just as good as yours."

I gulp in breaths and try to calm the fury of my heart. My eyes close. The magic calls to me, promises me rest, promises to reveal secrets that only the greatest magic-wielders have ever discovered. It's a lie, I tell myself. Magic is wily and cruel at its heart, but it speaks to me so sweetly that I almost falter.

"Steady, Leander. Your mate. Remember your mate." Gareth's voice comes to me as if from a long distance.

"I am your mate, your true one," the magic dances around me. "Come and I will teach you forgotten ways. Things no other immortal knows. You will truly be a king then, never to be defeated."

Its whisper is like the kiss of silk. I want to know the deepest ways of magic. Maybe I could go with it, just for a moment. Just for a glimpse of what lies in the otherworld.

"Yes." The voice turns into a dainty fairy made of blue embers. "Only for a moment. Take my hand and you will know the treasured secrets that can save your kingdom."

I raise my hand, though it seems to carry an almost unbearable weight.

"Leander." Another voice, this one soft and sweet.

"Who—"

"Shh, take my hand." The fairy reaches for me.

"Leander, please." A gentle touch across my forehead, and the sweet voice comes again, "I need you."

"Don't listen," the fairy hisses.

"Leander. It's me, Taylor. Please wake up."

"Taylor." I step back from the fairy. "My mate needs me."

"Your mate," the fairy snarls and snakes into a looping swirl of pure magic. "Your downfall. The downfall of your world."

"What? What do you mean?"

The magic laughs and fades, the blue embers disappearing. "You will only know if you come to the otherworld. If you let go and take my hand."

"I can't let her go."

"Then you shall learn what I mean soon enough." The magic evaporates, and I open my eyes.

"Leander." Taylor strokes my cheek.

The mate bond roars back to life inside me, and I sit up and pull her into my arms.

I cup her face with my palm and kiss her.

She squeaks with surprise, but I can't go another second without this connection. I'm too rough, too fierce, but I can't stop this. She grips my tunic and holds on as I run my fingers into her hair. Her lips—at first hard and closed—soften as I tease them with my tongue. Her eyes flutter closed, and I caress the seam of her mouth, urging her to open for me.

When she does, a low purr rumbles through my chest, and I delve my tongue into her slowly, touching and tasting the sweetness of my mate. Where she is hesitant, I am hungry, starved for her touch. I take her mouth like I want to take her body, feeling every bit of her, making her mine and leaving my mark.

She melts in my arms, pressing against me as I stroke her tongue and squeeze her silky strands between my fingers. My cock is so hard it almost hurts, and the need to claim her fully beats like war drums in my veins. When I slant my mouth over hers even more, she moans in her throat. I'm balancing on a razor's edge, and that sensual sound threatens to send me careening headlong into mating her.

"My lord?" Gareth clears his throat.

I can't relinquish her, not now. Not when she's in my arms, her soul grazing the edges of mine. I clutch her to me, the primal instinct to shield her from any other male taking over. She's not marked, not fully mine. That means she isn't safe. Some other male could try and take her. I growl and my fangs begin to lengthen.

Taylor pulls away, her eyes widening. She tries to scramble off my lap, but I hold her still.

"Leander!" She can't escape my grasp.

Claim her, mark her, take her. The primal fae roars inside me, demanding I take what is rightfully mine.

"You're scaring her, Leander." Gareth's voice is gentle. "Old friend, please."

"She's mine." The words are guttural. I can't let her go even though she's trying to push me away.

"I know." Gareth steps closer. "But you're suffering from magic withdrawal and blood loss. You aren't thinking straight. You need to release her."

I look into her eyes, and it's like a kick in the gut. Fear. Her sweet scent of arousal has changed to one of terror. And I'm the one who is scaring her.

Even though my instincts rage, I release her and set her on her feet. She backs away to Gareth, who is wise enough not to touch her.

"He needs help." Gareth hurries over to me and examines my wounds.

"I'm fine." I feel the urge to shove him away, to barrel right past him and to the one who can ease the ache inside me.

"Leander." He takes a deep breath. "Look at her. She's not used to any of this. It's all terrifying to her. And you're not helping right now."

"She's my mate," I argue, but my fangs retract, and my mind begins to clear. I hadn't hurt her, had I? Guilt burrows under my skin as I look at her, her teeth chattering as she hugs herself. What have I done?

"I'm going to do my best to heal some of these." He points to the cuts along my back and arm.

"Oh, Ancestors, no," I groan. Gareth is great with a destruction spell, if a bit wild, but his healing can go either way. I once saw him try to repair Grayhail's broken leg. When Gareth was done, Gray had two broken legs.

"I have to try. You aren't healing."

"No." I lean away from him.

"Hold tight." A blast of green shoots around me, the magic teasing along the edge of my depleted stores. My wounds burn, and I fear he's ripped them open even more. Another blast of green, and more stinging pain have me gritting my teeth.

"Not so bad." Gareth sits back and inspects me. "Still need some time for them to heal all the way, but at least the bleeding's stopped."

The fog lifts all the way, my senses snapping back into place. "Taylor." I look up at her, anguish in my heart. "I'm so sorry, little one."

She nibbles her bottom lip and shakes her head a little.

"I'm sorry I scared you."

"You have fangs." Her voice trembles.

Gareth gasps, and I can only stare at her.

"You speak fae?" Gareth barks.

"I do now. The witch—she wanted to talk to me, and she couldn't do it in changeling, so she—"

"Gave her that knowledge for free," the witch grumbles. "Thought I'd eat her before she could put the language to use, though."

I rise to my knees, and Gareth helps me to my feet.

The poison is fading, my body growing stronger with each breath.

"Fangs," Taylor says again, and stares at my mouth. That look sends tendrils of heat licking along my skin. She has no idea what a delicious lure she is.

"And you ... you changed." Her brows knit together. "Like you were—"

"Feral." I move toward her, and the relief I feel when she doesn't back away is a salve on my wounds more powerful than magic. "When a fae has lived for several ages, the feral part of us grows stronger."

"Feral?" She asks. "Like a cat?"

"A cat? More like a primal creature that relies on instinct and basic needs."

"So, a cat." She nods.

"The only cats I know of are the shifting panthers of the Twisted Pines, and I suppose they are somewhat feral, but are more known for cheating at cards than anything else." I stand in front of her and press a hand to her cheek where a scratch veers toward her ear. "I'm so sorry you saw me like that, little one. Are you hurt?"

I hold my breath, fearing she will say *I* hurt her in some way.

"No. The witch just talked to me, really. I mean, she pulled me out of my bed and had me walk through the woods. But, considering all that's happened in the past few days, chatting with her was probably the least dangerous thing I've done." She glances behind her at the witch who's still encased in my ice up to her waist. "But don't get me wrong. She's creepy as all hell."

"I could've eaten you, girl." The witch sniffs.

"Could've feasted on your bones and fresh meat. I didn't, yet you call me names."

I step between Taylor and the witch. "Threaten my mate again, black one, and I will finish you."

"Not a threat. Just saying what I *could have* done, but *didn't* do." She spits on the ground, and the spot sizzles. "Not creepy. Magnanimous!"

"You promised me a boon for your life. Are you prepared to give it?" I move closer to her, my strength returning and relief that Taylor is unharmed buoying me.

"Compelled." She spits again. "Compelled by the king beyond the mountain. But I drew blood." She grins, her sharp black teeth like a wild animal's. "I drew royal blood. An Obsidian witch does not break. I will not break, and I did what I was compelled to do. I no longer feel it. But I do feel the tether of our agreement." She grumbles and tries to pull one leg free to no avail. "Cold."

I point at the frost around her. "I'll free you only after you've granted the boon."

"I promised the boon for your mate. Not you." She taps the side of her nose. "But I can grant you one as well, if you'd like to bargain for one."

"I don't bargain." No fae will volunteer to make promises, and if one does, it never bodes well.

"I could tell you such things, winter king." Her tone turns dreamy. "About yourself, your mate, the king beyond the mountain. Valuable information. Priceless."

"Then tell me."

She tsks. "Not for free. Nothing is free."

"I don't bargain."

"Pfft." She sweeps her white hair from her black

shoulder. "Perhaps not today, winter king. But you will. By the end, you will beg me for a bargain." Her pointy teeth clack against each other again. "Maybe I'll give you one, maybe I won't."

My hand itches toward my blade, but I don't draw it. "Get on with the boon."

"It's for your mate only. Not you. You must go."

"I'm not leaving her alone with you, witch."

"Selene. Selene is its name." She wrenches one leg from the ice, but the other remains stuck.

"I'm not leaving, and I'm beginning to rethink this boon."

"You can't kill me now. We both know it." She bares her teeth. "No more winter in you. Not enough."

I regret sparing her. "Maybe I can't shatter you, but I can make you hurt. And I've recently come up with a theory." My voice drops to lethal levels. "The only known way to kill you is to shatter you with cold. But perhaps we're missing something. Maybe I simply need to experiment. Shove a sword down your throat, take a diamond axe to your head, roast you over a fire until the obsidian gets hot enough to melt. There must be some way to—"

"I gave my word and you dare threaten me? Dare question my oath simply because I am Obsidian?" A phantom wind stirs the witch's white hair, and she narrows her black eyes. The tension rises around us like floodwaters, and I raise my sword.

"Selene." Taylor hurriedly steps to my side. "I apologize for calling you creepy."

The witch's white eyebrows twitch, and I get a glimpse of what she could have been had she not fallen into the twisted evil of the Spires. Witches like her were once fae, but they followed the call of the dark and wound up changed by the mysterious forces that inhabit the Wasted Lands.

"Apologize to me?" Selene peers at Taylor as if she's confusing and entrancing all at once. "No one has ever apologized to Selene." She taps her chin. "Begged? Yes. Demanded? Yes. Cursed? Certainly." She cackles. "But apologized? No." She points one long finger at Taylor. "You are a special one, and not only because you were foretold."

I want to ask her what she means, but I can't. Making another deal with a loathsome creature like her would end badly.

"Well, I mean it." Taylor shrugs, innocence in every move she makes. "I don't know what's happened to you or anything about you really. And you were forced to come after us. So, I can't blame you for it."

"Yes, yes. All true. Wise one, you are." The witch nods furiously.

"Little one." I lean down and kiss the crown of Taylor's head. "You are new to this world, and your heart is purer than anything I've ever beheld. But an Obsidian witch is nothing to pity. Selene has likely shed more innocent blood than you can even imagine."

She meets my eye, her blue ones sparkling even under the night sky. "You're right. I don't belong here."

I wince and want to tell her she belongs here with me, always, but she continues, "And Selene has said some things that make me—" She swallows hard. "Uncomfortable, to say the least. But I don't know what she's been through or why she's like this. So, I'm going to reserve judgment."

"You don't understand. Your heart is too pure for—"

"You don't know me, Leander." She straightens her back. "You don't know anything about me. However pure you think I am, I can assure you that's not the case."

Her sharp tone cuts me to the quick. "I know you." I take her hand and place it over my heart. "I know you as the other half of my soul. And one day, I hope to know every minute detail about you. When we're settled in the winter realm, I'll happily spend all my time learning you." I hold my tongue before I say I hope all of that time is spent in bed.

She drops her gaze.

I know what she's thinking as surely as I know the snows are falling fast and thick on the High Mountain. She longs for her old life, for the land of the humans. It is up to me to show her that this is her home. That I am worthy of her, that she belongs atop the throne of the winter realm, ruling alongside me. I make a promise to myself that I *will* prove to her that she belongs with me. That's one bargain I have no trouble making.

The witch rips her other leg free from the frost and rushes forward. I pull Taylor behind me and brandish my sword.

"*E*nough heroics, my lord." The witch rolls her eyes at Leander. "I was only testing out my parts, making sure you didn't frost them into oblivion." She dusts herself off, icy flakes flying. "And you're not necessary. Go, go, stalk away and be kingly elsewhere. I'd rather speak to the pretty one who is far more level-headed than your dark fae heart ever could be."

"I'm not leaving." Leander holds his blade to her throat.

"Your threats are wasted on Selene, winter king." She winks. "Drained. Your magic only whispers to me now, and it dances away from you and back to the otherworld. And oh, how it pesters! The otherworld calls and calls and calls you." She presses her hands to her ears. "Always pulling at me, too. Wanting to show me even more than I already know. But I know too much as it is." She cackles, the sound painful. "So you can go. And I will grant my boon."

Leander—still wounded and clearly exhausted—is ready to fight to keep me safe. Endearing? Yes. Unnecessary? Also, yes.

"I'm not leaving, black one," he growls.

"Leander." I put a hand on his forearm. "Please. We have an arrangement, right, Selene?"

"We do." She picks at her nails and scrapes one clean on her teeth.

I refuse to think that she just ate a piece of the skin she scratched off Leander. Nope. Not thinking it.

"I'll be fine." I pat Leander's arm again, though he doesn't lower his sword.

"She's dangerous."

"I am." Selene grins and flicks another bit of carnage from her nails into her mouth. "But not to you, young one. And I gave my word." She cuts her gaze to Leander. "You know what that means."

"Give her a chance." I don't know what I'm doing, but I do know that if I don't calm this situation, the battle will start all over again, and from the looks of Leander, he might not make it out alive.

He finally lowers his blade, and I let out a deep breath.

"Only because you wish it, little one, I'll go. But I'll be close. So close that one wrong move will be disastrous for you, witch." He gives her a hard look, one that would probably make me pee myself if it were aimed at me. But it isn't. I don't fear him, and after that kiss—*that kiss*, my insides tremble—I feel so many things toward him that I can't even decide on one.

He leans down and whispers in my ear. "I know what you are thinking about, little one. And I intend to *discuss* it more very, very soon."

When he says "discuss," I get a mental flash of the two of us beneath soft furs before a roaring fire as a winter wind howls outside. I clench my eyes shut for a second. *Dear Horny Thoughts: Please go away. Xoxo, Taylor.* I let out a huff of breath and force a smile. "All good here, Leander. Don't worry."

After giving Selene one more face-melting glare, he turns and strides back toward camp.

"Just us girls." She twirls, her white hair flying out, and then we're both back in the clearing—her leaning over her cauldron, me sitting on the log. At least this time I'm not bound by her magic.

She opens one hand and blows on it, as if she's blowing a kiss, and the air shimmers faintly. My ears pop, and I get a slight sense of vertigo before everything returns to normal.

"That'll keep your pesky mate from listening in."

Darkness lingers, and the ground here has a faint layer of frost. I stare down at it. "Leander did all this?"

"He has the heart of the cold winter wind." She produces a large wooden spoon from thin air and stirs her pot. "And to think, his power is dimmed here in the southern realm. He almost did Selene in. When he crosses the border into the winter realm." She shivers. "He'll be unstoppable. No wonder he took the throne. What a strong mate he will be."

"He's not my mate."

She wrinkles her nose. "He is."

"No—"

"Fate, young one. Fate. Can't change it." She huffs. "Many a time I've tried to change mine, but everything comes to pass as it's meant to. Your mating was written long ago." She cuts her gaze to me. "You feel the bond already."

"I don't feel a bond." I shrug.

She stares at me, her black eyes glinting in the moonlight.

I squirm under her gaze. "I mean, I do feel *something*."

"Lust." She nods and returns to her cauldron, her stringy white hair hiding her face. "You feel lust for him."

I press a hand to my reddening cheek. "I don't know."

"Don't you? A fine warrior from the winter realm like that? Big and strong, broadest shoulders I've ever seen, face so handsome it must be a trick of the Spires." She smacks her hard lips. "Back in my fae days, I would have ridden him until I had blisters on my thighs."

"Wow, that's TMI." I press both hands to my cheeks.

"TMI?"

"Too much information."

Her cackle rockets through the trees. "I used to think there was no such thing as too much information. But now, Selene knows too much. So much I wish I could get —out—of—here." She punctuates each word with a smack to the side of her head, the sound of glass on glass. "But I can't get rid of it, so I stay in my cave, hidden. No one tells me anything else. I sit in silence with my lovely bones." She sighs, as if picturing her home. "It's beautiful."

I lace my fingers together as she stares off into the woods for a while, her hand slowly stirring whatever sizzles in the cauldron. It has a smell, but I can't place it. One minute bitter, the next sweet, the scent keeps changing.

"A boon!" She claps her hands and the wooden spoon continues stirring even though she's let it go. "I am to give you a boon, and then I can return to my bones."

"A boon means something good, right?"

"Good. Yes." She sits next to me on the log, her joints crackling. "What would you like?"

I open my mouth to respond.

She presses her finger to her lips. "Shh. You don't get to pick."

Utterly confused, I cock my head at her.

"Selene gets to pick. Those were the terms. I promised a boon, but didn't say you could pick. I know what you want. Or at least it's what you *think* you want."

"To go home."

"Yep, that's the one."

I grow breathless at the thought of returning to the human world. Home! Back to my books and my dorm and my exams. Sadness trickles through the thought as I realize it means leaving Leander behind. Maybe I don't feel a bond, but I have warmed to him in the past few days. There's something about him that draws me close. And the kiss we shared—I grip my fingers tighter—was the most exhilarating moment of my life. The way his lips moved over mine, the possession in his grip. I've never felt so desired, so needed.

"Mmhmm." Selene clasps her hands around one knee.

I try to keep my tone light, despite the distinct lack of air in this part of the woods. "What?"

"I know the thoughts in your pretty head. The bond. That's what it is. You just don't realize it yet."

I stand and cross my arms over my stomach. "Okay, so about going home. That's the boon I want."

"No." She rises and waves a hand at me. "That would be a terrible boon indeed. Not worth the trouble. Besides, do you believe your mate wouldn't come for you?" She laughs, a bit more agreeable than her usual cackle. "He would come on the winter wind and whisk you away in a storm of snow and ice the likes of which the human world has never seen. You'd wind up right back in Arin, probably in his bed, screaming his name."

"So that's a 'no' then?" I sigh.

"I choose the boon."

"If it's all the same to you, why not just give me what I want and send me home?" I puff my breath out, sending a lock of my hair floating up.

"Because ..."

I sink back down beside her. "Because what?"

"You apologized." She looks directly at me, and I swear I could sense something underneath the black skin and sharp teeth. Or maybe it's some*one*, someone who isn't quite as evil as billed. "And no one has ever done that to Selene. Not since I became..." She glances down at her black body and the shredded gray dress that barely covers her.

"What happened to you?" I can't stop the pity that blooms in my breast.

"That's an old story. One that I will tell you one day." She presses her palm to her forehead. "Yes, I have seen it. Only forgotten. I go to my cave to forget, to silence the voices. To make it all stop." She snaps her teeth. "Out here it all comes alive again—the knowledge, the T-M-I you spoke of."

I snort at her TMI reference.

She stands and peers into her cauldron again. "And now I remember your boon. What is promised, what I must give."

"So, not a way home?"

"A way to live."

"I don't understand." I rub my face and realize how tired I am. This ordeal doesn't seem to end, not since I first woke up in that cell, and it's taking a toll on me.

"I followed you through these trees as if you were a dark orb, flickering purple and emerald. A shiny sparkle that drew me ever closer." She blinks slowly. "That aura is part of what you are."

"And what's that?"

"TMI." She waggles her finger at me. "You are a beacon to any creature from the Spires. Spirits from dark lands will come for you. Maybe out of curiosity. Maybe for a taste of whatever shines so beautifully in midnight tones."

I chew my lip. "I don't like being seen. This place is

scary enough without this glow that you're talking about, making me a magnet for bad things."

"Not bad. Evil."

Exasperation doesn't begin to cover what I'm feeling. If she knows so much, why won't she just tell me instead of talking in riddles? But I can already tell that any direct questions will get me nowhere. Doesn't stop me from trying. "Why do I glow for evil?"

"Didn't say *for* evil. Just said you glow, and it's a lure to dark ones like me." She grabs the spoon again and reaches deep into the swirling, smoking cauldron. "There it is." Straightening, she pulls a pea from the end of the spoon.

"What is it?"

"Eat it." She hands it to me.

"What is it?" I take it from her and inspect it. It looks just like a pea. Green, round, and my least favorite vegetable.

"It's like a—" She pulls a tattered hood over her hair. "Cloak. Hides your glow. Hides you until you are ready to no longer be hidden."

"When's that?" I hold up a hand. "TMI, I know."

"T-M-I." She nods. "Eat it."

"It's safe?" I peer at the little green thing. Seems harmless. But I've read enough fairytales to know you shouldn't eat anything a witch gives you.

She clacks her teeth. "Eat it!"

I wish Leander were here to help me, to tell me if it's poison or just a regular gross pea. But maybe this is a decision I can only make on my own.

I take a deep breath. "I trust you, Selene." Popping it

into my mouth, I give it a single chew, then swallow it down.

"Trust?" Her eyebrows rise, and her sharp teeth clack. "You should never trust. No one. Certainly not me, young one. *Never* trust a witch."

My throat closes up, and I clutch it as my eyes begin to water. It must have been poisoned. Oh, god, what have I done? I can't breathe.

The witch simply stares with a look of satisfaction as my vision darkens.

3

LEANDER

I've considered several different ways of torturing the witch, even voiced a few to Gareth as I've waited for Taylor. I was a fool to let her be alone with the witch. The blood loss must have dimmed my reason. For the hundredth time, I curse my weakness and continue pacing.

When she emerges from the shadowy wood a few moments later, I rush to her side. "Are you hurt?"

"No." She rubs her eyes. "I'm fine. But I was shiny, apparently? And now I'm not."

"Shiny?" I wrap my arm around her shoulders as the strange stillness caused by the witch evaporates. Fairies creep out from hiding, their bright lights flickering here and there amongst the trees.

"Yep." She yawns. "She's gone now. Back to her cave."

"What boon did she give you?" I stop her and turn her toward me, searching her for any wounds. Each second she was gone was acute torture. And when the witch put up a barrier spell? I went wild with rage, cutting and hacking at the wall between us with all my might. But the witch's power is ancient and runs far deeper than mine. I couldn't get to my mate. It gutted me. "I will never leave you again, little one."

"I was fine. She didn't hurt me." She shrugs. "I mean, I thought she did, but I guess the magic was a little hard to swallow."

"I need you to explain." I gently tilt her chin up.

"I ate a pea from her cauldron."

I swallow hard. "Taking food from a witch is a bad idea."

"I know. I guess some things are universal." She gives me a tired smile. "But there was something about her. Something that made me trust her, even when she told me not to."

I send a barrage of thanks to the Ancestors that Taylor is unharmed.

"Anyway, she said my aura has a weird glow to it, and that I wouldn't last in this world unless she dampened it. So, she gave me a pea—I hate peas—and I ate it. Now, I'm not so shiny. But she said I can be shiny again when I want to be." She rubs her eyes again. "I'm not really sure what that means. But at this point, I'm kind of just rolling with the punches."

"Punches? She struck you?" A growl lofts from me, and I reach for my sword.

"No." She presses her small hands to my chest, my shirt still spotted with blood. "It's just a figure of speech. I just meant that I'm doing the best I can with all the weirdness. Honestly, I can't even think right now. I'm so tired."

I scoop her up. She doesn't protest as I carry her back to camp, her eyes closed as her breathing slows.

Beth sits next to the fire, worry in her eyes as we approach. "Is she okay? Where's the witch? What happened?"

"Everything's all right, changeling. Rest."

"Rest?" She throws her hands up. "I woke up to find Taylor gone, and then I got frozen to the ground! I can't rest, not when there's an Obsidian—"

"The witch is gone, and I have no reason to frost the ground again." I sink to my knees on my bedroll and lay Taylor down as softly as I can. My wounds still burn, the witch's claws perfect at slicing through skin and sinew. But, thanks to Gareth's magic, I will be healed by morning. The next time we leave the High Mountain, I'll be sure to bring Valen with us. His healing magic would go a long way to ease my mind when it comes to my mate's safety. Not that I intend to expose her to danger any more than I already have. She will be safe in the winter realm.

She moves a hand to her side, clutching something in the folds of her dress. Her breathing is low and soft, her mind already wrapped in a comfortable dream.

Carefully, I ease my hand along hers. When my fingers graze something oddly warm to the touch, I know instinctively what it is.

"By the Ancestors." I can't stop my exclamation as I pull the obsidian blade from Taylor's dress.

"Is that a ..." Gareth kneels down next to me and

touches the hewn black blade, the hilt rounded and small, perfect for Taylor's hand.

"An obsidian shortsword." I hold the blade up to the moon. It sucks in the glow around it, as if devouring the light.

"The witch did this for her." Gareth rubs the scruff on his jaw. "I've never heard of an Obsidian willingly giving her hide for such a gift. Not even her promise of a boon could have encompassed this."

I stare at the sword, a legend. It is said that a weapon forged from the flesh of an Obsidian witch can slay *any* creature—no small feat—and the obsidian blade will feast on the souls of its kills.

"Never have I seen such a blade." Gareth peers at it with the same reverence I feel. "They say the last one ever made was lost in the Battle of the Spires eons ago."

"She gave it to me." Taylor's sleepy eyes are open just enough for me to get a glimpse of their blue depths. "Not to fulfill her promise—that was a spell to dim my shine—but because she liked me. And maybe because I almost choked on her pea." She rolls to her side and rests her face on her folded hands. "Selene's not so bad. You should give her a chance." With a light sigh, she goes back to sleep.

I don't know what to make of any of it—neither the aura spell nor the blade. But one thing is certain, my mate is formidable enough to gain an ally from the darkest corner of our world. I stroke her hair.

"I'll just—" Gareth hitches a thumb over his shoulder and returns to the fire.

I lie down next to Taylor and tenderly pull her into

my arms. She doesn't stir, simply melds into me, her body relaxed as her breath tickles along my throat. Again, my body reacts, demanding I claim her. But I tamp it down and simply enjoy holding her. Even with her safe in my arms, an oily feeling still slinks around inside me.

I sense Gareth prowling through the woods, making one final check of our perimeter. The threat of the witch is gone, her ominous presence lifted. Fairies flit here and there, and an owl hoots its approval high above us.

The unsettled feeling remains.

What will happen when the next threat arises? I must protect Taylor at all costs. I should never have left her with the witch—promise or no promise. I can't put her in harm's way again. For her sake ... and for mine. It hits me then, what the feeling is. Fear. I didn't recognize it. The wars I've been through, the things I've done for my realm—I stopped feeling fear centuries ago. It was a waste. No point fearing death, not when it was around every corner, waiting with a dagger between its teeth. But now, I have a real reason to worry. I kiss Taylor's hair, and she snuggles closer.

There's only one solution. I need to keep her so close that nothing can touch her without going through me first. I close my eyes and let myself go, my mind quieting with nothing left but thoughts of her.

"*P*sst."

  I open my bleary eyes to find Beth close by and waving me toward her.

  "What?"

  "Shh!" She presses a finger to her lips.

  Leander slumbers beside me, one arm draped across my waist, his body tight against mine.

  Beth beckons again.

  "*Fine,*" I mouth and gently scoot away from Leander.

  He pulls me back to him but doesn't wake. Beth rolls her eyes.

  I go slower this time, lifting his arm and easing away from him. Once I'm at the edge of the furs, I lay his arm down and roll away.

  Beth helps me to my feet, and, with one finger still pressed to her lips, tiptoes past Gareth who is sitting against a nearby tree, his eyes closed. I follow, taking care not to make any wrong steps. They must have been exhausted from their duel with the witch, because neither of them wake as we creep from camp.

"Where are we going?" I whisper.

She just waves me onward. The sun slants through the trees, the warm air caressing us as we cross the flower-strewn forest floor.

The sound of water draws my attention, and Beth stops and points.

Through the trees, I see a shimmering pool that reflects the bright day. I'm suddenly parched. Taking a sniff of my underarm, I wrinkle my nose.

Beth takes off at a faster clip, shedding clothes as she goes. After a quick glance around to make sure we're alone, I follow. The fragrant flowers grow denser, deep purple blooms dusted with morning dew. I kick off my shoes, then pull my dress over my head. It comes away easily, partly because one seam is loose from the stable fae's attack and partly because I've lost a little weight since I've been here.

Beth sheds her last garment, some sort of an under-shirt, and I gasp. Fang marks cover her entire body, not just her arms.

She looks over her thin shoulder and shrugs. "I told you I'd rather die than go back to being a chew toy for my master's vampire hounds. Now you see why."

"I'm so sorry. I had no idea."

She shrugs. "What's done is done." With a leap, she splashes into the clear water, cool droplets spraying my bare skin.

I shed my panties and follow her, though not quite so jubilantly. I've always been modest, verging on painfully shy, so skinny dipping in the woods with a new friend—I pause at the thought. Beth is my friend. I've managed to do something in this new world that always evaded me back in my old one. I had study partners, sure. But an actual friend? No. Not like this.

"Don't just stand there, jump in!" She swipes her arm across the surface and splashes me.

I squeak and ease into the pool, my feet tentative as I step along the sandy bottom. She submerges completely as I get to the center, the water up to my neck. It's chilly, but I know once I get used to it, I'll never want to leave. I'd kill for a bar of soap, but the water is enough.

Kicking my feet up, I float a little and paddle around. Birds sing throughout the green woods, and the skitter of animals in the underbrush reassures me that nothing dangerous is nearby. Everything became so still when the witch was on our trail. Now, the forest is alive. I let out a deep, soul-cleansing sigh and dunk my hair, letting the strands twine away from me in the cool water.

Beth finally reappears and swipes her wet hair from her face. "I've needed this."

"You can say that again." I laugh.

She grins and splashes me. "You don't smell so great, yourself," she says in fae.

"I understood that," I reply in the same tongue.

Her eyebrows shoot to her hairline. "How?"

"The witch wanted a chat." I waggle my fingers along the surface of the water. "So she zapped the language into my brain somehow."

"Powerful magic." She cocks her head at me. "And

you need to give me details of what happened. But first, I would like to reiterate that we do, in fact, stink."

"I know." I grimace. "I've been wishing for soap."

"Can do." She dog paddles to the edge of the pond and swipes some of the purple flowers from their stalks.

"What's that?"

"These are blumerin. They crush these up and mix them with some other ingredients to make the palace soap."

I take a handful from her and squeeze them. A slight bluish tint leaks from the leaves, but the scent is amazing. I'll accept looking like a smurf if I get to smell like a blue-berry tart.

"Like this." She rubs them between her palms. "They don't get super sudsy, but they bubble a little."

The soft petals are almost spongelike as I roll them around in my palms and start lathering up my neck and shoulders.

"This is heavenly." I scrub behind my ears and take more of the flowers Beth offers. By the time we're done, we've washed our bodies and our hair.

She douses herself with palmfuls of water one more time, then tips her head back and lets a ray of sun play across her features.

"You're young," I blurt. "I mean, you're younger than I thought you were. All that dirt made you seem older."

She laughs. "Thanks, I think. I'm probably about twenty-five or so?"

"You don't know?"

"No. Our ages aren't important. We're either young enough to work or old enough to discard."

"Discard?" I pluck a piece of flower from her hair.

"When changelings grow old, their masters throw them out." She paddles to the edge of the pool and reaches over to grab our dirty clothes. "Send them to live on the streets until they die."

I hug myself. "That's horrible."

"Just the way it is." She begins scrubbing my dress in the water.

"Changelings never try to escape?"

"They do." She nods. "I did but didn't get far. But even if I had managed to get out of the palace, the Catcher would have come for me."

"The Catcher?"

"A vicious fae who returns runaway changelings to their masters." She rubs her palms on her biceps. "He's relentless once he's put on our trail. All changelings learn about him from the time they arrive here, and the ones he catches ... they never come back the same, not after he's had a turn with them."

I can't fathom the horribleness of Beth's history, but I know she's strong to have survived it. "I'm sorry."

"I am, too, for all those he's caught." She clears her throat and continues washing our clothes.

"I'll help." I reach for her underthings.

"No." She splashes me away. "I like laundry. Hate all the other chores, but laundry is my thing."

"Really? I hate having to load the washer in my dorm, mainly because it means I have to scrounge around for quarters to feed the machine. Oh, and half the time, someone will come along and dump my clothes out and put theirs in."

She peers at me. "I have no idea what you just said, but—"

"First world problems." I shrug. "I've never washed clothes the way you're doing it."

She rubs the cloth against itself and adds some of the blue flowers. "This is the only way I know."

"At home, we have machines that do all the washing."

"Home." Her chin drops a little.

"Right." I float over to her and rest a palm on her shoulder. "I know you don't remember it. I'm sorry."

She clears her throat and shrugs off my touch. "A home doesn't exist for me. Clean clothes, though, that's something I can control."

I go through several ideas of responses, but nothing seems right, so I let it drop. But I know there's a home for her somewhere. And I'm beginning to suspect that home might be with me.

After a while, she asks what happened with the witch. Grateful for the reprieve from the awkward silence, I tell her the details as she washes then drapes our clothes over a low-hanging branch.

"I'm getting pruny." I show her my fingers.

"We can get out." She spins in the water, sending little ripples across the surface.

"It's sunny over there." I point to a spot beyond the flowers. "Maybe we can lie there and dry off for a minute?"

"I like it." She climbs out of the water, the bite marks once again coming into sharp relief. Her ribs show through her skin, and I make a mental note to ensure she eats enough at every meal.

I follow her across the flowers and to the grassy, sunny spot. We lie down, the warm sun drying the droplets along my skin. I'm exposed, but the woods are quiet, and Beth hasn't given me a second look. We are doing this whole "we're naked in the middle of nowhere" thing like a couple of pros.

"Has anything ever felt this good?" I sigh and close my eyes.

"Not that I remember, no."

A whisper reminding me I'm far from home tries to sneak in, but I block it out. I'm here now, safe and warm with a friend. It's a pleasure I never had in the human world.

The sun heats us, cutting through the chill of the lingering water and tickling along all my exposed nooks and crannies. I've never laid out completely nude before. It makes me feel like a bad girl, and I rather like it. "This reminds me of this stupid TV show back home. It comes on one of the reality TV channels and is called 'Naked and Afraid' or something like that."

"A show? Like a play?"

"Sort of. But it's on this little rectangular device and you can watch all sorts of things, look at other people's lives, be entertained with fictional movies. They use a camera, which records everything."

She shoots me a perplexed glance.

"It's hard to explain." It really is. There's simply no way to put it into words, so I plow onward. "Like a painting that moves. But anyway, there's this show where they drop two strangers off in the middle of like, a desert, or on an island, or in the deep woods, and they're naked.

The camera follows them around—it's kind of like you're watching through a window, and they don't realize you're there—and show what they do once they're stranded. See what decisions they make, stuff like that."

"Why do they do this?" Her voice is low, drowsy.

"To see if they can survive. They have to live in this isolated place with the stranger for a month or so, I think. Fighting off the elements and bugs and animals and scrounging for food. But if they realize they can't hack it, they can call for rescue."

She snorts. "It sounds like my life—danger, fear, scrounging—until you got to the rescue part. No one ever came to save me from Granthos."

"You saved yourself, I'd say."

She smacks my arm. "Winding up in the dungeon wasn't saving myself."

"Well, you met *me* in the dungeon, and your kindness is what got you saved, so I count that as you saving yourself."

"Kindness?" She makes a pfft noise. "I was just trying to get you to stop yelling and drawing attention."

"You're deflecting." I return her smack. "You warned me, remember? Tried to help me, even when you were in a bad situation. No matter what you'd been through, you were still kind. That's why we're here, lying around in the warm sun, free as can be."

"Naked as can be, too." She stretches her arms over her head. "I could get used to this." She sighs, and after a long pause, says quietly, "I'm glad I met you that day."

"So am I."

Her snore punctuates my sentiment, and I smile a little. At least she's predictable.

I yawn and stretch my arms out, too. The sun peeks through my eyelids and promises me the day is just as bright as ever.

I don't know how long I doze for, but I know what wakes me: a guttural roar that slices through my dreams with a petrifying echo.

I wake cold and uncomfortable. She's gone. Gone from my bed, only her scent and the obsidian blade remaining.

I'm on my feet immediately. "Gareth!"

His eyes fly open and he looks around. "I fell asl—"

"Gone." I kick a log in the dying fire. "That changeling has kidnapped my mate!"

"Hang on, now." He spins, peering through the trees. "They can't be far."

My heart twists, and my primal need to find Taylor is like a thorny arrow wedged in my gut. I taste the air, trying to find some trace of her.

"This way." Gareth takes off through the trees.

I follow and catch the same scent that drew him. Blumerin. It grows in this cursed forest, but the smell is loud, out of place, and underneath it—I can get the faintest hint of Taylor.

I barrel past him and draw my dagger. How could I let her leave in the night? What sort of mate am I? First the witch and now this. She keeps slipping through my fingers, no matter how hard I try to hold her close.

A stream trickles ahead of me, a wide pool glinting in the sun. The ground is disturbed, flowers bent. She came this way. I'm wild, my body rushing before my mind can even catch up. But then I stop.

I. Stop. Dead.

Her eyes closed, hair damp, face peaceful, skin tantalizing, body delectable—she lies nude, her breasts offered to the sun, the pink tips soft, her stomach fair and then the slight tuft of neat hair between her thighs. My mind goes blank, and the bond snaps tight. My cock pulses and my mouth goes dry. I must claim her, must mark her as mine before any other male sees her. I will do it now.

I step towards her.

"What—" Gareth gasps as he catches up.

Gareth. Gareth is looking at my incomparable mate. I turn on him and draw my sword with a roar that shakes the trees.

He draws his blade and holds it across his body. Defensive. "Leander, the bond is turning you—"

"She is mine!" I rush him, my sword flying with a fury that seems to infuse the metal with extra bite.

He falls back, his blade dancing with mine as I swing and thrust, each step sending him farther onto his heels.

"Leander!" he yells when I strike a particularly hard blow that would have felled any other fae. "I'm your friend."

"You looked upon Taylor!" I swing again, and he blocks.

"I wasn't looking at *her*!"

"*A lie*," the feral fae whispers. "*He wants our mate. She is not claimed, not marked, fair game.*"

I advance again, putting all my might into an onslaught that lights up the woods with the sounds of battle. With a final, spinning blow, I knock his sword from his hand, and he falls back against a tree, his hands up.

My breath heaving, I raise my sword to hew his head from his body, ending his immortal life.

"Leander!" A cry from behind makes me blink.

"What are you doing? Let him go!" Soft footsteps through the flowers, a scent that twines through my dreams. *Taylor.*

I turn to her and sheath my blade. Gareth was just a distraction. Claiming my mate is more important. Once I've marked her, there will be no challengers for her.

She stares up at me, her damp dress clinging to her body. I know what every inch looks like. Now I just need to taste her. I advance, my blood thundering through me, her presence calling to me from every direction.

She steps back, her hands out in front of her. "What is *wrong* with you?"

"You are my mate." I swipe her hands away and pull her into my arms. "*Mine.*" Kissing her is the only thing I've ever done that has felt absolutely right. There is no error here, no shortcoming or doubt. Her mouth was made for me, and I am her devoted slave. I will kiss her until she knows those truths in her deepest heart, can feel me in there. She mumbles against my lips, and I slide my tongue against hers, taking advantage of every opening as I lift her against me.

Her small hands clutch my shoulders as I back her against a tree. When my cock nudges against the warmth between her thighs, I groan and delve my tongue even deeper. She opens her mouth wider, and I take the invitation, kissing her with a passion that engulfs both of us.

I palm her bottom, then hike up her dress. Her legs open farther for me, her heels digging into my backside.

She pushes against my chest lightly, then pulls back. "Leander, wait."

I follow her and press my forehead to hers, my fangs grazing her lips. "Can't you feel it?" I growl. Her heart pounds, the vein at her throat fluttering.

"I feel ..." She stares into my eyes. "I admit I feel something. I want ..." She shakes her head. "I don't know what I want."

"I can taste your arousal, little one." I push my hips against her and hiss at the contact. *Claim her, claim her.* "I know what you want."

"This is just too fast." Her gaze strays to my lips, and her body tightens for a moment. "I mean, I want this." Her cheeks redden. "I can admit that. But I'm not ready."

"Fast?" I scoff. "I should have claimed you the second I saw you, thrown you down on that table and made you moan."

She frowns. "You can't just take whatever you want like that."

I press her harder into the tree and grip her thighs. "I am the king of the winter realm. I take what is mine."

The frown deepens. "Now you're just being an ass."

"An ass?" I laugh. "No one has called me names in quite some time."

She pushes against my chest. "Maybe you need someone to call you names to remind you when you're acting like a big douche."

"What is a douche?"

"It's what you are. Now, put me down."

"Let you go?" I tighten my grip. "Never."

"Put me down. Now." The bite in her tone cuts through my mating haze.

I set her down gently, even though I want so badly to keep her in my grip.

"What is wrong with you?" She crosses her arms and glares up at me. "One minute you are gentle and kind and, and *hand-feeding* me, for Chrissakes, and then you're all alpha asshole and growly and insane!"

The mating haze begins to clear, and my head begins to work again. I scrub a hand down my face. Her anger is dissolving the fog, bringing me back to myself, sending the feral need back into my recesses. By the Ancestors, she's right. I have behaved like an ass.

"It's not his fault." Gareth eases around to my left. "It's the bond. In the old days, you would have felt it and mated with him by now. But now, with the curse, who knows how the bond is affected. I can't be sure, but the longer he goes without claiming you, I'm afraid the more feral he'll become."

Gareth. The world snaps back into focus. I just attacked him. Almost killed him. My best friend. "I am so sorry." I step back, away from them lest I try and harm them again. "I don't know what came over me." I think back and get a glimpse of fair skin, pink nipples, a thatch of neat hair, and— "No." I rub my eyes. If I dwell on that,

I'll go mad again. "I saw you, and I became a creature of instinct. A douche, as you said."

She smiles a little. "Douche may be a tad harsh."

"It was just a little skin." Beth walks up and finger-combs her hair. "You really need to learn how to be a gentleman at all times, nude or otherwise, your majesty."

Gareth clears his throat. "It was a lot of skin. Too much. Acting like two nymphs. And I know you were the one who led Taylor astray." He shakes a finger at her but doesn't meet her eyes.

I look more closely at him. Is he ...blushing?

"I led her to a *bath*," she counters. "You fae brutes may be perfectly happy romping around without cleaning up, but we aren't."

"Fae brutes?" Gareth narrows his eyes. "For a changeling slave, you have a mouth on you."

"I know. I catch you staring at it," she deadpans.

Gareth looks stricken, and a belly laugh rolls out of me.

Taylor laughs, too, then holds out her hand and opens her fingers. "Mic drop right there."

"Mic drop?" I cock my head at her.

"It's a human world thing. Just saying that Gareth started it, but Beth finished it."

"Hmm." Humans have such odd terminology, but I want to learn more.

"We need to break camp," Gareth grumbles, his eyes downward as Beth turns and saunters off through the trees.

"We will." I grab the hem of my tunic and pull it over my head. Satisfaction filters through me as Taylor's gaze rakes across my bare flesh. "But first we need to wash ourselves." I reach to untie my pants, and Taylor spins quickly, her dress flying out around her.

"You can't just strip in front of me!" She bows her head.

"Why not?" I shuck my pants off, my erection proud and thick. "This body is yours, my mate. Everything about it. It was created only for you." I stride to her, but she doesn't turn.

"You're naked. Right behind me. Being naked."

I lean close, my lips to her ear. "You can look all you want. I don't mind. Besides, I saw you, and I'll be dreaming of your beautiful skin, perfect breasts, and creamy thighs for the rest of my life."

She shivers, her breathing speeding up. I run a finger along her delicate neck, then press my lips to the spot gently. So gently. Her breath hitches as I suck lightly, then move closer to the skin beneath her ear.

A loud splash breaks the moment, and I turn to see Gareth's dark hair disappearing beneath the water.

"We'll continue this." I nibble her ear lobe.

She hastily turns toward camp. "I need, um. I need to ..." She doesn't finish the sentence, just hurries away through the trees.

I stretch and head toward the pool. Gareth splashes towards the far edge to grab some blumerin. As I wade in, I can feel Taylor's eyes on me, and when my crisp wind carries the scent of her arousal to me, I groan and sink beneath the sparkling surface.

*W*e spend the next three days travelling through the forest, the horses no longer running at breakneck speeds. Gareth and Leander still keep a wary eye out, stopping at times just to listen to the wind soughing through the trees. Sleeping next to Leander becomes a little more comfortable each night, his warm body and gentle touches easing my worries.

"Is there a damn town anywhere around here?" Beth rubs her lower back.

"There are towns." Gareth leans away from her elbow. "But we aren't stopping in them. Too dangerous."

"And the forest isn't?" She twists, her back cracking, and sighs.

"The forest hides us from prying eyes." Gareth stares through the trees. "But we'll enter the Red Plains in two days' time. We'll have no choice but to take shelter in a village along the way."

"Nice. Maybe that'll give me a chance to get away from your surly grunting."

"I don't grunt." Gareth's offended tone makes Beth smile.

"Sure you don't." She loves getting him going. And it works, because before long, they're sniping at each other.

Leander pulls the reins a little so we drop back from the repartee on the other horse. "Are you tired?"

"I'm okay." Truth be told, my ass is sorer than it's ever been in my life, I'm hungry, and I long for another bath.

"Do you ... miss the human world?" He keeps his voice soft, as if tiptoeing around a grave.

I sigh. "Yes."

He stiffens a bit. "Hmm."

"But the human world isn't all roses," I hasten to add. "It has plenty of room for improvement."

"Were you unhappy there?"

How do I answer that? My entire childhood was a nightmare that I still have damage from. My relationship with my mom is terrible, I can't even remember what my father looks like, and Steve still has a starring role in all my bad dreams. But then again, I was finally beginning to feel like I was on the right path. I was doing well in school, excelling in my chemistry classes and impressing my professors. Things were looking up until Cecile sent me here.

I realize I've been lost in thought instead of answering his question. "It was a mixed bag."

"How so?"

I shrug. "Some things were bad. Some were good."

"Tell me about your life. I want to know everything."

"Everything? That's a lot."

"We have time." He leads the horse around a sinkhole littered with ivy and odd pink blooms shaped like corkscrews.

"Um, well I was born in Indiana. Went to school there, graduated high school and then left for college."

"School? Magical or elemental?"

I turn and peer at his dark eyes and handsome face. "Huh? It was just like regular school. You know, history, math, reading, writing, science, things like that."

His brows knot, but he says, "Interesting. Please continue."

"I had a knack for the sciences." There isn't a word in fae for what I'm trying to say, so I have to switch to English. "Chemistry and physics especially."

"What are chemistry and physics?" The words come out funny with his thick accent.

I smile at his pronunciation. "Physics is the study of matter—basically all tangible things—and how it behaves. The planets, the stars, a rock, water, you, me—it's all matter. It can be as small as atoms under a microscope or as large as the universe. Physicists try to figure out why matter behaves in different ways and what that means. Once you figure something out about matter, and you can prove it applies to all matter, it will become a law of physics. Like gravity."

"Gravity?"

"Gravity is an invisible force that pulls matter together."

His arms tighten around me, pressing me against him. "Gravity."

"Something like that." I smile.

"And chemistry?"

"That's the study of how different elements can combine to make other substances, and more importantly, how matter reacts with energy. It's the basis for most of the scientific breakthroughs since the earliest humans existed."

"Ah, I know this one. You're an alchemist." He nods. "We have one in the winter realm, a member of my court. You and Branala should meet and discuss your magics when we arrive."

"Not magic." I find myself staring at the dark hair along his jaw. So masculine. What would it feel like against my skin, especially in sensitive spots? I shake my head. Where are these thoughts coming from? "I mean, it's science. Not magic at all."

His plump lips split with a grin, and I swear his dark eyes sparkle in their depths. "Like gravity? Science." He leans closer, his lips within a breath of mine. "Pulled together by an invisible force."

I don't move away and can't seem to stop staring at his mouth. "This isn't, um..." What was I saying? I can't think when he looks at me like this, like there's nothing else in the world but the two of us. Heat rockets along my skin, and my nipples tingle. The ache from my backside fades as my core tightens, the rocking of the horse doing nothing to stop the sensation.

"I want you." He strokes his thumb down my cheek, his voice deep and hypnotic. "Can I have you, little one?"

I close my eyes when his thumb brushes my lower lip.

"I've thought of taking you so many ways. Every night as you lie next to me, your sweet arousal perfuming the air. I want to taste you, to make you moan and quiver as I press my tongue deep inside you."

I grip the saddle so hard my nails hurt.

"I would have you writhing for me, little one." His hand slides down my waist. "I would kiss every bit of this beautiful body. And then I'd take you, thrusting so deeply that you will feel me in your soul and know you are mine." When his fingertips graze my panties, I bite my lip to stop from moaning.

"Would you like that? Would you like to be fully mine?" His fangs have lengthened, but their tips don't frighten me. Just the opposite. I want to feel them grazing along my skin.

"Leander." I'm breathless, my mind fuzzed, my body fully awake and needy.

His fingers delve lower, teasing beneath my panties. When he strokes the skin between my thighs, I let out a low sigh.

"My little one is already wet for me." He presses his cheek to mine, his mouth tickling my ear. "You feel the bond."

I feel ... something. But lust is probably a more accurate word for it.

"Leander." Gareth clears his throat. "Best to not tempt the feral."

Leander turns quickly and snaps his teeth at his friend. "She's mine."

"Hey," I say softly.

He meets my eyes again, his gaze so intense it's like staring into a volcano.

"Hey, let's just slow this down a little." I pull his hand from my panties. "We got a little carried away, that's all."

"You feel it." He presses his palm to my chest. "In here."

"I don't know what I feel." I take a deep, shuddering breath. "I just need to focus on getting back home, not—"

"With me, you are home." His fangs retract, and he loses some of the wild quality in his eyes. "I am your home, Taylor."

"You keep saying that, but it doesn't change anything. I don't belong here."

Gareth seems to relax, though Beth wrinkles her nose in disappointment. I guess she was looking forward to the mating show. Not happening. I don't care what my body says, my brain is in control and it says no. Or at least, not yet.

They canter ahead of us again, cutting a path across a ravine and up a slight hill.

Undeterred, Leander keeps his grip on me, his body taut at my back. "What of your parents?"

"We're not going there."

"Where?"

"I mean we aren't going to talk about my parents."

"Why not?"

"What about your parents?" I counter.

"My father was a bladesmith. My mother was a high fae noble that ran off with him."

"Ran off with him?" Interesting.

"She happened to meet him as he was delivering a sword to King Shathinor."

"He was the king before you?"

"Yes." His tone sours. "His evil was not so apparent back then. My father served him as did everyone else in the winter realm."

"Was he mad when your mom eloped?"

"She was the daughter of one of his old rivals for the throne. He pretended to be furious, of course, but only to cow my grandsire. And they didn't elope. There was no official mating ceremony."

"Even naughtier." I smile.

"When she came back heavy with child, my grandsire relented and allowed the match. Fae children are so rare that even my father's low birth could be overlooked. But it was quite the scandal in those times. I'd like to think things are different now, but I can imagine a few of my nobles might react just as badly, even though it's been twelve hundred years since—"

I turn my head so fast my neck pops. "Twelve hundred *years*?"

"Since my parents mated? Yes." He cocks his head to the side. "Why?"

"You're twelve hundred years *old*?"

"Yes."

I sputter, no words coming to mind.

"Is that a problem, little one?" He sits a little straighter. "I assure you my bloodline is strong. My father and mother lived well beyond five thousand years and chose to join the Ancestors together after I won the throne. Our children will—"

"Whoa." I scramble to dismount. "Whoa, whoa, whoa."

Leander grabs me and sets me on the ground, then follows. "What is it?"

"You're talking about centuries and children." I stalk back and forth in the high grass, hands on my hips as my mind races. "Centuries and children!"

He runs a hand through his midnight hair. "Yes."

"I'm twenty!" I yell so loudly that a flock of strange blue birds take off from a nearby bush. "You think I'm your mate, your queen. I'm twenty. I'm not supposed to be here in the first place. And you're like, I don't know, old enough to be my-my-my, what even would that be? My greatest-great grandfather?"

"Taylor." He looks down at me with so much warmth. "I've lived a long time, that's true. And I realize you are quite young, even for a changeling, but none of that matters to me."

"It matters to me." I cover my face with my hands. "This wasn't going to work anyway, but a twelve-hundred-year age difference is kind of an issue."

"Why?" He pulls my hands from my face. "Would you have known the difference if I hadn't told you my age? How old did you think I was?"

I huff. "I don't know. Like maybe thirty or something? You look so young. Everyone here looks young." I haven't been paying attention, because when I think about it, I've not seen the first old person since I've been here. No wrinkles, no nothing. "So everyone here is really old?"

"Fae freeze into their immortality when they reach their peak. After that, we age extremely slowly." He takes my hand and runs it along the faint laugh lines next to his eyes. "These have formed over centuries."

"So you can't die? But I saw you kill Tyrios."

"We can die. Either by injury or choosing to go to the Ancestors."

"But if you're never injured or suicidal, you just keep on ticking like a clock?" My fingers stray to the pendant at my throat, the feel of the cool stone calming me.

He follows the movement. "Why do you do that?"

"Do what? Freak out about insane age differences?"

"No. Stroke your throat when you get agitated."

"Oh." I drop my hand. "It's just a habit."

He stares for a moment, as if searching my neck.

"Look, your age just took me by surprise is all." I shake my hands out, as if that will somehow rectify the utter weirdness of all this. "I've never imagined someone could live that long." I don't say the rest—that I will age and die, that Leander's claim on me isn't real, that we can't be mates because how could fate be so cruel to put such different people together?

But it doesn't matter that I don't say any of it, because he strokes my cheek gently. "Don't worry, little one. I will find a way for us. I've waited for you for centuries. This is just our beginning. You will not perish, not in a mortal's death."

"How?" What he's saying is impossible, utter fantasy. "Do you happen to have the Sorcerer's Stone or maybe a pitcher of unicorn blood?"

His brow wrinkles. "The winter realm is home to many magical stones, but unicorn blood? They are far too proud to ever offer such a gift."

I hold up a hand. "Wait. Are you saying there are *unicorns* here?"

"They roam freely in the spring realm," he says matter-of-factly. "We have a few in the stables at the High Mountain, mainly because they were exiled from the spring realm for reasons that aren't entirely clear. I'd let them run free, but they wouldn't survive the cold."

"Unicorns." I jump up and down a little. "I have to see them!"

"You will." His bemused expression is ridiculously cute. "Just be warned that the ones at the High Mountain have mouths on them that could shock even the hardest soldier."

"They. Talk?" My eyes feel too big for my face.

"Of course." He lifts me back onto Kyrin and climbs up behind me.

I chew my lower lip as we catch up to Gareth. "And another thing, Leander. You know ... you know I'm not staying, right?"

"That's what you've told me, little one." He kisses the crown of my head. "But we'll see if I can't make you change your mind."

I'd get mad at his smugness, but I've already learned there's no point.

"Is it lunchtime yet?" Beth swipes a long hanging branch aside. "Because I could eat an entire sunstag at this point."

I glance at her gaunt cheeks. "I'm beginning to suspect you have a tapeworm."

"What's a—" She gasps.

Both horses rear as a giant gray bear emerges from the trees ahead of us, its teeth bared and its roar rattling the forest.

I scowl at Thorn as he laughs, his bear form shaking with mirth as he gets down on all fours.

Taylor intakes a huge breath, preparing to scream.

"Don't worry, little one. We know this beast."

"What?" She leans back against me, as far away from Thorn as she can get.

"You can go straight to the Spires!" Gareth spits out a few choice curses before stroking Sabre who is still backing up.

Kyrin snorts, then saunters past the bear, all of us pretending Kyrin wasn't just scared witless by Thorn's foolishness.

"Don't be mad." A flash of light and then Thorn is walking along beside us, his dark silver hair in a ridiculous bun, and his mismatched eyes glinting.

"You're a bear." Taylor shakes her head. "You're. A. Bear!"

"A tired bear. I've been running for days. Sorry I

jumped out like that, but I needed a little fun." He turns his full gaze to her, his lips ticking up in the same flirtatious smirk I'd seen on his face a thousand times over. "And it looks like I just found some."

A low growl rips from me, and I tighten my grip on Taylor. *Kill him*, the feral fae demands.

"Thorn, back away from there before Leander rips you apart." Gareth jumps off Sabre and rushes over.

Thorn's dark eyes widen. "Is it—"

"His mate. Yes. Back up before things get serious. He barely has the feral side of himself under control."

A chilly wind whistles down through the trees and swirls around Thorn. My magic reserves are back to normal and hovering on the edge of a knife.

"A mate? After all this time?" Thorn lets Gareth pull him away, but he still looks at us with open wonder.

"Stop gawking at her," I snap.

Gareth spins Thorn around, and they disappear behind a large tree.

"Does this mean we get to eat now?" Beth yawns and slides off Sabre. "I'll get the fire going."

"You have to stop doing this." Taylor smacks my hand.

"Doing what?"

"You know what." She shoots me a sassy glare, and Ancestors help me, I become instantly hard.

She continues, oblivious to the need shooting through my veins, "You have to relax. I'm not going to, you know, just 'mate' with you right now, so you need to get used to that. We barely know each other. I don't just jump into the sack with people I don't know. And I've never even

—" She stops herself and clears her throat. "For another thing, you're scary when you're all feral and crazy. And, *and*, I'm freezing!"

Guilt hits me deep in my gut. I've frightened my mate and punished her with the bite of winter.

I jump down and help her off Kyrin, then wrap my arms around her for warmth. "I'm so sorry. I'm failing as your mate."

"Dooooon funf nandin." Her voice is muffled against my chest.

I loosen my grip. "What was that?"

She turns her head and presses her cheek against me. "I said that you're doing fine. And I'm okay. The air is warm enough. You don't have to hardcore snuggle me right now."

"But what if I want to ... '*hardcore snuggle*' you?"

She laughs a little, putting my heart at ease. "Well, I've become used to the overbearing PDA."

"PDA?"

"Public display of affection."

"Is this not what is done in the human world?" I stroke her hair. Though I'm loathe to disappoint her, there is no way I will stop the "PDA." She is my mate, and I am proud of it. Everyone should know her as my queen, my bonded lover. *But you aren't bonded, not yet,* the feral whispers.

"People do, but they've usually known each other longer than a week."

"I don't need a week to know you." I gently set her back a little so I can meet her eyes. "I knew you the moment I saw you. The moment I *felt* you in that palace.

You've been in here ever since." I tap my chest. "And I will do everything in my power to show you how much you mean to me."

She sighs. "Arguing with you about this is pointless, isn't it?"

"It's about time!" Beth calls from where she's kneeling to start the fire. "She finally figures it out."

"You don't have to be a dick about it." Taylor turns and heads toward the other changeling.

A dick? What's a dick?

"I tried to tell you, an alpha fae who's found his mate cannot be reasoned with. The sooner you accept that, the better off you'll be. He's practically losing his mind because he hasn't claimed you yet. You are his entire world. Get used to it. It's never going to change."

"Leander." Gareth waves me over to where he and Thorn are talking. "You calm?"

I crack my neck. "As long as Thorn respects—"

He kneels, his head bowed. "Forgive me, my king. I didn't realize she was your mate."

My brows shoot up, and Gareth looks like he's been gut punched. Thorn is a jokester, not the sort who offers to kneel or speaks so seriously.

"Rise, Thorn."

He does, and we grip forearms. "I want to offer her my oath as soon as possible."

"You are welcome to, but first, tell me why you're here." Crossing the boundary line between winter and summer is forbidden without express leave granted by both rulers.

"We've had a breach at High Mountain." Thorn's

face hardens. "Right under my nose. A shadow crept in, slashed the throats of two guards, and entered the throne room. Ravella sensed the darkness and sounded the alarm. By the time we arrived, the intruder was gone. But there was a ... message."

I don't like the foreboding in his voice. "What was it?"

Gareth grits his teeth. "Yvarra's head."

Thorn nods. "Left on your throne. The tree brand burned into her cheek."

"The king beyond the mountain." I flex my fists.

"Yvarra was last seen in Silksglade. She was investigating a family of missing lesser fae. Her last correspondence was that she had a lead on them as well as some changelings who crossed the western border only days before."

"She was one of our best trackers." I let my sad sigh escape. "And a true blade of winter. She will be mourned."

"I came to give you this news. The threat is growing. I can feel it." Thorn peers westward, though there's nothing to see but trees. "Eyes are turned toward us, seeking hands weaving invisibly through the land."

"We've gained the alliance we came for. The summer queen will work with us to discover what has become of those who are missing. That trail will lead to the king beyond the mountain. I'm certain of it."

"And then?" Thorn rests his palm on the haft of his axe.

"And then, war." Gareth sounds tired. He's been a soldier for most of his life, just like me. When I became king, I'd hoped that the fighting days were over, that winter and summer could live in peace with each other as well as the other realms. But that dream is dying, and Yvarra's end is just the beginning.

"But now there is hope." Thorn glances at Taylor. "A royal mate."

My chest swells with pride. "She is a gift from the Ancestors, to be sure."

Thorn rubs his clean-shaven jaw. "Perhaps she is already with child. Can you imagine the joy in the winter realm for a new babe?" His smile is genuine, all pretense gone.

Gareth quickly claps a hand on Thorn's shoulder and leads him away. "Let's get some lunch."

Gareth is a good friend, but Thorn will know soon enough that I haven't claimed my mate. I send a request to the Ancestors for patience, then kneel as I say a prayer of peace for the soul of Yvarra.

When I get to the fire, Beth is roasting some root vegetables and Thorn is kneeling before Taylor, the Winter's Oath on his lips.

"This isn't necessary." She wrings her hands.

"You could always decree his death." Gareth shrugs. "I'd be more than happy to shut up this claptrap for eternity."

Thorn shoots him a grim look but keeps his head down. "It is your decision, my queen."

"He's a bear, Taylor. Don't you want a pet?" Beth snickers.

Gareth's lips quirk in a subdued smile.

"Fine. I'll say the words, but you must call me Taylor.

Got it?"

Thorn nods.

"*Blade thrower.*" She squints. "Is that it? It goes something like that. It's not in the fae words that I know."

"This oath and your response are in the tongue of the ancient fae, not the same that we speak now." I stand behind her and watch the sunlight play along her chestnut strands of hair. "*Bladanon thronin.*"

"*Bladanon thronin,*" she repeats. "That's what I meant."

Thorn rises and bows low again. "Thank you."

"How do you change into a bear?" Curiosity coats her tone.

"My magic is transformative. It runs in my line. My sire could turn himself into anything you could imagine, even other fae."

"Wow." She presses a palm to her cheek. "That's unbelievable."

Thorn would usually parlay a comment like that into a joke about his sexual prowess, but he abstains, which is good, because it would end in a brawl. One that I'd win.

We all sit around the fire as Beth hands out the small bowls of food. I scoop some of my carrots into Taylor's bowl. She gives me a long-suffering look but eats without complaint. My feral side is appeased that I've provided for my mate, even in this small way.

I chew my food, my mind working over the news of Yvarra's death. She was a strong tracker, skilled with the bow and blades. For someone to get the drop on her, there had to have been seriously dark magic at play. This will require more than a simple spy.

"Send Brannon to Silksglade." I stare into the fire.

Thorn whistles. "You sure we shouldn't start smaller?"

"No." I set down my bowl. "Yvarra's death can't go unanswered. Brannon will be able to track the dark magic if there are still traces of it in Silksglade. He can then report back. Maybe this is our chance to finally find the trail that leads to the king beyond the mountain."

Gareth sucks on his teeth. "Last time we set Brannon loose, we almost lost an entire village."

"I'm aware of the risks. But we need a wielder of the dark. It's the only way. Brannon is loyal to me and to the Phalanx."

"He's dangerous, Leander." Thorn shakes his head. "What if he takes innocent lives this time around? He's changed, sure, but how far can anyone stray from their roots?"

"Far." Taylor's soft voice resonates. "People can change." She lowers her gaze. "But not always for the better."

Where did that come from?

"So Brannon was bad before?" she hurries to ask.

"Bad is a massive understatement." Thorn passes his bowl to Beth. "He was born from the Spires, and he has a particular talent for the dark magics. His powers are without equal, save for perhaps a necromancer or an Obsidian witch—" he shudders "—but what are the chances of a run-in with one of those?"

Taylor laughs, the sound a little too gleeful, and gives me a knowing glance.

Thorn, though perplexed, continues, "Brannon is a

member of the king's guard, the Phalanx, but he's had to prove himself, to show us he's truly turned from his old ways."

"What made him turn?" Beth scoops the dredges from the cooking pot.

"Leander." Thorn inclines his head toward me.

Taylor turns and peruses me with her impossibly blue eyes. "What happened?"

"It's not important. We should be on our way—"

"Don't be so modest." Thorn waves me off. "Brannon was in league with Shathinor, the previous king of the winter realm. He was the bane of realms, burning villages, terrorizing and pillaging wherever he went. A vicious creation of the Spires. When Leander began the winter realm uprising, Shathinor sent Brannon to kill him."

Taylor clutches her hands in front of her. "Go on."

"Brannon shows up at our war camp with over a hundred shadow warriors at his back. We had thousands, of course, but shadow warriors cannot be killed by simple combat. They can strip a soldier's flesh in seconds and move on to the next. We were on the verge of a battle that could very well have ended our rebellion. Brannon strolled into Leander's tent, and Leander ordered all of us out. It was the hardest thing I've ever done—walking out of that tent and leaving my king with such a vicious creature. Our soldiers were surrounded by the shadow demons, all of them screeching for blood but waiting on word from their leader."

"I think I lost a century off my life that day," Gareth grumbles.

"What went on in the tent?" Taylor's wide eyes hold so much wonder.

"That's the thing." Thorn punches me in the arm lightly. "He never told us why Brannon sent his shadow warriors back to the Wasted Lands and joined our cause."

"That is for Brannon to divulge, not me." I've gotten used to deflecting their inquiries on this point.

"And Brannon won't say?" Taylor asks.

"Brannon isn't particularly talkative." Thorn smirks. "Besides, most fae take one look at him and run in the other direction."

"Something wrong with him?" Beth grabs the stew pot.

"He looks … interesting." Gareth has grown more diplomatic in his age.

"Why won't you let me help you with that?" Taylor reaches to collect the bowls.

"No way." Beth grabs them before Taylor can. "You're the queenie of the winter realm."

"I'm your friend." Taylor darts forward and lifts the pot. "Let me help."

This time, I agree with Beth. Taylor is my mate and queen. She shouldn't feel the need to perform menial tasks. "Taylor, you aren't expected to—"

She shoots me a hard look over her shoulder. "Don't you start, too. I'm not helpless, and I'm definitely not royalty. It's time I pull my weight on this little adventure." With a hard stride, she stalks off through the forest.

Beth collects the rest of the dishes and grins. "Taylor," she calls and hitches a thumb behind her. "The stream is that way."

"Oh." My mate's cheeks color a sweet pink as she huffs past lugging the stew pot.

"Spirited." Thorn nods.

"She's certainly got a mind of her own." I stretch out my legs and rise, my senses attuned to each of her steps.

"I'd expect nothing less of your mate." Thorn clears his throat. "But, perhaps you haven't noticed, she's a changeling."

"Of course he's noticed, Thorn." Gareth kicks dirt onto the low flames.

"I meant that in a charming fashion."

"Charm somewhere else." Gareth finishes snuffing the fire.

Thorn picks a piece of gristle from his teeth. "I'm only saying that it's an interesting pairing and one that might cause some issues with a handful of the old guard nobles."

"She's a changeling." I shrug. "But she's my mate. If anyone has a problem with her, then they have a problem with *me*. And as you know, I'm a problem solver." Aggression boils through my tone.

"And then there's the little problem of longevity." Thorn tucks his dark gray hair behind his ear. "She will die."

"There has to be some way to change that." I glance over my shoulder to make sure she's not listening in. "There are magics that can reshape her fate."

Thorn whistles. "Only the dark can do that. And the price you'd have to pay—"

"Would be too high." Gareth stands and meets my eye. "You know how magic works, Leander. It takes and takes and takes. Something like this? I've never heard of it being possible, but if it is, you can be sure it will have a terrible price."

"Then I'll pay it," I snap. "I will never allow her to suffer and die, not when I've finally found her."

Gareth shares a warning look with Thorn.

I force myself to lower my tone. "One thing at a time. We need to get across the border. The winter winds will soothe my feral fae, and I'll be able to think more clearly about her and deal with the trouble building along our borders. Thorn, fly back to High Mountain and send Brannon to investigate. Give word that we're returning, but keep the information about Taylor to yourself. Have the rest of the Phalanx wait for us at the Timeroon border crossing. We'll be there in a fortnight at the latest. Go."

"Yes, sire." Thorn gives me a brief lowering of his head before turning and running. In a flash, he turns into a silver hawk and pumps his mighty wings, shooting up through the trees and wheeling away into the sun.

"Why does he always have to do a dramatic exit?" Gareth peers after him. "Showboat."

"He's loyal." I rub my temples. "But he's an ass."

"Same can be said for the entire Phalanx." Gareth smiles. "I like to think I'm the most stubborn of all of us, though. Pride myself on it."

"I tend to agree." I clap him on the back, my dark mood lessening. "Let's get ready to ride. The winter realm beckons."

"I feel it, too." He pounds his chest. "Ice calls to ice."

I stride through the woods as Gareth packs up camp. Beth and Taylor are returning from the stream, Taylor complaining that Beth barely let her wash a dish. I can't see them through the trees yet, but I can hear them arguing.

Beth lets out an exasperated sigh. "Look, girl, I've been doing cooking and laundry and scrubbing since I was a wee one."

"So?"

"So, your technique needs work."

Taylor grumbles as they appear just up ahead. "I washed dishes some when I lived at home. But in college I didn't have to do dishes or cook. I mean, I subsisted on Hot Pockets and ramen most of the time. Give me a microwave and some paper plates, and I can show you what I'm made of."

"You speak fae, but nothing you just said made any sense."

Taylor wrinkles her nose. "It's technology. It makes life easier."

"Sounds like nonsense to me. Give me a good pot and a fire, and I can make anything your heart desires." Beth brushes past me.

I put out a hand to stop Taylor. "A word?"

Beth takes the bowls from Taylor and continues toward camp.

"What is it?" Her irritation with Beth bleeds over to me.

"I wanted to ask about..." *About what you said about people changing, but not for the better.* But the way she looks now—slightly dejected and frustrated—has me changing my mind. "About Hot Pockets. What are they?" When she said the phrase the first time, a certain image came to mind, but surely that's not what she's referring to. Couldn't be.

"Oh." She smiles, some of the tension leaving her. "They're food. Like sort of bread wrapped around ham and cheese or pepperoni pizza—cheese and tomato sauce. They're super easy to cook and best of all, cheap. Like ramen. Those are noodles that don't cost a lot."

"Did you go without in the human world?"

She shrugs as a bird sings overhead, its song bright and warm. "I didn't always have food to eat, no." Her gaze falls, as if she's hiding her face from me. "My mom was gone a lot when I was a kid, so I had to take care of myself. And in college, I'm there on scholarship, but I didn't have extra money. I worked, but what I made got spent on books and my dorm room."

No easy life for my mate. I should have guessed. "I'm sorry."

"It's fine. Plenty of people had less than I did. And I was lucky enough to get into college."

"Lucky? I don't think so. You worked hard, even when it wasn't easy for you." I push a little further. "And your father?"

"He was never around. Left when I was little. But my mother always had boyfriends." She tangles her fingers together and squeezes. "And I had a stepfather for a short while."

Just the way she says the word 'stepfather' has me bristling. Something is wrong there. "Your stepfather, was he kind?" I keep my tone light despite the vengeance pulsing through me.

"He's dead." Her head tilts even lower. "What about you? I'm sure you've had hard times in all your years."

A deflection, but one I have to let go for now. She's opening up to me bit by bit. But her question takes me off guard. How can I answer? Should I describe the terrors of war, the fae I've killed, the many lives that have been lost under my command? Should I tell her of the weeks when my soldiers and I starved on the fields of battle after Shathinor's forces destroyed our provisions and burned the surrounding farmlands to ash?

Like her, I choose to deflect. "Nothing worthwhile is ever easy." I cup her face with one hand. "And that includes us. I know it's a lot. When I step back and try to think about it from your point of view, it's overwhelming. A new world full of strangers with one of them claiming to be your eternal mate. But you are strong. You've shown me that time and again since I met you."

"I think you've got me wrong." Her cheeks pink. "I'm just a student looking for a way back home."

I don't say that I'm her home. It's in my heart, though, and one day she will know it's true. "We should get going. The forest will start to clear from here on out, then we'll pass over the Misty River and into the Red Plains."

"Two more weeks until the border, right?" She wipes a stray strand of hair off her brow.

"Two more weeks," I agree.

We make our way back to the camp in a comfortable silence, though my thoughts push ahead, imagining the day we enter my lands. Two more weeks before the winds of winter soothe me, fuel me, and give Taylor a taste of the power lying dormant inside her mate.

*T*he Red Plains are aptly named. Stark and forbidding, the landscape stretches out before us, the ground bloodred and covered with twists of brambles and something akin to sage. This morning we emerged from the trees and rode until we found a narrow lane.

"We'll stick to the road from here on out." Gareth peers into the distance where I can almost see dark jagged peaks.

"I feel so ... exposed." Beth pulls her ratty shawl around her shoulders. "And the merchants gawk at us when they pass."

"It's safer on the road. More traffic here. If we wandered out into the plain, we'd be far too obvious, not to mention, the land is full of pitfalls, sinking red sands, and a number of other dangers." Leander pulls my hair from my nape and blows cool air across my skin.

I almost moan with relief. How does he know what I need before I do? The sun has grown hotter, the sanctuary of the trees now a dense green wall at our backs. Here, there is no respite, no fairy lights flitting around, no lazy streams. Ahead, a dark river cuts a slash against the encroaching crimson, and a ramshackle town—almost like something out of the Old West—sits on the opposite bank.

"What's that?"

"Blood Run," Gareth offers. "The only town in the Red Plains. Full of schemers, travelers, and outlaws."

"So it's Mos Eisley from *Star Wars*." I smile at my faint geek knowledge, well aware that no one else will get my reference to the spaceport where Luke and Obiwan meet Han Solo for the first time.

"Sounds like my kind of town," Beth says after giving me a blank look. "Too bad it's ugly."

"Inside and out," Gareth agrees.

"Are we stopping there?" I stretch, and Leander grips my waist.

"For supplies, but not for the night. It's not safe. We're better protected on the road where we can see what's coming." He slides his palms upward, as if committing my shape to memory.

"I was really hoping for a bed." Beth frowns. "I haven't slept in a bed since ..." She pauses and stares into the middle distance. "I guess it depends on if a pile of empty grain sacks counts as a mattress."

She's had such a hard life. The bite marks on her body only tell one part of her harrowing story. I want to know more, but she deflects every time I ask about her life as a changeling slave. I do the same when she asks about my past, so I can't blame her for it. Some parts of a person's history are better left alone, though they're never forgotten.

"Your master was Granthos?" Gareth asks.

"Yes," she says tightly.

He grunts in response but doesn't say anything else about it.

Beth shoots me a questioning glance, then shrugs and turns back toward the town. "I hope they have bread."

"Me too." That is a train I'm happy to ride. "Carbs are life."

"Carbs?" Leander blows against my nape again, and I want to moan.

"Carbohydrates. What bread is mostly made of."

"Spoken like a true alchemist." He says it with pride.

"I'm not an alchemist. Just an almost-chemist. Not the same. And besides, it's pretty common knowledge that bread has carbs. It's why I love it so much. Carbs are my jam."

"I know jam. We have an entire store room at High Mountain full of it." I can hear the smile in his voice. "Any flavor you'd like."

I laugh and lean against him. His chest has become my back pillow and his arms my seatbelt. "In that case, I'll be sure to raid the jam room when we arrive." But then I'll go home. A pang of hurt slashes through me at the thought. The idea of leaving is still my goal, but somehow, each day I spend with Leander, it gets harder to think about. Not to mention the bonds I've built with Beth and Gareth. I don't have anything like it back home —my only pseudo-friend, Cecile, is the one who sent me here, so she's more of a backstabbing enemy. I still ponder why she did it but haven't been able to piece it together. Then a thought stings me like wasp, and I almost jump off the horse.

"Hang on. HANG ON!" I yell so loud that Kyrin startles.

"What?" Leander tenses and draws his sword.

"*Byrn Varyndr.*" I clap a hand over my face.

"The capital of the summer realm?" Leander's voice is tight and wary. "What about it?"

"It translates to Long Island." I grit my teeth as some pieces of the puzzle click together. "I didn't realize it until I learned fae, and I didn't think about it until right this second. But in English, it means Long Island."

"You lost me." Beth's eyebrows crinkle.

"Cecile always said she came from *Long Island!*" I take a breath and try to keep my voice calm; I've scared Kyrin enough. "And see, I thought she meant Long Island, New York, but all along I think what she really meant was *Byrn Varyndr.*"

Beth's eyebrows unknot. "So your roommate is a summer realm fae?"

"Yes!" Kyrin jumps a little, and I pet his mane. "Sorry, buddy. I'm going to be quieter. But yeah, I think that must be it. She's a summer realm fae, maybe some sort of exchange? I don't know."

"Exchanges don't realize they're fae." Leander stows his sword. "She's something else. Fae, but not a traditional exchange."

"Then what is she doing over there?" Beth gnaws on her thumbnail. "I've never heard of anything like it."

"Neither have I." Gareth frowns. "We'll need to

speak with Ravella about it when we get to High Mountain. She's the only one who may know how Cecile is in the human world, and why she sent you here, for that matter."

I sigh and settle down. One thing has become clear, but the rest of it is still hidden from me. All these questions bumping around in my skull are beginning to tangle with each other, the wires crossing. Leander seems to hear the noise in my head and rubs my upper arms slowly, pulling my thoughts away from the mystery until I focus on his gentle touches instead.

Gareth leads us to the river, the surface covered in a low fog dotted with whorls, as if something spins below the surface. A wide bridge made of splintering timbers and mossy stone is the only way across from what I can see. A buggy approaches, and a man with a pair of skeletal wings jutting from his back gives us a simple nod as he passes.

"What was that?" I try not to stare.

"Lesser fae. They can be a mix of different races but have a line of high fae blood in them."

"Why do you call them lesser? Seems sort of ... snobby."

Leander sighs. "It's simply the way it's always been. An easy way to delineate between full-blooded high fae and those with mixed heritage."

I wrinkle my nose. "Even if you don't mean it as an insult, it doesn't mean it's right. 'Lesser' has a negative connotation, no matter how you say it."

"I agree." Leander steers us to the side of the road as another, larger buggy passes.

"Leander tried to change the classifications of beings in the winter realm long ago, but the distinctions still persist." Gareth leads, his broad back hiding Beth from view. "He wanted to do away with the separate classes and simply have 'fae'." Gareth grumbles under his breath. "The nobles, though, would not have it, threatened outright rebellion. We didn't need more bloodshed, not after the centuries we'd already spent at war. At least, that was my counsel. Leander wanted to decree it, the nobles be damned."

"They're fools," Leander says matter-of-factly.

"They are. But we need stability," Gareth's words seem like pieces of an argument the two fae have had quite a few times. He waves a hand. "That discussion is for another day. For now, Taylor and Beth, be on your guard at all times. Don't speak to anyone."

"We'll come back to the discussion, and my queen will have a voice in it." Leander squeezes my hand. "But Gareth is right. Blood Run is a pit, one we can't afford to fall into. Gareth and I will conduct our business, gather supplies, and then we'll be off."

"Sounds like a real good time," Beth snipes.

The road gets busier as we ride into town. Creatures that defy imagination mill about on either side of the lane, entering shops or arguing with each other. Some of them are high fae, their stature and ears giving them away. Others are more of a mystery, though I can see what I think are a few changelings scattered around on wooden porches stained red from the dirt. We cross an alleyway, and I see two bare-chested males fighting, both of them swinging huge axes, their battle yells ignored by everyone. The view is gone as we continue down the road. Maybe Gareth wasn't exaggerating about how dangerous this town is.

Pulling up in front of a storefront, Gareth jumps down and peers around the street. Plenty of fae watch us, some of them whispering to each other. I suppose seeing two winter realm fae with a couple of bedraggled changelings isn't a common occurrence.

"I need a hat." I glance up at the too-bright sky. "The trees shielded me in the forest, but out here I'll burn to a crisp."

"Clothes, too." Beth throws a leg over her mount and jumps down. "You need to cover up. So do I."

"We told you to stay put and—" Gareth groans when I start to dismount. Leander grabs my waist and lowers me down slowly.

"Beth is right. We need clothes. Is there a store like that here?"

"This is the goods merchant, and you two aren't going in." Gareth looks at Leander with a stern expression.

Leander shrugs. "If my ma—" He glances around at the busy street. "My *friend* needs clothing, then she shall have it."

"Fine. Let's get inside before we draw even more attention to ourselves." Gareth leads the way onto the porch and into the store, grumbling under his breath about females the entire time. Leander smirks and offers his arm. I get a little thrill as I take it and we enter the shop.

I wrinkle my nose as we step inside. "Why does it smell?"

"Meat." Gareth points to a row of carcasses hanging behind a rough-hewn wooden counter.

"What sort of animals are those?" I peer at one ribcage that looks a little too human.

"You don't want to know." Leander sweeps me to the back of the shop as Gareth goes to speak to the fae with the beak at the counter.

"Not much to choose from." Beth runs her hand along a rack of clothing, all of it dusky brown with black stitching. "But it'll do." She snags a couple of long-sleeved tunics.

"Oh my god, pants!" I pull a pair off a spindly wooden hanger.

Beth grabs another set and holds them up to her narrow hips. "These will do just fine. And look, new undergarments, thank the Ancestors!"

"Is there a dressing room?" I look to the back of the shop, but the dark door leading farther inside isn't particularly welcoming given that it has odd pelts nailed all around it.

Leander steps away, and a filmy barrier appears around Beth and me. "I've cloaked you. No one can see."

Beth and I strip down.

"No one but me." He meets my eyes but doesn't let his gaze drop to my naked body.

A shiver tickles up my spine, sending jolts of heat shooting through me. How does he constantly manage to turn me into a horndog? When his lips tug into a smirk, I know he knows what I'm thinking. Mortifying.

"Looking good." Beth smooths my tunic down.

"You're going to need a belt." The brown fabric sags around her waist.

I turn to look for one, and Leander already has two in his hand, which he offers to me.

"Thanks." I take them, and Beth and I finish up. "Wait, shoes?"

Once again, Leander already has two pairs ready.

"Can fae read minds?" I kick off my worn and dirty slippers and slide on the leathery ones Leander chose.

"Some can. But it's super rare. Most fae can't wield magic at all."

"Seriously?" I just assumed they all could.

"I mean, most fae have a talent of some sort or other." She grimaces. "My master had a talent for creatures. Not magic, exactly, but Granthos could communicate on a basic level with most beasts. And he could tell them what to do." She doesn't mention the scars that mark her body, but she doesn't have to. Her master had commanded some sort of vampiric dog to feed on her. I only hope that one day he will receive the punishment he deserves.

She stands and works her dark blonde hair into a big knot. "Anyway, magic isn't so common—and the magic Leander and Gareth have? It's unusual." Swiping a couple of wide-brimmed hats from above the meager rack of clothing, she hands me one. "These will have to do. They don't have anything else to choose from. Maybe they'll last us through the plains." She doesn't sound too sure.

"We'll make them work." I test Leander's barrier with my finger. It sends a tingle up my arm. "We're ready."

The barrier disappears.

"Is there anything else you'd like?" Leander asks, his dark eyes gleaming as he inspects my new outfit.

"Toothbrush." I don't think the shop has any. It's more of a wilderness store, not one too concerned with hygiene. "Oooh, and a hairbrush." It's funny, but back home, my fiercest desire was a set of Baron Fig Squire pens. I was certain if I had those fancy pens, I'd actually journal everyday instead of once a week when I thought about it. Pipe dreams. Or, pen dreams, more accurately. But now? A simple toothbrush would make my day, week, year.

"Tired of the twig toothbrushes I make for us?" Beth asks almost petulantly.

"No, of course not." I think fast. "But in the plains, there won't be any trees, so you can't make fresh ones."

She considers for a moment. "Good point." Turning to Leander, she says, "We need toothbrushes."

Gareth is still arguing with the shopkeeper, though he's amassed a small pile of goods on the counter.

"Not here." Leander leads us back to the door. "The inn across the street might have a few items like that. I'll take you."

"Leander, this son of a yakhound is trying to charge us double simply because he doesn't like my face." Gareth towers over the shopkeeper, who snaps his beak.

"I wouldn't let my ugly sister sit on a face such as yours." The shopkeeper has a row of green feathers along the top of his head that stand up in challenge.

Leander sighs. "Wait here."

He strides to the counter. "We need supplies and are

happy to pay a fair price for them. If you'd prefer to deal with me—"

"You winter realm fae aren't welcome here."

"I have coin. You have goods. Let's discuss—"

"Come on." Beth tugs me out of the shop and onto the dusty porch.

"Shouldn't we wait for Leander?" I glance back into the shop, but it's too dusky inside to see when the sun is so bright out here.

"It's just across the street. We'll be fine. They're a couple of over-protective ninnies." She steps to the edge of the porch as another buggy passes along with a few horses. "Come on, here's our chance."

I let her pull me off the porch and into the dusty road. We hurry across, avoiding all the creatures on the opposite porch as we step up.

"See?" Beth smiles.

"Okay, but let's hurry. You know how Leander gets."

"Insanely possessive?" she says brightly.

"Yeah, that." I snug my hat down tightly on my head, mainly to ward off the prying eyes of the nearby fae.

"We can handle ourselves." She leads the way into the inn. "Don't worry so mu—" Her shriek cuts her words in half as a large fae grabs her and shackles her wrists.

"Let her go!" I rush forward as the creatures in the inn scatter, knocking over tables and chairs. Grabbing Beth's arm, I try to pull her from the fae. He's almost as large as Leander, strength rolling off him. He wears a bandanna around the lower half of his face. When I see his dark eyes, I suspect he's a winter realm fae.

"She's mine." He keeps a hard grip on the chain between her shackles as she struggles to free herself, then he pushes up the brim of my hat. "Are you a runaway, too?"

"Run!" Beth kicks him in the shins, but he doesn't seem bothered. "It's the Catcher!"

"Leander!" I think my yell is loud enough to be heard all the way back at the summer palace.

The inn darkens, a chill blowing through the building so quickly that my teeth chatter. Leander enters behind me, his presence like a tangible fist of cold.

"Release her." He holds his sword with lethal ease and softly maneuvers me behind him.

"Get him!" I pat him on the back. It's pretty much the extent of my usefulness in this situation.

"The Catcher, is it?" Leander's voice is coated with ice, though he lowers his sword.

The Catcher dips his chin just a bit in Leander's direction. Was that respect?

Gareth rushes in, blades in each hand. The inn has completely cleared out, as if we're having a showdown in a ghost town.

"Release the changeling." Gareth advances, his ire even greater than Leander's.

I peer around my fae warrior. No, not 'my.' I try to shake the possessive thought free, but it seems stuck in the net of my mind.

"She ran from her master," the Catcher says, as if it explains everything.

"And she is now a citizen of the winter realm. Free." Gareth stands just out of reach.

The Catcher palms a blade. "I hate to quibble, but

you see, she isn't *in* the winter realm. Therefore, she's not free. Here, she's just a runaway changeling."

"Quibble all you want, but you will release her." Gareth raises his daggers.

Leander reaches back and puts one hand on my hip, the other still holding his sword. Is he sitting this one out?

"Release her?" The Catcher lifts her chain, then drops it. His hand flies out, far too quick for me to see anything other than a blur.

I gasp, but Gareth easily deflects the blow, then counterattacks with a hard kick to the Catcher's stomach. He flies backwards and out a glassless window into the street.

Gareth storms past, and I rush over to Beth.

"You okay?"

She rattles her metal cuffs. "Never better."

"Leander, can you get these off her?"

He reaches for them, but his skin sizzles, and he frowns. "They're enchanted. Only the Catcher can open them."

"Great," Beth deadpans.

A rough yell draws us out to the street, though Leander keeps both of us behind him.

Gareth is spinning and striking like some sort of murder dynamo. The Catcher stumbles back, though he puts up an impressive defense.

"Gareth is mad." Beth cocks her head to the side. "Like, really mad."

It's my turn to smirk at her. "I think he's got a crush."

She makes a pffft noise and continues watching the fight. The street is bare, but plenty of creatures are gathered on porches watching the fray.

"You aren't going to help?" I grab Leander's forearm.

"He doesn't need me." He places one hand over mine. "Have I mentioned how much I enjoy it when you touch me?"

"Only a few ... *hundred* times."

He grins down at me. "Get used to it, little one."

"Are you two really going to do this when Gareth is fighting for his life?" Beth goes to step off the porch, but Leander holds her back.

"Gareth is my deadliest warrior. You have no need to fear the outcome of this duel."

"Oh? No need to fear, eh?" Beth shakes him off. "Tell me, smart king, if Gareth kills the Catcher, then who will get these cuffs off?"

Leander shrugs. "He won't be killed."

"How do you know?" Beth groans, then steps into the street. "Hey, assholes!"

My eyebrows pop up. I've never heard her curse before. Gareth and the Catcher pause.

"I need him to remove these cuffs, so don't kill him."

"He harmed you." Gareth narrows his eyes.

"No, he just tried to kidnap me. I'm not hurt." Beth holds up her hands. "But these have to go."

"All right. That's enough." Leander raises his hand and sends a blast of icy cold shooting through the street. The spectators disappear into the buildings or turn tail and run toward the bridge.

Gareth whirls and aims a blow for the Catcher's throat, but the Catcher manages to stop it with his own blade just before contact. I grip Leander harder. I don't know if I'm ready to see this. Tyrios still flits around the edges of my mind, not haunting me exactly, but the way he died isn't something I can simply erase. Am I ready to see another death?

Leander shoots me a concerned glance, then calls, "Phinelas, that's enough."

"Phinelas?" Gareth yanks the bandanna away from the male's face.

A handsome grin fills in the blanks. "Gareth."

"What in the Spires is going on?" Gareth roars.

"Okay, now I'm beyond confused." Beth leans against me.

Leander waves the two males over. "Let's go inside. It's not something we want to discuss out here."

*G*areth is still steaming when he walks into the barren inn, but he relaxes a hair when Phin releases Beth from her cuffs.

"Why are you on a first-name basis with the Catcher?" Taylor asks as I set a chair to rights for her.

"I've never met the Catcher." I flip a table onto its legs and a few more chairs, then sit beside her.

"I'm lost." She stares at Phinelas, but not as hard as Gareth glares at him.

"Phin is one of ours, a member of the Phalanx, but I was under the impression he was investigating the disappearances." Gareth splits the glare evenly between Phinelas and me.

Phin pockets the cuffs, then hops over the bar at the back of the room and returns with a few bottles. "I am investigating ... in my way." He sets the bottles on the table along with some glasses.

"By parading around as the Catcher?" Gareth leads

Beth to a chair and holds it for her. I don't think he even knows he's doing it.

She grins and takes her seat, then pretends to fluff a fancy skirt.

Gareth notices and grits his teeth, then takes his usual grumpy tone toward her. "And you! Going around and getting yourself caught, putting Taylor in danger. I ought to take you outside and—"

"Gareth, calm down." I kick a seat out toward him.

Gareth catches it.

"Phin is here on my orders." I await Gareth's outburst, but he sits and crosses his arms over his chest.

Silence from him is never a good sign.

I hurry on with my explanation. "When the disappearances began increasing, especially among changelings, I decided the best way to question changelings from the summer realm would be for one of ours to take over the role of the Catcher. That would give us unfettered access to changelings, maybe even ones who intended to set off for the Gray Mountains."

"That's all well and good." Gareth snatches a drink from the table. "But you didn't think to tell me? I'm your second in command, and you hide this from me?" He takes a drink, then sputters, "And you've allowed Phin to catch these poor changeling slaves and return them to their horrible masters?"

"No." I sniff Taylor's drink before letting her taste it. "He doesn't return any of the changelings to their masters. He takes them to the winter realm and sets them free."

"Then how does he ever get any work? If he doesn't deliver?"

Phin salutes me with his drink. "I never deliver, but there's a very real Catcher out there who does. The trick is for me to get his assignments before he does. He knows about me, or at least he knows he has an impersonator. But, as we suspected, he isn't divulging that information to clients. It would be a sure way to kill off business. Instead, he's been chasing me whenever he's in-between jobs, trying to take me down quietly."

"Why not tell me about this?" Gareth is still a thundercloud.

"Because you would have said no." Phin downs his drink and pours another.

"You're damn right I would have said no!" Gareth is close to bellowing. "You put our truce with the summer realm in danger by freeing their changelings!"

"But it's the right thing to do, old friend." I put my hand on his shoulder. "You know it is."

"Maybe it is, but strategically—"

"Don't think about strategy. Think about how you felt when you saw Beth in irons."

"Well, that's—" He shakes his head. "That's different."

"Because you like me so much, right?" Beth grins and drinks her whiskey as if it were water.

Gareth's bluster dies a bit as he sputters out a vague denial that ends with "damn females" and a chug from one of the bottles.

Under the table, Taylor takes my hand. "You've been freeing changelings?"

"Technically, Phin has." I grab my drink and raise it. "To Phin."

Gareth grumbles but lifts his bottle. "This isn't over. We are going to discuss this, Leander."

"Let's do it on the road." I can feel the townspeople scurrying around just outside of our presence. "We've attracted enough attention. Phin, keep the work going and save as many as you can. I'll get word to you once it's time to return to High Mountain."

"One more thing before we part." Phin levels his gaze at Taylor.

A sharp tingle spikes along the back of my neck, the feral fae taking issue with Phin's direct stare.

"Why are you taking these changelings to High Mountain?"

"That's not your concern." Gareth rises.

I stand and offer Taylor my hand. She takes it and rises beside me.

Phin's eyes open wide, his countenance puzzled as he tries to piece together why I would be so familiar with a changeling. "Is there a reason to hope? Is the curse finally..." He rises so fast his chair falls over. "Your mate. This changeling is—"

"Not another word, Phin." Gareth peers around at the walls.

"My spell has muted our talk, but we can't be too careful." I put my arm around Taylor, and to my never-ending pleasure, she leans into me.

Phin smiles, and it takes such a weight from him. "This news is—I can't begin to describe it." He strides to us, pulls out his blade, and kneels before Taylor, his oath pouring out of him as he bows his head. My most trusted warriors never disappoint me, and their unerring loyalty is worth more to me than any riches the summer realm can boast of.

"*Bladanon thronin.*" She says the words without hesitation and with a quiet strength that runs through her from head to toe. Though she doesn't know it yet, she will be a formidable queen, one I will always be honored to call my mate.

The sky is so huge, pounding down to the ground in shades of deep blue, and a crimson dust devil twirls off in the distance.

"Does anyone live out here?" I pull the brim of my hat down low.

Leander shades his eyes. "These lands are home to the Vundi, a nomadic band of lesser fae. I've heard tales of a vast network beneath the surface of the plains, roads of iron and halls of stone, a Vundi community, but I've never seen it."

"Doesn't exist." Gareth leads his horse down the right side of the narrow, red road. "Someone would have seen it by now, come back and told us. Besides, the Vundi are violent and territorial. They don't have what it takes to build some sort of vast underground cavern like that."

"Sounds like the Mines of Moria."

"The mines?" Gareth points to his left across the Red Plains. "Those are far away to the south."

"No." I smile at my tidbit of human knowledge—even

if it's fiction. "The Mines of Moria are in a book. Well, I didn't read the books, but I saw the movies. It's this huge underground place, up under a mountain, and they have enormous halls and rooms and an entire city. It's fancy and has dwarves."

"Hmm." Leander blows on my neck again. "Sounds somewhat like the caves of the Wyvern Range. They're a set of mountains along the winter realm's northern border. I've been beneath Caron's Cap, the tallest of the peaks, but I can assure you that dark, dank place is nothing like what you've described."

"Sounds scary." I turn back to look at him.

"We have no reason to venture there." His grip tightens on me almost imperceptibly. "You will find safety at High Mountain and have no need of travelling farther."

"What's at High Mountain? A city? Or, like, a big castle?"

Leander laughs. "It's like nothing you've ever seen. Stone walls that no spell can touch, high turrets flying the Gladion flag, and a keep that has never been breached. It was built eons ago and still stands as proud as it did then. A city, Cold Comfort, rests at the base of the mountain. It's protected from the vicious winds and the harsh bite of the cold that dances along the peaks."

"Are there many people there?" I don't know why I'm so curious. I intend to leave as soon as I get there.

"Cold Comfort is the biggest city in the winter realm, but it still doesn't have the numbers of the summer realm."

"But didn't you win a war against the southern

realm?" She arches a brow. "How, if you have so fewer people to fight?"

"I won peace, yes. And I think you'll find that the fae of my realm are a hardier people than those who inhabit the summer lands."

"If they're anything like you, then I'm not surprised you won." I smile as his chest puffs with pride. He can be so cute sometimes, even though he's a hulking warrior. "Hey, speaking of battles, I want you to teach me how to use this." I pull the obsidian blade from the makeshift scabbard Beth crafted for me.

"You have no need of that." Gareth shakes his head. "Your king and the Phalanx are your devoted protectors."

"Sure, but you aren't always with me. Remember Tyrios?" I suppress a shudder. His memory is one I fear I'll never be rid of. "He caught me alone, and it's been dangerous ever since. I need to be able to defend myself. I mean, at home I could use my car keys between my knuckles or aim a kick between the legs, but here, that's not enough."

"You've kicked a male between the legs?" Gareth pales a little beneath the road dust on his skin.

"No, but I will if I need to."

"She's right," Leander says. "She needs to be able to defend herself."

"By the end of this journey, you'll be able to cook, clean, and flay a man alive," Beth says brightly.

"Certain skill sets never go out of style." I return her wry grin.

"Ouch?" I palm my butt as Leander darts past me. "Do you really have to spank me with that thing?"

He twirls a short sword in his wrist. "I'll happily do it with my hand, if you like. Perhaps put you over my knee when you underperform?"

My stomach clenches at the image he puts in my head, and a low growl rips from him.

"Careful, little one." His bare arms flex under the hot sun.

"You be careful!" I rush him and stab forward with the obsidian blade.

He dodges with ease and smacks my ass again with the broadside of his sword. "You're getting a little better."

"I'm not." I huff and realize maybe I should've utilized my free gym membership at the student rec a little more. "But I will."

"That's the spirit." Beth raises a skin of water in toast before drinking.

"Maybe you should try? Practice with me?" I raise my sword. "Maybe it wouldn't be like shooting fish in a barrel the way it is for Leander."

"You have the oddest expressions." Beth takes another gulp.

My mouth waters.

"Focus." Leander grabs my throat.

I drop my sword and try to pry his wrist away.

His palm tightens. "Never drop your weapon. *Never.* You're a changeling in a world full of creatures that are stronger and faster. I've been at a tiny fraction of my usual speed with you. Don't let it fool you."

I reach out to smack his bare chest, but to my embarrassed horror, I can't even reach him when he holds his arm out straight.

He smirks as I swing again and hit only air.

"Asshole!" I scratch his wrist, drawing blood.

When his pupils blow, I know I've screwed up.

"I'm sorry," I squeak.

He yanks me to him, and I'm crushed in his arms as he pulls me up to his height.

"Gareth!" Beth yells.

"My mate seeks my blood." His fangs lengthen.

"Leander, you're doing the feral thing again." My voice trembles.

"I will give you all you desire, little one." His voice is low and gravelly, and I can feel his erection pressing against my thigh.

My breath quickens, and I can't seem to focus on anything except his lips. "I didn't mean to—"

He stops me with a kiss, his lips rough and demanding. That wire that seems to run between us tightens, and I open my mouth, letting him in, giving in to the pleasures of his mouth. I've never been kissed like this, never felt such a fever in my soul from the simple touch of another's mouth on mine. How does his tongue manage to stroke mine until I'm keening and wrapping my arms around his neck? One of his hands strays to my ass and squeezes, while the other holds me steady with firm pressure on my back. I should stop this, tell him to put me down. I don't. Instead, I wrap my legs around him and sigh as his low purr rumbles between us.

"My lord?" Gareth stands a few paces away.

"Mine," he grits out before returning to our kiss.

"She drew blood," Beth says amusedly.

"Damn." Gareth steps closer, and Leander's purr turns to a growl.

"Taylor, when a mate draws blood, it's a... well, it's—"

"An aphrodisiac," Beth calls. "You may as well have licked the point of his ear or stuck your hand down his pants."

Leander kisses down to my neck, his tongue dancing over the sensitive skin as goose bumps rise along my arms and back.

"I can take you here under the sun. Give you so much pleasure. Spend hours with my mouth between your legs, even longer with my cock deep inside you until you beg me for release." He squeezes my ass, and my core heats, growing wet as his words set off sparks in my imagination.

"This is what I came for," Beth crows.

"Stop that, changeling." Gareth steps closer. "My lord. Leander. This is not the time or the place. We're in enemy territory."

"I can protect my mate." He pulls the neck of my tunic down and kisses along my collarbones.

I know I should protest, should tell him to let me go. I can't. Those words don't come to my lips. None do. I can't think when he's touching me like this.

"We are *exposed*," Gareth hisses. "Think of your mate's safety!"

"He-he's right." It takes more effort than it should for me to force those words out.

"Taylor." Leander runs his fangs lightly along my throat. "I want to pleasure you, to give you everything you deserve."

"We can't." I shake my head, trying to snap out of it. "Gareth's right. We need to focus on getting to the High Mountain."

"We can do both," Leander whispers. "I can focus on tasting you every night, while still making good time to the winter realm."

"No." I push away from him and glance around. Do I want my first time to be in an inhospitable red landscape with two witnesses? No, thanks. "This isn't right."

"I can make it right." His lips feather across my jaw, and I want to give in so badly I start to tremble.

"Please, let me down." I bite my lip to stop the quiver.

He growls low and long as he eases me down his body, making sure I feel every hard inch of him. When my feet hit the ground, my mind clears somewhat, and I back away. He matches each step, refusing to allow any distance between us.

Gareth advances. "Leander, how about we get the horses ready? It's time for us to go."

Leander whirls on him. "*I* am your king! We do what I say, when I say it. Unless you intend to challenge me? You come between me and my mate. Do you dare try to stake your claim on her?"

"No." Gareth looks hurt, his brows drawing together. "I would never do such a thing. You know that. My loyalty is—and always has been—to you. I know you're struggling right now, but this isn't you."

"Leander." I put my hand on his back. "Gareth is your friend, not a rival. Stop this, okay? I don't like it when you act this way."

He turns to me and blinks, his pupils shrinking and

his face falling. "I-I'm sorry, Taylor. I never want to disappoint you."

"I know it's the feral thing. And you can't help it. But maybe try and be a little less suspicious? Poor Gareth has never been anything but kind to me, and in case you haven't noticed, it's pretty clear that he'd follow you to hell—err, the Spires—and back again if you asked him to."

Taking my hand, he kisses the back with a tenderness that I've grown to enjoy. "Please forgive me."

"I'm fine. Talk to Gareth." I jerk my chin toward him.

"The horses," Gareth offers with a grateful glance my way.

"Of course." Leander kisses my crown and strides off, the two of them talking low. After a while, Beth and I hear them laughing, and I sag with relief as we pack up the bedrolls.

"I thought this was it." She frowns. "I thought I was going to experience a mating and replay it in my mind whenever I got alone time."

"That's kind of disturbing." I try not to laugh. It would only encourage her. Okay, so I laugh a little.

"You're almost there, Taylor. That time was even closer than the last. When you give in—" She sighs dramatically. "It's going to be a night to remember."

"You have some real issues, you know th—"

"Shh!" She holds a hand out toward me.

I freeze and mouth "*what?*"

She taps her ear, and then I hear it—a low whistle off in the distance. Could it be a bird? Come to think of it, I haven't seen a single speck in the sky since we've been in this odd red world.

Leander pounds up on Kyrin and jumps down. He doesn't even need to say anything. We're in danger. Again.

Beth flies into action, wrapping up camp as Leander leads me to Kyrin and lifts me with ease. With a few quick movements, he loads our supplies and climbs up behind me.

"What's going on?" I hold on tight as we take off toward the road, Gareth and Beth at our backs.

"The Vundi."

"They're coming?" I peer across the empty crimson expanse.

Leander spurs Kyrin into a run. "They're already here."

11

They've been tracking us for days, ever since we emerged from the Greenvelde. But they did the same when we arrived from the winter realm, and never approached us. This time, though, is different.

Movement to my left catches my eye but disappears just as quickly. The Vundi have mastered this land, melding into the red ground as if they are part of it. I can sense them all around, hiding in plain sight.

"Ahead," Gareth calls.

I snap my eyes forward. An entire contingent of Vundi appear on the road, seeping into view like blood from the dirt. Taylor tenses, but keeps her head up. With one arm I lift her and pivot her around my body so she rides behind me. Her arms go around my waist, and she presses her forehead into my back. I want to tell her she's safe, but I don't take my eyes off the Vundi or utter a word.

A leader emerges, her red scarf covering most of the

tan skin of her face and leaving only her silver eyes visible.

I ease Kyrin to a stop a few yards away. Gareth is close behind, ready to shed blood if need be.

"Odd for winter realm fae to grace the Red Plains with their presence, don't you think?" The leader keeps one hand on the hilt of a curved blade at her hip. A whip is looped on the belt that cinches her red dress close to her body.

"Only passing through." I let one blast of coolness pulse from me, coating the air around me with tiny shards of ice.

"See, that's a problem." She's smiling beneath her scarf, laugh lines appearing beside her eyes. "Because there's a price for anyone travelling in my land."

"Your land?" I look down my nose at her and the contingent of two dozen red-garbed warriors at her back. "These lands are within the summer realm and under the control of Queen Aurentia, to whom you owe your allegiance."

The leader lifts her scarf and spits, a grave insult. "We answer to no supposed queen."

"If you don't let us pass, you will answer to the bite of the winter wind." I don't make threats lightly, and she seems to understand this, because the smile fades a little.

"Not without the toll."

"Give us your price." Gareth saunters up, Beth at his back.

The leader cuts her eyes to him, then re-focuses on me. "You might want to call off your dog, your *majesty*," she sneers.

They know who we are. But, of course, word that the winter realm's king had crossed the border would have spread rapidly.

"Your price," Gareth presses.

She traces her fingers along the whip. "No small talk? Fine by me, my lord." She steps toward Kyrin, who snorts his disapproval. "You know what the king beyond the mountain wants."

"You won't take my life." My fangs lengthen as I eye her numbers. "Plenty before you have tried. I've killed each, sometimes with more relish than I should have."

She arches a brow. "You? It seems your ego precedes you, my lord. I'm not here for your head. My price is simple. We require the changeling hiding behind you. She will stay with us, and the rest of you are free to go on your way. A reasonable price, truly, since it ends with all of you breathing even though you trespass in our lands."

"Your price is death." A sizzle of cold ripples through my skin. I'm barely keeping my magic at bay, everything inside me demanding I destroy the threat to my mate.

"Why do you want her?" Gareth dismounts and hands his reins to Beth, then positions himself between them and me.

The warriors tense, some of them drawing their curved blades, but the leader doesn't move at all. Steady like a snake waiting for its prey.

"The bounty on her head."

"What bounty?" I ask.

"The king beyond the mountain has promised enough coin to fund my people for generations. Anyone who can deliver this changeling alive to the Gray Mountains will receive the reward." She flicks her whip free. "And I intend to claim it."

"Maybe I'm the changeling you're looking for. You ever think about that?" Beth calls.

The leader doesn't even look at her. "The one I want is coveted by the king of the winter realm. I can assume, based on the way he's fawning over her, it's the one on his horse."

Taylor fists the material at my sides. "Why would he want me?" she breathes.

I squeeze one of her hands. "They won't take you."

The leader shrugs. "That's cute, but I'm not walking away from the reward. So, I *will* be taking her, even if it requires killing the rest of you."

"Then you will be disappointed." Gareth draws his sword. "And your warriors will be dead. Or you could let us pass. The choice is yours."

"For this sum, I have no choice." The whip lights with magical fire, orange flames licking along the leather. With a vicious crack, she launches it through the air, and Gareth ducks out of the way. All the warriors go into motion, their blades drawn.

I jump from Kyrin, hand the reins to Taylor and guide both of them to Beth. "Go back down the road. Keep to it, and ride hard. Flee to the Greenvelde and then to Queen Aurentia. She will keep you safe. I will come for you when I can."

"Wait, Leander." Taylor reaches for me, but I slap Kyrin's flank, and both horses take off. The fear in her eyes tears me to pieces, but I can't ease her. Not now. Instead, I turn and engage the warriors, each of them fast and cunning. But they are no match for my magic. Even in the summer realm, my powers are formidable. With a vicious push, I shove a wave of cold into the nearest soldiers, and a frost creeps along their red clothing, slowing their movements.

I jump into the fray, slashing with my sword as Gareth engages with the leader, the crack of her whip a constant threat. More of them emerge from the low brush along the side of the road, all of them coming straight for us with their curved blades held high. They fight well, not as a unit, but separately, each of them spinning and engaging with lethal efficiency. I cut them down, the ground absorbing their blood as they fall, crimson on crimson.

One lands a blow to my arm, the skin separating as the blade cuts to my bone. I yell and parry, attacking the fae soldier with an onslaught that leaves him badly wounded as another emerges from the brush and comes for me. I'm used to fighting wounded. It keeps the stakes fresh and fuels my magic.

The whip cracks against the side of my head, the fire scorching my temple. I send a wave of blistering cold into the mass of fighters. Two of them fall dead, their eyes frozen open, as the others slow but do not stop.

"Gareth." I spin and roll out of the way of another crack of the whip. "It's about time you dusted off your magic."

The leader is grinning, her sword red with Gareth's blood. "I've never killed a winter realm fae." She drops and does a spinning kick, knocking Gareth off his feet. When she slashes at him with her blade, I block the blow as he scrambles to his feet. Her silver eyes narrow as I stare down at her, our blades locked, though she's losing ground.

"And you won't kill one today." I shove her back, and she sprawls on the road.

With a hiss she summons a large ball of red flame and throws it at me. I blast it away with my ice. She's already panting, her magic stores no match for mine.

Another blast of cold from me, and she curls in on herself, the freeze turning the tips of her fingers black with frostbite.

"Back up." Gareth grabs my shirt and yanks me away as the remaining warriors rush us. "Shield!"

I throw up an ice barrier just as Gareth unleashes his magic. The air explodes as if it's made of glass, and the red warriors scream as bits of their flesh are ripped away. Gareth's magic is destructive and wild, so vicious that despite years of practice, he can barely control it. And in situations like this, he can only use it when assured his allies aren't within range.

Several of the warriors fall to the road, their lives bleeding out onto the hungry ground. Others limp away and disappear into the red wastes. The leader struggles to her feet, whip still in hand. The scarf has fallen from her face, revealing a comely female with high fae features.

"You brought this end upon yourself." I advance with my sword out beside me. "Joining with the king beyond the mountain was a foolish choice."

She holds her blade out defensively. "My people are starving. I'd happily ally with anyone who could put food in their bellies." Kicking her chin up, she cracks her whip, the flames flickering. "Come for me, king, and I will show you the sting of the Vundi."

I raise my sword and swing. The blow cuts her blade in half and severs her whip. She staggers back, gasping as she pulls a dagger from the folds of her dress. I would spare her, but she made the mistake of threatening my mate. The feral fae will not stop until her blood runs cold on the dusty ground.

Reaching for her, I take her by the neck and lift her off the dirt. She slashes my arm with her dagger, but I barely feel it. All I have to do is close my fist, and she's done. But a sound catches my ear. Hooves.

The female's mouth spreads into a grin as I turn and see Kyrin galloping toward me. A Vundi sits astride him, in his hand the obsidian blade. Taylor is draped across the saddle, her body limp.

My battle cry erupts in an icy wave, and I taste blood.

BITE OF WINTER

FAE'S CAPTIVE BOOK 3

1

"Release her." The Vundi warrior astride Kyrin raises the obsidian blade and points at me.

I hold the Vundi leader in my grasp, her death only a whisper away. All I have to do is squeeze and her neck will break in my palm.

"I wouldn't do that." Gareth takes a step toward Kyrin, but the warrior brings the blade down to Taylor's side, almost touching her with it. My mate.

Another blast of cold whips through the air around me, and the leader groans. The feral fae in my breast demands I kill them all and take back what's mine. I want to agree. I'm almost there, my bloodlust welling inside me with a sweeping vengeance I've never felt before.

"That female?" Gareth risks another step. "Is Leander's mate. And he hasn't claimed her yet. Do you have any idea what he will do to you if you harm her?"

I lift the Vundi leader higher as she claws at my arm. Killing her will be a pleasure. And the one who touched Taylor? I will end him slowly. Tie him to Kyrin and drag him through the Red Plains as we make our way to the winter realm.

"Release Para." The Vundi juts his chin toward me.

A few warriors rise from the road, their wounds not enough to keep them down. They should have stayed on the ground. I'm done talking, done negotiating, done with anyone or anything that tries to keep me from my mate.

"Easy now, Leander. We can solve this." Gareth holds a hand out toward me, his entire posture reminiscent of a wince, as if he knows the murder brewing in my soul.

"Yes, we can." I whistle a sharp burst of three notes.

Kyrin bucks hard. I throw the Vundi leader to the ground and rush forward. Taylor lands in my arms as the Vundi with the obsidian blade flies off the back of my horse.

Her eyes flutter open. "What the—"

The Vundi warrior must have bespelled her to sleep. Gareth backs to me, his blade in front of him as the Vundi warriors regroup. A tall red cloud grows in the distance, a sense of foreboding on the already-tense air.

"Are you hurt?" I kiss Taylor's forehead.

"No." She blinks hard. "I was riding away, but then I saw the Vundi. He has the strangest eyes. And then I … fell asleep somehow."

I put her on her feet and keep her behind me as I turn to face the Vundi leader. She's grasping her injured neck. I should have snapped it. There are too many Vundi warriors, and now that Taylor is in the thick of it, there's no way for us to get out without risking her. But I can't give her up.

The leader, Para, straightens her shoulders and grabs one of the blades from her slain brethren. Her soldiers advance. Hooves catch my ear as Beth pounds up on Sabre, but she slows as she approaches the fray.

"Stand down, proud Vundi." Though it takes every bit of self-control I have, I lower my blade—but not all the way. "If we continue like this, more of your people will die. I don't want that. But you must know that I will kill you all to keep my mate safe." I motion to Gareth, and he holds his hands up, a maelstrom of wild magic swirling between them. The red cloud behind the Vundi grows, the sun turning a shade of crimson as dust rises high in the air.

Para winces and holds up her hand. "We can't let you go. Not with her."

"Seems we're at an impasse." Gareth lets his magic expand, but not too much. If it gets any bigger, he won't be able to control it.

Ice builds in my veins, choking my thoughts, the feral fae ruling me and demanding vengeance against anyone who would harm my mate.

Para's eyes widen as she looks at the two of us, but she doesn't back down.

"Wait." Taylor tries to step from behind me, but I don't let her. She growls a little, and my cock hardens despite the circumstances.

She leans out a little so her voice will carry. "Can we at least talk about this? If we can't solve it, then fight after, okay?"

"There's nothing to talk about." Para coughs, her throat no doubt raw. "I can't let this opportunity go. If I give you to the king beyond the mountain, he's promised crystal and coin. Enough for my people to survive, even thrive. No more going hungry, no more sending what little we have to that bitch on the throne. And all I need is you."

"You go hungry?" Taylor's voice softens.

"It's a hard life out here." Para lowers her weapon just a hair. "Harder when the fae at Byrn Varyndr demand what little we're able to farm." The bitterness in her voice could kill a woodland fairy. "We keep our warriors fed, but others ..." She shakes herself and raises her blade. "I won't watch another child go hungry when all I have to do is turn you over. I'm prepared to die for it."

My cold seeps through the ground, snaking toward the warriors. She's prepared to die. I will grant her a quick end.

Taylor pulls on my arm and leans forward, her gaze locked with Para's. "Para, is it? I know what it's like to be hungry. Not the sort where you've missed a meal or wake up too late for breakfast. I'm talking about the kind where it *hurts*. The kind that makes you wonder how long you can stand it. And the kind where, eventually, you don't even feel it anymore. You've gone so long without that you can barely feel anything at all."

Para blinks, then nods slowly. "Yes. That's exactly what it is. Too many of my people suffer it, and you're the way to change all that. I can't let you leave."

My ice grows, coating everything and cracking the red dirt beneath it. I should slay them all and leave nothing alive. And then I will comfort my mate, assure her that she will never go hungry again.

Taylor squeezes my arm and whispers, "Hang on. Give me a chance, please."

I keep the magic at bay, the ice stopping like the edge of a frozen lake just in front of the Vundi.

Taylor raises her voice again and addresses Para. "I don't know you, but I don't want you to die. And maybe you haven't noticed, but Leander is on the verge of freezing all of you to death. Can we all just pull back and talk about this? Everyone put their weapons down."

Para finally breaks her eye contact with Taylor and looks up at me. Her brows furrow and she lets out a low sigh, as if she's defeated, disgusted, or just tired. Based on the circles under her eyes and her gaunt cheeks, no longer hidden by the scarf, I would guess the latter. She seems to weigh Taylor's words, then says, "Winter king, give me your word you will keep your magic in abeyance during our talks, and I will have my people stand down. But I make no promises, not to you or your changeling, about what happens after we meet with the council and the high priestess."

"We can't trust her," I growl.

"Leander, please. Hasn't there been enough death?" Taylor rests her forehead against my back, her warmth soothing the cold heart of winter inside me. "If there's a chance we can talk our way out of this, we should at least try."

I wrestle with my need to destroy them, to freeze their hearts until the threat is gone. But the non-feral part of me is yelling to stand down. With every day that passes, that voice gets quieter and quieter, the feral side of me growing louder.

"Leander." She strokes her hand down my back. "Please, for me."

"Anything for you." Even the feral fae can agree to that, though it still sneaks in a whisper of *"claim her, here on the ground in front of them all"* before dissipating along with my ice. "Gareth." I give him a nod.

"Weapons down, all of you." He shrinks the ball of destruction between his palms until it disappears.

Para whistles high and sharp, and her warriors sheathe their blades and drop back, but not far.

"The storm is almost here." The warrior who wields Taylor's obsidian blade steps to Para's side. Light brown scales fan out from beneath his crimson scarf, ending along the lower parts of his cheeks.

"We've called destruction to us with the scent of blood." He surveys the dead along the ground.

Para spares a glance over her shoulder. "The Ancestors are punishing me."

"Dust storm." Gareth whistles, and Sabre hurries to him. "We need to make camp before it hits."

Kyrin walks over and nuzzles Taylor. She rubs his muzzle like an old friend.

"So we're running from the storm, yeah? Because it doesn't look like fun." Beth peers into the distance.

"You can't run from the wrath of the Ancestors." Para motions to her warriors. They disperse, dragging their dead with them and seeping into the red oblivion on either side of the road before disappearing. The one with the scales and the obsidian blade remains, guarding Para's back.

"Wait. I need your oath." I'm asking for more than simple words. An oath among the fae is so serious as to be unbreakable. Any fae who ignores this fact will be branded an outcast and never allowed to speak amongst their brethren without reproach. And if the oath is serious enough, it can kill the fae who breaks it. "A promise to the Ancestors that we will be safe in your realm and that you will not attempt to take my mate."

Para bristles, then gives a curt nod. "I will give my oath to the Ancestors that you shall not be harmed and will be treated as honored guests if you promise to never speak of what you see during your time with the Vundi."

"And my mate?"

"She will not be harmed."

"And you will not attempt to take her." It's not a question.

"We will allow you to speak to the high priestess and the council of elders. You have my word that she will not be taken before that time."

Her companion's eyes, now slitted like a snake's, narrow, but he doesn't interrupt.

"And after?"

She presses her lips into a fine line.

A growl rises in my chest, bloodlust bursting in my veins.

"She can't promise that, Leander. Not yet," Taylor says softly. "But that's what the talks are for. It gives us a chance."

A guttural shriek tears across the wide plains.

"Decide quickly," the male Vundi says. "There's more in the storm than simply dust."

"Do you agree, winter king?" Para presses.

Taylor leans against me, a silent promise that she isn't going anywhere. "Please, Leander."

I bend to the will of my mate, because she is the only reason my heart beats and my breath stirs. "I agree." The sizzle of magic whips through the air, and the deal is struck.

"Follow me." Para turns and heads into the low brush as her companion eyes us.

"You will return my mate's blade." I glare at him.

He doesn't respond, but motions for us to follow Para, the sword still in his grasp. I'll retrieve it later and may use it on him for good measure.

Gareth shoots me a look. "I don't trust her."

"Neither do I." I lift Taylor onto Kyrin and climb up behind her. "But we need to beat this storm. I've heard enough tales of what lurks in the swirling dust to know we need shelter. We must follow, but keep your wits sharp and your magic ready."

"Always." He settles behind Beth, and we follow Para into the red wastes as the storm bears down, promising ruin.

2

TAYLOR

"Are you certain the Vundi didn't harm you?" Leander asks for what seems like the dozenth time.

"I'm fine. Really." I squeeze his hand. "It was weird. One minute I was awake and then, *bam*, snooze-city. That guy is like a creepy-eyed sandman, or maybe the Lunesta-Man. He could make a killing back home."

"I would never allow him to kill you or anyone you cared about." His arm tightens around my waist.

"No, I mean he'd make a lot of money. Humans have a ton of anxiety, so they sometimes need help falling asleep."

"You don't seem to have trouble." He guides Kyrin through the brush and gently sloping red dirt. Para walks ahead of us, her back straight as she navigates the terrain like she was born to it.

I shrug. "I used to toss and turn, but now ... Now that I've been here, it's been easier."

"You mean now that you've been sleeping with me." I don't miss the cockiness in his voice.

"Don't get ahead of yourself." But yes, I think it's him. Before, I'd run through shadows from my past, every worry I had, even some that verged on imaginary, before I could fall asleep. Now, in his arms, I seem to drift away so peacefully that the transition is nothing more than a ripple across clear water.

I peer into the distance as the red storm grows taller by the second. We've been traveling away from the road and perpendicular to the storm for half an hour. Now I can hear the rumble of the wind, the rush of dirt brushing against dirt, and every now and then, a peculiar screech. Para doesn't seem to notice it as she forges ahead of us. But Kyrin tenses beneath me and Sabre lets out a huff.

I finally get up the nerve to ask, "What is that sound?"

"Wind wights." Beth's eyes are wide. "I thought they were a myth, just a stupid story told to us changelings to keep us in line, but—" Another howl cuts through the air, louder now.

"Wights?" I stare as the heightening maelstrom turns the sun a vicious shade of crimson.

Beth's creeped-out stare intensifies. "Spirits so malevolent they couldn't pass to the Ancestors and refused to enter the Spires. They say they're huge monsters formed from the blood and bones of ancient warriors."

"Seriously?"

"A great war was fought on the Red Plains almost three thousand years ago," Leander says. "Some of the greatest warriors of fae legend perished here, millions of dead on either side."

"Why?" I can't imagine the enormity of a battle like that. "What were they fighting over?"

"All of Arin." Leander says it so matter-of-factly, as if world domination is as sensible as the sun rising in the morning. "It was a clash of seelie and unseelie fae. They say the plains used to be a beautiful land of farms and plentiful crops. But that battle created such evil that the ground turned to sand, forever stained crimson from the blood of the children of this world, the rivers dried up, and the wights rose from the mounds of the dead, their dark magic feeding from the strife."

"That's kind of intense." I hug myself and try not to think of the sheer horror of war, the propensity for evil that exists in the hearts of all creatures—human, fae, everyone.

More piercing cries sound, and Beth leans forward in her saddle. "Hey, Para lady, how much longer? Because I really don't want to feel my bones being crunched in a wind wight's maw."

Para shoots a glance over her shoulder but continues walking. I can't see a path. The entire landscape looks exactly the same, as if someone took a stamp and pressed it all over the world until it meets the horizon.

"Soon. I'll just take that to mean soon." Beth sits back, and Gareth rests his arm around her waist. Comfortable. They look used to each other. Close, even. I can't help my smile.

"What?" she asks.

"Nothing."

A cacophony of screeches burst from the storm to our right, and I cover my ears out of sheer reflex.

"Don't worry, little one. I won't let anything harm you." Leander's voice rumbles through me, stroking my fears until they relent.

Para takes a sharp right, and the horses follow, though their movements are getting a bit jerky, the shrieks eating away at their confidence. I don't blame them. The storm is a red wall rushing toward us, and if I stare hard enough, I could swear I see enormous skeletal fingers emerging from the redness every so often, like giants running full speed at us.

"God," I breathe out hard at the sight.

"Safe, little one. Always safe with me." Leander has one hand on the haft of his blade.

Para seems unhurried, and her companion at our back doesn't rush us, just follows along. She walks a little while longer, then stops and steps to the side, motioning us onward.

"What is this?" Gareth stares at the landscape, which is exactly the same as the one behind us.

"Safety." Para crosses her arms over her chest. "Hurry, before the storm hits."

"Hurry into what?" Gareth sputters. "There's nothing here. No shelter! We'll be set upon by the wights and ripped to shreds."

Para hitches a dark eyebrow. "You can either wait here and perish or follow my instructions and live." She gestures for Gareth to continue onward. "I suggest you save yourselves. The wights sound particularly hungry, especially now that they've scented royal blood." She looks to Leander. "It's their favorite."

Gareth glowers. "If this is a trick—"

"Suit yourselves." Para shrugs and marches forward into the red waste. And then she ... disappears.

I lean forward, my eyes likely popping out of my head. "What the hell?"

Beth yelps as if she's been struck and stares at the spot where Para vanished. "She's tricked us!"

"Not a trick." Her companion strides past, my sword strapped to his side, and disappears right in front of us. The more I stare at the spot, the more something strikes me as off. This piece of land doesn't quite fit with the rest of the landscape, as if the stamp on this area had a crack running through it.

"Hang on." I tap Leander's hand. "Let me down. I want to see something."

He jumps down, his eyes wary, and then helps me to my feet. "Stay close."

"I think ..." I sidestep and turn. "Wow."

Leander has already drawn his sword as he hews close to me. "What is it?"

The shrieks are almost constant, and the low hum of the wind has grown to just under a din.

"An optical illusion." I point. "Look."

Para and her companion stand just inside a tall, rectangular doorway. "It's masked to mimic the landscape, painted too. Look at it from any other angle, and it seems like just more of the same." I take one step farther to the right, and the doorway disappears. "That's kind of genius."

"What magic is this?" Gareth frowns.

"Not magic. Perspective." I reach out and touch the layered edge of the doorway, each inset like a piece of the horizon. "Art. No one would be able to find it if they didn't already know where it was."

"If you're done, we'd like to get inside." Para points to the roiling wall of crimson.

"Watch your tone when you speak to my queen." Leander's growl rivals the fury of the storm.

"It's okay." I turn and look up at him, his dark eyes filled with nothing but me, my reflection. Something inside my stomach flips. "We should go."

He takes my arms and pulls me away from the door. "If anything happens, always run to me. I will keep you safe. We can't trust the Vundi, especially not now. But they won't take you. I will always protect you."

"I know." I hold his gaze, though worry twists in my gut. If it's true that there's a high bounty on me, how could Para resist turning me in? Especially if she's telling the truth about her people going hungry.

A particularly sharp roar sends ice cascading down my spine, and Kyrin whinnies.

"In." Leander motions for Gareth to ride forward.

Gareth can't see the door, but he doesn't question Leander. He and Beth disappear as Leander grabs Kyrin's reins and we all walk into the red stone world of the Vundi.

The wind howls as the storm hits, bits of red dirt filtering down through the layers of rock and silting the floor as we walk deeper into the heart of Arin.

"I thought they were rumors." Gareth reaches out and touches the rough-hewn rock. "But it's true. The Vundi have a city of stone."

"Your horses can stay here. Deep enough to be safe, but close enough to the surface for them to feel somewhat at ease. Cenet." Para motions to her companion, who takes Sabre and Kyrin's reins and leads them into a hallway to our right.

Kyrin gives me a long look, but I nod to him. Hay thickens along the floor as he goes, and I can see the stables farther down. I make a mental note of where we part ways and endeavor to keep a map of where we tread.

"Come." Para leads us down the slope.

Taylor slips her hand into mine, and I force my purr to stay locked inside. The Ancestors must be testing me, putting her right within my grasp but withholding our mating. I keep my other hand on my sword. The deal has been sealed, and my mate is safe, but that doesn't stop me from being ever on the lookout. She must be protected.

"At least it's cooler in here." Beth sighs. "And no wind wights. Always a plus."

We continue down until the walls begin to smooth out, their red hue darkening and the lights burning bright and high above.

"Did the Vundi build all this?" Taylor stares at the rock that curves away from us as we enter a large chamber with two ornate doors at the end.

"Long ago, after the war that left these lands barren."

"But the Vundi are nomads. They don't build, only trade." Gareth shakes his head.

"You don't define who we are," her companion, Cenet, says gruffly.

Gareth glowers but falls silent as we reach the wide doors. I would gloat about how wrong he'd been, but it will have to wait until we are back in the winter realm. Here, I must be on my guard.

Para waves a hand, and the doors begin to open inward with a near-silent whir. What lies inside defies even my vast knowledge of Arin. It is a wonder, one that lies hidden beneath the inhospitable red wastes above.

"*I knew it was Moria!*" Taylor's excited whisper almost draws a smile from me, but the line of warriors on either side of the wide walkway temper it.

An immense cavern lies beyond, and a crystalline waterfall pours from a great height, the water refracting and creating rainbows in the spray before it lands in a basin far below. Large white crystals line the sides of the waterfall and cover the ground below where the water splashes and flows away.

"Water." Gareth lets his disbelief show. "But the plains have no water source, only the Misty River far to the east. This isn't possible. None of it is." His gaze lifts to the ceilings, its surface glittering with veins of gold and white. Opposite the waterfall, an enormous silver statue of a nude fae rises, her gaze fixed on the entryway and her mouth in a mischievous smile.

"Who's that?" Taylor appears transfixed.

"Delantis. The Vundi matriarch." Para motions one of the guards to her, and they engage in a quick back and forth before the guard takes off across the long bridge between the statue and the waterfall.

I keep my eyes on the line of soldiers ahead of us, their curved blades honed. Some of them are bloodied, likely the same fighters we encountered on the road, and they eye us with suspicion.

Para removes her scarf and head covering, revealing a cascade of white hair. Cenet watches her closely. Are they mated?

"So, when's supper?" Beth rocks back and forth on her heels and rubs her arms. "And where's the fire? I think this is the coldest air I've ever felt."

Gareth snorts. "This is cold to you?"

Beth rolls her eyes at him. "Is this the part where you brag about how cold the winter realm is? Because I'd rather skip it and go straight to the Vundi food part."

Para gives her a sideways glare, then turns and heads across the bridge. "This way."

We follow, though I'm on edge, aware of every sound

and movement even though the waterfall muffles much of what goes on deeper in the cavern.

"What's that stone?" Taylor points at the statue's necklace.

"Soulstone." Para doesn't even look at the egg-shaped stone that graces the statue's ample chest.

Taylor's hand strays to her throat. "Does it come from—"

"Para!" A fae emerges from the arched doorway at the end of the bridge.

"Vanara." For the first time, Para picks up her pace. This must be her commander. The fae is tall and wiry, and her age is beginning to show in the wrinkles along her upper lip, as if she spends her spare time in a scowl.

"What have you done, Para?" The woman, her face severe, eyes all of us. "Your mission was quite clear."

"I know, but there were—" She clears her throat. "Unforeseen complications."

"You come back with dead and wounded warriors and call it 'complications'?" Vanara swipes past her and stops in front of us. "The changeling, is she here?"

"Yes, we brought her." Para, cowed, stands just behind her leader.

Vanara looks down her nose at first Beth, then Taylor. "The changeling must not be harmed. That's part of the deal with the king beyond the mountain. I must inspect her straightaway."

Taylor straightens. "Standing right here. I can hear you, you know?"

"Then hear this." Her silver eyes narrow. "Delivering you to the king beyond the mountain is what must be done—what *will* be done—no matter what you say to the council."

Her threats must be answered. I begin to draw my sword, but Gareth reaches over and stays my hand.

"Vanara, is it?" His tone is laced with contempt. "You aren't going to *inspect* anything, and if you don't back off, I can guarantee that Leander will take your head. Taylor is his mate. And I don't know what sort of ramshackle hole in the ground you're running here, but no one has afforded my king the respect befitting his station."

My grip tightens on my blade, and I step forward. "Perhaps the Vundi prefer battle and blood to tradition and hospitality. In that case, I am happy to oblige them."

Gareth doesn't release my wrist. "Even the high fae of Byrn Varyndr treated us better than we've fared at your hands."

Nothing fazed Vanara. Not a word. Until Gareth's final gripe. Once hostilities on the plains were ended and the pact was sealed with magic, we should have been afforded some semblance of a welcome. Instead, they offer threats.

"The pretenders at Byrn Varyndr cannot rival the warmth of a Vundi hearth." Vanara backs off and even dips her head a little. "My apologies, King Gladion."

"Never speak to my mate again. Don't even *look* at her." I sheathe my blade.

Para clears her throat. "Your rooms should be ready. Please follow me." Even her tone has softened. "This way."

I keep Taylor at my back, hemmed in between Gareth and me, as we leave the waterfall chamber and enter an even larger one. A city slumbers here under the dark stone ceiling that soars away high above us. Thousands of homes are carved into the walls and along the floors as far as I can see. Several of them seem abandoned, but the ones nearest the ground level are occupied, light and voices humming along the rock. More buildings line the cave floor, some of them large enough to hold hundreds of fae—gathering places and possibly businesses. Stone bridges criss-cross the cavern and foot paths wind up each side. An entire civilization lies hidden beneath the red wastes.

"How many people live here?" Taylor stops and stares down from our bridge high above the stone buildings below. A handful of children, lesser and high fae, play amongst the ruin of a dwelling beneath us, their laughter high and ringing as they chase each other. But their clothes are shoddy, their bodies thin, and one of them has a cough that would concern any parent.

"We used to boast great numbers. After the conflict that ruined these lands, we rebuilt and thrived underground." Para follows her gaze to the children. "But when the war with winter ended, not enough of us came home. What little farming we were able to do along the banks of the Misty River was pillaged by the high fae at Byrn Varyndr. Now, we have very little. We're able to trade with the gems we mine, but we can't support ourselves without turning to ..." She chews her lip. "Other avenues."

"You mean brigandry." Gareth crosses his arms over his chest. "Vundi bandits."

"We must survive however we can," Para snaps and turns on her heel.

"Has anyone ever told you you really have a way with females?" Beth cuts in front of Gareth and keeps pace with Para.

We turn sharply to the right and enter another, smaller room, this one lined with fine, if worn, tapestries.

"These are your rooms." Para leads us down a corridor and into a round room with a fire pit in the center, the smoke escaping through a chimney hewn into the rock above. Divans, pillows, and a dining table fill the space, and doorways lead deeper into the stone maze. "There are two bathing rooms and two bedrooms. Will this be sufficient?"

I have no doubt these are the finest apartments the Vundi possess, but my approval is contingent on my queen's. "Taylor, are these to your liking?"

"It's lovely. Thank you, Para." Taylor feels the nearest pillow, its silky crimson fabric highlighting her small, fair hand.

Gareth strides down the first hallway, doing a sweep.

"I'll have food brought in and return when the council is ready to speak with you. Until then, please make yourselves comfortable. Cenet will stand watch outside your chambers should you need anything."

Beth plops down on a deep emerald divan. "I'd say this arrangement is better than being eaten alive by wind wights, right?"

"We went from enemies to honored guests." Taylor shakes her head. "I don't understand this place."

"We're still enemies." I follow Gareth, checking every shadow and hallway. "Be on your guard."

"Hospitality is a big deal among fae." Beth takes on a conciliatory tone with Taylor. "When Gareth said that stuff about the snobby high fae treating them better, that's pretty much as if he smacked the Vundi across the face with his glove."

"Oh." Taylor hovers around the entry to the hallway where I am, as if keeping me in her view. My chest expands a bit, but I keep up my search. I must know these chambers are safe before I can let her wander.

"That tradition is why they went all welcome wagon on us?"

"Welcome wagon?" Beth asks. "You and your weird human sayings. But, yes. Now they have to play nice or have their honor besmirched forever." She adds an echo effect on the last word.

"Forever?" Taylor laughs lightly. "Seems sort of harsh."

"Turn away or mistreat a guest—that stuff sticks with fae. You'll see. And they live a long time and have memories that only fade a little. They can pretty much recall anything. When they sleep, they can access memories."

"I had no idea. That explains how Leander's English improved so quickly overnight."

"Yes." Beth prattles on as I finish my sweep.

Once satisfied that the rooms are safe, I return to the common area with a tantalizing bit of information for my mate.

"Taylor." I can't keep the purr off the 'r' of her name. Not when I'm about to give her this gift.

Her breath quickens as she turns toward me. "Safe?"

"Safe." I pull her into my arms and lean down until my lips are grazing her rounded ear.

She clutches my biceps in surprise, and then that sweet scent of hers perfumes the air and pulls my feral side to the fore. "What—"

"There's a bath. Hot water. Fine soaps."

Her tiny nails dig into my arms. "Are you shitting me right now? Because if you are, I might kill you."

"No, I'm not ... shitting ... you. But—"

"But?" She pulls back and peers into my eyes.

I smile, knowing full well my fangs have lengthened. "It's too dangerous for you to bathe alone."

She swallows hard, her pupils growing as she stares up at me. "Beth can—"

"No way." Beth leans back on the divan and closes her eyes. "I'm waiting right here until there's food."

"She can't protect you." I pull her down the hall and usher her into the bathing room. "I can."

She walks to the ivory tub and runs her fingers through the water I've already poured from the fire-heated bucket above. "Oh my god." Her tone is decadent, and I want to indulge her so much that it's frequently on her tongue. "You can guard the door, and—"

"No, little one." I reach behind me and pull my tunic over my head and drop it to the cool stone floor. "Not this time. I won't risk you."

She gawks. "What are you doing?"

I can't help but grin when her eyes widen as she stares at my chest and abs.

"Leander!"

I stalk to her and I admit, blow a hint of cold around her. Running my fingers along the water, I say, "So warm. It'll go cold soon enough, and it'll take hours for more water to heat."

"You're a bad man." She eyes the water.

"Fae, little one. I'm a bad fae." I kiss her crown.

"You really won't leave?"

"Last time I left you alone in a bathing room ..." I stop. I don't want her to re-live Tyrios's attack.

When she shivers, I pull her into my arms. "I'm sorry. I shouldn't have said that."

"It's okay. I mean, you're right."

"I am?"

"Yes." She lets out a long breath and says the words I need to hear. "You can stay."

I take a deep breath. Having Leander in the room with me won't be so bad. He can face the wall or something while I bathe. Besides, he's already seen me naked. Not a big deal. Fabric hits the stone floor, and I turn to find Leander climbing into the tub.

He settles down, then runs his fingers along the surface. "Come, little one, before the water goes cold."

I slap one hand to my face. "I said you could stay. I didn't say you could take a bath with me!"

"Don't be ridiculous. Of course I'm bathing with you." He leans back and spreads his knees against the sides of the tub. "Why waste the hot water? Besides, I can get you perfectly clean."

"I can get myself perfectly clean." I cross my arms.

"Taylor."

I kick up my chin.

"Little one, please."

"No."

"I already told you this body is yours." He sounds almost hurt. "Do you think I'd use it to harm you?"

"Well, no."

He stills. "Do you find me ... unpleasant?"

"No!" I sigh. "Not at all."

"Then why can't we bathe together?"

"Because that's private time. Private stuff." I wave my hand in front of me in a way I then realize looks ridiculous. "I've never been naked with a man, and I don't think—"

"That pleases me more than I can say." He stands and steps from the tub, his arms out toward me.

I look. *I. Look.* And it is large. Are they all this large? And hard. Oh my god. Desire snakes through me like a poison, and I can't look away.

He takes me in his arms. "I assumed you were coveted on earth. Men likely fell all over themselves for you." His grip tenses, a growl in his throat. "But none of them were worthy of one such as you. You are a queen, no matter where you are."

He clearly hasn't realized it, but I'm no great beauty. Next to the golden Cecile, I was practically invisible. I rest my forehead against his damp chest. "Why do you say such nice things?"

"I say only the truth. And if you wish to bathe alone, I will respect your choice." That last part comes through gritted teeth. "But I can't leave you alone. I fear too much. Fear never lived inside me as it does now."

"You were never afraid?" I can't begin to fathom living a life without fear—fear of others, fear of failure, fear of the unknown. My list goes on and on.

"For my people, my soldiers, and my friends, yes. But for me? No. Now that I have you. Now that you are my heart, I am afraid all the time."

"You don't have to be afraid for me."

"I can't stop. Because if I were ever to lose you ..." He buries his face in my hair. "I couldn't survive it."

Did I say I wanted to go home? To return to my college dorm room with the Hot Pockets and the bitch roommate? Because right now, I don't want any of that. I want the fae standing in front of me. The one who's baring everything, inside and out.

I step back, though the haunted look in his eyes almost breaks me. "Get in the tub."

His face brightens, his eyebrows rising. "Do you mean—"

"Get in before I change my mind. And no funny business!"

He smiles, and my sweet stars, I can't seem to feel my toes. Does he have a clue how gorgeous he is?

With preternatural quickness, he settles in the tub, his thick arms lying along the sides.

I fiddle with the hem of my shirt. "Don't look, okay?"

The smile dims a bit, but he turns his head as requested. I strip down quickly and climb into the tub. The water is amazing, so warm that it almost burns. I moan as I sink down, and he pulls me so my back rests against his chest. But there's something else lurking beneath the water.

"Um, your uh, you've got a ... It's kind of pressing against my ... Never mind." I turn crimson and not just from the heat.

"My apologies, little one." He doesn't sound the least bit apologetic. "I can control many things, but that is beyond even my magical abilities."

A thought rebels against me, careening around my mind and whispering, "*Imagine how good that would feel inside you.*" I bite my lip and reach for one of the blue soaps next to the tub.

"I said I would clean you, my mate." He grabs it with his big paws and begins to lather it up between them. "Relax. Ease your mind. I agreed there would be no amusing business, and I meant it."

"Funny business."

"Yes, like I said." He scoops water into my hair with one hand.

I sigh and close my eyes. When he begins to massage the soap into my strands, I let myself go, resting against him as he meticulously rubs my scalp, washing away the worries of the road and our most recent life-or-death skirmish.

"I keep thinking about when I first saw you." His voice rumbles through the water.

"When I was terrified?"

"You were, yes. But magnificent all the same."

"That's a new one. I don't think anyone has ever called me 'magnificent.'"

"Why did you surround yourself with fools on earth?"

I laugh. "I think you are overestimating me just a bit."

Strong hands grab me and turn me around until Leander and I are face to face. His is stern, but there is a softness to his eyes. I've never seen him bestow that look on anyone else but me.

"You are far more remarkable than you give yourself credit for. Beautiful, strong, intelligent, an alchemist, no less. You are a queen. I knew it from the moment I saw you. I *felt* it."

My voice sticks in my throat, and all I can manage is a soft "oh."

"Why do you feel less than you are?"

I shrug, feeling exposed in every way possible. "I guess I just... I'm not special."

"Who told you that?"

"I don't know." I do know. "People, you know?"

"Who?" The warmth in his dark eyes turns steely. "Who said such things to you?"

My mother. Steve. I try to banish the thought of him.

"What was that?"

"What?"

"I could feel your fear." He tilts my chin up so I have to meet his direct gaze. "Why are you scared?"

"I don't want to talk about this." I try to turn around, but he doesn't let me go.

"Did someone hurt you?" His face turns stony. "Tell me who hurt you. I will find them, and I will make them pay."

I reach up and run my thumb down his cheek. "You really would do that, wouldn't you? For me?"

"I would do anything for you." He says it with such clarity, as if it's as simple as 'water is wet'.

"Someone did hurt me—"

"I will—" I press a finger to his lips.

"But he's dead. And I don't want to talk about him while I'm naked in the tub with you, okay?"

He opens his mouth to retort, but then snaps it shut. "I will respect your wishes, but one day soon you must tell me what happened to you. Why you went hungry, who hurt you—I want to know everything."

I know what promises mean here, how unbreakable they are, but I make one all the same. "I swear I'll tell you everything one day."

"I'll hold you to that, little one." He gently turns me back around and rinses my hair, his touches immeasurably kind. Working up another lather, he runs his wide palms along my neck and then lower down my back. He kneads as he goes, and what little tension still resides inside me spills out into the clear, warm water.

"That feels so good."

His low purr is instant.

"You're like a cat. Why do you purr?"

"Not a cat." He runs his thumbs in circles along my lower back. "It's a high fae trait. A reminder of a time when we were more animal than anything else. Mostly, it's a signal between mates."

"A signal for what?" I realize the answer right as the question disappears into the air.

His low, sensual laugh surrounds me. "I think you know."

"Yes." I decide that maybe talking is a bad idea, especially when I'm tired and saying foolish things. Not because his touch is making me have filthy thoughts. Not because his purr is vibrating in all the right places. Not because, despite the impossibility of the situation, I want him.

He lathers up the soap once more and holds his hands in front of me. "May I? Not funny business, little one. Just getting you clean."

Not funny business? He's asking for what, second base? If that's not funny business, then I don't know what is. But would it be so bad to feel his touch all over me? He's already worked wonders on my back.

I bite my lip and relax my shoulders. "Go ahead."

"Are you certain?"

I know what he's asking. "Yes."

The purr increases as he soaps my shoulders, down to my collar bones, past my necklace, and then lower to the swells of my breasts. He goes agonizingly slow, sweeping his fingers back and forth across the tops of my breasts, the soap bubbles fanning out on top of the water. I can't seem to focus on anything but his touch, the way the pads of his fingers are callused, the way he makes my breaths hitch and my core tighten with each pass. Can anticipation kill a person?

When his fingers finally brush my hard nipples, I moan. And when he cups my breasts in his palms and rubs the stiff peaks with his thumbs? I combust.

I dig my nails into his thighs and turn my head. "Leander." I put everything I'm feeling into that one word, and he answers it like a prayer.

His mouth crashes into mine, taking, demanding. I part my lips, relishing the sweep of his tongue against mine as he keeps one hand at my breast while the other skirts down my stomach. I can't think, can only feel, my desire like a flame burning too bright.

When his fingers delve lower, I allow him to spread my thighs apart.

"How you please me, little one," he growls against my lips, then claims me in another fierce kiss.

I jolt when his fingertip presses against my most sensitive spot. With another little stroke, he has me melting for him. He twists my nipple as his fingers play beneath the water, and I let my legs fall open all the way, giving him access to the parts of me no one has ever touched before.

Our kiss deepens, his tongue caressing mine as my body tightens, my mind spins around the central contact of his hands on me. I've never done this with another person, and his fingers on me are so much *more* than anything I've done by myself. My entire consciousness folds in on itself, everything focused on the rising tide inside me, the heat that unfurls and turns every part of me molten.

My release comes from everywhere and nowhere all at once. My thighs shake, and I moan as I fall beneath waves of pleasure, my entire being swallowed up by the perfect bliss Leander has drawn from me so easily. Stars burst in my vision as I grip his arms and moan into his mouth.

More funny business, please.

When the last tremor leaves, I'm completely bone-less, floating in Leander's grip.

I don't protest when he turns me in the water and

pulls me to him. His fangs are long, his eyes dark, and his desire hard.

"I must claim you." His voice is lower, and I realize I'm speaking to the feral side of him. He pulls my hair, arching my back, then runs his fang along my throat. "I will pierce you, mark you so hard that no male will ever doubt whom you belong to."

I can't catch my breath, can't think when he touches me like this. But I know I'm not ready.

"Leander, I can't—"

"Just let me fill you, little one. I can give you everything you've ever wanted." His voice weaves around me like a spell. "My cock was made for you. I will give it to you again and again. As many times as you want. I want to taste your pleasure on my tongue, devour you like the treat you are."

"Oh god." I dig my nails into his shoulders.

"Taylor, my perfect queen." He runs his hands down my chest and cups both breasts. "I will worship you until the Ancestors call me home."

I tremble when he feathers kisses along my neck, each touch growing more passionate. I want to give in. To say yes. To give him every part of me. But what will that mean? Being truly mated, will it change things? My mind says yes, even though my body wants to continue down this path, running into Leander's arms and letting him give me the pleasure he promises with each kiss.

"I can't." I force the words past my lips.

He retakes his grip on my hair and bites my throat gently, not enough to break the skin. "I can give you so much."

"Leander, please."

"If I don't claim you, other males will try to take you from me. Don't you understand?" His growl is full of longing, wild just like the feral fae inside him.

"No one will take me."

"I will kill any male who tries." Another growl rips from him. "I must have you, must mark you." His grip tightens. "It's the only way to keep you safe."

My scalp begins to prickle from his rough hold. "Leander, my hair."

Like lightning, he releases me and jumps from the bath, water sluicing down his body as I grab the sides of the tub to stay upright.

"What—"

"I can't." He clutches his chest, his fangs still long, his eyes wild. "I can't be in here with you. The feral is too strong. I never want to hurt you. I'm so sorry, little one."

"I'm okay." I reach out my hand. "A little hair pulling can be fun, right?"

He doesn't laugh, his chest heaving with his labored breaths as his magnificent body glistens with water droplets. "I'm sorry." His tone is anguished as he turns and stalks from the bathing room, leaving me panting in the rapidly cooling water.

"She deserves better." I cradle my head in my hands.

"You didn't hurt her, Leander." Gareth sits next to the dining table, his feet up on a tufted ottoman as he faces the stone entry.

"I shouldn't have scared her like that. She said no funny business and then I—"

"Funny business?" He scratches his chin.

"You know, mating play." I scrub a hand down my face. "But her body, the scent of her, the way she felt in my hands."

"She's fine, my friend. She and Beth are sleeping peacefully." He glowers. "After they had a giggling fit or two. I think you can guess what they were talking about."

I nod. I can hear her breathing. She's sleeping nearest the door, lying on her right side, her hands folded beneath her cheek. I can smell the soap on her, can almost taste her.

"You kept the feral in check. That's all that matters."

He grabs a tomato and takes a bite. The provisions the Vundi served would be considered meager in the winter realm, but here I suspect they are worth a small fortune.

Gareth finishes the stunted tomato. "Though we may need a new plan once we reach the border."

"What do you mean?" I should eat, but I can't. Not until I apologize more thoroughly to my mate.

"I've been thinking about it, and if you haven't claimed her by the time we enter the winter realm, there may be trouble."

"Speak plain, Gareth." I lean back in the rough-hewn chair and rest my head against the stone wall.

"Your power will be back to normal levels. The magic will have more sway over you, and so will the feral. You could lose control. The feral might ..." He trails off, but I can hear the unspoken words. He worries the feral could force the mating.

"I wouldn't do that."

"I know you wouldn't, but there's no reasoning with the feral."

Just the thought of hurting her like that twists my insides. "It won't come to that."

"You don't know that for sure, not when—"

A short knock at the door has both of us on our feet, hands on our weapons.

Gareth strides to the faded wood. "Yes?"

"May I come in?" Para's voice carries.

Gareth opens the door and stands back so she can enter. Her white hair is neatly plaited on top of her head, and she wears a more formal dress, though still in the Vundi crimson.

"I've spoken to the elders and the high priestess."

"And?" I glare down at her, even though she isn't the true object of my ire. I am. I pushed Taylor too far.

"And the council will meet with you in the morning."

"Why not now?" I need to get Taylor out of this rock prison and to the safety of winter.

"The council will have to deliberate amongst themselves for a while before hearing from you."

Gareth blows out a hard sigh. "Fine. We could use some rest."

"And there's another item."

"What's going on?" Taylor stretches, her white bedclothes loose on her frame. She doesn't seem angry with me. But that's fine. I'm angry enough with myself for both of us.

"Para was just leaving." I stride to Taylor, keeping myself between her and the Vundi.

"The other item?" Gareth broaches.

Para eyes me, as if she's waiting for me to blow up. Her instincts are dead on.

"The high priestess would like to meet with your changeling—"

"Taylor. Her name is Taylor," I correct her.

"Again." Taylor rubs her eyes. "Standing right here."

"Taylor. Yes. Our high priestess would like to speak with you alone."

"No." I've had enough of creatures with questionable motives speaking with my mate alone.

"You are under Vundi protection. Nothing will happen to your mate." Para's brows draw down, two dusky thunderclouds on her tan face. "Or do you question my oath?"

"We don't question it." Gareth is quick to intercede. "But we are, naturally, protective of Taylor, especially given the circumstances."

"I gave my word—"

"No. The answer is no." I turn my back on Para.

"In that case, I may as well speak to her in front of you." A wizened fae appears in the doorway, her silver eyes dimmed with filmy white, and her back bent. I've never seen a fae this old, not when peace awaits with the Ancestors. Power seems to emanate from her, her skin covered with a gossamer glow and the tips of her fingers nigh on translucent with light.

"Delantis." Para bows low.

"Aren't you an ornery king?" Delantis grins up at me.

"Delantis? You're the one from the statue." Taylor steps forward.

"Wasn't I something?" Delantis takes the nearest cushioned chair and motions Taylor over. "Hips for days and a cushy rear that made many a male beg for my attentions." The sparkle in her eye verges on lascivious. "And you're the changeling I've heard so much about. The one the king beyond the mountain covets." She wrinkles her nose as she mentions his name. Good.

I keep to Taylor's side as she sits across from the ancient fae.

Lifting her gaze to me, she says, "My, my, you're half feral right now, aren't you winter king?"

I bare my fangs. "Twice as dangerous to anyone who threatens my mate."

"Leander." Taylor shakes her head at me, the scolding in her tone just as adorable as her disapproval. "She's an elderly woman. Don't scare her."

"Don't be fooled, little one." I keep my gaze on the white fae. "She's far more than she seems."

Delantis laughs. "No threats from me, my lord. Though I must warn you, I've followed the magic to the otherworld, learned its secrets and danced to the forbidden music of the moon and its guardians. The son of a rebel noble and a swordsmith does not frighten me, no matter how kingly he might be."

Despite my misgivings, I rather like this Delantis.

"Now." She turns back to Taylor. "I've come to talk about the stone."

"Stone?"

Delantis waves a hand across her throat and reveals an egg-shaped stone with veins of silver and pearl, a large opal.

"What about your stone?" I peer at it.

"Not mine." She points at Taylor. "Yours. Where did you get it?"

Taylor's hand goes to her throat the same way it's done so many times over the past weeks. Whenever she's uneasy, she strokes her neck. I've assumed it was just a cute tick. Because there's nothing there. Only her bare throat.

She looks down at her hand as if she's holding something. "I've had this necklace for as long as I can remember."

"Wait." I stare at Taylor's neck, the skin alabaster and bare. "You've had what necklace?"

Taylor turns to me. "What do you mean?"

"There's no necklace."

"Yes there is. Right here. I've had it on this whole time." She pulls at air between her collarbones.

Gareth's brow furrows. "Nothing there, my queen."

As Gareth and I search Taylor's bare throat, Delantis laughs, her mirth loud and full. "You fools have no clue what's going on, do you?"

Perhaps I don't like her so much after all.

"You really can't see this?" I hold out my pendant, the stone warm in my hand.

Leander kneels down and looks hard—almost comically so—at the stone. "No. I've never seen a necklace on you."

"But you've looked at it when I touch it."

"No, I've looked at you touching your throat. I've never—"

"What'd I miss?" Beth strolls into the main room, her eyes sleepy.

"Do you see this?" Taylor holds the supposed amulet toward her.

"See what?"

"This necklace."

"What necklace?" Beth walks over and frowns. "You got jewelry from king feral over here?" She pushes my shoulder. "You are really trying to get that mating on, aren't you? I respect that."

"Changeling." Gareth rubs his temples in frustration.

"What?" Beth sits on the arm of Taylor's chair.

"What is the gem? Is it dangerous?" Leander eyes my fingers as if they might be holding an adder.

Delantis sits back and runs her finger along the large gem at her own throat. "It's a shard of soulstone, and it can be dangerous if wielded by the wrong hands."

"Take it off." Leander wraps his arm around my shoulders. "Please, Taylor."

I reach behind my neck to undo the clasp, pressing the mechanism beneath my fingernail, then bring my hands back around to the front.

The necklace is still on.

"Taylor?"

"I didn't get it off somehow." I try it one more time, but once again, come up emptyhanded.

Delantis nods. "You've never taken it off."

"I ..." I pin my lips between my teeth and think back, but my memories of the necklace are almost fuzzed over in my mind. "No. I mean, I can't remember a time when I've taken it off, no. It's weird, I guess, that I never have. But I don't think about it. It's sort of out of sight, out of mind." A creepy crawly sensation skips up my throat, and I try one more time to remove the necklace. It doesn't come off. "What do I do?" I attempt to push the rising freak-out back down, but it doesn't stay away. I pull at the stone, trying to break the chain.

"Calm, Taylor." Delantis reaches out and takes the stone in her hand and closes her eyes. "The one who bestowed it on you had powerful magic, so strong that the stone keeps itself hidden. A disguise within a disguise." The wrinkled skin on her forehead scrunches up as she seems to concentrate on it, the stone glowing in her palm, light shooting out between her fingers. "But someone else will remove it." She winces. "Someone from the dark."

My ears begin to burn, and my back itches, and my lungs feel too small.

"I can't—" I grip the sides of the chair as the light intensifies. "I can't breathe."

Beth gasps and scrambles away from me.

"What's wrong?" Tears stream down my cheeks, and I can feel everything, the texture of the chair's fabric, the humidity in the air, the heat of Leander pressing against my side. "Leander."

"Release her," he demands.

"Wait." Delantis, concentrates harder, the glow from the stone spreading through her until her hair verges on neon white.

"Please." Spots dance in my vision, and my lungs burn. "Lean—" I fall.

And I keep falling. Through stars and oceans and trees and veins and neurons and swirls of ember and night. When I land, it's on a tuft of the greenest grass beneath a perfect azure sky. I reach for my necklace, but it's gone.

Sitting up, I feel a cool breeze rushing down my skin and rustling the grass at my toes. My ears hurt, and my back is itching so badly I contemplate lying down in the grass and wriggling.

"Leander?" My voice seems to carry impossibly far and echoes back to me despite the wide open emerald field.

"Here you are." A wisp of blue shoots up from the grass in front of me and coalesces into a female form.

"Where am I?"

"You know you're giving off sparks? Dark bursts of starlight." She leans down. "It's beautiful, but dangerous."

"The witch said she dimmed it."

"Nothing's dim here." The blue smoke twirls around and returns, this time taking Leander's form. "Everything is possible here. Stay." He offers me his hand, the streaks of blue eddying inside his long fingers.

"But where is here?"

"The place where all magic-wielders must come if they want to become powerful." The voice changes into Leander's. "And you, little one, could be the most powerful of all."

"I'm just a human. No magic. No—"

"Wrong." It tsks.

"No, it's true. I can't do any magic. I'm a college student. I—"

"Lies don't become you." The creature morphs again, this time into my mother. "Stop fibbing about Steve, Taylor. He's a good man. He'd never hit you. And I don't see a mark on you. Go to your room!"

"Stop." I shrink back, my skin going cold and clammy. I'm not supposed to be here. Where's Leander?

It swirls again and takes on Beth's shape. "Don't worry. Just take my hand. I'll show you all you need to know."

"You've got the wrong person."

It sighs hard and long, then changes into a tall fae with a stern brow, one I recognize.

"Remember me? From the stables?" It pulls down the top of its tunic and shows me black streaks spreading from where I struck the stable fae with my blade.

"I don't—"

"Magic." It snaps its fingers. "This is magic. The darkest kind of all."

"It came from the knife! It was Leander's. He gave it to me. There must have been some sort of poison on the blade. I don't know." I wrap my arms around my knees.

"No simple poison can inflict instant death." The black spreads farther, dark lightning streaking along its chin and into its cheeks. "But you can."

"No." I scurry back across the grass, but the blue smoke keeps up with me, hovering along, its hand out yet again. "Come with me. We shall dance with the darkest denizens of night. I am not afraid of you. Not like the rest of them will be."

"Afraid of me?"

"Yes." It oozes closer. "When they find out what you are."

"Wh-what am I?"

"I will tell you all, show you all, *give* you all. Just take my—"

Someone calls my name, the sound growing louder until I see an orb of bright white light. "Taylor, come now before the magic drags you down." It's Delantis's voice. But can I trust it?

"Stay here, little one." The blue is Leander again. "I can protect you."

"Don't listen to it! Come, girl. Run!"

I jump to my feet and, with one more look at the blue smoke, I dash toward the white orb. When I hit it, my body goes numb and my mind silent, but I can hear the shriek of the blue smoke, its anger vibrating in notes of frustration.

I wake encased in granite. No, not granite. Leander's arms. He rocks me slowly, a song lilting off his tongue. The words must be in old fae, because I don't understand them. His voice is deep, the low notes soothing. I hold my breath, not wanting him to stop.

But he does, the sound fading away. "You're awake."

"Hi." I look up at him.

"Thanks to the Ancestors." He crushes me to his chest.

"Can't breathe," I grit out.

He pulls me away and peers at me. "Are you hurt?"

"I'm fine." My ears aren't bothering me anymore, and my back isn't itchy. Winning on all fronts, really. "What happened?"

"Your stone." He looks at it.

"You can see it now?"

"Delantis broke the visual enchantment, but we still can't remove it." He reaches for it but can't touch it. It repels him the same way it repelled the obsidian witch.

"Hey, that reminds me. Selene could see the necklace, but she couldn't touch it."

He frowns. "She is a powerful creature of the dark. I

have no doubt her powers could overcome most enchantments. But if even *she* couldn't lay a finger on it." He shakes his head and presses his palm to my cheek. "Do you have any idea how worried I was when the magic took you?"

"Magic took me?"

"To the otherworld. Delantis didn't realize undoing the stone's spell would create a magical connection straight to the otherworld."

I press my palm to my forehead, my memory surfacing like a sea monster. "I remember. There was this blue smoke creature that could become anyone, and it wanted me to go with it."

"Never follow the magic," he says starkly. "Never. If the magic seduces you, you could become lost in the otherworld forever."

"I don't even know what it is. Or where it was. Or what I was doing there." My heart races as I remember it changing from one person to the next, always with its hand out to me. "Why do I have this stone?"

"Delantis doesn't know. Or, at least she's not telling. Removing the enchantment drained her, and she had to be carried out of our rooms."

Jeez, I almost broke the oldest fae ever made. "I hope she's all right."

"She should have known better." His voice is rough, fatigue written on his face. "She put you in danger."

I glance around, but it's impossible to tell night from day this far below ground. The ceiling glows the same as it did when we first walked in. "How long have I been asleep?"

"All night."

"What?" I thought he'd say fifteen minutes. "All *night*?" I brush his dark hair off his forehead. "Were you awake the whole time?"

"I couldn't sleep. Not when you were ..." He shakes his head, as if tossing away whatever he was going to say.

He held me all night. I stroke his cheek and lean up, placing a soft kiss on his lips. "You are too much."

"Is that a bad thing?" A cocky smirk turns the corner of his lips before he returns my kiss, not softly. Not gentle or tentative. He takes me.

I wrap my arms around him as he grips the back of my neck, holding me just how he wants as he lays me on the bed, his hard body pressing against mine.

He nips at my bottom lip. "I would've followed you to the otherworld. I will always come for you, no matter what happens."

"I know." And I really do. Leander has proven again and again that he will never give me up. A fissure opens in my heart when I think about returning home.

"What is it?" He kisses down my jaw line. "I can read you, mate. And soon, you will find you can read me like one of your alchemy textbooks you were telling me about."

"It's just that I have an entire life back on earth." I try to focus on my words even as his lips trail to my throat.

"And?"

"And I can't just—"

"You can." He sucks on the spot between my neck and shoulder. "You can stay here and be my queen, rule the winter lands and have a strong—" He nips at my flesh as punctuation. "Dedicated—" Another nip. "Loyal fae king at your disposal."

"I can't think when you do that."

"Good. Don't." He moves on top of me, one knee between my thighs as he returns to my mouth, his kiss a heady distraction that I'm beginning to crave.

I stumble onward, pulling from memory. "There's more. The magic said I have death in me. Or something like that? It wasn't really clear. There was that stable fae who I cut with the knife and there was this black stuff that I thought was poison on the blade and—Oh!" I moan as he pulls my sleep shirt down and licks the top swell of my breast. "And." My voice is breathy, and I have the distinct need to rock my hips against him. "And the stone. Why couldn't you see it? Why do I have a fae stone? I shouldn't have—"

"After what happened with Delantis, I suspect you're something more than a changeling. The witch said as much in the forest. The stone could be the key to discovering what."

My mind refuses to believe it. "I have human parents. I've lived a normal human life. Only a human. Not magical, not—"

He stops my mouth with his, then says against my lips, "We'll discover what it all means. Together. In the winter realm surrounded by my Phalanx where you'll be safe. And I don't care if you turn out to be a three-headed fire viper from the Burning Woods of Galendoon, I will never stop loving you."

"Love?" My eyes water instantly. He's called me his

mate, told me I'm meant for him—but he's never dropped the 'L' bomb on me.

"You're surprised that I love you, Taylor?" He twists a lock of my hair around his finger, his dark eyes devouring me. "I admit that sometimes fated mates aren't in love at first, but I thought it was clear how I feel about you." He kisses me again, hard and strong until I'm senseless.

"But you love me?" I struggle to clear the lust haze. I can't lose the plot. Not now.

"More than my own immortal life." He smiles, the harsh planes of his face turning almost boyish. "Didn't you know?"

"I ... Well I just sort of thought, you know, that maybe you ... I don't know?" I end weakly.

He laughs and buries his head in the crook of my neck, his fangs brushing my skin. "Will you ever stop being adorable?"

"I certainly hope not." I run my fingers through his hair, my nails against his scalp.

"Careful, little one." His voice is low, gravelly. "The feral is already demanding I take you. Any more encouragement, and I'll have you right here and now."

Maybe I want to be taken. Maybe it's time. That nightmare spent in the otherworld reminded me how soon I could be gone. This isn't my world, and I'm not guaranteed another day, not even another minute. I should live for now. I open my mouth to say as much, but a knock sounds at the door.

"Para is here," Gareth bites out.

Leander sighs. "What does she want?"

Gareth opens the door and quickly turns his back with a cough. "The council is ready for us."

Leander groans. "Fine. The quicker we get this done, the quicker we can cross the border." He crawls off me but makes sure to drag his fingers down my thigh before standing.

Goosebumps erupt all over me, and I clutch the sheet.

He pauses at the foot of the bed, the predatory look in his eyes still there. "I know I almost had you, little one."

I blush all the way to my toes. "No, you didn't."

His sexy smirk reappears. "I did."

I yank the crimson blanket over my head.

"Come, Taylor." He pulls the blanket down until our eyes meet. "It is time to show the Vundi the queen of winter, the bite of the icy wind, and the cold fury of the storm if they dare to defy us."

I stride into the Vundi council room, a grand hall with every inch of dark stone carved with whorls and ancient fae symbols. Seven fae sit along the back wall, their gazes fixed on Taylor at my side. She wears a dress of crimson, a black sash at her waist in Vundi fashion. No queen has ever been more beautiful.

Para and Cenet stand to the side, their expressions giving nothing away, and the high priestess sits at the very center of the room, her white glow a testament to her age. A fae this old doesn't exist in the winter realm. What would cause her to stay on Arin instead of fading to be with the Ancestors?

"Welcome, honored king. I am Keret, head council for the Vundi people." A lesser fae that appears to be mostly lizard-like stands and bows, the other councilors following suit.

"Thank you for your hospitality." I don't bow but give a slight dip of my chin.

The rude one from yesterday, Vanara, sits at the end of the row and is careful not to look at my mate. Good.

"Please, make yourselves comfortable." He gestures to the table where the high priestess sits.

I don't move. "I'm afraid I cannot be comfortable until you tell me that my mate is safe here. Para made clear that her forces attacked us on the road at the direction of this council. Your intention was to steal my mate—"

Vanara shakes her head. "We did not know that she was—"

"You will let me finish." I don't raise my voice. I don't have to. Vanara snaps her mouth closed. "As I was saying, you sent Para and her forces to take Taylor, the future queen of the winter realm. In the fairest light, this was a mistake. In the darkest, an act of war against my realm."

Keret shifts in his seat, his long tongue darting to his lips, but he doesn't interrupt. Perhaps he's noticed the temperature of the room has dropped so low that ice creeps along the carved walls of stone.

"I agreed to a short truce while we discuss these matters, but I must warn you that any further acts of aggression against my mate will have dire consequences."

"Our circumstances are already dire." Para steps forward, her voice strong. "We cannot continue like this. No food, no way out for our people. Our crops have failed again, the roots decaying and the fruits withering. We will not survive it. The children already suffer from maladies we've never seen before, and I can't bear to watch them go another day without food in their stomachs. This is our one chance."

My ire swells like a river during a thaw. The room grows even more frigid, and Taylor squeezes my hand.

"Your crops failed?" Taylor addresses Para. "The ones you mentioned that are near the river?"

"No." Para glances to the council, as if unsure she should continue. Keret waves her onward.

"We created a system of underground farms by bringing dirt from the river bed during dry spells when the water receded. Light comes in through funnels carved in the plains above, and we have plentiful water in the caverns—water that used to run through the plains before the great war."

"Can I see them? The farms, I mean?"

I turn to Taylor. Her eyes are bright, intelligence sparkling in their blue depths. I want to pull her close to keep her tucked under my arm, but she is strong enough to stand on her own. And as queen, she must.

"You want to see the crops?" Keret looks left and right at the other council members.

Taylor's cheeks pinken. "Yes. I mean, I'm not super into agriculture, but I've taken a few classes in organic chemistry, a botany elective, and worked in the university greenhouse over the summers. Maybe I can help."

Vanara grips the arms of her chair. "The way you can help is to allow us to turn you over to the king beyond the mountain."

"If you want to keep your life, you will never speak in my presence again." I maintain my hold on the heart of winter while the feral seeks to unleash its fury.

Vanara, eyes wide, turns to Keret, but she doesn't open her mouth. It's the only smart choice she's made.

With a disgusted huff, she rises and storms from the room.

Keret blinks slowly, his reptilian shoulders rising in a shrug.

Delantis chuckles. "I knew I wasn't the only one who's grown tired of her voice. Thank you, King Gladion." She rises, her posture bent and her eyes watery. "I'll show Taylor to the crops, if that's okay with you. We have some things to discuss." Without waiting for approval from the council, she hobbles to Taylor, who offers her arm.

"Thank you, child." The elderly fae takes Taylor's elbow, and they turn to leave.

I can't let her out of my sight. Can I?

"You have things to discuss here, my lord." Delantis pauses. "So I will make this easy for you. I give my oath to the Ancestors that I will not harm your mate or allow anyone else to harm her while she's with me." Her fingers glow bright white, the magic so strong within her that it has to escape. When she gives her word, magic ripples through the air between us, sealing the deal.

"Taylor?" I loathe letting go of her hand.

She steps up on her tiptoes and kisses my cheek. "I'll be fine. Maybe Delantis can give me some information on the stone, or what I am, or what's going on, or the two million other questions I have."

I kiss her forehead, my need to keep her near almost overcoming even Delantis's oath. But I have to let her go. She must be seen as capable of handling herself ... No matter how much I want to hide her away and keep her to myself.

"She's safe." Delantis pulls her gently. "I know well what it means to have a mate and feel the bond. But you must trust in her. And I can assure you, if anyone threatens her ..." She lets the magic seep from her fingertips until a gryphon forms next to them, its body of white smoke, but its talons of silver. Delantis's feral fae in corporeal form. How old *is* she? She pats the gryphon on its eagle head. "We will handle it." The gryphon blinks, and its lion's claws click on the stone floor.

"A gryphon?" Taylor's fingers twitch to pet it, but she keeps her hand at her side.

"Isn't she beautiful?" Delantis smiles.

"As soon as you're done, meet me back in our rooms." I let go of Taylor's hand, even though it feels wrong.

"I will." She gives me a confident look and leaves the room with Delantis on her arm. The gryphon follows, its tail whipping out the door.

I turn back to the Vundi council, the mix of high and lesser fae eyeing Gareth and me with an apprehension that borders on fear. While I admit I will destroy anyone who threatens my people, I'm not a despot. I see the plight of the Vundi. Though the heart of winter beats in my chest, I am not cold, not ice, not unmoving.

Striding to the table, I sit down, though my attempts to put the council at ease don't seem to have any effect. Half of them still look ready to bolt.

I lean back and graze the hilt of my sword with one hand. "Before we engage in any hostilities—which is exactly what will happen if you continue with your fool-hardy plan of kidnapping my mate—let's discuss possibilities for peace and cooperation between our peoples. Gareth, you have the floor."

He clears his throat. "As you know, the winter realm does not have the bounty of the farmlands to the west that supply a great deal of the summer realm. However, we are not without means to assist a neighbor in need, especially one that is ... let's say, *underappreciated* by Byrn Varyndr, as are the Vundi. Now ..."

As Gareth launches into our plan for diplomacy, I monitor my subconscious link to Taylor. For the councilors' sakes, I hope they don't intend to double-cross me. Because if I get so much as a hint of fear from Taylor, I will turn this room as red as the plains above.

"*T*hat mate of yours is a real bruiser, isn't he?" Delantis and I walk slowly down a stone passageway.

"He can be sort of aggressive, I guess you'd say." I glance at the gryphon. "But I guess most fae have some fight in them."

She laughs, the sound brittle like fall leaves. "You are correct about that, young one."

I want to rattle off so many questions, because if anyone here has answers, it's Delantis. Even Leander seemed taken aback by her age and power.

I clear my throat as we turn a corner. "Can you tell me more about the soulstone I wear?"

"It was mined right here under the Red Plains." She pauses and turns, eyeing the necklace with affection. "I remember when I birthed it from the same gift of stone that my own jewel was created from."

"Wow, so you recognize it. How long ago was that?"

She cuts her eyes to the side, the silver flashing in the dim hallway. "Is that a classy way of asking my age?"

"No." Yes.

"Let's just say it was quite an age ago." She smiles and pats my hand. "But I can't forget the stones. And yours has a peculiar history."

Answers. She is offering answers, and I'm surprised my mouth isn't watering at the prospect. I try to play it cool. "Oh, it does?" The words come out in a whoosh, not cool at all.

A few Vundi pass by, their eyes glued to the smoky gryphon that stalks along behind us.

She doesn't seem to fault me for my eagerness. "Your stone was a gift."

"To whom?" I feel like I would have remembered a glowing old lady with pointy ears handing me a magical necklace at a birthday party.

"Queen Aurentia."

I stop, confusion gumming up my works. "What?"

"Given to her upon her ascension to the throne. Yes. A gift of the Vundi, one that should have cemented good relations between us. And I suppose it did for a while." She nods and pulls me with surprising strength. "Keep up."

I force myself into motion. "If you gave it to her, how the hell did I wind up with it?"

"That's a good question." She laughs again, and her gryphon caws lightly behind us.

Here I was thinking I'd finally get answers. Turns out, I just have more questions. Did Queen Aurentia see the necklace when I was there? Why didn't she say anything about me wearing one of her jewels?

"Do you know what I am?"

"What are any of us?"

I pinch the bridge of my nose.

"Don't do that. Wrinkles." She smiles again, and despite her age, she's still beautiful. Also, mischievous.

"So you aren't going to tell me?"

"I have suspicions. One such as you was foretold, but how can anyone know the object of a prophecy until the prophecy comes true, eh? No one, that's who."

"You remind me of a witch I met."

Her white brows furrow as we turn again, the underground corridors a maze. "Is that an insult?"

"Not at all. I rather liked her. And she helped me out."

The air becomes heavier, humid and with an earthy scent. We must be getting close.

"I saw Cenet with an Obsidian blade. Was it the witch who gave it to you?"

"Yes. She also gave me a pea that dimmed my sparkle."

"Hmmm. I did notice your aura is muffled, like someone threw a black blanket over you." She sucks on her teeth. "She's the one you should've asked all your questions. She's danced with the magic of the otherworld even longer than I have, and on top of that, has the devious intelligence bred by the Spires."

"Well, she went back to her cave and she told me to be scared of TMI—too much information."

Delantis nods. "She was wise, and I'm impressed you made it out of that encounter with all your skin intact."

I shudder. "I'm good like that, yeah."

"Can you tell me about the prophec—"

"Here we are." She turns into a wide carving in the rock and leads me along a walkway a few stories above a wide, flat cavern. Several football fields worth of dirt and crops expand into the distance, and light shines through shafts from above that hit the rows of plants perfectly.

Vundi workers walk along the rows or group around work stations placed at intervals.

My mouth may be hanging open a bit. "This is amazing. I've never seen anything like it."

"We can't survive in the plains anymore. This was working for a while, but now we can't produce enough to feed ourselves. Not since the plants began to die off."

"What happened to them?" We ease down a set of stone stairs, and the gryphon takes flight and lands below us, its smoky white tail high in the air.

"We don't know. Mainly because we aren't farmers by nature. Centuries ago, we sent spies to the western farmlands who brought back basic farming knowledge as well as seeds and a few plants. From that, we were able to thrive. Until it all went bad." She frowns at the wilted plants all along the rows we approach. "We keep ourselves hidden, never allowing outsiders to enter our caverns, so there's no help. Only what we can do. And—" She motions to the failing greenery. "As you can see, we've reached the limits of our abilities."

"You let us in. Surely, you could let the western farmers you mentioned come to help?"

She cocks her head to the side a bit. "The king of the winter realm is a little different than just anyone, especially when his changeling is the one thing that could save our people. You're an exception. The rule is that we hide our numbers. It's safer that way. No outsiders."

The scent of rot is heavy here, the withering green stalks limp and barren.

"May I?" I gesture to the nearest plant. I don't recognize it, but I assume horticulture works the same way here as on earth. After all, the plants grow in dirt, need sunlight, and have a rough irrigation system via narrow water ducts running in a grid through the fields.

"Go ahead." She reaches out and strokes her gryphon's feathers.

"What's your gryphon's name?" I kneel next to the nearest plant.

"Delantis." She runs her finger down its beak.

"Oh." I try not to sound as confused as I am and focus on the withered yellow leaves.

"She is me. My feral."

I turn back to her. "That's your feral fae?"

"She manifests physically now. The older a fae, the stronger its feral. It seems your mate is on the verge of manifesting his own. I can hear it inside him, desperate to claim his mate."

I swallow hard. "Wow."

"Indeed." She points to the plant. "This is supposed to produce dwarfberries. It's a vining plant but hasn't been able to branch out." Looking at her white-tipped fingers, she frowns. "All this power, and I can't do anything about it. Life is its own particular magic, and not one I can control."

"Let me take a look." I dig into the dark brown earth at the plant's roots. Rotted ooze covers its damp roots.

"Delantis." A woman approaches, her hair tied up in neat knots, and her face something like a deer's. "I didn't know we'd have such an honor this day." She bows low.

"Chatara, I just brought Taylor by to see if she had any thoughts on our problem. She's an alchemist."

"Chemist," I correct and peer more closely at the goo on my fingertips. It stinks like decay. "Are they all like this?"

"The plants? Yes." Chatara eyes me curiously. "It started in the back reaches of the fields and spread in a matter of months. We eventually set fire to everything in an effort to stop the plague and planted new seeds, but they still fell ill."

"Did you treat the soil?"

"Treat it?" Chatara blinks, her doe-like eyes big and brown. "It was on fire. Nothing survived."

I stand. "Do you have a microscope?"

Chatara blinks even harder. "A ... A what?"

"It's a ..." I chew on my lip and hold my dirty hands out in front of me ... like an idiot. "It's where you use glass lenses to magnify something."

"Magnify?" Delantis peers at my fingers.

"I need to see what this is. But up close. Like the tiny stuff it's made of." I hold up the dark green sludge. "If I can see what's in here, I can maybe figure out a solution. I'm suspecting fungal by the looks of it, but I can't be sure."

"But we can all see it." Chatara points. "It's rot."

"The rot is a symptom. There's a microorganism attacking the roots, which results in the decay. Like when you have a skin infection and a sore shows up. The sore is the symptom. That's what this rot is. I need to see the tiny organisms of this in order to tell what it is."

"Ahhh." Delantis nods. "I see." She holds out her hand and touches the tip of my finger, then looks up at the stone ceiling far above. The white light grows so bright around her that I wince, but then she holds her hand to her face and blows on the bit of rot on her fingertips. It floats on a phantom white wind and expands, filling the space above our heads as it grows and grows. From unintelligible dark green mush, it stretches and expands farther and farther.

Some of the workers yell and run toward us, cowering as Delantis's magic unfurls. She's created a microscope larger than an iMax theater, zooming in until I can see the fine detail.

"Holy shit." I stare at the strands of plant matter that float huge and bright over my head. Her white light shines through all of it, highlighting everything wrong. "Whoa, Delantis. Stop there." I point to a particularly nasty spot. "Fungus. Like I said. Looks like fusarium wilt, though it could be any number of other fungi. Can you go deeper, Delantis? I'd like to see the cellular level."

She obliges, not even breaking a sweat as she increases the magnification.

"Yep. That's it." I walk down one of the rows and point over my head to a patch of cells. "This here? These are vascular cells, but these dark spots are paired arbus-cules." I look back at Chatara.

Her silver eyes are blank. "I don't know what—"

"It means the rot is affecting the plants' vascular systems. Basically, the water processes and eventually photosynthesis. The fire didn't work because this fungus hides in the soil. You can't stop it because it's everywhere down here."

"In the soil?" Chatara wrings her hands. "But we spent a century moving this dirt here from the Misty River. If we had to remove it and start over, we wouldn't survive."

Delantis blinks and lowers her hand, the image above our heads fading.

"That was kind of amazing." I walk back to her.

"I have tricks, young one." Her silver eyes twinkle.

"We're doomed." Chatara leans against the damp wall.

"Not at all." I shake the dirt from my hands. "We can fix this. Do you have more seeds or seedlings?"

"We do but we've been holding them back because of —" She gestures at the dying fields.

"Good. How about shovels, pickaxes, laborers?" I didn't think Chatara could look more confused. I was wrong.

"The work begins." Delantis smiles and starts climbing the stairs back the way we came.

"Yes." Chatara points to the closest Vundi. "Get all the things she says." Turning back to me, she asks, "What are we going to do?"

"The waterfall."

"The waterfall?"

"When I came in, I saw that beautiful waterfall, but what I also saw was the mineral nahcolite. The white crystals along the stone beneath the falls—that's likely a mix of limestone and nahcolite. I'd need a closer look to be certain, but I'm pretty sure it has what you need."

"Nahcolite?"

"It's the rock form of sodium bicarbonate." I smile. "Baking soda. It's naturally anti-fungal. So is lime. You need to load up with it from the walls of the waterfall, bring it over here, smash it until it's a fine powder, and then lace the dirt with it. It might even be better if you mix it with water and add it to your irrigation system. There will be an eventual calcium buildup doing it that way, but better to do a clean-out every so often than have a fungal issue. It'll take time, and you'll likely lose these plants, but when you re-seed, the problem should have abated."

"How do you know this?" Chatara is a mix of dumbfounded and wary.

"Trust her, Chatara," Delantis calls. "The Ancestors brought her here for a reason."

Chatara straightens, her doe-eyes sobering. "We'll get to work immediately." She takes a few steps away, then turns. "Thank you. If this works, you will have saved countless Vundi."

"Happy to help. I just know fungi and minerals. You're the ones doing the saving. I'm not the savior, um, person. Anyway, gotta go. Yep." I try to cover my awkward by following Delantis up the stairs and back into the hallway.

I offer Delantis my arm again. She takes it, but she seems energized, her steps lighter than before. Even her gryphon prances along behind us.

"Now that we did our dirt, back to the prophecy." I'm not about to let her get away with not telling me anything.

She laughs. "Tenacious. A good trait for a queen." She turns those silver eyes on me, but trouble haunts the creases beside them. "Perhaps the prophecy was wrong. It doesn't fit. Not with you."

"Tell me the prophecy. Please." I need more to go on than a necklace I can't remove and a dark, sparkly aura. I need to know what connection I have to this world.

She pauses. "Prophecies are strange things. They never mean what they say or say what they mean. Keep that in mind."

"It's in mind." Can't she tell I'm on pins and needles here? "Spill it."

"It isn't pretty, but I will tell you. We owe you. And I sense that the Vundi will be even further in your debt once the fields are replanted." She sighs. "This prophecy —few know of it, and fewer still believe in it."

I bounce on the balls of my feet. "I'm ready. Hit me."

"It was foretold long ago by a seer who could sense the coming of the great war that decimated Arin. She saw another conflict, one just as great, that would be heralded by the arrival of a particular creature. 'A child of many worlds, clothed in light, will come home.'"

I chew my bottom lip. "That doesn't sound so bad."

"I'm not finished." She gives me a wry smile. "'On

wings of death, the child will glide to sit on her throne of bone.'"

I frown. "Okay, that's a little darker than I thought it was going to go, but we're getting somewhere, I guess. Please continue."

"The realms will bend—"

"I'm afraid it's time for you to surrender, changeling." Vanara appears ahead of us, my obsidian blade in her grip and resolve in her eyes. "The king beyond the mountain will have his due."

I shout Leander's name in my mind and hope he can find me in this stone maze. If he can't, things are about to go terribly wrong.

"You don't want to do this, Vanara." Delantis glows, the white light flowing from her in waves.

Her gryphon wraps its large talon around my waist and pulls me back before standing in front of me.

"Step aside, crone." Vanara brandishes the obsidian blade and advances. "The changeling bitch belongs to me."

"*T*he council came around in the end, at least. I'll have to talk to the harvest master in Cold Comfort and figure out logistics, but we should be able to get enough food over the border to sustain them until we can figure out the crop situation." Gareth leads the way back to our rooms.

"We should send an envoy to the farmers in the west, see if they can assist with the underground fields. Maybe the Vundi will let them in."

"I can arrange that, though we may run afoul of the queen."

"Better to ask forgiveness than permission, right?" I turn the corner toward our rooms. "Besides, maybe Taylor has already figured out a solution. My mate is quite a clever alchemist."

Beth stands at the door, her gaze on Gareth as she taps her foot impatiently. "About time. Where's Taylor?"

"She should be—" The hairs on the back of my neck

stand up, and the feral howls inside me. I take off running.

"What is it?" Gareth follows at my heels.

"She's in danger." I draw my sword as I navigate the dark passages, each second an agony as I try to find my way to her. Her fear coats me like the tang of blood, but there's something else crackling down our bond. Something cold and dark.

A shriek echoes through the dark stone hallways, the sound covered in pain and impending death.

"What was that?" Gareth keeps to my heels.

"I must find her!" I roar as I race past some wide-eyed Vundi carrying shovels, bowling them over as I go. She's closer, but I can't get to her, and the darkness is growing.

"Leander!" Gareth shouts. "That way's a dead end." He points to the right.

I rush past him and catch her scent, which spurs my steps even faster.

When I turn the next corner, I see her. She sits cradling Delantis's head in her lap as Vanara lies to the side, her body convulsing as black streaks trace across her skin. She shrieks, but the sounds quickly die on her tongue as she folds in on herself, the darkness covering her. The proud gryphon lies on its side, a cruel slash in its chest.

Taylor looks up at me, tears glittering in her eyes.

"Are you hurt?" I rush to her as Gareth stands next to Vanara, his blade at the ready.

"No. But Delantis—"

"Your aura." Delantis reaches up and waves her

fingers around Taylor's shoulder. "It's beautiful. Dark and starry. I can see it now."

"I'm sorry." Taylor strokes Delantis's cheek. "I'm so sorry."

A deep red stain mars the front of Delantis's dress, spreading from her heart.

"It's my time." The old fae smiles but doesn't move, her life draining away as she struggles to catch her breath. The gryphon lets out a mournful sound as it struggles to crawl closer to Delantis, its body fading as it drags along the cold stone floor.

"Can you save her?" Taylor's lip quivers as she turns to me. "Heal her?"

The obsidian blade lies nearby, and I can smell Delantis's blood on it. It can kill any creature. Even a fae as old and powerful as her. There is no saving her, but I will try anything to ease Taylor's pain.

"Gareth?" I motion him over but keep Vanara in my peripheral vision. She's not moving, her skin turning black and desiccated. What did Delantis do to her?

"I'll do my best." He holds his palm out, summoning a healing spell.

"You can't." Delantis closes her eyes. "The obsidian has a hold on me now. I can feel it pulling me away."

Gareth tries anyway, pressing the green magic to her chest. The blood doesn't stop, and Delantis sighs. The gryphon cries low and weak, then fades from view.

"Please don't go." Taylor's tears fall on Delantis's white hair.

All I can do is wrap my arm around her and hold her as she holds the dying fae. The workers we passed earlier have caught up, all of them dropping to one knee as Delantis's light fades, her long life ending as my mate cradles her close.

"The stone will protect you, young one. Keep it for as long as you can."

Taylor strokes Delantis's cheek. "I'm sorry I couldn't save you. I-I didn't know what to do."

"Shh now." Delantis's voice drops to a whisper, her breathing slow. "You did fine. I will be with you. The stone, the blade—each of them is yours, and each of them harbor a part of me."

"No, no, no." Taylor's tears are coming faster now. "Please don't go."

Gareth toes Vanara, but her body turns to black soot, crumbling into nothing. He looks at me with stark eyes. "What magic did Delantis unleash?"

The injured fae coughs weakly. "He will send for you. Do not forget who you are. Do not reject the bond." She opens her eyes one more time and pins Taylor with an intense stare. It's an act of sheer will. She's lost too much blood and is fading fast. "It will save you."

"What?" Taylor sobs.

Delantis closes her eyes again and breathes her last breath, the light fading from her like the setting sun, and everything going cold.

"What happened?" I murmur into Taylor's hair as I hold her close, carrying her back to our rooms as Gareth takes point, both of us attuned to any rising threats. We need to get out of here. The delicate trade deal we just struck will be blown apart by the deaths of Delantis and, to a lesser degree, Vanara.

She hitches in her breath. "Vanara came at us, and then Delantis used her magic, but Vanara had some sort of defense and slashed the gryphon."

I hate seeing her tears and wish I could take her fear away.

"She was coming after me. Vanara wanted to hand me over to the king beyond the mountain, but Delantis defended me. And now sh-she's—" A sob catches her words and won't let them free.

"She is with the Ancestors." I kiss her forehead. "The Glowing Lands were made for a fae such as her. She defended you, gave her life for yours, and defeated Vanara."

"No." She pulls back and looks into my eyes, her gaze haunted. "She didn't kill Vanara. I ... I think I did. I felt something when she died. Like a surge. I don't know how. I don't understand."

"What did—"

"What is going on?" Beth sprints toward us, a row of Vundi soldiers at her back, their weapons drawn.

"Behind me. Now." I set Taylor down, then draw my sword. It's close quarters, but I'll use it to my advantage and cut a way out of this place. The feral clamors in agreement. "Gareth, watch our flank."

He's already there, a blade of winter, cold and deadly.

"You slew Vanara and Delantis." The first soldier advances, his curved blade out to his side.

Ice creeps along the floor toward him. "Vanara betrayed our truce, and Delantis died trying to defend it. Now, you can let us leave, or you can die." I keep my voice steady, the calm before the storm.

He doesn't stop, the ire in his eyes showing he's already made up his mind. "You will pay for your crimes."

"You choose death." I send a vicious blast of cold shooting down the corridor.

Charging ahead, I raise my blade to shatter the soldiers as I go.

"Halt!" Keret shouts.

I look up and find him on the ceiling, his lizard-like claws gripping the stone.

He drops down in front of me, his tail sticking out behind him.

"We are leaving." I don't back down. I'll kill him if I have to. Getting Taylor out of here is paramount.

"Wait." He holds out a hand. "Delantis sent her feral to me as it died. She told me what happened. Vanara turned traitor."

I advance on him and press my blade to his throat. "Did she? Or was she acting on council orders?"

"No!" He blinks one eye and then the other. "The council is prepared to stand by the agreements we made. The Vundi word is good." The sizzle of magic reinforces his promise and tells me he didn't order Vanara to break the Vundi's oath.

"And what of Delantis?" The feral rides me hard, telling me to kill them all to keep Taylor safe. "There will be no retribution for her life?"

"Not against you or your companions. And I believe Vanara has already paid the price for her mistake." He yells to the soldiers, "The council demands you all stand down. The winter realm is an ally, and they have done no wrong. Vanara betrayed us. She served the king beyond the mountain, not the Vundi. The winter king's mate, Taylor, has given us a way forward with the crops, and the king has agreed to help sustain us until such time as we produce enough food to support ourselves. They are *not* our enemies."

I wait and allow the winter freeze to retreat inside me, but it's right on the edge, ready to explode should anyone make a wrong move. "We're still leaving." I pull my blade from Keret's neck.

"The treaty?" he asks.

Movement has me tensing for a fight again, but Cenet appears behind Keret, his hands out, weapons stowed. "I came to help."

"Your soldiers could have used it," Gareth says wryly. He hands Taylor the obsidian sword, the blade cleaned of Vanara's blood.

"I meant that I came to help *you*." Cenet glares. "But I see Keret has it handled."

"The treaty?" Keret presses.

"It is still good as long as we are allowed to leave." I can't keep the ice from my tone. "The Vundi shouldn't suffer because of Vanara's treachery."

"You may leave as soon as you wish, and I'm happy to send Cenet with you to make sure you reach the border safely."

"No, thank you," Gareth's voice carries down the hall. "I can see to the king's security."

"May we at least send provisions with you?"

"We don't want to take what you have." I eye the nearest soldier as the ice falls from him, and he's able to move.

He steps back. Wise choice.

I hold one hand out behind me, warmth infusing me as Taylor takes it without hesitation. Leading her through the soldiers, I glower at them as they part for us. We return to our rooms, and Gareth guards the door as Beth and Taylor throw clothes and food into bags. I don't leave Taylor's side, my instincts attuned to every move she makes.

"Leander." She pauses as she's stuffing her hat into the bag and turns to me, her eyes troubled. "When Vanara came for us, it wasn't Delantis who killed her. That magic, the black veins on her skin—it came from *me* somehow."

A wave of foreboding cascades through me. "Are you certain?"

"Yes." She stares at her pale hands. "I barely touched her. I was trying to get the obsidian sword from her, but when my hand grazed her arm, she sort of froze. Her eyes —" She shivers. "They turned black, and then she fell. I never meant to kill anyone. But I did, didn't I? I took her life. It was as if there was something so dark inside me, almost like another person, and she *wanted* to kill Vanara. I could feel it under my skin somehow—that need to inflict death. Wh-what was that?" She stares at her hands again, as if they're alien to her, as if they belong to another.

I've seen that sort of dark magic before, but only once. And I never thought I'd cross paths with it again—at least I hoped I wouldn't. I don't let my suspicions show, but I have some—ones that I dare not speak aloud. Pulling her to me, I wrap her in my arms where I know she's safe. "Vanara wrote her own fate when she decided to turn on her own. You did nothing wrong."

"You say that." She presses her forehead against my chest. "But I can't agree. I don't know how to live with it. Can I?" Her eyes are brimming with tears when she looks up at me. "Can I accept that I took a life?"

"Put your burden on me, Taylor. Give me that worry and let me carry it for you. At least for now. When we're safe in the winter realm, we can take it out of its box and examine it together. But for now, let me have it. All right?"

She sniffs and nods. "I can try."

"And let's keep this between us for now. At least until we return to High Mountain and speak with Ravella."

"Who is she? You've mentioned her before."

"A powerful fae with expertise in some peculiar areas. She's a valuable member of the Phalanx. Now, we must hurry. We'll discuss it all later, I promise."

"Okay." She takes a deep breath and lets it out. "I trust you."

Has my heart ever beat this hard? "Good. That's what—"

"Leander, we must go!" Gareth calls from the front entry.

I kiss her forehead, then grab a few more items and hurry her out the door.

Back out in the hall, Keret waits for us. Alone. His guards have dispersed, but I can still feel unease in the air. Some of the Vundi may have been in league or agreement with Vanara. We need to leave before the situation boils over even further.

"Para will lead you out. She has your provisions, and Cenet will bring your horses. You will be safe." Keret gestures down the hall. "Para will show you the secret way that leads to an entrance near the walls of Timeroon."

"Timeroon is at least a week's ride from here." I glance at Gareth.

"Week and a half, at best," he adds.

Keret nods. "Our ways are underground, faster than the road, safer too, but it will still take you five days to get there."

We can take our chances on the plains, risk another storm and the wind wights, or remain trapped in this stone world for a few more days.

I tense as Para appears down the corridor.

She kneels in front of me, her head low. "I swear on the soul of High Priestess Delantis that I will see you safely to the walls of Timeroon."

"Why this allegiance?" I, like any fae, distrust an oath so freely given, though the sting of magic is just as potent.

"You tried to save her, didn't you?" Her eyes meet Taylor's, and I realize she isn't kneeling for me, but for my mate.

Taylor steps to my side, and I let her stay there despite wanting to keep her safely back.

"I did. I tried to stop Vanara, but I wasn't able to keep her from—" She chokes up and puts one hand to her mouth.

Para's mournful voice reverberates from the walls. "Delantis is—was—our guiding light. That you fought to save her means more to me than I can give voice to." She takes a deep, shuddering breath and bows her head again. "I offer you my sword for as long as you wish it. To the walls of Timeroon and beyond, I will serve you. Upon my life and honor, I make this vow."

"You don't have to do that." Taylor steps forward and offers her hand. "Please."

Gareth clears his throat. "My queen, her oath is as sacred as the one sworn to you by the members of the Phalanx. You can either accept and honor her by doing so or decline and leave her to her shame."

Taylor looks at me, her gaze questioning. But this is a decision she must make on her own. I am her king, but she is strong in her own right and grows more so each day. She seems to realize that and returns to Para.

"Your pledge is honored. *Bladanon thronin*." She holds her hand out again, and this time, Para takes it.

*W*e travel for what feels like a day in the unending stone world. Over bridges and through tunnels, we find abandoned mining equipment and mushrooms that bloom wide and translucent along the walls. Water is plentiful—so different from the dry, dusty landscape above. It makes me wonder if there is some way to pull the water from underground and recreate a farming oasis on the plains, restore it to its former state.

Too often, my thoughts wander to Delantis's death. It has weighed on me each moment as we trudge along, the horses following behind. Even more than that, Vanara haunts me—the way she looked when the darkness crawled up her arm. I wince when I remember it. The darkness that came from *me*. Leander has given me so much comfort, but I haven't been able to shake the feeling that something is wrong with me, and taking a life has made it even worse.

"We can camp here for a bit," Para says as we enter a medium-sized cave covered with glowing crystals overhead. "We're making excellent time. I didn't intend to reach this crystal cavern so soon. After this point, we should be able to ride the horses. The ceilings are much higher."

"Are you all right?" Leander keeps a steady hold on my hand. He's offered to carry me about a dozen times, but I'm fine. At least I am, physically speaking.

"It'll be nice to have a rest." I squeeze his fingers.

He drops a kiss on my hair and strides to Kyrin, unloading our supplies with unnatural speed. Before I've even had time to stretch, he's got a fur pallet set up for me.

Beth plops down on it and pats the spot next to her.

Leander frowns, but doesn't order her away. "I'll be back, little one." He gives Beth a hard look. "And you will be gone so I can attend to my mate."

"If 'attend to' means 'mate with,' I'm all for it." She gives him a thumbs up.

I snicker despite myself. I must be tired.

He stalks off to Gareth, who's unloading Sabre.

"Why do I always miss the good stuff?" She kicks her feet out and lies back. "Come on. Tell me what happened. Begin at the beginning."

I lie next to her and close my eyes. Somehow, telling her about the council, the crops, Delantis, and Vanara lifts a weight from me. I suppose her exclamations of "you're so smart" and "Delantis knew you were special" and "that bitch Vanara got what was coming to her" helped a bit. I hold back on the details about the blackness that destroyed Vanara, the way it seemed to come from somewhere inside me.

"What am I?"

"Huh?" She turns to look at me.

"Didn't mean to say that out loud." I sigh and snuggle deeper into the fur. Leander arranged it so I don't even feel the stone floor beneath us.

"I know what you are."

My eyes pop open. "What?"

"A cock block."

I snort. "Not this again."

"I want to see the mating." She sighs dreamily. "Is that so wrong?"

"It kind of is, yes."

"I bet it'll be like, pretty much the most amazing sex ever."

"How many men have you been with?" I blurt.

She arches a brow. "We're going to have *that* conversation, are we?"

"I just." I shrug. "You know." I shrug again. "You don't have to tell me."

"Are we talking the males I slept with on purpose or the ones who ..." She tries to keep her tone light, but I sense the pain beneath it. She's such a deep river of history and layers. Maybe I'll never get to know all of her, but it won't stop me from trying.

I take her hand. "I'm sorry," I whisper.

"Eh, it was a long time ago. Besides, I was more prone to getting beatings than anything else."

My throat constricts. "I know what that's like."

"You do?"

"I had a stepfather." My skin crawls just talking about him. "He was kind at first. Or, at least I thought he was. But then he changed. And he would ..."

"Bastard." She says it so low it verges on a Leander-growl.

"He was good at it. He knew where to hit me where it hurt but didn't leave many marks. He'd just, I don't know, get mad about traffic or a sports game or maybe his coffee wasn't quite right. He would somehow work it around to being something I did, and he'd hit me. My mother never believed me when I told her. Or maybe she did." That's the part that draws a tear from me. Knowing that my mother likely *did* believe me but wanted Steve more than she wanted me. I blow out a long breath. "I've never told anyone about all that."

"Sometimes, you can only tell someone who knows the pain the same way you do." She closes her eyes but doesn't let go of my hand.

"Where is this man now?" Leander's lethal voice is right next to my ear, and I jump.

"Fae hearing is a bitch." Beth sits up and glares at him. "Not to mention that you need a bell or something. Damn."

He cups my face in his hands gently, his soft touch at odds with the murder in his midnight eyes. "Where is your father? I swear on the throne atop the High Mountain that I will find him and make him pay for—"

"He's dead. I mean, my father died when I was really little. Steve was my stepfather." I press my palms to his hands. "He died in a barfight when I was in high school."

He grits his teeth. "I would kill him again."

"I don't think that's a thing." I press my forehead to his. "But I appreciate the offer."

His gaze turns heated, and he leans into me until his lips brush mine. My heart jumps, leaps, and falls. But he catches me. He always does.

"You know I will murder any enemy you have. Send them to the Spires with a smile on my face." He kisses me slowly, his tongue worshipping mine with slow strokes as one of his hands trails through my hair. "Any command from your lips is one I will follow until the Ancestors call me home."

Why does his murder talk turn me on? I fear this whole "darkness inside me" thing is starting to make sense.

I shake my head. "I don't want anyone dead."

"Tell me what you want." The feral fae is in control, Leander's fangs long and his pupils blown. "I will give you an empire, a crown, every jewel you desire. You have but to ask." He kisses me again, pulling me down into the bottomless depth of desire.

I need him in ways that I can't comprehend, and that scares me.

I pull back and take a breath, my gaze straying to Para and Gareth, both of whom pretend to be inspecting the crystals along the ceiling. "They're watching us."

"So?" He moves closer until I fall back on the fur. "Let them." His mouth claims mine again, one possessive hand sliding down to my waist.

My worries disappear, my thoughts vanish. He fills my entire world, my heart and mind. I wrap my arms around his neck as he moves on top of me.

"Leander!" I gasp when his hard length presses against my thigh, but he prevents any discussion with another wicked sweep of his tongue.

"When I claim you, little one, you will squeal with pleasure." His feral fae growls as he palms my bottom.

"Oh my god." I grip his hair as he pulls me against him, his thigh pressing between my legs and heightening every sensation.

"Let me claim you." He licks my throat, his fangs tickling along my skin. "I can scent your desire, taste it."

"*Yessss*," Beth's hiss sounds next to me.

My eyes open. "No." I shake my head and push his chest. "Not happening."

Beth groans. "You can't be serious right now."

"For once, I agree with Beth." He stares down at me, desire writ large across his handsome face.

"I'm serious." I sigh and roll out from beneath him, then elbow Beth.

Leander collapses face-first into the furs, and I have no doubt he and his feral are having it out inside his skull.

"Changeling, come away from there." Gareth shoots Beth a scowl as he yanks provisions from one of the packs. "We need a meal."

"Oh, and I'm the food preparer? Your little changeling slave to boss around?" She stands and practically bounces over to him, always happy to squabble.

Para stares at them as if she believes they might truly

come to blows. I suppose it will take a while for her to get used to us.

Leander groans a little.

I pat him on the back. It's as awkward as it sounds. "Sorry. I just need ..." More time? More nerve? Less of an audience?

"I will wait for you, little one." He turns to look at me. "I will wait as long as necessary." He leans closer, his lips at my ear. "But I must tell you, the longer it takes, the more desperate I will be for you when I claim you."

I shiver, and not from the chilly underground air. "I should, um. I should... Gotta go do a thing." Climbing quickly to my feet, I hurry away.

He groans as I walk over to Para.

"Hi." I stuff my hands into my dress pockets. "I love it when dresses have pockets, don't you?"

"What imbecile would make a dress without pockets?" She raises one eyebrow.

"Right?" I cough and relax as the sexual tension eases.

"So, how did you learn how to use that whip?" I point to the leather looped at her hip.

"It's a tradition for the female Vundi. The whip is the first weapon we're taught."

"Do you think you could teach me?"

She finally focuses on my eyes. "You'd want to learn the ways of the Vundi?"

"Sure. I don't have anything against the Vundi. I mean, other than Vanara trying to kill me and ..." My words fade away as I remember her death, the darkness that seemed to devour her.

"It's not your fault," she says quietly. "Vanara was beholden to a power beyond her control, and she acted foolishly."

"The king beyond the mountain?"

She nods.

"Do you know why he wants me or who he is?"

"All I know is that he is a great evil, one that will spread if the winter and summer realms don't ally to stop him." Her voice is backed with iron, but also resonates with a sadness I don't understand.

I put a hand on her arm, her brown skin smooth and warm. "Are you all right?"

"I'm fine. Just ready to get out of the caves." She pulls the whip free from her hip and hands it to me. "Would you like to learn?"

"Please." I take it and flail it around a bit. "I am the new Indiana Jones."

"No." She grabs my wrist. "You'll end up without an eye doing it that way."

"Oh." Maybe I was a tad premature on that Indiana Jones declaration.

"Here." She stands behind me and holds my wrist, and we're suddenly in a romcom montage, but in this one she's teaching me how to kill a man with a leather rope. "Like this."

She guides my hand, and we flick out the lasso's tip and take off a chunk of a mushroom on the cavern wall.

"Okay, that's fun."

"Let's go again." I can hear the smile in her voice.

Leander looks on from his spot on the furs, pride in his eyes as I learn the basics.

Eventually, Para seems assured I won't put my eye out and lets me do a few strikes on my own. I manage to smack a mushroom, but don't do any damage.

"Good work for your first lesson." She takes the lasso and fastens it to her hip. "You learn fast."

"Thanks for teaching me." I have a newfound appreciation for the strength of her forearm. Mine is on fire.

"Get some rest. We'll get going soon." She smiles, but I can still sense that sadness in her. Is it because she had to leave Cenet?

"Come, little one," Leander calls to me and pats the furs. "You've done well."

I return to him and collapse. "I need to start lifting."

"Lifting?"

"Weights. You know, get pumped." I try to make a muscle with my bicep.

"I've been offering to pump you for weeks." He darts in and kisses me, his tongue seeking at the seam of my mouth.

I crinkle my lips. "That was a terrible pun."

He laughs, then rolls to his side and pulls me into his arms. "Rest your weary mind and delectable body."

"My mind is pretty weary," I admit and close my eyes.

"I know. I've been listening to your churning thoughts for the past few hours."

The blood leeches from my face. "Oh my god. You can hear my thoughts?"

He laughs low in his throat. "Of course not. But I can feel the pressure of them, of your worries. We agreed I would carry them, so let them go." He pulls the fur over us. "Now get a little sleep. Beth will wake us when it's time to eat."

I snuggle closer, already well aware of my favorite sleeping spot against his warm body.

Right as I doze off, I feel him stroke my hair and the breath of winter at my neck. "Soon, little one."

hen we emerge from the tunnels, I flinch against the sun and the pervasive heat. So different from the cool, dark caverns that run beneath the plains like spider webs. I mark the entry though it's disguised just as well as the other entrance. All the same, I'll be able to find it again if I ever have need of it.

The plains stretch out behind us, two dust devils dancing along the road. Kyrin surges ahead, happy to be out of the depths of Arin.

The high walls of Timeroon beckon, and beyond, I can see the white peaks of the winter mountains. The border is finally within my reach, the cold bite of winter calling to me. My joy is dimmed by the thoughts that weigh heavily on Taylor's mind. Perhaps I was foolish to think she'd lend me her cares so that I could shoulder them for her.

I pull her hat from my pack and snug it down on her head. Maybe I can't protect her from her thoughts, but at least I can shield her from the sun.

"Thanks." She gives me a smile, the one I've come to crave.

"Of course." I kiss the side of her neck. When her pulse quickens, I pull away, lest I tempt the feral.

"I thought I missed the heat." Beth shades her eyes with her hand. "I was wrong. Ugh."

"Always complaining." Gareth digs around in the pack behind him and yanks out her hat. "Here."

"Thanks, lover." She takes it.

"I am *not* your lover." He sounds angry. But I can sense the frustration beneath it. I've known him for too long. The tension between he and the changeling is the sort that could rival the heat wafting from the Spires. When they finally come together, I fear an explosion.

"Better stow that grin, king of winter," Taylor whispers. "Gareth will blow a gasket."

"You're quite the diplomat." I nip at her neck and squeeze her waist.

"When I need to be." She grips my knee with her small hand. "Now stop the funny business before you wind up the feral."

"The business I want with you isn't funny at all, little one. It's serious." I smooth my hand up her stomach, stopping just beneath her breasts. When the memory of how she came for me in the tub surges inside me, a low growl rips from me.

"And there it is." She sighs and threads her fingers with mine. "You're going to get us in trouble."

I pull her hips closer so she can feel exactly how much trouble she's in for.

The goosebumps along her skin and the sweet scent

from between her thighs tell me her walls are falling. Soon, she will be mine. Marked and mated.

"Taylor, don't be a horny horny hippo," she says under her breath.

"Horny hippo?" I slide my index finger along the bottom curve of her breast. "Is that a beast from your world?"

"You weren't supposed to hear that." She shakes her head.

Teasing her is fast becoming one of my favorite pastimes. "I want to hear more about these hippos and what the horns—"

"What form is your feral fae?" She chirps the question, her cheeks pink.

I let her get away with the subject change. "I've never seen it manifest, so I don't know."

"But you can feel it inside you?"

"It's never been so close to the surface before. It grows stronger as I age. Our bond also feeds it, gives it power."

"How?"

"Because of the link between us. Two bonded mates are a power unto themselves."

"But we aren't bonded."

Not yet. "Let's revisit this in a few—" Movement in the red landscape has me jumping from Kyrin and drawing my sword.

Gareth hits the ground only a moment after I do. "Show yourself!"

Para's whip lights with orange flames as she slides from her mount and crouches low, melding with the landscape. She's almost invisible, the subtle pattern on her crimson dress creating a perfect camouflage. We could be surrounded with Vundi warriors and not know it. The thought doesn't sit well with me, but I focus on the slight mound of scrabbly plants ahead of me.

It moves, and I raise my sword, ice crackling through my veins.

"Cenet?" Para stands, and the fire along her whip dims.

The Vundi male loosens the kerchief hiding his face and steps forward.

"What are you doing here?" She hurries to him and stows her whip.

"I wanted to make sure you emerged." He glances up at Gareth and me. "I'm here for Para and to ensure the treaty stands."

"You need to leave." Gareth loosens his stance but doesn't sheathe his blade.

"Cenet is a friend and ally." Para turns to Taylor.

"Is he your mate?" Taylor asks.

Beth snorts. "Oh, my Ancestors, Taylor, you can't just go around asking people if they're mates."

Taylor's brows draw together, then she laughs. "That was a very '*Mean Girls*' moment."

"What?" Beth cocks her head to the side.

"It's a movie. And, oh my god, I really hope we get to watch it together some day."

"One of those moving painting things? I'm all for it. Does it have sex in it? Can you touch the people while they are inside the painting or do you—"

Gareth pointedly clears his throat, his glare unmistakable. "Cenet, we appreciate your care, but we cannot take another Vundi to the winter realm."

"I have no plans to enter the winter realm." He glances at Para. "Only to say my goodbyes in Timeroon."

"It's settled then." Taylor motions Cenet forward. "If Para vouches for you, then you're all right with me. Para?"

She nods. "He is a true friend."

"Then I'm cool with it." Taylor smiles. "He can accompany us into town."

I climb up behind her. Gareth turns his scowl on us.

"You heard your queen. She's 'cool' with it." I guide Kyrin toward the road and the stone walls of Timeroon and keep one eye firmly on our newest companion.

he doors of the city are wide open, weary travelers covered in crimson dirt arriving while others venture forth into the plains. Soldiers stand on either side of the high, metal portico, but they don't seem particularly invested in the goings on. Instead, they chat amongst themselves and talk to the pretty fae who often pass by. Even so, one of them stands at attention as we approach, his gaze fixed firmly on Leander.

"Captain Tavaran." Leander nods in his direction.

"You're back sooner than I expected." He glances at me, then stares. "And with more cargo."

Leander's grip on the reins tightens, and I get the feeling he's debating whether to flay the fae captain.

"Hi. I'm Taylor," I blurt.

"Well met." His silver eyes don't stray from me.

Leander's knuckles turn white.

I look to Gareth with a silent *"help me."*

He takes the hint. "Tavaran, good to see you manning the gate."

The captain finally looks away. "You've got a changeling, as well? Are they giving them out in Byrn Varyndr and no one told me?"

"Oh, you're funny," Beth says, though her tone makes clear she finds nothing about him amusing.

"And two Vundi?" He eyes Cenet and Para.

"We're popular." Beth shrugs.

"Mouthy for a changeling." Tavaran's disposition sours.

"We're for the crossing as soon as possible." Leander guides Kyrin forward.

"Always a pleasure." Tavaran doesn't stop us, but he watches us until we're swallowed up by the bustle of Timeroon.

This city is the busiest I've seen, though to be fair, Byrn Varyndr may have been busier if it weren't for a couple of dark fae warriors fighting in the streets. The red road widens and cuts through the center of the town. Stone buildings rise on either side, thatch roofs holding off the unforgiving sun.

Changelings, fae, lesser fae, and creatures I've never seen before travel along the roads or lounge on the narrow front stoops. Horses pull wagons and carry travelers as we make our way down the main street. Smells of food, exotic spices, and the ever-present scent of horse manure coat the air. Turbaned vendors shout their wares, and people walk by chowing down on street grub. My stomach rumbles.

Leander whistles to Gareth who guides Sabre closer. "My mate is hungry."

"I can arrange something with a street cook." Gareth

peers at a booth set up on a small side street with some sort of roasted fowl hanging along the front. "That way we don't have to stop and can cross as soon as possible."

My mouth waters. The Vundi root vegetables and dried jerky sustained us in the caves, but the scent of cooked, delicious food is a lure I can't resist.

I'm about to ask Gareth for one of the tasty-looking birds when my breath catches in my throat, and then I scream so loud that Leander has to rein in Kyrin before he bolts.

"What?" Leander already has a throwing dagger in his hand. The street pauses for only a moment, then the creatures go about their business as if nothing happened. Are they nuts? Or blind? I squeal again and throw one leg over Kyrin's side but can't go anywhere when Leander grabs my dress with his bear paw. "Let me down!"

"Little one." He lifts me with one hand until we're at eye level. "What are you doing?"

"Isn't it obvious?" I turn and see it again.

"What?" Beth follows my line of sight. "What is it?"

It's the necklace all over again. "Is it invisible to everyone but me? Don't you see it?" I point.

Leander arches a brow. "Ah."

"Right. Ah. Now let me down! I have to pet it!"

He pulls me to his chest and dismounts, keeping me under his arm as we walk along the dusty street.

"Leander?" Gareth calls.

He points to what looks like an inn to our left. "Set up a room with food and toiletries. We'll be along shortly."

I prance forward and press my hands to my cheeks. "I can't believe it. A real. Live. *Unicorn!*"

The white beast is loosely tied to a hitching post, its bright blue eyes surveying the road, its horn iridescent and catching the light. I've never seen anything so beautiful in all my life.

"Careful, Taylor."

"This is just like '*Legend.*'"

Leander gives me a blank look.

"It's this amazing eighties movie. It has Tom Cruise. And that girl from '*Ferris Bueller.*'"

The blank look doesn't abate.

"In the movie, there are two unicorns; the last ones. And the lord of darkness wants them killed so the sun will never rise again. The princess screws up and gets one de-horned and one captured, and—"

Leander's nose wrinkles. "The princess doesn't sound very bright."

"Oh, but she is!" I step closer, and the unicorn focuses on me with his big blue eyes. "In the end, she defeats darkness by sacrificing herself. The unicorns are saved, and the sun rises."

I reach out toward the unicorn's mane. "May I—" I take a deep breath. "Pet you?" I expect it to simply eye me haughtily or bow its head in gracious assent.

Instead, it speaks! "Sure." It's a deep, beautiful tone that reminds me of a clarinet, and I almost fall over dead from excitement.

"Thank you." I run my shaking hand along his mane. It's soft like rabbit fur instead of coarse like Kyrin's.

"You didn't ask me where." He blinks.

"Oh." I pull my hand back. "I'm sorry. Where may I pet you?"

Leander puts a hand to his mouth.

"What?" I ask him.

"Nothing." He gestures to the unicorn. "Go ahead."

I swear he's hiding a smile or perhaps a laugh, but I don't have time for him. Not when I'm standing next to a real, live unicorn. Best. Day. Ever.

"Put your hand gently on my back," the unicorn instructs.

I run my hand along him, and he gives a low nicker. "Like this?"

"Perfect. Now run up to my mane slowly."

"All right." I slide my fingers along his rabbit-soft hair and up to the crown of his head.

"Now down my muzzle." His voice drops even lower.

A snort escapes Leander.

I ignore him. He's clearly jealous that I've charmed the unicorn. "Like this?"

"That's it." The unicorn nuzzles against me, his soft hair like a perfect pillow along my face.

"You're so soft."

"Thank you." He stamps one hoof. "Now up to my horn."

A thrill runs through me. "I can touch it?"

"Please."

I gently run my fingers along it, the iridescence sparkling along my fingertips. "It's beautiful."

"Wrap your hand around it."

"Really?" I peer into his eyes, and he blinks slowly.

Leander clears his throat, but when I look at him, he's sharing a look with Kyrin.

"It's magical," the unicorn coaxes.

I grip the base and slide my hand along it.

He nickers. "Again."

Leander grabs my wrist and pulls my hand away. "All right. That's quite enough."

"Hey, man." The unicorn turns and stares at Leander. "You don't see me slapping pussy out of your mouth, do you?"

"What?" I stumble back, and when I glance down, I gasp and clutch Leander. The unicorn is excited. *Really* excited.

"Where are you going?" He lowers his head, his horn in front of my face. "Keep it up. I was getting there."

Leander shoves his face away. "I think she's learned her lesson on unicorns."

"You got a problem with unicorns? Over here interrupting my handy like a swat twat." He stamps his hooves, his nostrils flaring. "Bend over and I'll shove this horn where—"

"Oh my god." I stare in horror at my hand, the palm still iridescent. "You are disgusting!"

"You think I'm going to turn down some loving from a pretty little changeling like you?" He snorts again. "Next time lick your palm first. I like that better."

Before I can even think, I slap him.

Leander bursts out laughing.

"I just slapped a unicorn." I let Leander pull me behind him.

"You've had your fun. That's the end of it, beast." Leander backs me away from the pervy unicorn.

He tugs at his reins. "You're lucky I'm hitched up. I'd take your girl right out from under you, winter realm trash. She'd be neighing all night long."

"Unicorns are bad. So, so bad." I'm dying. I just slapped a unicorn.

"Your loss, baby. In case you haven't noticed, I'm hung like a horse."

Kyrin snorts disgustedly.

I clap my hands over my ears. But it's too late. Unicorns are ruined for me. My childhood dream just got crushed by a unicorn's boner.

"*S*carred. For. Life." Taylor plops down at the table Gareth arranged for us at the back of the inn.

"I'm sorry, Taylor." I wrap my arm around her shoulders. "But that's the way unicorns are."

"You could have warned me!" Her blue eyes flash.

"I did. Remember? I told you unicorns were foul-mouthed creatures, no good beasts. As you say, 'just the worst.'"

She grumbles. "Maybe."

I reach over and load her plate with bread, butter, fruit, and slices of rich meat. "I shouldn't have let it go on as long as I did." The feral wanted to gouge my eyes out, but I have to let Taylor learn this world on her own terms. Did I want to strangle the unicorn with my bare hands? Yes. Would Taylor have forgiven me for it? Maybe.

"Shouldn't have let it go on, huh?" She smacks my arm. "You think?"

The feral roars to life, and I sit still for a moment.

"Sorry." She grimaces. "Didn't mean to do that." She blows a stray strand of hair from her face. "And I probably wouldn't have believed you about the unicorns if I hadn't seen it for myself." Her grimace deepens. "And boy did I *see* it."

Beth snickers. "All the new changelings are like that. Think the unicorns are noble and magical and amazing." She devours a piece of bread, then cants her head to the side. "Then again, the new changelings are always children. You don't have that excuse."

"Whatever." Taylor grabs another piece of bread. Then she drops it with a gasp, horror in her eyes. "Oh, god, Leander. What if your feral fae is a *unicorn?*"

The tickle starts in my throat and explodes through me. I laugh. No, I *howl*. Beth joins in, her laughter verging on a cackle.

"I'm sorry." I try to settle myself, because Taylor doesn't seem quite as amused. "But I don't think you have anything to worry about."

"Oh, but you don't know *for certain*, do you?" A smile finally emerges as she takes a drink of water. "You *could* be a unicorn in there. A nasty, freaky unicorn."

"I suppose that's possible, but—"

"I guess we'll just see who has the last laugh on that subject."

"Taylor, I meant no offense."

"Oh, none taken," she says too quickly, then juts her little chin out, the picture of pique. Does she have any idea what that does to me? How badly I want to throw her over my shoulder and take her to one of the rooms upstairs?

"Come on." Beth swipes half the loaf of bread. "You know that was hilarious."

Taylor huffs a bit, but I can see she's suppressing a smile.

"Just think. If he *is* a unicorn, you can ride him on both ends." Beth grins and pops a grape into her mouth.

"Stop." Taylor's smile breaks through, the color high in her cheeks.

I take her hand and kiss it. She grumbles a little more but leans against me.

Cenet and Para, their faces tight, walk in and sit across from us.

"You two are killing the vibe," Beth says through a mouthful of food.

"You really intend to cross the border tonight?" Cenet ignores Beth and focuses on Para.

"Yes." She doesn't look at him. "We've been over this."

Cenet stands and stalks out. Para sighs and follows.

They aren't mated, or at least I can't see the bond, but there's obviously something between them.

"Leander." Gareth jerks his chin toward the hall.

I add a few more pieces of fruit and some vegetables to Taylor's plate, then rise and follow Gareth out the door.

He closes it behind us. "Crossing the border could be dangerous."

"You have news of trouble?"

"Not exactly." He glances at the door and pulls me toward the rear of the inn near the kitchen, pots and pans clanging in the background.

"What is it?" What could possibly harm her in the winter realm? The king beyond the mountain wouldn't dare send an assassin to High Mountain while I was there. I would kill any such interloper with nothing more than a thought.

Gareth scrubs the weeks-old beard along his cheek. "It's you. Remember when we talked about the danger your feral poses once you cross?"

I stare up at the thatch ceiling. "Not this again."

He doggedly continues, "When you cross the border, your powers will be at full force."

"I know." I clap him on the shoulder. "That's a good thing."

"Generally speaking, yes, but—"

I sigh. I shouldn't fault Gareth for his practicality and carefulness, and I don't ... mostly.

"The feral." He crosses his arms over his chest. "Look, you'll cross that border and become the winter wind. Your feral will have more power than it's ever known. You don't think that will present a risk to Taylor?"

"I would never harm her." I try to keep the ire from my tone. I fail.

"I know *you* wouldn't." He meets my eyes. "I know you better than anyone else. And I know you'd never force her or hurt her. But the feral fae isn't something you can control. I didn't even know they *could* be controlled until I saw how Delantis handled hers."

I wave his concerns away. "I can handle myself and my feral."

"But what if—"

"I *must* go to the winter realm, and I *must* take Taylor there." I stab my fingers through my hair. "What would you have me do?"

"Don't overreact, but I was thinking maybe it's best to keep you separate when you cross."

"I can't go without her."

"I know." He moves to the side as a harried servant carries a platter full of food past us. "Look, how about I take Taylor through the crossing and continue with her toward Cold Comfort. You give us a head start. Let's say until sunup tomorrow. Then, when you cross, she'll be a safe distance away. You'll burn off some of the power while you're playing catch-up. By the time you reach Taylor, you'll be back to an even keel." He hitches up one shoulder. "What do you think?"

The feral rages inside me, demanding I drag Gareth outside and beat the Spires out of him for even suggesting such a thing. But I try to think about it through his eyes. And, more than that, I try to see it through Taylor's. If Gareth's fears are correct and the feral takes over, she could well be in danger. As much as it stings to think I would be a threat to her, it's not worth testing the theory, not when Taylor could get hurt.

"Fine."

Gareth's dark eyebrows almost hit his hairline. "Really?"

"Yes." The feral howls in disagreement. "It's probably for the best, and there's no one I trust more to watch over my mate."

"I will guard her with my life." His gaze turns even more serious.

"I know you will." I lock forearms with him. "Thank you for your wise counsel, old friend."

"You realize I'm going to tell the rest of the Phalanx you called me wise, right?" The side of his lips quirk up in a smirk.

"I expect nothing less." I release him and return to the dining room where Taylor and Beth are engaged in a heated discussion over which is worse, the Red Plains or Byrn Varyndr.

"—don't have fae that dress like overdone chandeliers." Beth points her fork at Taylor. "So I'm saying that's a point for the Red Plains."

"Sure, but Byrn Varyndr had, ummm, pretty flowers."

"Weak." Beth waves her hand in the air and makes a pffft sound.

"You're right." Taylor throws her hands up. "Byrn Varyndr sucks ass."

Beth whistles and raises her cup. "I'll drink to that."

Taylor toasts with her and downs the rest of her water. The table is almost cleared of food.

Beth pats her stomach. "Best meal I've had in ... ever? I guess?"

"If you've had your fill, then it's time to cross the border." Gareth looks down his nose at Beth, who gives him a saccharine smile in return.

"To the cold, desolate wasteland we go." Beth stands.

Gareth grunts his displeasure. "Bad-tempered changeling."

Taylor rises and nods, seemingly to herself.

"You all right?" I take her elbow.

"I think so." She smooths her dress down. "I mean, this is what we've been waiting for, right? Your realm. And then ..."

"Home." I tilt her chin up. "Your home."

She quirks her lips. "I know you mean *your* home."

"My home is with you." I take her hand and lead her out of the inn.

Cenet and Para stand next to their horse, Cenet's look and tone urgent as Para crosses her arms over her chest. A lover's quarrel, no doubt.

"Members of my Phalanx await us just over the border. Thorn should have supplies—everything you'll need. Gareth will keep you safe." I help Taylor onto Kyrin.

She casts a wary glance to where the unicorn had been hitched. He's gone, thankfully.

"Hang on." She grips my forearm as I climb up behind her. "Why are you saying that like you won't be there with me?"

"I will be there, but I have some business to attend to here in Timeroon first." It's not a lie. It's just that the business I speak of is me not mauling my mate.

Her grip tightens. "I can't go without you."

My mate, my heart—her need for me is the sweetest sustenance. I can live on it for the moments when we're apart.

"It will only be for a short while." I guide Kyrin down the main road, the cobblestones bathed in starlight and the glow from the buildings on either side. "Gareth, Beth, and Para will accompany you."

She stiffens. "No."

"Taylor," I purr in her ear. "I only part with you because I must. But I will catch up with you." *Hopefully not too quickly.*

"What if something happens to you?" She turns in the saddle and locks eyes with me. "Maybe you haven't noticed, but trouble seems to follow you around like a puppy. A vicious, bloodthirsty one."

"I tend to think you're the one who attracts trouble, little one." I nip at her lips.

Her lashes flutter, but then she pulls back. "Stop trying to distract me."

"What can a simple male do? You're distracting. Gorgeous, intelligent, fiery—appealing in so many ways." I let my gaze drop to her throat where her heartbeat taps against her flesh in rapid strokes.

"Stop it, mister. You aren't dodging the subject." She turns around, but she's breathless.

I want her so badly I fist my hands, then relax. "It will only be for a short while."

"Why?"

"It's for your protection." Gareth rides up next to us.

"That doesn't make sense. You and Leander go nuts whenever I'm out of your sight, so why would Leander let me wander off into the winter realm without him?"

The pearly wall between realms appears before us, a garrison of summer realm soldiers standing guard along a stone parapet set back from the shimmering magic. The barrier is thinner between two stone turrets that flank the opening on either side. The crossing.

"Holy shit." Taylor presses a palm to her face. "How is this even possible? It's *snowing* over there. Snowing!

Like, fifty feet away. I'm this close to breaking a sweat over here."

"I'm going to need a coat." Para looks down at her crimson dress. She and Cenet argued a bit more before they parted, but she seems steady now.

"Snow." Taylor shakes her head. "How?"

"Magic divided the lands in the ancient times. To maintain balance, it created the realms of summer and winter. There are other realms across Arin, night and day, spring and fall—but they're far away beyond the Ocean of Storms. I have enough troubles on this continent to worry about others, though we do have infrequent trade with them."

"That's great and all, but there's *snow!*" She points.

"I think you broke your changeling." Beth grins, but I can sense she's more than a little awed as well with the way she stares across the barrier.

I look beyond the shimmering wall. Shadows ease from the wooden structures of the small town on the winter side. They coalesce along the main road, members of the Phalanx armed to the teeth and ready to bleed for their king. Some of my tension releases. No threat can stand against them. I ignore the feral's rejoinder of "*we can.*"

"Now I must wait here." I throw a leg over Kyrin and drop to the dusty cobblestones. The soldiers are bored, most of them playing dice while others drink and carouse. Only a couple of them watch us, and they focus solely on me.

"You never said why I have to go without you." She reaches out for me.

I take her hand. I always will. "Just in case my feral gets a little too strong when I cross. I don't want to ... hurt you. You see?"

"Oh." She bites her lip, then says again more quietly, "Oh."

"Yes. It's for your safety." I squeeze her hand. "But it won't be for long."

"Do you promise?"

I close my eyes, a promise between mates being an aphrodisiac all its own. "I promise I will follow you into the winter realm and wherever you go from now on."

The zing of magic shocks between us, and her eyes open wide. "Wow."

"That's nothing." I kiss the back of her hand but dare not do more. Not when I'm this close to the winter realm, the feral howling just beneath my skin.

"Gareth." I turn to him. "She is in your care."

"I will keep her close, my king. You have nothing to worry about."

I'll worry all the same. But I've put my life in Gareth's hands more times than I can count. He won't let me down.

"I'll watch out for both of them." Beth pats Gareth on the knee. "He could use some direct supervision."

Gareth's usual scowl reappears.

Para pulls her dress closer around her throat.

I meet her gaze. "Don't worry. There will be furs aplenty once you cross. Hospitality is the way of the winter realm."

She gives me a curt nod and looks away quickly.

I still hold Taylor's hand. I have to let go. Looking up

at her, my heart constricts when I see the wetness in her eyes. I can't leave her like this.

One pull and she's in my arms, my mouth pressed to hers. The feral be damned. She wraps her arms around my neck, her feet dangling off the ground as I kiss her with all the love I possess. Her tongue searches mine, both of us lost in each other. My worries fade as I taste her sweetness, and I want this moment to last forever. But, too soon, it must end. She has to go.

When I break the kiss, the feral rakes its claws down the inside of my chest.

"Go, now, before I change my mind." I set her on Kyrin, her tears still salty on my tongue.

"Leander." She wipes her eyes and straightens her spine. My queen. "I'll see you on the other side."

"It's a deal." I slap Kyrin's flank, and he takes off through the barrier.

Gareth and the others follow, but I don't take my eyes from Taylor, not until she vanishes in a swirl of snow while surrounded by my warriors.

*T*he cold seeps through my clothes and plays along my skin with frigid fingers. A row of soldiers in silver armor line the road on either side of us. They're stationed like the ones on the other side, but they are far more formal and verge on scary. They don't look at me. Their eyes are forward, hands clasped behind their backs.

Snow coats everything, fat flakes falling all around as ice dangles like fancy earrings from nearby trees. "*Narnia,*" I whisper and rub my arms against the cold. Gareth doesn't seem bothered by it as he rides slightly ahead then stops in front of a line of fae. Four of them, each looking at me with thinly veiled curiosity.

"Who's the changeling riding Leander's horse?" A female steps forward and throws her hood back revealing close-cropped curly black hair and piercing eyes.

"Ravella, this is Taylor." Gareth dismounts, helps Beth down, then walks to me.

"Why is she on Leander's mount?" She cocks her

head at me, something like a predatory bird who's noticed a tasty bug.

I take his hand, and he lowers me to the ground. Ravella keeps her gaze on me.

Trying not to let my teeth chatter, I say, "Hi, I'm—"

"There you are!" A familiar face appears as Thorn saunters up and hands me a thick black fur. "For you, my *queen*." Then he takes a knee.

"Showboat from the Spires," Gareth gripes under his breath.

Ravella's eyes round as I fasten the toasty cloak around me.

"So much better." I rub my cheek on the soft fur. "I'm Taylor." I hold out my hand to her.

She looks at it, then immediately drops to her knee. The three fae behind her do the same.

"Don't." I wince. "You don't have to do that." I reach out, but what am I going to do? Pat her on the head? Pulling my hand back, I change tactics. "I've been looking forward to meeting all of you. Leander speaks so highly of his Phalanx."

They don't rise. I look helplessly at Gareth.

"You can offer your oaths in the morning. For now, we must get moving." He grabs the back of Thorn's shirt and yanks him up. "What else did you bring for the journey?"

"Granite is loaded with all manner of weapons, furs, food—everything." He whistles, and a dark gray horse trots out from beside one of the log cabins.

Glancing around, I assume this is what an old-school Aspen would look like—a street of cabins, wood smoke on the air, snow everywhere, unbelievable mountains in the background, and so many trees. After the flat expanse of the Red Plains, this place is a wonderland.

"A fated mate?" One of the males—this one with shiny black hair and dark, sparkling eyes—rises to his feet. "How? And why isn't Leander here?"

"We'll discuss it on the way, Valen. Mount up, everyone. Form a wall around Taylor. Nothing touches her."

He smiles, and he looks boyish, like maybe he isn't as old as Gareth and Leander. "I can't believe Thorn managed to keep his blabbermouth shut about this."

"I was saving up for the big gesture." Thorn winks and pulls a small bouquet of slightly crushed lilies from inside his fur cloak. "For you, my queen." He hands them to me with a flourish.

"Um, thanks."

Gareth continues grumbling about showboats as he lifts me onto my horse, then takes the ailing flowers and tosses them over his shoulder with a harrumph. "Taylor, you already know Thorn, and that's Ravella." He points. "Valen is our healer."

The fae waves as he mounts a midnight steed.

"Hi." My voice is quiet, shyness overcoming me.

"This is Grayhail." He points to a particularly surly warrior who wields a warhammer bigger than my head. "And this one here is Branala, our alchemist." She gives me a small salute, her silver eyes marking her as a summer realm fae. How did she end up here?

"Very nice to meet all of you." I fake some confidence.

It seems to work, because they all give me a deferential nod and mount their horses.

"We're missing Brannon. He's off to Silksglade. And you met Phinelas in Blood Run."

The Catcher, right. I mentally tick him off the Phalanx list.

Gareth hands Para a fur from Thorn's stash. "And everyone, this is Para. She's a Vundi warrior who's sworn allegiance to Taylor."

Para's back is straighter than an iron rod, and she takes the openly suspicious looks from each of the fae with nothing but strength.

"Forget about me?" Beth waggles her fingers at him from her spot astride Sabre.

He tosses her a fur. "This is a changeling with a profane mouth. You may call her Beth."

"That's it?" She frowns at him as he mounts Sabre behind her.

"Phalanx, form up," he barks.

They position themselves around me as Kyrin takes off at a lazy pace.

"Faster, beast." Gareth reaches over and smacks his flank. "We need to be well into the Kingswood before sunup."

Kyrin snorts but increases his pace, carrying me into a new world—this one white, cold, and full of wonder.

I can't sit still. The inn is too confining. The air outside too warm. She's only been gone an hour, and I'm not sure how I'm going to make it till morning. But I must. For her, I must. So, I stalk around Timeroon, walking the narrow backstreets and counting the moments until I can cross into my lands. It doesn't help that the feral howls inside me, demanding I go to her, claim her, take her.

A lesser fae with a scorpion tail eyes me as I pass his leather shop for the third time. "What's winter realm garbage doing in Timeroon?"

"Only a summer realm fae would rise to your pitiful taunt." I continue on my way even though pummeling the lesser fae into the red ground doesn't seem like a particularly bad idea. Too easy, I remind myself.

I keep going for an hour more, each step adding another knot of tension to my body. When I hear rumbling along the main road, I alter my course and creep along the darkened stone buildings until I get a view of the border crossing garrison.

Captain Tavaran lines up his soldiers in front of the barrier's opening until they're four-fae deep. He's brought every warrior in Timeroon to guard the way. Why? Is there a problem?

I weigh my options and realize I have none. This is the only crossing for thousands of kilometers. I *must* go through when the sun rises.

After a quick weapons check, I stride out onto the road and head for the barrier. "Tavaran." I keep my hands at my sides. No need to draw a blade until I get a handle on what's going on. After all, this may have nothing to do with me. The feral snickers at the very suggestion.

Tavaran turns, his eyes growing beady. "It's *Captain* Tavaran. Where are your changeling companions?"

"Why?" I stop about twenty meters away and size up the small army before me.

"Where are they?" He advances, one hand on the hilt of his sword.

I turn and look around, then up, then down, then back at Tavaran. "I don't see them. Do you?"

His countenance hardens. "Queen Aurentia demands the return of the special changeling. The one who bears the soulstone." He motions to one of his soldiers. "Take ten men and turn this city upside down."

They take off, and it isn't long before I hear doors being kicked in and frightened screams. The other fae close ranks in front of the barrier.

"Well, as you can see, I don't have a changeling on

me." I move forward, trying to judge how many soldiers stand between me and the crossing. "Stand aside."

"Not a chance. Queen Aurentia's orders were clear. We are to escort the changeling back to Byrn Varyndr. You can cross, but not with her, and I'm sure you understand I can't let you go until she's found." He raises his hand, and his soldiers draw their swords. "She must not be allowed to pass to the winter realm."

"You know, Tavaran, I've never liked you."

"My heart breaks." He draws his sword and bangs the hilt against his gold armor. "An unseelie dog doesn't like me. What ever shall I do?"

His soldiers laugh. More rumbling behind me is the harbinger of additional summer realm troops. I'm trapped. But I will never break my promise to Taylor, no matter the cost. I must get through the crossing. Once I'm in my realm, the soldiers won't dare follow.

I step closer, ice crunching beneath my feet. "You summer realm fae and your insults." I shake my head. "But perhaps you're right. I *am* unseelie." A frigid wind whips my hair back, and I crack my neck.

Tavaran's confident sneer falters, and he backs up a pace.

I take another step, the ice building inside me until all I can hear is the roar of the winter wind. "But not just that." I hold out my hands, ice spiking from my fingers. "You seem to forget, I'm the unseelie *king*."

My blast of winter knocks Tavaran on his ass and sends his soldiers flying backward.

I have to go, and it has to be now. I send a prayer to

the Ancestors that Taylor is far enough away, and I launch myself toward the crossing.

"*Y*our aura." Ravella rides next to me, her hood keeping her face in shadow. "It's subdued. How did you do it?"

"I swallowed a witch's pea."

She turns her head toward me sharply, her eyes open wide. Too wide.

Oh. "Pea," I say quickly. "Like p-e-a. Not p-e-e."

Her face returns to stoic, though I can almost sense a hint of amusement in her dark eyes. "Is that where you got the obsidian blade?"

"You saw that?" I thought I'd hidden it in the folds of my dress and then under the fur.

"I see a lot of things." She glances at the forest all around us, the tall dark trees hiding the starlight as a light snow falls.

"Well, yes. Selene gave it to me. She actually pulled it off her body." I'm glad I closed my eyes when she did it, but I can still hear the sharp cracks. I shiver.

"You must have impressed her for an obsidian to grant you such a gift."

I shrug, though the thick fur muffles the movement. "I tried not to judge her, is all."

"Well, you weren't eaten, so I say that's a win."

"So, do you have any magic?" I shake my head. "Sorry, was that rude? I know I'm not supposed to ask if people are mated, but can I ask about magic?"

"You can ask me anything." Her frank tone backs up her assertion. "And yes, I have magic. I'm a mystic."

"What's a mystic?"

"I can travel through the vale, read auras, do a few other handy tricks."

"What's the vale?" I feel like a child with all my questions, but Ravella doesn't seem to mind.

"Think of it like the world behind this world, or perhaps more like a mirror of it. I can travel there, unseen. There are shortcuts, and sometimes there are other creatures or wisps of knowledge."

"Sounds like the otherworld."

"You've been to the otherworld?" She eyes me, this time with a bit more curiosity.

"Once, and I'm happy to never go there again."

"Interesting." She hides her face in the shadow of her cloak again.

Awkward moments pass until I'm compelled to press my palms to my frigid face. "Does it ever get warm here?"

She laughs, quiet and lovely. "You'll get used to it."

A thought strikes me. "How do you grow food?"

"Hmm?"

"We made a deal with the Vundi to trade goods with

them, provide food. But if it's forever winter, how do you grow anything?"

"We're a hardy people. Excellent hunters." She smiles, a hint of pride in her profile. "But some of us are rather ingenious, as well. When we get to Cold Comfort, you'll see most buildings there have a greenhouse atop them. And if you venture to the east and into the Aurora Fields, you'd find long stretches of fields and crops, all safe and warm inside stone walls with latticed wooden roofs. We burrowed deep beneath the frozen surface to create vents of heat from the depths of Arin. Not even the hoarfrost can touch the plants we tend there."

"Geothermal energy. Wow." Here I was thinking it was all barbarians and nothing to eat but snowcones. "That's pretty advanced."

"We feed our people. It isn't always easy, and there are lean times, but ever since Leander became king we've made huge leaps in just about every area." She shrugs. "But it will always be cold."

"As long as there's plenty of furs and fire, then I think I—"

A howl pierces the night air, and an electric tingle runs up my spine. "What was that?"

A frosty wind picks up, swirling the snow around us, and the flakes fall heavier.

"What—"

"You must go. Now." Gareth rides up next to me, his face pinched.

"What is it?"

"Leander is through the barrier. He's here, and he's out of control."

Beth wrinkles her nose. "How do you know he's—"

The howl rips through the night again, and my insides turn molten. Is this fur hot?

"That's how." Gareth leans over and checks my grip on Kyrin's reins. "It's his feral."

"Like separate from him? Like Delantis?"

"Yes. We'll try to hold him off. But you must ride swiftly. Stick to the road, Kyrin. You know the way." Gareth, satisfied with my hold, rears back and slaps Kyrin's flank. "Fly!" he cries as Kyrin takes off, his hoofbeats muffled on powdery snow as I lean forward. I hold on, my eyes stinging from the cold wind.

The howl is closer this time, the sound sending tingles through me until I'm panting as hard as Kyrin. Trees blur past as the snow falls harder, the wind like a tangible fist pushing us back. We run and run, the landscape hilly and full of trees. Eventually, Kyrin slows, his breath coming out in steamy bursts.

"It's okay." I run my hand down his mane. "It'll be okay."

The wind forms a white funnel ahead of us, and Kyrin halts. I'm not afraid. Not of winter. Not of my mate.

"It's him." I can feel it down to my toes. "He's come for me." Holding onto the saddle, I slide down Kyrin's side, and my feet hit the snow with a soft crunch.

"Leander." I step toward the funnel of wind and snow.

The vortex dissipates, and I see him. The feral. A huge white wolf—bigger than Kyrin—with ice blue eyes. It rears back and howls, the sound burning me up. I push the fur cloak off my shoulders, and when the wind wraps around me, I can feel its cool fingers sliding along my skin.

The wolf approaches, and through the snow, I see another shape. Leander, his chest bare and his gaze fixed on me.

"I warned you, little one." He stalks closer as the wolf circles me. His fangs are long, the tips impossibly sharp.

I swallow hard and clench my thighs together. "I know."

"Waiting for you has been the sweetest agony of my life." He reaches me and presses his cool palm to my hot cheek. "And I can wait no longer." The wolf howls its agreement, and I can't seem to catch my breath. Hot, so hot. Leander's hand snakes around my neck, cooling my overheated skin, and his mouth meets mine in a bruising kiss that rocks me off my feet.

He swoops me up with one arm and crushes me to him, his possession complete. I open my mouth as he ravages me with his tongue, teasing and taking as I hold onto him and the vortex forms around us. Snow and ice spin and dance as we kiss, and I feel his claim on me, seared into my heart and written on my soul.

Pulling back, he strokes my cheek. The wolf is gone, and I can sense it inside him. His low voice is almost guttural. "I want you, Taylor. All of you."

His dark eyes sparkle in the night, and ice sits atop his head like a crown. He is the winter, the bite of frost and the crackle of ice, but I've never been warmer in all my life.

"I want you." I kiss him softly. "I feel it, too." The

connection I've been denying for so long roars to life inside me. "Please, Leander."

"I can never deny you, my queen. My heart." He kisses me again, his fangs grazing my lips as he lies me down on my fur cloak. "But I cannot be gentle. Not with this claiming." He swipes my hair from my neck and kisses along my throat. "I must mark you so that every male knows you belong to me, to the king of winter, to the one who will bring their death if they dare harm you." He reaches down and hikes my dress up.

When his fingertips delve into my panties and stroke my sensitive spot, my back arches. "Wet for me, little one." He kisses my chest, then moves down my body. With a yank, he rips my panties away. The low growl that rumbles through his chest sets me alight, and I moan when he presses my thighs apart with his big palms.

"Perfect." He kisses me.

I jolt, but he holds my hips and presses his face against me. His tongue moves along my flesh, tasting every bit of me before swirling around my clit. I grip the silky fur as he delves lower and presses his tongue inside me.

"Leander!" I gasp and writhe, my core tightening with each move he makes.

He moves back up, his tongue committing delicious sins against me as I moan and clutch at his hair. This is what it means to be devoured. My breath hitches, and my hips lock, my legs spread wide. He laves me with the broad side of his tongue, then focuses on my clit again. I can't stop the tension, the heat. I cry his name as I shatter under the stars and the snow. He growls against my skin as I fall again and again into the bliss he's giving me. I pull his hair as my back arches again, my body under his command as he pulls aftershocks from me.

When he prowls back up my body, he licks his lips. "Your taste is honey on my tongue, little one."

"Oh my god." Greedy for more, I lift my hips to him.

He smirks, cold and feral but also scorching hot. "My mate must have what she wants." He grips the front of my dress and with total ease, tears it down the middle.

Chest to chest, he takes my mouth again, sharing my taste with me as he cups a breast with one hand. His thumb rakes over my hard nipple, and I squirm under his touch. He does it again and again, sending shockwaves through me that all end between my thighs. I can feel how wet I am, but I'm too far gone to care.

He kisses to my neck, nibbling below my ear. I dig my nails into his shoulders, unable to keep my passion inside. He throws his head back and howls, and I lean up and bite his chest. With another growl, he grips my hair and holds me in place as he kisses to my breasts.

So much sensation rushes through me, and I wonder if I can survive this. When he claims one hard nipple in his mouth, I cry out. A deep purr rumbles through him as he licks and sucks each breast until I'm panting again, my body desperate for more. When he returns to my throat, heat coils inside me as his hard length presses against my thigh.

"I can wait no longer, my mate." He sits back and reaches down to his pants.

"I want to do it." I sit up and press kisses to his bare chest, the skin warm despite the maelstrom of ice swirling around us. My touches are tentative at first, but when I brush my tongue over his nipple, he grips my hair, pulling me closer and urging me on. I nip at his abs as I slide lower along his taut body. Gripping his pants, I tug at the leather tie. With confidence borne of sheer desire, I pull them down.

He takes my hand and guides it to him, wrapping my fingers around his thick shaft as I stare at it. "The way you look at me, little one. I can feel what you want."

He guides my hand up and down along the smooth, hard skin. A small bead of wetness appears on the tip, and I lean down, dabbing it with my tongue. His grip on my hair tightens as I give it another taste and run my tongue along his head. When his hips jerk forward, I feel powerful, in control, and more than anything, desperately ready for the rest of him.

"You tease me." He pushes me back and prowls on top of me, his mouth taking mine again as he presses between my thighs, rubbing up and down along my wetness. Each time he grazes my clit, my need for him grows. He knows it, too, because he speeds his pace, his head hitting me just right as his tongue masters mine.

I spread my legs wider and hold onto his shoulders.

"My mate." He stares down at me as he lines up at my entrance. "I prayed for you for so long." His hungry eyes fill with a tenderness that takes me by surprise. "You are so much more than I ever dreamed."

I lean up and kiss him, sharing my breath, my soul, my love. "I've wished for you too." Lying back, I hold his gaze. "Take me."

The tenderness falls away, and the feral takes over,

pure desire lighting his eyes and setting my pulse on a reckless course. I want all of it. All of him.

"Mine," he growls.

With a hard shove, he seats himself inside me. The link between us snaps tight, and a rush of emotion crashes into me. Wonder, need, and love—all of them so intense that I can't catch my breath. And then I realize these are *Leander's* emotions. At the same time, I *know* I'm his and he is mine. And then? The pleasure that floods me is like a supernova. Our joining heightens everything—my senses, the feel of him against me, the love that blossoms in my heart.

I arch against him, my breasts pressing into his hard chest as I claw down his back. Pulling out, he pushes in again. I expect more pain, but all I feel is a slight pinch and the incredible sensation of fullness.

"Leander." I move my hips, and he growls against my skin. "Please." I don't know what I'm asking for. I just know I want more.

"My perfect mate. Give me everything." He starts a rhythm, his body contracting and surging forward as I take everything he gives me. He claims my mouth again, his tongue working in tandem with the rest of him, taking and filling me as I open myself to him. He groans and pushes harder, faster, his body owning mine as the snow intensifies around us.

I close my eyes, and focus on his touch, but he nips at my lip. "Open your eyes, little one. I want to see you come apart for me."

I meet his dark gaze, my insides molten and my core tightening with each stroke. His fangs seem to lengthen even more, the tips lethal. Why does that make me hotter? I lean up and lick one. He growls and kisses me, tasting the hint of blood from my tongue. With an animal roar, he thrusts harder, and I hang on, my nails digging into his back as I give myself over to him.

Each impact hits me just right, sending me higher. And when he stays deep and grinds against me, I think I might lose my mind.

"I can feel you clenching me, begging for my seed." He holds my gaze as he pumps his hips, and my legs begin to shake. "I will give you what you want, little one. I will coat you in me so that no other male will ever doubt who you belong to. Would you like that?" His low voice is gravelly, sex in a sound.

"Yes." I shudder, my heels digging into the backs of his thighs.

"Mine, little one. You're mine forever. Say it." He grinds against me, stealing every bit of thought until I run on nothing more than animal instinct.

"I'm yours, forever."

"Promise me." He runs his lips along my jaw.

I already know it's true, the bond between us unbreakable. "I promise."

"I love you, Taylor. My mate. My queen. And I will be yours forever. I promise."

The sting of magic ripples across my body, and he thrusts hard and deep, then sinks his fangs into my shoulder.

I come so hard that my vision goes black for a moment. Everything inside me falls apart, pleasure shooting through me like fireworks across a dark sky. The bliss comes in waves, rolling over me and drowning me in the most perfect sensations—release coated in love and sealed with completion. I hold onto Leander as he thrusts again. His body tenses even more, and he roars against my skin as he comes, his hot seed filling me as my body is caught in the delicious throes of ecstasy. He doesn't release his hold on my shoulder, his fangs marking me so deeply that I can feel his claim on my soul. His pleasure filters through me, and I feel his love as it dances and entwines with mine.

When the orgasm slows and only pleasant echoes remain, I relax, my arms falling to my sides. I gulp in the chilly air and try to calm my rampaging heart.

He gingerly releases his bite, and I can't be bothered to care about the hint of pain. Staring down at me, his mouth twists into a satisfied smile, my blood lingering on his lips. Why is that hot? It shouldn't be. But it is.

"Mine." He kisses me gently.

"Mine." I lean up and bite his bottom lip.

His answering growl turns me to mush. He pushes me back down onto the fur and kisses me into a stupor all over again as the snow swirls, the icy wind blows, and I give my heart away—all at the king of winter's command.

17

———

LEANDER

"More?" I offer Taylor another snowberry.

"I'm stuffed." She snuggles down in our furs as a roaring fire crackles nearby.

"Just one more?" I wave it in front of her plump lips, bruised from my kisses.

"You are always trying to fatten me up." She opens her mouth, and I slide the berry onto her waiting tongue.

"I must provide for my mate." I watch as she chews, and my gaze travels to the bite at her shoulder. It's still red, the skin angry, but my mark will never be questioned. She is mine as I am hers.

"You're a giant wolf." Her eyes drift closed.

"At least I'm not a unicorn, right?" I kiss her forehead.

Her nose wrinkles. "Ugh."

"So you like the wolf?"

"I love him." The wrinkles flatten out. "I think I'll keep him."

I kiss her, the snowberry tart and Taylor sweet. Claiming her again is on my mind, but as it was her first time, I know I must give her time to recover. Surely, no more than an hour at most. I run my fingers along her pink cheek as she falls asleep. I can feel her slumber through the bond, the quieting of her mind. It's so much stronger now, and I only hope it grows more so each day.

Gareth and the others are gathered by the fire, and they sneak glances at us every so often. I can't blame them. Beth has been complaining loudly about missing the mating ever since we made camp.

I rise quietly and steal over to them.

Gareth stands and joins forearms with me. "Congratulations."

I can't keep the smile from my face, the pride impossible to hide. "She is everything I ever hoped for."

"I'll drink to that." Ravella raises her cup, and the others follow suit. "To our queen."

I grab a cup of wine and join them. "To Taylor."

We drain our cups.

"You marked the ever-loving Spires out of her," Thorn says appreciatively.

"No male will mistake that mark." Valen nods.

"I can't believe I missed it." Beth drops her head into her hands.

Valen pats her on the back. "Maybe you'll catch the next one?"

Gareth lets out a low, barely-audible growl.

"Whoa." Ravella turns to him, her eyes narrow. "What was that for?"

Valen withdraws his hand and gives Gareth a knowing smile. "I have an idea."

"What?" Beth looks around, baffled, as if expecting a wraith to come swooping out of the trees. "What is it?"

Gareth grumbles and pours himself another drink. I hide my smirk in my cup.

"Does this mean the curse is broken for all of the winter realm?" Branala ignores the tension.

"I don't know." I run a hand through my hair. "Do any of you feel the bond?"

"No." Valen shrugs. "But maybe our mates are elsewhere."

"Could be. Have you had any reports of mates in Cold Comfort?" I keep Taylor in my view as she slumbers.

Branala frowns and tosses the remains of her wine into the fire. "No."

"Has anyone heard from Brannon?" I need a rundown of everything that happened while I was away, but I'll settle for the highlights. Finding out what happened to Yvarra is paramount—because she deserves justice and because her death is linked to the king beyond the mountain.

"He's gone quiet. Set out for Silksglade as soon as I gave him your orders. Haven't heard anything, but that doesn't mean he hasn't decimated the entire town by now." Thorn stands and stretches.

"He wouldn't do that." Branala scowls. "You never give him a chance."

"A chance to knife me in the back? No thanks."

"That's enough, Thorn." I'm not having this argument again, especially not on the night of my mating.

"The sun will be up soon. I intend to make good time to High Mountain. There is much to do."

"You mean the mating ceremony?" Ravella asks.

"Yes." My heart jumps at the thought of presenting Taylor to the winter realm. "But we have other troubles. Queen Aurentia sent Tavaran to stop me at the border. And he was looking for Taylor in particular. I had to fight my way out."

"Why?" Gareth stands and crosses his arms. "She let us go, let Taylor leave Byrn Varyndr without objection."

I shake my head. "I suppose she changed her mind. I don't know the reason, but I intend to find out."

"Raising arms against you could be considered an act of war." Thorn peers into the fire. "One that would start conflict all over again."

"We won't let it. I can't let the realms fall into ruin and infighting again. I just need time to figure out why she—" The winter wind whispers to me, telling secrets from the border.

"What?" Gareth tenses, and one hand goes to his sword hilt. "What is it?"

"The summer realm soldiers have crossed the barrier. They're engaging our guards and pouring into our lands." My hackles rise with each word the wind imparts. "There's already been blood shed on both sides."

"What is this madness? The queen can't have sanctioned such a break." Ravella rubs her temples.

"This has to be some mistake. But it doesn't matter. I can't let it stand. I have to get to the border, try and stop this skirmish before it goes any further."

"I'm with you." Gareth turns toward Sabre.

"No. Gareth, Para, and Beth, stay with Taylor. Thorn, Ravella, Grayhail, Valen, you're with me. Branala, make haste to Cold Comfort and stop any rumors about this incursion before they begin. We have to solve this before the old hatreds reignite."

"I can't stay behind." Gareth swears with a vehemence.

"You must. The rest of you, go." The ring of command is back in my voice, the tones of war.

Thorn takes off at a run and changes into his owl form, Ravella fades, travelling through the vale to reach the crossing, while Branala, Grayhail, and Valen mount their horses and gallop into the night.

"What's happening?" Taylor clutches my fur around her shoulders and runs to me. "Where is everyone going?"

"Something's wrong. The summer realm is invading our border." I pull her to me and kiss her forehead. "I must go and defend our realm. Stop this before it gets started."

"No. Don't go." She clutches me to her.

"I must." I stroke her soft cheek. "These are your lands now, just as much as they are mine. And we must defend them."

Her bottom lip quivers. "Please be safe."

My heart aches as her worry resonates down the bond. "I will come back for you, little one."

"Promise?" The fear in her eyes is almost too much to bear.

"Always." I kiss her hard and fierce, the promise sealed between us.

"Take care of her." I pin Gareth with a hard look.

"On my life." He draws his sword and directs Beth and Para to break camp. "We ride for High Mountain."

"Be careful." Taylor cups my cheeks and pulls me down to her. "I can't lose you. Not now." She kisses me again, and it takes every strand of willpower I have to pull myself away.

"I love you, little one." I back away and call the winter wind to my aid. It swirls around me and lifts me off the ground, carrying me over the trees and toward the Timeroon crossing where fae blood already stains the snow.

J think my mouth hangs open for a good thirty seconds as Leander disappears into the sky that lightens with the coming sunrise. "So, he can fly?"

"He can command the cold winds, yes." Gareth throws the rest of our supplies across Sabre's back. "You'll find there isn't much Leander can't do in the winter realm."

"Did I say 'wow' yet? Because, wow." My amazement is tempered by the fact that he's headed straight for a bloody conflict. "Why is Aurentia doing this?" I help Beth gather her fur around her shoulders.

Gareth leads her to Sabre and helps her up. "No way to know. But we have to stop them before the rest of the winter realm finds out. Because if we haven't beaten them back by then, it will be all out war." He motions me to Kyrin. "Come, we must hurry."

I take his hand and he helps me up. "Ready." I cast a glance back the way we came, back to where Leander is fighting, and a shard of worry spears my heart. I can still feel him, the tether between us tightening and thinning the farther away he is. But he's there, and I don't feel fear, only strength. "He's going to be okay," I reassure myself. "He'll straighten out this mess with Aurentia, and we are all going to be fine."

Gareth lets out a pained cry and keels forward in front of Kyrin.

"I'm afraid not." Para pulls her knife from Gareth's back and grabs Kyrin's reins.

"Gareth!" I scream, my insides twisting as his blood turns the snow crimson.

Beth scrambles off Sabre and runs toward Gareth as I climb from Kyrin.

"What are you doing?" I pull the obsidian blade from my fur and hold it out. "You swore allegiance to me!"

"I did." She wipes at her nose as blood drips from it. "And I will pay for breaking my oath."

Cenet creeps from the trees behind her, his face hard, his eyes on me, and his sword drawn.

"Why?" I keep my blade up even as Cenet advances. "Why?" I demand.

Beth screams and cradles Gareth's head in her hands.

"I already made another deal. Before I met you. Before—" Para drops to her knees, blood spilling from her eyes, nose, and mouth as her oath breaks. Regret coats her words. "There was no going back. There never has been. Not for me."

Cenet advances into camp, his steps sure, his demeanor triumphant.

Para gasps, her silver eyes darkening. She blinks as they go gray and then black. "I'm sorry, Taylor. I'm sor—"

Cenet strikes Para, taking off her head in one stroke, and then he stalks to me. "Your father would like a word."

I swing the obsidian blade at him, but all I hear is his hissed command – "Sleep, princess."

I drop to my knees in the cold snow, and darkness falls as the sun rises.

BEYOND THE MOUNTAIN

FAE'S CAPTIVE BOOK 4

1

*S*omeone is crying.

I blink my eyes open and find I'm sitting at a long, dark table, my arms bound to a chair, though I see no rope. A cavern soars above me, the roof covered in icy stalactites. I shiver as a cool wind whips by. Turning my head, I see the cave is open on one side. A dark sky glowers beyond the opening, and a wizened, leafless tree grows in the very center of the cavern, its black roots oozing along the stone floor.

The sniffle comes again, but I can't see anyone. Where am I? The last thing I remember—Gareth bleeding on the ground, Para's death. Klaxons blare in my mind. I have to get to Gareth. He needs help. I struggle to pull myself free, but my wrists don't budge.

"No use." The voice comes from above.

I twist around and peer up between the stalactites. A gasp whooshes out of me. "Cecile!"

She hangs upside down, her long, golden hair flowing, and her hands bound. Someone else hangs beside her, and a creeping sensation tiptoes through my gut as she spins slowly from the chain attached to her ankles. Her arms hang limp, eyes closed—my eyes, my everything—it's the girl who looked like me. It *is* me. My mind spins a little, vertigo and nausea rocketing through me.

"Where are we?" I stare up at Cecile as she rotates.

"Gray Mountains. May as well be the Spires."

"You *are* fae." I knew it.

"Of course I am." She takes the same snotty tone I've heard so many times. It's like resting bitch face, but in her voice.

"Why did you send me here? Who is the one that looks like me? Why are we in the Gray Mountains? *What is going on?*" I run out of breath on the last question and try to swallow my rising panic.

"Why are we here, you ask?" She cranes her neck back so she can glare at me. "We're here, Taylor, because you're a screwup. You had *one job*. ONE JOB. Serve my father as his changeling slave. But could you do that? No. You fucked that up right out of the gate and—"

"Your father?" I shake my head. "Tyrios was your father?"

Her now-silver eyes narrow. "What do you mean by 'was'?"

She doesn't know he's dead. This is an 'oh, shit' moment buried inside another 'oh, shit' moment all tied with a 'we're screwed' bow.

"*Leander!*" I scream in my mind, but the link between us seems almost severed, a dead end where there was a vibrant highway before. What could make the bond feel this way? Is he ... I can't think about that. Leander is strong. He's fine. But if I can't escape this cave, I won't be.

"Your father doesn't matter. We need to get out of here." Something tickles across my consciousness, echoing the word 'father' back to me. What had Cenet said to me before he put me to sleep?

"*We need to get out of here,*" Cecile mimics my voice. Poorly. "You think?" She rattles the chains at her wrists. "This is iron. My skin is on fire, I'm upside down, and you are saying stupid things as usual. And all of this is your fault. Do you have any idea what sort of trouble you've caused me? I'm supposed to be partying with the ..." She blathers on.

I grit my teeth. I took her crap for far too long back on earth. But now? Now, things are different.

"Cecile!" I snap. "Shut your mouth for once in your life and listen."

She stops talking, her mouth hanging open.

"We need to get gone before someone comes. I'm pretty sure we aren't going to make it out of here in one piece if we don't escape. So, unless you want to be torn apart, tortured, or straight-up sent to the Spires, why don't you pull your head out of your ass and work on getting free?"

She blinks, her expression so surprised it's as if I've slapped her. And I suppose I have. No one talks to Cecile that way. At least, no one did. Oh boy, the times, they are a-changing.

The more she gawks at me, the higher my anger rises. "And how *dare* you blame me? You're the reason I'm here in the first place. Why? Why the hell did you send me here?"

She glances at the other me, her eyes softening just a bit. Just enough for me to understand.

"For her?" I look up at me, I mean *her*, a bruise on her forehead and her skin pale.

"She's my friend." Cecile's voice is almost a whisper now, and there's a tremor in it. Before, she was running on empty bravado. But now I see her clearly. She's afraid. But not for herself. For my twin. "The only friend I've ever had. She was stuck here with my father." She swallows hard, and I suspect she knows just what sort of fae her father was. "And he sent me to earth to keep us separated. But then I saw a chance to make the exchange between you two, so I took it."

More questions surface, but we don't have time. Not now. When we get out of here, I intend to sit her down and ask her everything.

I try to twist my wrists out of their invisible shackles even though it causes Leander's bite on my shoulder to ache and burn. A frustrated cry rips from me, and I have to force myself to stop fighting. I need to think. What tools do I have? I glance up at Cecile again, her long hair hiding her face. "Let's focus on blowing this taco stand, okay? What sort of powers do you have?"

"I don't have magic," she says quietly.

"No talents, no nothing?"

"I have a talent, but it won't help."

"Why? What is it?"

She shrugs. "I can ... keep things alive."

"Huh?"

"You know that plant you brought home from the greenhouse and put on our windowsill?"

"Yeah." I have a green thumb. That little houseplant flourished under my care.

"It would have died ten times over if I didn't save it."

"That's not true." Pride, thou art gravely wounded. "I'm great with plants."

"Maybe, but you aren't great with paying attention to plants when you're busy doing your nerd stuff. You didn't water it and left it to bake in the windowsill." She shakes her head, her hair flying. "But I kept it going just for fun. Or really, just to troll you into thinking you were any good at houseplants."

"So you can heal, too?"

"No. It's just a talent, something small I can do. It's not infused with full magic, not powerful enough to work on much more than that small plant."

"Look, not to brag, but I just saved the Vundi's entire farming system, so maybe it wasn't your magic that—"

"Stow it." Her petulance is back in full force. "Accept I'm better than you at plants, and everything else, and get me down from here."

I grumble a few choice words about the clearly lying louse hanging above me, then ask, "What about the other me? What is she? Does she have powers?"

"She's a human. No powers."

"A human?" I never considered for a moment that my creepy twin was a human like me.

"How did you get here?" I glance around, but no one else is in the cave. Just the three of us. Not even a guard.

If only we could get free, we could disappear right out of the cave entrance.

"Someone came for us through the ley lines. I was in our dorm room with Taylor, and someone knocked at the door. I opened it, and saw a lesser fae that looked kind of rough, I guess? He had snake eyes."

"Crimson clothes? Scales?"

"Yes."

"Cenet. He's a Vundi warrior."

"I tried to slam the door on him, but I ... I think I fell asleep."

"He's pulled that crap on me twice. I'm kind of over it." I strain so hard I think I'm going to dislocate my elbow and rip my shoulder open. Nothing. "Have you seen anyone?"

"No." She kicks her leg a little so she spins around. "Taylor!"

"What?"

"Not you." She wriggles again. "The real Taylor."

I watch as she tries to face the other me. "I am the real Taylor."

"I mean *my* Taylor!" she snipes, but then her tone softens. "Wake up. Come on, wake up. You're scaring me."

Oh, god, what if I'm dead?

I put one hand to my face. *What if the other me is dead? Also, how am I touching my face?*

I squeak and rocket up out of the chair. "I'm free!"

"How?" Cecile spins back to face me.

"I don't know." I feel my wrists.

"Get us down!" She wobbles with excitement.

"Okay, let me think." They're hanging at least ten feet over my head. How in the hell do I reach them? "I'm going to find a ladder or something."

"A ladder?" Cecile grips her hair with her chained hands and pulls it out of the way. "You seriously think there's a ladder in here?"

"I don't know, but your tone isn't helping your cause." I scoot along the edge of the table and peer into the dark recesses at the back of the cavern. Nope. Not going into the pitch black. "They got you up there somehow, right? Let me look around." I head toward the opening that leads out into the night.

"Don't leave us," Cecile hisses.

"I'm not leaving you. *Even though you sent me to a scary fae world where I was held captive in a dungeon, almost eaten by an obsidian witch, and kidnapped by a Vundi sandman,* but that's neither here nor there, is it?"

She lets her hair drop, hiding her face from me again.

I turn my back on her and pick my way through the white stalagmites that jut up from the stone floor. Giving the tree a wide berth, I move faster, though I keep glancing around as though someone might run out and bust me. But the place is barren. Who captures three people and just sticks them in an empty cave? Doesn't matter, because I intend to get us out of here.

Creeping to the edge of the cave opening, I stop and peer over. It's a sheer cliff. Damn. And that's not even the worst part. Far below the mountain peak and along the valley floor, thousands of fires are burning. Campfires. And in the background, carried on the wind, is the unmistakable drumbeat of war. Is this what happened to the disappearing lesser fae and changelings that Leander has been searching for? Are they an army?

"What do you see?" Cecile calls.

"Nothing good. We need to go. Now." I turn and almost run into a man.

No, not a man. A tall, wiry fae with black hair, even blacker eyes, white skin, and enormous raven's wings spread out behind him.

I stumble backwards, a shriek caught in my throat.

He grabs my arm before I fall off the cliff and sets me on my feet. A chilling cold leaches from him, along with a darkness that seems to coat the air with black soot. Evil. There's no other word for this creature.

When he smiles, fear twists in my gut like a serrated blade.

He takes my hand and pulls me back into the cavern, now filled with dozens of warriors that weren't there only moments ago. *What the—*

Cenet stands at the fore, the snake scales along his face glistening in the low light. His crimson scarf is gone, revealing a brand on his neck. It's an image of the tree in the center of the cavern.

The black fae pulls me forward, his grip unbreakable and one of his ebon wings at my back. I pull against his hold but get nowhere. As he leads me into the unrelenting darkness at the rear of the cavern, he says, "It's about time we got to know each other, Daughter."

*T*he snow at the border is already red with blood, my guards falling back from an over-whelming summer realm force. Grayhail and Valen are thundering this way, but they won't be here soon enough.

Ravella materializes beside me. "Ready."

I can't risk magic, not when my guards are so deeply engaged. This must be done with direct combat. "Let's go."

I draw my sword and enter the fray, slashing and battling through the golden-armored soldiers, mowing one down, and then another, and then more until my guards are able to rally and push them back.

Too much blood is spilling, the truce between winter and summer breaking right before my eyes. Our tenuous peace, gained only after centuries of fighting, lies broken on the snowy ground.

Ravella ghosts through the fight, her silver knives glinting before finding home as she weaves in and out of the vale.

Captain Tavaran swings for her but misses as she disappears and reappears behind him. Her blade is swift, but I'm swifter. I stop it with my sword before she plunges it into his neck.

"Tavaran," I roar and send a gust of winter down the ranks, one that will frost the summer fae but leave my warriors unbothered.

He spins, and Ravella darts into the fight behind me, her sneaky blades doing untold damage. Something tickles in the back of my mind, an ugly feeling that I can't place, but then it goes quiet. I focus on Tavaran, on ending the mess he's created on my doorstep.

"You've broken the truce!" I send spikes of ice shooting up from the ground, caging him in.

He swings, but his sword glances off the slick surface. The spikes build and join until he's caged in an icy prison.

Thorn charges by in bear form and tackles the nearest summer soldier.

"Give us the changeling." Tavaran rams his armored elbow against the bars. Bits of ice crack along the surface, but they don't break.

"Never." I raise my sword. "It would be so easy to kill you now. To freeze your heart and shatter you. To simply ram my blade through you. Call off your soldiers, or I will end you here and now."

He scowls, his silver eyes hardening.

Fool. I could destroy them all. But I am not my predecessor.

I try to calm the vengeance in my blood, the frigid rage this invasion has pulled to the surface. I can't give up our hard-won peace so quickly, despite the fact that summer has committed a grave sin against us. I speak as earnestly as I can. "We may yet have time to stop another war between our realms."

"You stole the changeling, killed Lord Tyrios, and fled Byrn Varyndr. If anyone's broken the truce, it's you." Tavaran's sneer is trying to convince me that saving them isn't worth it.

I send another spike of ice through his foot, talking over him as he howls. "Then it's war. Perhaps this time I will wipe summer off the map and claim it as my own."

"Unseelie garbage! You will—"

With an easy shove, I slide my sword through the icy cage and into his side at a joint in his armor. I'm well-acquainted with the summer realm's weaknesses, though I'm surprised the war taught them nothing about how to create better defenses.

Tavaran screeches and struggles to free himself. More ice forms around his neck, holding him still while I press my sword into him.

"Call. Them. Off." I won't ask him again. "You seem to have no idea how close I am to destroying all of your soldiers and sending their corpses back to Byrn Varyndr with your head perched on top of the stack." I twist the blade. "Now sound the retreat."

He grits his teeth, but I can see him cracking like the ice of a frozen lake.

"Summer, retreat!" His yell is loud enough for the nearest soldiers to hear. Word spreads quickly through the skirmish. Thorn backs away, his maw dripping with enemy blood.

"Blades of winter, let them go." I send my voice whistling down the line on a frigid breeze. "Do not follow."

The golden soldiers hesitate.

"I said retreat!" Tavaran's cry is more desperate this time, my silver blade hewing close to his liver.

The soldiers back down and flow toward the crossing, some of them carrying their wounded.

"Captain?" One approaches, a bloody slash on his face.

I tap on my sword, the pain immediately showing in Tavaran's gasp. "All soldiers must leave my lands immediately."

"Go! Retreat, I said!" Tavaran leans his forehead against his ice prison.

"But, Captain—"

I turn to him. "You only live because I allow it. Would you like me to change my mind?"

His face pales. "I—No. We will await your orders beyond the barrier, Captain." He turns tail, leaving Tavaran to his fate.

"Look upon your death!" Grayhail rides up on his mount, his warhammer held high. Valen follows close behind.

Ravella rolls her eyes and stows her blades before seeing to the nearest wounded.

Gray jumps down and rushes toward the last of the summer realm soldiers.

"Gray, they've retreated." I send a harsh wind that pushes the stragglers through the shimmering barrier.

He turns to me, disappointment in every corner of his

deep frown. "I didn't get to slay anyone." Glancing past me, his glower lightens. "But you've got one left. One for me." He strides up, and Tavaran's brows rise high as he takes in Gray's hulking body and thick warhammer.

"Valen, help the wounded." I gesture toward the fallen winter realm guards.

"On it." He kneels and begins to pull healing magic from inside him that casts a green glow on the muddied snow.

"Now, Tavaran." I cross my arms over my chest. "You're going to tell me what this is about in very specific terms."

He spits blood onto the ice. "You killed our noble and stole the changeling. I've come to retrieve her."

"Queen Aurentia sent you for Taylor?"

"Yes."

"You spoke with her?"

"No."

"Who told you to attack us?"

He cuts his gaze to Gray who is doing some practice swings behind me. One hit with his warhammer, and the ice and Tavaran would be nothing more than pulp.

"We received a message from Byrn Varyndr. It was from the queen."

"Tell me what it said."

He pauses for a moment, but another test swing by Gray loosens his lips. "It said the changeling stole a stone from the royal treasury. A soulstone she wears around her neck. And ..."

"And what?" I twist my sword. "I tire of your withholding. Spit it out, Tavaran."

"And the queen had a vision that if I allowed the changeling to reach the winter realm, the summer and winter realms would fall."

I don't like the sound of any of this. What does Taylor have to do with the realms falling? "What else?"

"Nothing else. That was it. When I learned she'd already crossed, I came to try and retrieve her. Not to start a war."

I shake my head. "Invading my lands—for whatever reason—was going to start a war. You're a military captain. You know that."

"It was that or let both our realms fall." He grunts in pain.

Unease settles in my gut, the same odd sensation I had only moments before, but stronger this time. I send out a feeler to Taylor, running a piece of my consciousness down the bond between us. But instead of sensing her on the other end, I feel nothing, as if the link has been cut. My heart goes dark, a howl echoing in my mind. *My mate.*

"Gray, keep Tavaran prisoner. Valen, heal him. Thorn, guard the crossing." I pull my sword free of Tavaran and lift off the ground on the winter wind. "Ravella, I need you back at the camp."

Gray laughs at Tavaran's agonized groan, then asks, "Where are you going?"

"My mate. Something's wrong." I don't have time to explain. Every second is precious where Taylor is concerned. The wind rushes me over the dark trees and snowy landscape as I try to reach her, to feel her beating heart and clever mind. But I can't. *Please, Ancestors, don't take her away from me. Not now.*

The camp appears just ahead, the fire down to embers and foreboding on the air. The scent of fresh blood hits me, and I howl, the feral strong within me.

"Where is she?" I yell before my feet hit the snow. Para's head lies on the ground, her body nearby, and Beth sits with Gareth cradled in her lap, his blood seeping out and staining his tunic. Worry turns into terror, filling my heart with fear for both my mate and my best friend.

Beth sobs. "He took her. Cenet. And Para stabbed Gareth in the back. He won't wake up."

Ravella appears beside me. "What the—"

"Get Valen. Now." I kneel next to Gareth and inspect his waxen face, then the wound that cuts through his gut. Ravella sends Gareth a worried look before disappearing again.

I press my hand over the bloody rip in his skin.

"Save him." Beth turns her teary eyes on me. "Use your magic. Please, save him."

"I can't." I keep pressure on the wound, using a little chill to try and slow the blood. "I don't have the gift of healing. Never have." My eyes sting as I stare down at the greatest friend I've ever had. We've been through so much. I can't let him pass to the Ancestors, not like this, not from a traitorous blade through the back.

"Someone has to save him." She strokes his white cheeks, her tears dropping like rain onto his dark hair. "Please."

"Where did Cenet go?"

She shakes her head. "He put Taylor to sleep, then

carried her off." She juts her chin to the side. "That way. But he said something when he took her. He said that her father wants to see her."

"Her *father*? That's impossible. Her father is dead. She said he died when she was a small child."

"I don't know." Her voice crackles as more tears well. "That's what he said. Her father. I don't know any more than that. Except." She blinks the tears free so they roll down her cheeks. "Except I saw him. Without the Vundi scarf. And he had a symbol on his neck. It was a—"

"Twisted tree?" I grit my teeth.

"Yes." She sniffles. "How did you know?"

I lean my head back and roar to the rising sun, my despair and anger mingling into one vicious sound that shakes the trees and promises swift vengeance on the king beyond the mountain.

*T*he scary fae doesn't release his grip on my arm as I stumble into the pitch blackness at the back of the cave. Leading me through an arch, he turns to the right and winds deeper into the rock.

"You're the king beyond the mountain." My words barely make it into sound, and my hands and feet are like ice.

"I'm the king. Yes." His tone is even, his voice deep but silky.

"I'm not your daughter," I blurt.

He laughs. My skin crawls.

"Come now, Taylor. Are you trying to hurt my feelings?" Taunting and ugly, the words wrap around my throat, constricting it. "Of course I'm your father. That mating mark on your shoulder doesn't change anything. The pretender on the winter throne doesn't have a claim on you. Not like I do. We're blood, after all. Besides, don't you like being a princess?"

"My father died." I cringe when his wing brushes against my back. "And I'm not a princess."

"You had a human on earth who thought he was your father." He leads me into another cavern, this one decorated like a swank house that's fallen into disrepair. Guards stand along the walls, but there's something wrong with them. I look at the nearest one, but he doesn't look back. He can't. His eyes are white, covered over with some sort of cataract. Where there should be a nose, there's only a gaping hole, and I can see his yellow teeth through his cheek. When his head turns toward me, I jerk back.

"Dead." I clutch the stone at my throat as I look down the row of guards, each one rotting and grotesque. "They're dead, aren't they?"

"The dead can be quite useful." The black fae leads me deeper into the room even though everything inside me is screaming that I should run. A huge fire burns to the right, the jumping flames a deep purple. He leads me up wide, stone stairs. A white throne comes into view at the top. No, not simply white.

I stop. "Is that bone?" Delantis's words bubble up in my mind. *"On wings of death, the child will glide to sit on her throne of bone."*

"You like it?" He smiles though there is no joy in it. "It's a favorite of mine, something that is as unique as it is effective."

"Yeah, it really ties the room together." I force myself to climb, because I'm afraid he'll drag me if I don't.

"Was that humor?" His dark eyes cut to me.

"N-no?" I don't know what answer the monster wants, but I'm almost certain humor isn't allowed here.

"I'm not devoid of amusement, daughter." He tsks. "When you get to know me, I think you'll find I can be quite humorous. Though I admit, my sense of humor might be a bit ... dark." He smiles with his fangs showing. They're crimson at the tips. Stained. From blood?

My steps falter, and I cry out for Leander again. As I feared, the dark fae wraps his arm around my waist and pulls me up the rest of the way.

A large black pillow rests at the foot of the throne. He sits on the bones, a set of skulls lined up behind his head, and points at the pillow. "Sit, my child, and I'll tell you a story."

I glance around, but there doesn't seem to be a way out of this. At least, not one that doesn't involve zombie guards, a host of warriors, and a pissed off, scary father-fae person.

"Sit." His voice has an edge this time, as if he isn't accustomed to asking twice.

I lower myself to the pillow, tucking my legs under me and trying my best to keep one eye on him and another on the creepy guards.

When his fingers sift through my hair, I bite back a scream.

"Long ago, there was a great king." His tone verges on dreamy. "He ruled his realm with a firm, but fair hand. The kingdom prospered. It became so great that its neighbor grew jealous. This neighbor, you see, believed theirs was the *better* realm. Warm, fertile, filled with prattling, simpering nobles who doused themselves in jewels and pretended they were gods."

"The summer realm," I offer.

His jaw ticks. "Do *not* interrupt me."

Sorry, psycho.

"This realm of foolishness thought they were better. They roused their citizens against the good king with words like 'unseelie' and 'dark magic' and 'evil.' So, the king went to war for his people. He fought with honor and bravery." He grasps my hair tighter, twining it between his fingers until my eyes water. "But there was a traitor in his midst. A fae who thought he could be king. The traitor raised a rebellion and challenged the good king for his throne. Through treachery and deceit, the pretender slayed the king and left his body on the battlefield."

He's talking about Leander. Has to be. Leander killed Shathinor, the former king.

"But the pretender didn't know everything." A smile cracks across his lips, ugly and smug. "And he should never have left the body of a necromancer to rot." He pulls open his black shirt.

I pin my lips together to hold in the scream. His guards aren't the only undead in this place. The scary fae is disintegrating, his rib bones exposed and his heart beating beneath a layer of damaged white flesh.

"Shathinor. You're him." When I try to scoot away, he takes a fistful of my hair. "Let me go." I grip his wrist but pull my hand away quickly. Something moved beneath his skin when I touched him. No, it *slithered*.

"I'm not done with my story." His tone is as gentle as

his touch is brutal. "Before I was betrayed, I carried on an affair with a summer realm noble. She fed me information to aid my war efforts, and I promised to make her queen of the summer realm." He shakes his head. "I wouldn't have, of course. Callandra was far too weak, proven by the fact that the great fool Tyrios was her mate."

His story has familiar threads that weave a tapestry of my memories. "Tyrios—Cecile's father."

"Yes. I hear the pretender to my throne slew him." He loosens his grip and strokes my hair again. "But you already know that, don't you, dear heart?"

I cringe at the term of endearment. "Yes," I answer quietly. "I was there."

"What *I* didn't know, because that whore Callandra never told me, was that she bore a child during the long war. *My* child. And hid her away in the summer realm."

Prickles race up my back like a thousand needle sticks. I don't want him to go on. The promise of doom grows as he speaks, and I don't know if I can handle what else he has to say. I turn to my mate, the only one who was able to defeat the evil creature that now holds me captive. *Leander, please! I'm in a cave on a mountain. Shathinor is alive. Please, come get me!* I scream in my mind, but it's like speaking underwater; the sound doesn't go anywhere, and I feel like I'm on the verge of drowning.

Shathinor's gaze slides to my throat. "This child was protected by a soulstone, one that Callandra stole from Queen Aurentia's treasury. A powerful artifact, the soulstone kept the child alive, but asleep, and hidden in the summer realm. There you slumbered, just as I slumbered under the muck of a battlefield, the worms my company as I slowly rebuilt the shards of my soul."

I shake my head. "I was born in Indiana. I have a whole life—"

"You have nothing but me, my child." His sharp snarl echoes off the barren walls. "You and I are everlasting, and we will always be together from this day forth." His tone softens, and something verging on actual warmth seeps into his words and multiplies my goosebumps. "I would have found you sooner, but Callandra sent you to earth as an exchange. I don't know why she chose to do so twenty-one years ago. Perhaps you were fading? Perhaps it was because Cecile came of age during that time?" He shrugs and continues running his cold fingers along my scalp. "Callandra went to the Ancestors soon after. I didn't know about you until you returned to Arin. Callandra hid you too well. The soulstone you bear, it disguised you from everyone but me. Blood calls to blood."

"That's not true." I clasp the stone in my hand. "I have a mother and father on earth—"

"Every changeling does," he chides. "And you were no different, but then again, you were completely different, weren't you? No friends, a distant mother, no other family, no one to care about, and no one who cared about you."

"I had friends." My protest is admittedly weak.

"And then you came home," he continues as if I hadn't spoken. "I didn't understand the why of your return until I questioned Cecile and the human version of you. Cecile wouldn't tell me at first. I must admit I had a good laugh when she cried as I tortured her *friend*." His tone turns teacherly. "Because humans are pets, my dear one. Not friends. Certainly not equals. But Cecile is a tender-hearted fool like her mother. Or, I suppose I should also say, like *your* mother."

"My mother." I can't contain the confusion, the utter shock that rocks through my mind like aftershocks that don't seem to end. "If Callandra is my mother, that would make Cecile my sister?"

He taps the tip of my nose. "Correct. Cecile didn't realize you were sisters. She only knew her mother instructed her to come to earth and find you once you'd aged twenty years. I suppose Callandra believed you two would hit it off. But her blood doesn't call to you, not like mine. You are a child of darkness and cold winter winds. When Cecile sent you to Arin so she could have her human pet with her on earth? I *felt* you arrive. Finally, an heir of worth." He strokes my cheek, and I have to fight my gag reflex. "My only daughter."

None of this is true. Is it? It can't be. My breathing comes too quickly, my lungs aching. I want to run as far and as fast as I can, but I'm frozen to this spot, locked to this impossible story told by the scariest creature I've ever encountered. "I'm human," I say weakly and tug on my ears. "I don't have fangs, my ears are normal, and I don't have magic."

"You don't?" He leans forward his black eyes almost level with mine. "You killed, did you not? In the Red Plains? I felt it."

I swallow hard, my mouth going dry. "I had to.

Vanara was trying to kill me. It was self-defense. Anyone would have done the same."

"Is that so?" A sneer creeps across his lips, the crimson-tipped fangs far too long. "Can just anyone kill with merely a touch?"

The blood drains from my face. "How do you know about that?"

"Did you feel anything then?" He runs his long finger under my chin and forces me to hold his gaze. "When you took her life? You felt it." His mouth widens in a grin. "The surge of power. Her bits of magic and life adding to yours, making you stronger."

"I-I don't know." I wrap my arms around my middle.

"Yes, you do." He sits back, eyeing me contentedly. "You know exactly what I mean. You have my power, my blood, my dark heart. You are the heir I've awaited."

Footsteps on the stairs behind me have me whirling to see what's coming.

"She's the one you've been waiting for?" Cenet gains the top step, and levels me with a malevolent stare. I cringe away until I hit the throne, the bones digging into my back.

Shathinor grips my shoulder as if reassuring me. I pull my knees up and hug myself.

"This sniveling child is your heir?" Cenet's forked tongue darts out and wets his lips as he lifts his gaze to Shathinor. "Did you forget about me, father?"

*G*areth sleeps, the color still drained from his face, his breathing labored as he lies on a table in one of the rough border cabins. I sit next to him as the wind howls through the trees, my rampaging thoughts creating the snowy din outside. Valen had already drained himself at the skirmish, and only had enough to bring Gareth back from the brink of death. But he struggles, his life like a fraying thread.

Beth sits across from me, Gareth's hand in hers as she stares into the flames. She hasn't said much since I found her, her usual saucy banter buried under a mantle of dismay.

Rising, I begin to pace again, the roaring fire doing nothing to warm me. Not when Taylor has been taken from me. Ravella sits cross-legged, her eyes white as she sends her feral self into the vale to seek out my mate. She's been like this for hours, and each second that ticks by is a particular agony.

My bond with Taylor is stretched too far, so close to

snapping. It was only just beginning to grow strong, to allow our minds to meet without saying a word. But I can barely feel her now. And it isn't enough to track her.

"Valen's resting." Gray stomps into the cabin, his broad shoulders brushing the doorframe on either side. "Thorn is a hawk watching the crossing, and Tavaran is on the verge of tears, I think." He grins. "So tough in his golden armor. But put him in a snow bank up to his neck, and he shivers like a new foal."

"Gray—"

He waves a hand. "I took him out ... After he cried." His expression turns solemn as he glances at Gareth. "No change?"

"No." My voice is a hoarse whisper.

Gray sits on the stone hearth in front of the fire and pulls his fur from his shoulders. "Plan?"

"Get her back." My hands curl into fists as a million worries trample through my mind. Is she injured? Terrified? Mistreated? Worse?

"Any idea where she was taken? The Gray Mountains are wide. So many peaks and valleys, places to hide."

"I realize that," I snap.

He nods. Gray has never been one to get his feelings hurt. Tough and resilient, he's the perfect soldier.

"Ravella can locate her. Surely." He scratches his red beard. "Only a matter of time before we go on the hunt."

"Who died?" Gareth's weak voice barely rises past the crackling fire.

The smallest bit of hope blooms in my chest as I turn to him. "About time."

Beth exhales, and her chin drops to her chest.

"Are you hurt?" Gareth tries to reach for her.

"I'm fine." She looks up, her eyes glistening. "I'm fine now."

"Worried for me, were you?"

Her impish smile returns, though subdued. "Worried you were going to die before admitting how much you like me."

"Good to see your false confidence is still high." He sighs but doesn't let go of her hand, the two of them sharing a moment that's shocking and tender all at once.

"Taylor." He turns to me, his eyes stark. "We must find her."

"Be still. You took a sword through the back."

He grimaces. "I told you we couldn't trust Para."

"You never trust anyone." I clasp his forearm, relief filtering down through the veil of grief that shades my soul.

"I know. That's the way to avoid a blade in the back." His breath catches on a cough.

I pour him a cup of water and lift his head. He drinks, then settles back down.

"Cenet took her." His hands curl into fists. "Bastard stole right out of the woods and took her. Killed Para—no loss there. But Taylor. Have you found her?" He looks at me with hopeful eyes, but he's a warrior too. Just like me, he knows that things are never simple. Never easy.

"Ravella is scrying for her through the vale." I resume pacing. "Did you see anything else? Any clue where she's gone?"

He shakes his head slightly. "Para took me out. That

shame rests squarely on my shoulders. I didn't protect my queen. I have failed her." He meets my gaze, his dark eyes giving way to sadness. "Just as I have failed you."

"Your oath is still good, old friend." I stop beside him. "We are going to take her back. We have to."

"Ravella can find her, right?" Beth chews her lower lip.

"I don't know." I hate the answer. "She's been able to scry before, but not in the Gray Mountains." Saying it out loud is a fresh dagger through me. Where is my Taylor? "She's tried to find the missing lesser fae and changelings, but her vision stops at the edge of those lands. Nothing passes through there, not even her spectral form."

"Maybe this time—"

"No." Ravella leans back against the cabin wall, her face wan, her eyes back to normal. "I followed the trail as far as I could, but I couldn't see past the mountains. The trail leads to those damnable peaks, but I can go no farther."

I can't stop the roar that rips from me, the sound shaking the timbers of the cabin and sending puffs of dust down from the rafters.

"Me too." Beth taps her heart. "But in here."

Ravella wipes the sweat from her brow.

Gray rises and pours her some water.

"Thanks." She drains it. "But I did see someone in the vale. Someone who could possibly help us." Her expression darkens even further. "But it will be costly."

"I'll pay any price to find her." No hesitation.

"I was afraid you'd say that." She drains another cup, then crosses her legs again. "I'll bring her. Brace yourselves." Her eyes turn white, and she's gone into the vale again.

Gray opens one of the provisions bags and starts setting out a meal. "We need to eat. Keep our strength in case the summer realm gets suicidal again."

I wave the food away. I can't eat, can barely function. What I need is Taylor. Everything inside me clamors for my mate, and the feral howls with longing. I won't sit idle. I must follow her, even if my path takes me to the darkest Spire.

"Gray's right," Gareth chides. "Eat while you can. When we set off for the Gray Mountains, there may not be food for—"

"We?" I arch a brow. "*You* aren't going anywhere."

"I damn well am." He sputters. "I watch your back, remember?"

"Might need to keep a better eye on your own." Gray snorts.

"You'll pay for that comment."

"Not till later." Gray cuts a hunk of bread.

"Then start counting interest." Gareth's tone is stronger, but still reedy.

"Stop getting him excited." I take a piece of bread from Gray's grip. "I'm eating." I point at Gareth. "You're staying."

"She's my queen, too, Leander. I am to blame for her capture. I must honor my oath to her."

"You almost died." I toss a crust of bread at him.

His reflexes are deadened, the bread bouncing off his tunic and proving my point. "You are no use to me like this. Stay here, recover, and wait for my return." I swipe the crumbs off him and down the bread. "That's the end of it."

His cheeks redden, his eyes furious. "That is *not* the end of—"

"She's here." Ravella sits forward right as a knock sounds on the door.

*a*n undead guard leads me down a darkened corridor, the faint lights hung at intervals barely revealing the path underfoot. Shathinor hurried me out of his throne room after Cenet appeared, and the two of them engaged in a heated argument as the guard gestured for me to follow. I was too dazed to disobey, not to mention the row of additional soldiers lining the damp underground hallways discouraged me from any escape attempt.

The guard turns abruptly and swings open a worn wooden door. He doesn't enter, but his rotting hand points the way for me. I step inside a crude bedroom, and the door closes behind me. When I turn to try the door handle, it doesn't budge.

"You're here." Cecile sits in a chair next to a small bed. The other me lies there, her eyes still closed.

"Is she alive?" I hurry over.

"Yes." Cecile holds her hand between both of her

own. "She's breathing." Looking up at me, her red-rimmed eyes are teary. "Why won't she wake?"

"I don't know." I run my hand along her forehead and try to ignore the creepy feeling that touching my own face elicits. "She's not feverish, but that lump on her head isn't so great." I pull her hair back and look more closely at it. "I don't see a dent or anything, so maybe it's just a superficial bruise. Your head has a really good blood supply, so any injuries there tend to look worse than they are."

"But she won't wake." Cecile's defeated tone hits a sad note inside me.

"Give her more time." I pull up the threadbare blanket and tuck it around her, doing my best to ward off the dank chill that pervades this stone prison.

"You're mated." Cecile stares at the mark peeking from beneath my shirt.

"Yes." My cheeks heat.

"I guess all you needed to finally get laid was a little push from me."

"*A little push?*" The pity I felt for her starts to drain away. "You call sending me to another dimension—or whatever this is—*a little push?*"

She shrugs. "Well, it worked, didn't it?"

I would strangle her, but that would leave me with one fewer ally. So, maybe later when I've gotten out of this mess.

I rub my eyes and plop down on the hearth where a small purple fire burns. "By the way, did you know we're sisters?"

She turns her head toward me, her now-pointy ears thrown in sharp relief. "Did you hit your head, too?"

"No." I lean back against the stones, though they aren't as warm as I'd hoped.

"Then why are you spouting nonsense?"

"We have the same mother. Callandra."

Her nostrils flare at the name. "Not possible."

"Maybe it's escaped your notice, but none of this is possible." I wave my hand at pretty much everything. "Shathinor is alive, I'm his daughter, I'm your sister, I have an evil brother, there's another me right here in this room, and we are trapped in a cave where the fires are purple and the guards are dead guys!" My voice rises with, I admit, more than a hint of hysteria.

Cecile glares at me. "Things are already bad enough without you harshing my vibe."

"I'm harshing *your* vibe?"

"Yes. And I need positive feels to help my girl get better. So, I'd appreciate it if you keep any and all negativity to yourself." She turns her back on me. "And we *aren't* sisters. I have a sister, and she's right here." She grasps the other me's hand again.

I don't even comment on how ridiculous she is to claim I'm not her sister, but somehow my doppelganger is? What a mess. I lean my head back against the wall and yell for Leander again. But he can't hear me. Our bond was so alive when we mated, but now that vibrancy has faded into black and white. He's too far away.

"Mother would have told me, you know," she says quietly. "She would have said."

"She was trying to keep me hidden. I was born a long

time ago, but she had to keep me away from my father. That's why you didn't know about me." A thought hits me, and I laugh.

"What could possibly be funny?" Cecile snipes.

"I'm your big sister." It tickles me for some reason, and I wheeze-laugh as Cecile scowls. "Maybe I can babysit you sometime." Raucous, inappropriate laughter boils out of me until I double over and hold my aching ribs.

"You're mental."

"Maybe." I sit back up and wipe my eyes, the (admittedly crazy) laughter fading. "Probably. But don't worry about me, little sister."

She rolls her eyes. "Mother sent me to find you." She smooths the other me's blanket. "I didn't know why. But before she went to the Ancestors, she told me to go to earth and look out for you. I had to promise her, swore on the Ancestors and the old magic. When the time came, I fought it, but father wanted to separate me from my Taylor, so he was happy for me to go. I told myself it would be easy, that maybe it wasn't so bad. After all, my Taylor is my best friend." Her eyes narrow. "But then I arrived to my dorm room and met *you*."

I ignore her barb. "All of it fits." I don't want it to. I don't want to be Shathinor's daughter, but there it is. I can't deny how well his story matches up to what's happened to me, but I still don't know why I'm here. What's his plan? To keep me around as a pet?

"My father is dead, isn't he?" It's a question, but she states it with such resignation that I can tell she knows the answer.

The question is an even gloomier change of pace. "He is."

"Did you kill him?" Her shoulders hunch a little.

"No." I don't intend to volunteer that Leander did.

"Okay." She nods. "I know he wasn't ... a good fae. But I'm glad you weren't the one—"

We jump when a knock rattles the door.

A female undead shambles in, her head bald in spots, and her blue dress torn and tatty, but she holds an emerald green gown that seems fit for a queen. Walking to me, she lays the dress along a wooden chair, then reaches for my shirt.

"Hey!" I try to scoot back but knock my head on the stones behind me.

She takes the opportunity to begin yanking my shirt off.

"Stop!" I throw my hands up, but she's surprisingly strong, and so is her stench.

Shoving myself to the side, I evade her grasp and hurry around the bed. "Go away."

She gestures to the dress, her white eyes droopy, and moves toward me again.

"Look." I hold my hands up. "I can dress myself. All right?"

She stops but doesn't leave.

"She *can* dress herself, but trust me, she doesn't have a clue *how* to dress." Cecile's usual snarky armor is back up.

"This is neither the time nor the place, Cecile." I edge around the bed and grab the dress.

"Whatever." She leans over Taylor on the bed and finger combs her hair.

I turn my back on them and the corpse and strip down, then stand and throw the velvety dress over my head. It falls almost to the floor and has a scoop neckline that isn't too low. Not bad.

"I'm dressed. Now what?" I put my hands on my hips and speak with an utterly false bravado. Is this dress what I'm about to be sacrificed in? My knees go to jelly at the idea, but there's nothing I can do except put my faith in Leander. He will come for me. He promised to the Ancestors that he would *always* come for me.

The woman shuffles to the door and opens it, then waits.

"She wants you to go with her," Cecile offers helpfully.

"I figured that out. Thanks." My fear hasn't killed my sarcasm, so that's a win, sort of.

I ease out the door, and one of the undead guards from earlier walks behind me, herding me down the dark hallway and up a flight of stairs that never seems to end. By the time I get to the top, I have to wipe the beads of sweat from my forehead and take in gulps of air. Apparently, more cardio is necessary to survive the evil mountain lair. The zombie behind me isn't even winded.

"Daughter." Shathinor's voice carries on a cool wind, and I shiver.

The guard gives me a light push. I turn to glare at him, but his gelatinous white eyes have me turning right back around.

With heavy steps, I walk toward the sound of Shathinor's voice. More guards appear, some dead, some alive, all of them stern. Soldiers line the stone walls that open onto a wide veranda jutting out into the cloudy night. There is nothing below but the valley of campfires that spreads as far as I can see. One misstep up here would spell doom.

"Come, daughter." Shathinor stands near the very tip of the stone peninsula extending from the side of the mountain. His black wings are folded neatly behind him, the tips peeking over his shoulders.

Cenet stands beside him, his gaze no less lethal than it was before. But they aren't arguing anymore, at least.

A wind whips past, and I stop as my gown flows out beside me and over the edge. *That first step is a doozy.*

"Come." Shathinor beckons with what passes for a smile on his face.

My heart thumps out of tune, and I want nothing more than to flee back down the stairs. But one look at Cenet tells me he'd catch me and hurt me. And worse than that, he'd enjoy it. He has my obsidian blade at his side.

I force my feet to carry me all the way and stop next to the rotting king.

He takes my arm and pulls me to the very lip of the stone. I clench my eyes shut.

"Look down." His voice slithers into my ear.

It takes effort, but I open my eyes and squint at the camps far below.

"All this is ours. Every bit of it." He wraps his arm around my shoulders, and for a moment, I ponder throwing myself off the cliff. "I had already begun my work to rebuild my army, but the moment I felt you here in Arin, I knew it was time. More and more join my cause, and now we can take the reins of this great slumbering beast and turn its jaws toward first the summer realm and then to the true prize, my former home. *Our* home."

I have to give it to him. He's trying to win me over with this "our" business. But what he wants to sell me is an evil empire with him as its king. No, thank you. "Look, you don't know me. I'm just a human—well, I guess a fae? —See? I don't even know what I am. I'm not evil. I don't want to take over the world. War sounds horrible." I cringe away from him a bit more with each word. "I just want to be me." *And I want to be with Leander.* I dare not speak that aloud, not when Shathinor has made clear that Leander is on his "Murder ASAP" list.

"You want to be you?" He pulls me closer, the scent of rot wafting to my nose. "That's what I'm offering. I can give you that. You can finally be yourself. Your *true* self."

"But I already am. I'm happy like this. Like a human, more or less."

"You're a high fae," Cenet practically spits. "Not a human."

Shathinor's white face crinkles a bit. "Don't mind your brother. He's just a tad jealous now that you've come to claim what's yours. He thought he'd be the one to rule with me. But he's a lesser fae, his mother a spoil of war. I enjoyed her but didn't intend for her to bear a child." He gives him a deathly glare. "But here we are."

I swallow hard as Cenet's eyes slit even more narrowly. "One big, happy family."

"Besides, he doesn't have your gifts." Shathinor takes my hand and holds it out. "Death lives in these fingertips and in your heart. You can take life with a whisper, with nothing more than the scantest touch."

"If that were true, Cenet would be toast by now." I pull my hand away. "I'm not who you think I am. I mean, maybe I'm your daughter. It's not like I can do a DNA test and find out. But that doesn't mean I'm, you know ..."

"Bad?" he offers, then smiles, his fangs even longer than I remember. "Bad is relative, my dear heart. Think about it. How were you treated in the summer realm? Did you fare well there?"

Imprisoned in a filthy dungeon, threatened, enslaved, smacked around, and almost murdered. I shrug. "I guess it could have been better."

"So many of those lesser fae and changelings that the summer realm mistreats? They're here." He stares down into the valley. "Both realms downgrade their lesser fae and changelings. Both realms commit grave sins against them. That's why they come here. To take their place in Arin, to gain equality. I have given them a way to fight for what they want."

I hold up a finger. "Hang on. I'm confused."

His jaw twitches, and he speaks in a painfully patient tone. "Why is that?"

"Just like, an hour ago, you said that changelings were pets and that lesser fae were ... lesser. So why would you help them?"

"Oh." He laughs, and I think some part of me dies at how ugly it is. Lowering his voice, he speaks in my ear. "They are a means to an end. Once they've overrun the realms and claimed their victory, I will take over and reorder everything the way it should be."

"The way it should be? And how's that?" I have a feeling I already know.

"High fae should always rule these lands and use lesser fae and changelings as servants and laborers. Their lives are disposable. Why else would I want an army full of them?"

I glance over the precipice. "And what if I don't want any part of this?"

Cenet hisses and crosses his arms over his chest. "She isn't worthy. I told you, Father."

"Silence!" Shathinor's yell seems to come from all around and echoes off the mountainside.

I shudder and try to pull away, but he keeps me tucked under his arm.

"It is time for you to evolve, dearest one."

"What?" I wrap my arms around my middle.

"This mortal form isn't you." He turns me around to face him, my back to the abyss.

"It's me." I look down at myself. "Same old me."

"Not quite." He tilts my chin up, then focuses on the soulstone.

"What are you—" I jolt as he holds his hand over it, green electricity crackling around me in bursts of lightning.

"Hold still, my heart." He winces and takes the stone in his hand. "The magic told me this will hurt both of us."

"Stop." I can't breathe, my lungs flat as a sensation like being sucked through a vacuum compresses the air around me. "Don't."

He pulls at the stone, the electricity growing and lifting me off my feet.

"Let go." My eyes water, pain ricocheting through me, my ears burning, my back ripping apart. "Please!" I scream, agony destroying me at a cellular level.

"Almost there," he grits out, his black brows drawing together as if he's under great strain.

"Stop!" My cry erupts in a burst of black sparks. Everything in me constricts, pulling in on itself. It feels like being born. Or dying. Maybe both all rolled into one. Pain and rebirth and the approaching promise of death.

With a yank, he pulls the stone off me, the chain breaking as he stumbles back. The green lightning expands outward, and agony bursts through me, blasting away my thoughts, my heart, and my soul in one searing explosion that ends in a comfortable, easy darkness.

"Daughter?" Shathinor's voice comes to me as if from a great distance. "Daughter?"

I breathe in, the first gasp of a newborn, and blink my eyes open.

Everything is more. The fine grains of black sand on the stone, the scent of smoke on the air, the sound of the breeze playing along the outcroppings of rock.

I am more. I unfurl from my place on the ground and rise to my feet. Dark wings fan out behind me, the edges dancing with the wind as I reach up and feel the pointed tips of my ears.

The world is sharp. So am I. I stretch out my arms, my fingernails hard and curled like talons.

"It's you." Shathinor's eyes light with awe as he comes to stand by my side.

"Kneel!" he yells, and all the soldiers follow his command, taking a knee and keeping their eyes down.

Only Cenet remains on his feet.

I point my long claw at him and bare my fangs. "Kneel, Brother."

His slitted eyes widen. "Father—"

My claws are at his throat before he can say more. "I. Said. Kneel." Blood runs onto my fingers, the tang of his life salting the air as death flows through his veins, streaking his flesh with black. The death I wield, the fate I hold in the palm of my hand.

I strip the obsidian blade from him.

The hatred that swirls in his eyes is like a fine wine, one that hits my palate just right. I like his hate. I want more.

He bends his knees, dropping to the stone as I step back and stand next to my father.

I flick the blood from my claws into the dark wind that whispers its thanks. "Now, Father. Tell me more about this war."

*T*he winter wind carries us to the western edge of my realm, the Gray Mountains looming in the distance. Kyrin hates flying, and taking so many through the skies drains my magic, but there is simply no time to wait, not when Taylor needs me.

Ravella stands below, a fire already roaring on the bank of a frozen river. I calm the winds, and the rest of us drop to the ground. Gray grunts when his feet touch the snow—he's about as fond of flying as Kyrin. Valen is a bit more graceful about it, but his color has a definite green tint. Thorn glides down as a white owl and changes form, landing on his feet at a slight run.

I sent word to Phinelas, but he may be too far away with Catcher duties to be of help. Branala is in charge at High Mountain while I'm away, and Gareth is recovering. I can't reach Brannon, and I haven't heard a whisper about him since I sent him to Silksglade to investigate Yvarra's death. The Phalanx is spread thin, but I have warriors at my side who are ready to fight and die for my mate. I can ask for nothing more than that.

Ravella stares across the vast wasteland that leads to the mountain range. "Maybe we should have brought the army."

"No." I rub Kyrin's muzzle. "We need to do this quickly and quietly. Get Taylor and get out."

"You need rest." Ravella points to a log next to the icy river. "We need full strength when we enter the Barren Lands."

"We do." I can't disagree. But sitting down isn't going to happen, not when I know Taylor is in those gray and black mountains. Possibly hurt and afraid. My hands curl into fists. If she's been harmed ... I shake the dark thoughts away and work on feeding Kyrin as Gray tends to his horse.

"You sure we can trust the information on where Taylor is being held?"

I lean against Kyrin. "We can. I made an oath that can't be broken, just as she did."

Gray runs a hand over his close-cropped hair. "She might break it out of spite, send herself to an even darker pit of the Spires."

"Your suspicion hurts me, warrior." Selene strides up, and the horses snort nervously.

"I don't think anything hurts you." Gray drags over a pail of water for his horse. "Though I'm happy to try it out and see." He straightens and looks at her. "Why do you watch me like that?"

She clacks her teeth, her black eyes glinting. "Just imagining what your hide would look like in my cave."

"I'm warning you, creature." He steps toward her.

"Stop." I put a hand to his chest. "We don't need division right now. Selene has sworn an oath. Her information is good."

She kicks her chin up. "Listen to your king, tasty warrior." She cocks her head to the side at an unnerving angle. "Did you know your bones call to me? They tell me how I could use them in a stew."

"I said knock it off." I cross my arms and stare her down.

"Of course." She does a curtsy with an imaginary skirt.

Gray glowers but backs away.

"Why did you insist on coming along?" I hold her shadowy gaze. "I gave you what you wanted. You gave me her location. What else is there?"

"I went back to my cave. My lovely, beautiful cave. Sat with my bones and flesh for a while. But then got the itch, felt the power in the air—" She sniffs like a hound. "Tasted it, I did. And I want to follow that scent all the way to the source."

"The king beyond the mountain?"

She cackles. "He's powerful, but there is one even more powerful. More glorious." She sounds almost ... smitten.

I didn't anticipate an even greater foe, but I will fight through whatever the Spires can throw at me to get to Taylor. "I don't suppose you'll share any information on the king beyond the mountain or the other threat you speak of?"

"What are you offering?" She spins and clasps her hands in front of her.

"No." I've already given up something of great value. I won't give up anything else to this dark creature.

She pouts. "Too bad."

"Let him rest, witch." Ravella dumps some vegetables into the stew pot. "We eat, and then we ride."

My magic is replenishing slowly, but we don't have time for it to rebuild all the way. I won't be as powerful out of the winter realm, but I send a prayer to the Ancestors that I'm strong enough to free my mate and get her to safety—even if that means I never return from the Gray Mountains.

"The Barren Lands." The witch dances back, hands still clasped.

Valen sits on the log and stares at her, a mix of curiosity and disgust on his face. He's never seen an Obsidian before, so I can't blame him.

"What fun those dangerous pits of sand and hordes of double-fanged snakes will be, and then the mountains." She puts the back of her wrist to her forehead, seemingly lost in reverie. "So much blood and bone, so much death to come. I want to bathe in all the—" She stills, then her head snaps around at an impossible angle, and her body turns slowly to match it.

"What?" I peer toward the mountains where she's looking, an ominous feeling growing in my breast. "What is it?"

"Don't you see it, winter king?" she crows. "The dark sparks, the purple blooms, the black bursts of death?"

Valen shades his eyes. "I see nothing."

"I see it." She dances a little unhinged jig, her feet nimble. "I told her she could free her aura when she was ready." Her head snaps back around to me, her eyes vicious. "And, oh my dark, rotting stars, she's ready."

TAYLOR

*T*he guards move aside as I sweep past, my wings aching and my heart pounding. I can feel each one of the dead, their lifeless husks silent and dull. But I can sense life nearby. That idiot Cecile and her pathetic human, the one who looks like me but not half as good.

I burst through the door, and Cecile stands from her spot at the bed.

Her eyes open wide. "What happened?"

I hold out my hand and watch as black embers spark and dance there. But it's not enough. Something is holding me back. I'm caged, the dark heart of me wrapped in razor wire and stuffed down, down, down. Closing my eyes, I concentrate on the piece of me that's bound, and I will it to let go, to free me, to release whatever hold it has. I cough, choke for a moment, then spit out a small, green pea.

My magic explodes through the room, tendrils of

gorgeous death reaching and swirling, diving to the ground and twining like the roots of the great tree.

Cecile screams, and I turn to her.

"You're a necromancer." She tries to ward off the black tentacles and backs away to defend her pitiful human.

I want to hurt her. To suck her life away and leave her a desiccated corpse. And why not? I can feel that power flowing through me, the ability to control life and death housed in my immortal frame.

Holding my hand up, I stare at it, at the black streaks through my veins and the darkness that rolls off me like a fog. "I am death incarnate." My voice is many, shaking the rock, shattering the glass water pitcher, and piercing the hearts of all who hear.

"A necromancer." Cecile's silver eyes brim with tears. "That's what you were all along. Just like your father. An unseelie monster."

My black tendrils wrap around her throat and lift her off the ground. "You throw those names around as if they might mean something to me. As if they could hurt me." I advance until we're face to face as she claws at her throat. I smile and treasure the terror that blooms in her. "I can smell your fear. I bet your father smelled the same way when he died. I remember his face, you know? How he looked when his throat was cut, his blood pouring all around." I press the tip of my finger to her chest, right over her heart, and watch as my darkness spreads within her.

She kicks, her eyes rolling back.

I stop her heart.

Then I start it again. For fun.

"*Stop.*" A voice not unlike my own whispers. "*This isn't you. Please, stop.*"

I step back, the blackness rewinding, spooling itself inside me. Cecile falls to the floor, her breath coming in great gulps.

I blink hard. "I'm so sorry." I kneel next to her and help her to her feet. "I don't know what that was."

She backs away. "You're a necromancer. Evil. Unseelie."

"No, I'm your sister." I step closer. "Please, I'm not bad."

"Stay back." She holds one hand out to ward me off.

"Cecile, please." I move closer. "It's me. You know me. I wouldn't hurt anyone."

"Are you back to normal?" She relaxes a little.

Gullible fool.

Normal. The word is so ridiculous. Was the weak version of me 'normal'? That pathetic Taylor who had to wear the soulstone to keep me repressed? She was a bad joke. It's a good thing my mother is with the Ancestors, because I would kill her for what she's done to me. Forcing me to remain locked in a silent, black cage inside a wretched changeling version of myself.

I turn back to Cecile. "Yes, I'm back to normal." I reach down and grab her pet's hand, crushing it in mine.

Cecile flies at me. I wrap her in death again, holding her off the floor as she struggles.

Her anger is laughable.

"Don't worry." I grin. "I can bring your human pet back. She'll just be a little ... different." I delight in

Cecile's horrified scream as I send death twisting through her human.

"Daughter." My father kisses my cheek as I enter the bedroom he's had prepared for me. "I hope everything is to your liking."

"It will do." I peer at the rack of clothes along the back wall. Mostly black items, and the shirts have clever notches in the back for my wings. Good.

I can smell everything—the leather from the pants, the mold on the rocks, the semi-fresh linens on the bed. So many sounds form the background of this place that I could go mad if I don't learn how to block them out. The groans from the undead are particularly unappealing.

"When do we march for Byrn Varyndr? I have a few scores to settle there." I pull a black shirt from the rack and a pair of black leather pants. "I want to bathe in Aurentia's blood. Is that too dark? Because I think it would be delightful."

"Perfectly dark." He smiles, his fangs lengthening. "You make me so proud."

I roll my eyes and strip out of my dress.

He doesn't look away. I don't care. I pull on the pants, then drop the shirt over my head. The slits go around my wings, and I'm able to fasten it with a tie at my waist. I wonder if I can really fly with these things. I suppose I'll find out soon enough. *Fly to Leander. He can help.*

"Did you hear that?" I glance around the sparsely-furnished room.

"What?"

"Nothing." I shake my head and strap my blade to my belt.

Shathinor strides to me and dangles a small pendant from his fingers. "I have a gift for you."

I arch a brow. "Another necklace. No, thank you."

"This one is special." He guides me to the mirror above a dressing table.

I suck in a breath when I see my reflection. My eyes are the same, but my skin is paler, my ears pointier than I imagined, my hair somehow darker. Not to mention the fangs and the wings. But I'm still me, right? I pause for a second and stare into my eyes. Who are you? I blink hard and try to place how I got here. Cenet, right? Cenet brought me here. I remember it all—but it's like it happened to someone else. Not me. To someone weak and foolish and silly. I'm none of those things. So why does this all feel wrong somehow? Like I'm forcing a puzzle piece in the wrong spot.

I shake my head and square my shoulders. Nothing's wrong. I want to be here. The other woman, the one whose memories I have, was an embarrassment. I'm not her. I'm something better. And I will rule this world and crush any who stand in my way.

The mark at my shoulder catches my eye. My mate. A hint of a smile creeps across my crimson lips when I think of him.

"The traitor marked you with a vengeance." Shathinor scowls. "The Ancestors are cruel to do such a thing, but there it is. He deserves a death so gruesome that it's whispered of for thousands of years. Instead, he takes even more from me."

"I won't kill him. Not for you." I can still feel him inside me, the way his body moved, the bite that sealed our mating. My fangs lengthen. I look forward to fucking him upon our next meeting, even if it's on a bloody battlefield.

"Mate bonds are ancient magic. They can't be broken, not without the greatest sacrifice." He taps his shirt where his rotted heart still beats. "I could have been whole. But I chose to salt the ground in the winter realm, destroy future mating bonds, starve them of children until I could return triumphant."

"Vicious." I hold his gaze in the mirror. "I'm impressed."

"Not as much as I am. You are a true beauty. Not unlike your mother was, though you are so much more than she could ever be." He gestures for me to lift my hair. "You were foretold long ago. Your wings of death and your power to destroy the realms."

"Tell me the rest of the prophecy."

"You don't know it?"

"The Vundi witch didn't finish it before she was killed."

"Very well. 'A child of many worlds, clothed in light, will come home. On wings of death, the child will glide to sit on her throne of bone. The realms will bend to her command, she has but to choose. She alone can start the war and be victorious, win or lose.'"

"That doesn't entirely make sense."

"Prophecies never do." He clucks his tongue and

holds the necklace up for me. "But it gives us enough. You are the spark we need to start the war, to end the summer realm and take winter back."

I lick my lips. "The summer realm will fall. They thought they could break me. My waves of death will roll over them like an unrelenting ocean." I pull my hair up and he drapes the necklace around my throat. It's a simple golden vial with what looks like blood inside. "What is it?"

He centers the pendant for me, his cold fingers sending ugly prickles along my skin. "A phylactery."

I stare at him blankly.

"It contains a small bit of my essence. Something of me that you can keep with you always." He squeezes my shoulders. "Do you like it?"

For an evil king, my father sure is turning out to be a pussy. I wonder how long it will take me to overthrow him. A day? Maybe two? Or maybe I should keep him around just long enough to take the realms, and then dethrone him in front of an audience. Taking his head will certainly set the tone for my reign. I force a smile.

It's enough to get one in return from him. "Now, how would you like a flying lesson as we discuss our battle plans?"

"I need lessons?" I scoff.

"I suppose we'll find out." He opens the door for me. "Flying is critical, and of course we'll need to practice reanimation and a few other tricks."

"I'd prefer to kill."

"Of course." He laughs. "That's the fun part. It's too easy. Reanimation is where the real work comes in, but you'll find it quite useful. We have a living army now, but we'll lose numbers as we march eastward. With our abilities combined, we can bring back quite a few of them to rejoin our numbers. But you need practice. I want you to focus on bringing them back, then the reward will be killing once we've begun our march toward Byrn Varyndr."

I follow him out toward the cavern with the tree, the undead snapping to attention as best they can when we walk past. Cenet stands next to the twisted trunk, inspecting its branches as if he's not listening to every word we say.

"Father." He turns toward us, his eyes back to looking almost normal. But he's a lesser fae. Utter trash. My father should be ashamed that he ever touched a lesser fae female, and even more ashamed of this filthy offspring.

"Aren't you supposed to be training with the troops?" Shathinor keeps walking past him.

"I would like a word."

"We're busy." I turn on my heel and face him.

"I wasn't speaking to you."

"Are we playing the usual sibling games?" I simper and let the darkness ooze from my fingertips. "Because I'm very interested in a contest. One where the winner pisses on her brother's corpse."

His eyes change, and his claws lengthen. "Let's do this, bitch."

"Stop!" Shathinor roars and steps between us. "I am *king* here. And you two will obey me. Cenet, stand down. You owe your sister your allegiance just as you owe it to me. She is chosen. She was *foretold*. On her wings—and mine—we will claim the summer and winter realms, and then *all of Arin*. She is the key to our victory." His tone turns icy. "And I will not have you challenging me on any of this. Do you understand?"

Cenet's lips press into a harsh line.

"I said do you understand?" Shathinor bellows, sending rocks and shards of stalactites crashing to the cavern floor.

"Yes, Father." He bows his head.

Pity, I would have enjoyed removing it.

"Come, daughter." He walks to the sheer cliff that looks out over the valley, the sun just barely tipping over the horizon.

I shake my wings, the new muscles sore and unwieldly. The world rolls out before me, everything there for the taking. All I have to do is claim it for my own. I peer over the edge. The fall would definitely kill me, but what if I could soar? The breeze picks up and ruffles my feathers, the sensation sending goosebumps down my back.

"Afraid, dear princess?" Shathinor spreads his wings and jumps, his power on full display.

I hold my breath as he dives a bit, then flaps and shoots up into the air, his dark shape marring the coming day. He makes it look easy.

There is no place for fear, no time for weakness. That was the old me, the one who was made to suffer and die. I am immortal. My reign will be forever. I back away and take a deep breath.

"*Yes, walk away. That's not safe.*" The nagging voice is there again. I want to kill it.

I plant my foot and stare out at the coming dawn. This is what I was made for. It has to be. I take off at a run.

"*Are you nuts? Noooo!*"

I jump from the cave and try to spread my wings. The wind pushes them back, and I plummet straight down like a fallen angel.

*B*lood spurts from the last viper, its melon-sized head dropping to the sand with a thunk. I sheathe my sword and wipe the sweat from my brow. The foothills beckon, the mountains casting long shadows that promise relief from the unrelenting heat, sand, and cracked dirt of the Barren Lands.

Sometimes I think I can sense Taylor, but then it's gone, like a wisp of smoke I can't catch.

Selene snatches up the viper's long, coiling body. "For my collection." She stuffs it inside a knapsack turned black with blood and filled with bits and pieces of the many vicious creatures we've had to slay to simply make it this far.

Ravella wrinkles her nose, but Gray laughs.

Thorn scouts out ahead, his gray eagle's wings melding into the dark mountains. He's been gone for over half the day, the burning sun a near-constant companion as we slog through the barren soil. What I wouldn't give for a dousing of snow and a brush of the bitterest wind. But I would give more for one moment with Taylor.

"We're getting closer." Selene stares up at the craggy peak ahead of us. "The darkness grows, and I can feel the drums." She thumps her chest in a steady rhythm. "Can you hear it? Can you imagine the treats left behind in the coming battles?" Her mouth crackles into a grin. "So much beautiful offal."

"Does anything else make you happy?" Valen guides the horses along behind us, careful to keep them on the path we tread lest they stray into the sinking sands. "Anything other than ... pieces of things?"

She fluffs her hair and twirls back to Valen. "Why? Do you think *you* could make me happy?"

"I don't—"

"Because you could." She runs her claw along his cheek. "Your guts would please me for days on end."

"That's enough." I shield my eyes from the sun and search the mountainside for any sign of Thorn.

"He'll be back soon." Ravella takes a swig from her canteen and hands it to me. "I still can't go through the vale. I keep trying, but something in this place blocks me."

"Ravella." I yank her behind me and cut the head off an enormous black scorpion that was poised to strike. "At least now we know why no one ever returns from the Gray Mountains."

"By the Ancestors!" She kicks its head into a thorny plant. "I'd rather face ten ice bears than deal with one more of these abominations. A week in this scorched waste has been plenty."

One week. I pour a little water on my hand and rub it on my face. One week since I last held Taylor, since I felt her warmth. My teeth grind as I go through a never-ending list of worries, of fears for her. If the king beyond the mountain has harmed her—no matter how little—I will add days, maybe weeks to his suffering. He will die for touching her. That is certain. The only variable now is how much pain I will inflict before I send him to the Spires.

"We'll find her, Leander." Ravella squeezes my shoulder. "I know it."

I nod. Emotion closes my throat. When I told Taylor I had never feared before I found her, I spoke the truth. The fear now? It guts me. Every day, every moment without her is a particular torture, especially when I can't feel her through the bond. I don't know if she's hurt or crying or wishing for me the way I'm wishing for her.

Shake it off. I do. For the millionth time. I keep walking through this ghastly desert, because each step brings me closer to the one my soul loves.

"Ahead." Gray pulls his warhammer from his back.

Through the hazy heat, a figure approaches, though it's oddly misshapen, one side higher than the other.

I draw my sword as Ravella palms her knives. "Keep close."

"Isn't he a handsome devil?" Selene whistles.

I can't see the figure, but I know the walk. That deadly prowl belongs to only one fae I know.

"Brannon." I sheathe my sword as he appears through the waves of heat, Thorn perched on his shoulder. "I didn't know you gave rides."

He grins. "I shot him down, so I thought it was the least I could do."

The eagle screeches angrily and makes a show of his bloody feathers.

"You shot him?" Valen hurries forward. "Where?"

"Just clipped his wing a bit. He's fine." Brannon shrugs the eagle off, his broad shoulders bare under the blazing sun, the black ink that snakes around him almost glowing in the light.

Valen takes Thorn and does a quick healing spell on the bloody feathers along his right wing.

"How did you find us?" I clasp Brannon's forearm as Selene prances up.

"Hi, handsome," she purrs.

He looks down at her. "Witch."

She bats her black lashes. "I'm Selene. Let's have sex."

Ravella caws out a laugh that echoes across the sandy expanse, and Valen's mouth drops open.

"Sorry." Brannon runs a hand through his raven hair. "I'm saving myself for my mate."

"What?" Selene stomps her foot on the sand. "I demand you fornicate with me forthwith, handsome one!"

The black ink that creeps up his neck pulses. "No."

Selene crosses her arms and harrumphs, her claws clacking against her sides.

Thorn flashes back into his fae form and doubles over, laughter rolling out of him, which then has Ravella starting up again. Then Gray joins in.

"Saving yourself?" Thorn guffaws. "Are you serious?"

"And what of it?" Brannon's hands fist, the darkness inside him threatening to emerge.

"Leave him be." I point at Selene. "Both of you."

She grumbles but drops back and resumes a one-sided conversation she's had off and on with Kyrin.

"What did you see?" I yank Thorn upright, and the laughter dies off. "The mountain. Tell me."

"A cave system at the top of that peak." He points to the highest one, the same one Selene had described. "Lots of movement up there, but that's only half of it. I found the missing lesser fae and changelings."

"What? Are they all right?"

"They're an army. I've been to the camps. Blended in under the cover of night." Brannon spits. "They've joined up with the king beyond the mountain, believed his tales of taking over the realms and remaking them. Most of them are there voluntarily. Some were conscripted, but not many."

"Why would they go?" Valen verges on flabbergasted.

"They want equality, freedom from the high fae."

"And they think the king beyond the mountain will give them that?" Ravella shakes her head. "I don't know who he is, but I can guarantee his purpose isn't peace and equality, not when he's been amassing a host of warriors."

"They left my realm to join him." It's a kick to the gut, but one I should have expected. When I tried to enforce equality amongst high and lesser fae, the disdain from the nobles of High Mountain may have been what pushed them away. When they saw that no matter what their new king argued for, the old ways still prevailed. They lost faith in me. "How many?"

"Thousands." Brannon sucks on his teeth. "Enough to take the summer realm with a surprise attack. They'll have to march long and hard to Byrn Varyndr, but they'll murder and burn as they go."

My hopes fall even further, sinking low into the pit of my memories of fallen friends and never-ending bloodshed. Please Ancestors, not again.

"And the king beyond the mountain?" I force myself to continue, to keep going, to do what must be done to reclaim Taylor and defend the realms. "What of him?"

"He's in the caves, I suspect." Thorn points. "Lording over it all."

"They say he has a weapon, a warrior who soars on black wings and who can kill with a whisper."

"Have you seen this warrior?" I don't want to think about Taylor in the clutches of a monster like that.

"No." Brannon shakes his head. "On the night I crept through the camp, I heard the beat of wings and spotted something high in the clouds, but it vanished."

"Anything else?" I trudge ahead, the sand falling away from my boots in little waves as I parse what information Brannon and Thorn have revealed.

"Leander." Brannon's voice is soft, eerily so.

I turn and meet his gaze.

"There's one more thing I found out."

"Yes?" A drowning weight settles on me before Brannon speaks, because some part of me already knows.

"The king beyond the mountain ... It's the old evil, the dark one."

I freeze, winter rampaging through my heart, and turn my eyes to the mountain. "Shathinor."

*T*he dead soldier flops on the ground like a fish, his arms splaying at odd angles.

"More." Shathinor stares as I pull magic from inside me and force it out and into the corpse.

A sweat breaks across my brow, and I concentrate on reanimating his heart, forcing it to beat with black blood. It oozes from the wound in his neck where Cenet's fangs ripped the soldier's life away. He flips to his back, and his white eyes open too wide, his mouth rounded in a scream as his body begins to function again.

"That's it." Shathinor smiles, his hollow cheeks stretching wide. "You have it."

I cut off my magic and rub my temples as the creature rises to its feet, its mind empty and ready for orders. "*I wish you would stop doing that. This is the thirteenth one you've brought back. We need to get out of here. Find Leander.*" I squelch the annoying voice that sounds far too much like my own.

"Cenet." Shathinor glowers. "Next time, make your

kill without injuring too much. She needs practice, but not the sort that drains her."

Cenet sneers. "Too hard for your precious Taylor?"

Shathinor strikes him so hard that Cenet's head whips around and the nearby soldiers murmur uneasily. "Do not test me, Son. Lest I have her make an example of *you*."

Cenet stalks away as Shathinor resurrects another soldier.

I swipe the back of my hand across my forehead and throw my shoulders back, the magic already replenished and ready for more. I'm always ready for more. All these days and nights spent training have honed my focus, and I know what I'm here for. I *will* fulfill the prophecy and bring Arin to heel.

"*Why?*" The irritating voice is back.

"*Because that is my destiny*," I think back at it.

"*It doesn't have to be. We don't have to do these things. Just because Shathinor is our father, it doesn't mean we have to be like him.*"

"*What if I* want *to be like him? Only stronger.*"

"*No one wants to be like him. Hate-filled and power hungry. It's not who we are.*"

"*I say who we are.*" I can feel her trying to wrestle her way free, to be on top again like she's been since we were born, since our mother cursed us with that stone.

"*If you would just let me—*"

With a yell, I rush headlong at the nearest cluster of changelings, their eyes widening in terror. Unfurling my wings, I leap into the air and flap them hard, the burn of my muscles a welcome reprieve from the headache I get each time I reanimate a corpse.

The clouds flow around me as I soar. I relish the damp chill, and my wings expand, gripping the air and pushing me up and up until the sun beats down on my face and the valley is nowhere in sight. The voice goes silent. Good.

"You're a fast learner." Shathinor follows me up, his black wings beating steadily. "That first day, I had my doubts."

"I've never had wings before." I shout over the wind. "What did you expect?"

"You're my child." He shoots in front of me. "I expect excellence."

"Does Cenet give you that?" I tuck my wings in tight and dive through the clouds, heading straight to the ground like an arrow from a bow. The roar of the wind is my companion as the valley reappears, the soldiers below running drills and sparring with each other.

Before I get too low, I spread my wings and let myself drift lazily, like a leaf in a stream.

"Cenet has his uses." Shathinor floats next to me. "You should make peace with him and work together to—"

"He's a mistake." I glare at him. "One that you made, and one that I don't intend to live with."

"You plan to kill him?" We loop up and around the camp.

"Isn't that obvious?" I won't let him live, not when he might try to challenge me for the throne one day.

He looks away, then roars with laughter, his wings

shaking. "The Ancestors were kind to send you to me, my dear heart. You do me proud."

"You won't interfere?"

"No." He points to a peak up ahead. "Let's set down there."

I want to keep flying to stretch out my sore wings even more, but I acquiesce. For now. Snow crunches under my black boots as I land a little unsteadily, and I turn to lean against the dark rock at my back.

A twisted, stunted tree grows from a narrow crack, its thin branches trying so hard to reach the sun. But it will die, just like the soldiers milling about in the valley below. Everything will die and be reborn, this world mine to shape as I please.

Shathinor lands and turns his gaze to the valley.

"When can we march?" I'm itching to start the war, to bring death to the summer lands.

"You are so like me." He tries to tuck my hair behind my ear.

I duck away.

He looks almost ... crestfallen, and his tone turns wistful. "I missed your entire life."

"You didn't miss much." The memories of my 'human' life disgust me.

"But I did." He sighs heavily. "If only I'd known you existed, I'd have ..."

"You'd have what?" I wave his words away. "Saved me from my stepfather's beatings? Brought me to Arin? Had me live with you and your undead in that slovenly cave for centuries? Is that it?"

Irritation flickers across his face, but he tamps it down

and continues, "If I had known when you were still a child, still here in Arin, think of how all that could have been different." He peers at me, his black eyes probing. "Maybe if you'd been allowed to grow and thrive, you could have fought by my side in the last war. You could have saved me from the pretender. We could have ruled together, and I wouldn't be in this state." He glances at his silver chest plate and to the ruin hidden beneath it. "You and I could already have the world in our grasp. But your whore of a mother took all that away from me, banished you to earth, and sent herself to the Ancestors to make sure that secret was never revealed."

I smirk. "What she didn't know is that Cecile is an utter moron and sent me to Arin anyway." I laugh, the sound harsh like crushing rock. "Good job, Sis."

"Perhaps it had to happen this way." He goes to reach for me again but lets his hand drop. "You are more powerful now than even the prophecy suggested. I can feel you, the darkness inside you seemingly bottomless."

"Jealous?" I summon a ball of black death into my palm.

"Proud." He swipes the ball away and tosses it at the stunted tree.

It withers and dies, its remains cascading down the unforgiving rock and into the oblivion below.

I run my fingers along my shoulder as I peer into my mirror. Leander's bite is healed, but the fang marks will never go away. Claimed. Just like he promised me. But

Leander claimed a foolish girl, one who believed in unicorns and fairytales. I press my thighs together as I contemplate our next mating, how much *more* it will be for both of us. He will be surprised, I'm sure, to find me in this vastly improved state. No matter. The bond is still there. I am still his. Soon I will show him how much better our mating will be now that I'm fully fae and imbued with my father's dark power. He will love me like no other, and I will reward him for his devotion.

I sigh and lean forward, the dresser's shoddy wood nicked and marred, though my father has laid out precious jewels along the top for me. Did he expect me to fawn over them? I swipe them aside but stop when my hand touches the soulstone.

The simple pendant has no power over me now. I run my fingers down its face, the smooth opal warm under my touch. Sometimes I think I hear it whispering to me in Delantis's voice. The obsidian blade does the same. But whatever she wants to tell me, I don't care to hear. I have everything I need. My army is prepared to march, and I'm ready to lead. Cenet plots behind my back, telling my father I'm not battle-tested, that I'm not ready. I close my hand into a fist. When the time comes and his head is on a pike, we'll see who was ready.

Cecile walks in, my laundered clothes in her arms. She doesn't look at me, and for the first time since I've known her, her confidence is drained away. Shoulders slumped, eyes down—she's beaten.

"I like you like this." I spin away from my dresser to face her.

She hangs my clothes without a word.

I smile. "How's your little human?"

Her motion stops for only a moment before she continues.

"I thought perhaps I'd killed her." I call the darkness into my palm and play with it, tickling the tendrils of death with my fingertips. "But I hear she lives."

When she doesn't respond, I send a wisp of black to curl around her throat. "I'm speaking to you, Sister."

"We're not sisters." She turns to me, the fire back in her silver eyes. "We will *never* be sisters."

"Blood is blood." I pull the darkness back inside myself, as if sucking it through a straw.

"You'll never take the summer realm." She hugs herself. "Queen Aurentia will—"

"Fall just like all the rest." I rise and walk to her, reveling in the dark circles beneath her eyes and her lackluster hair. A week in the caves has robbed her of all the beauty she used to wield on earth. "I never realized it when you were in the human world, but here, surrounded by your own kind, you're nothing special."

"And you are?"

"Oh, I don't know." I let my wings expand, the dark feathers iridescent in the low light. "I think I'm a bit more remarkable than you ever gave me credit for."

"You think any of this changes who you are?" She smirks. "You're still the same nerdy loner with daddy issues you always were. Now you have wings and a bad attitude. Congratulations. You've finally peaked."

I grip her throat and squeeze. "I took your shit for too long. You were nasty then, and you're nasty now."

"At least I'm consistent." She grits her teeth.

"No, you're just a bitch." I throw her backwards, and she slides across the floor on her ass. "A stupid one at that."

She climbs to her feet, her eyes flashing. "If you're finished insulting me, I have some more laundry to do."

"Not so fast, Sis." I advance on her, though she doesn't hold my gaze for long. It's as if she can't bear to look into my eyes. Good. "I have a little job for you."

*S*tone scatters under my feet as I climb to the nearest ledge, the valley floor falling away beneath me. Thorn wheels into the coming night, his shape transforming from eagle to owl.

"Ravella won't forgive you for this." Gray grabs the handhold I just vacated and hauls himself up next to me.

"Someone has to stay with the horses. We need them for our escape, and if they aren't there, we're as good as dead. Taylor can't make it through the Barren Lands on foot. She's too fragile."

"Still, she'll be mad for years."

"I'll deal with it." I launch myself up the unforgiving stone and grab another hold, my fingers aching.

"Shathinor." Gray spits a few choice curses in the ancient fae language. "How did he survive? I saw you ram your blade through his heart. Saw you *twist* it. He was dead. No doubt in my mind."

"Necromancers have tricks. So many fun tricks." Selene skitters across the rock above us, her legs spider-like as she makes easy work of the cliffs and sharp cracks in the rock.

"That's creepy." Gray stares up at her.

"Selene can hear you," she singsongs.

I pull myself up until there's a break in the cliff face, a ledge just wide enough to sit on. I help Gray up, and he collapses next to me, his large frame taking up half the ledge as he starts rummaging in his pack.

Valen's hand appears, and we both pull him up. He throws himself down and lies there staring up at the sky, breathing hard. "Climbing is not my thing."

"Where'd you send Brannon?" Gray hands me a piece of dried meat and what's left of our bread.

"He thinks he can do some more infiltrating in the camp, report back on planned troop movements, maybe give us a chance to break up the ranks before they get too far into the realms."

Gray grunts.

"Give him a chance." Valen reaches for the water. "You and Thorn are always so cynical."

"You're young." Gray hands him the canteen. "Too trusting."

"He's always been loyal."

"He shot Thorn in the wing two days ago. Remember that?"

"That was an accident." Valen shrugs. "Besides, I fixed Thorn right up."

I lean back against the cold rock as Gray and Valen have the old argument yet again. My thoughts stray to Taylor. Always her. I pray to the Ancestors that she knows I'm coming for her. That whatever horrors she's seen or endured, I will do everything in my power to make it right, to heal her wounds, to give her whatever she needs, and that I will enact vengeance on those who took her. I can see her, the way her mouth turns up at the corners, the sweet little sounds she makes when she sleeps, the way she fits so perfectly against me, the way she looked when I claimed her. I press my hand to my chest, feeling her loss like a tear in my heart. The bond is silent, but it's still there. Not severed, not gone, just achingly empty.

"Kingly fae," Selene calls. "Come up, up, up. I see a way. One even Valen can tread with ease."

"Thanks." Valen wrinkles his nose and struggles to his feet, then hands the canteen to Gray. "I'll go first so you can catch me if I fall."

Gray snorts. "You have a lot of faith in me."

"I was talking to Leander." Valen hoists himself onto the rock face and aims for where Selene clings to the stone, her body upside down and her black eyes glinting.

I pack my thoughts of Taylor neatly away, the edges worn from frequent use and the pages still warm from the last time. She's never far. I follow Gray, all of us struggling up the steep rock wilderness until we make it to Selene. When I get to her, she's snoring, yet still clinging to the stone.

"Selene."

She jolts awake and grins. "I was just chatting with my magic."

I take Gray's hand, and he pulls me up onto another, wider ledge. "It tell you anything interesting?"

"Oh, yes!" She follows, clinging to the rock and skittering sideways. "The best news."

"What news?" Gray's dark brows lower.

"We're going to have company." She jumps down and claps, then points at a crude stone staircase that hews close to the mountainside.

A summer fae appears from the top, her face weary and her steps uncertain. She stops when she sees us, her eyes widening.

Gray pulls his warhammer from his back.

"I'm looking for Leander." She fixes her gaze on me.

"You're a lure, female." Gray jumps across a narrow chasm and lands on the steps below her. "Sent here to destroy us."

"Does it look like I can destroy anything?" She holds her hands out. The attitude in her voice sounds faintly reminiscent of the way Taylor used to imitate her roommate.

"Wait, Gray." I jump across. "Who are you?"

"Cecile."

"What are you doing here?" I peer around for soldiers. This must be a trap. I throw up a quick cloaking spell around us, hiding my warriors from prying eyes.

"The short version? Shathinor kidnapped me, tortured me, used me to get his hands on Taylor, and now I'm pretty much a maid. They treat me like a changeling." She seems struck by her own words, her face souring. "They treat me like a changeling *slave*," she says again, the frown growing deeper.

"What about Taylor?" I grab her arms. "Is she all right? Is she hurt?"

"She's fine." Then she hurriedly adds, "Majorly scared, of course. *Terrified* of Shathinor and the undead and the soldiers and all that." She waves a dismissive hand. "Worried about you, naturally. She's sensitive like that. Caring and sweet. Changeling through and through, you know?" She stares at her feet, then continues, "Anyway, she asked me to come take you to her. So that you can save her."

"It's a trap," Gray growls behind me. "Shathinor sent her to entice you to your doom. He knows we're here."

"No." She holds out the necklace, Taylor's soulstone. "She said you'd be here, could feel you through the bond. I swear she sent me. She told me to give you this."

Gray advances. "Shathinor could have sent it—"

I take it and turn it over in my palm, warmth pulsing into my skin. The bond. "It's from her. I can *feel* her on it."

"Let's go, then." Valen gestures from across the chasm. "I'm ready."

"No. Just the king." Cecile shrugs. "I can only sneak one of you in. More than that, and I'll get caught." She shivers. "And I *definitely* don't want to get caught."

"Leander, no." Gray puts a hand on my shoulder. "It's a trap."

"Probably." I pin Cecile with a hard look. "Lead on."

Gray grabs my arm. "Wait."

"Bad plan, my king." Valen shakes his head. "Let's talk about this."

"The rest of you stay here and await my command. If I'm not back by sunup, leave this place and alert the realms of the coming war." I shake my arm. "Gray, I'll need that back."

"No." Valen jumps to the stairs. "If Shathinor gets his hands on you—"

"He'll kill me." I turn to look at both of them. "I knew that risk when I left the winter realm, but I will do anything to save Taylor. She is my sunrise and sunset, and if she asks for me, I will go to her, no matter what."

Gray scowls, Valen's face falls, and Selene is snoring again.

"I must see this through." I offer my hands. They take them, reluctantly, and grip my forearms. "Trust me. Trust that I know what I'm doing, and we will all be together again—either at High Mountain or in the Glowing Lands of the Ancestors."

"The second option doesn't seem like the best one." Valen pulls me into a hug. "Good luck." His voice is tight.

"This is a bad idea." Gray squeezes my arm and releases me. "I won't let you live this down. Not here or on the other side."

I smile for the first time since Taylor was taken. "I would expect no less."

"My king." Valen drops to his knee, his head bowed.

Gray's face sobers, and he does the same. "My king."

Cecile clears her throat. "If we're done here, I've got laundry and—"

I turn to her so quickly that she stumbles backward, barely catching herself on the wall.

Trap or no, my fate lies with Taylor. "Lead me to my mate."

ecile's steps are loud even as she tries to creep down the hallway outside my door. Leander barely seems to touch the stone floors, but I can sense him. Everything inside me goes taut. My mate his here. The one who will rule Arin by my side.

I face the door, smiling as it creaks open and Cecile hurries in, Leander on her heels.

He stops, the air growing cool and his body tensing. "Taylor?"

"Yes." I step forward, suddenly worried he won't recognize me, not as I am.

He rushes to me and pulls me into his arms, crushing me against his chest. "Thank the Ancestors. You're safe." He kisses my hair, his lips straying down my cheek and meeting my mouth with a fervor that sets off an ache inside me.

I wrap my arms around his neck and answer his tongue with mine, every bit of the passion I feel for him going into this kiss.

He pulls back, but not far. "I have to get you to safety. What did he do to you?" He glances at my darker hair, then runs a hand along one of my wings.

I shudder at his touch, every bit of me attuned to what it feels like to be near him again.

"Taylor?" Cecile waits at the door. "I did what you asked."

"Your pet is safe. Get out," I hiss.

Leander's brows draw together, but I don't have time to explain, not when my need for him blots out any rational thought. I skim a hand down his abs and reach into his pants.

"My mate." He kisses me hard, his cock in my hand like an iron rod covered with the finest silk.

"I want you." I back away and strip my shirt off.

He watches, his eyes hungry as I shuck my pants away and stand naked before him.

When I drop to my knees and pull him toward me, he reaches for my wings again. "You're fae? How?"

I don't want to talk. Not now. I pull his cock free from his pants and lick the head.

He growls and runs his hands through my hair. "Little one, we must leave. You aren't safe."

I take him to the back of my throat, my tongue pressed against his cock as I start bobbing my head.

His groan creates a sensual wetness between my thighs, and I reach down and rub my clit as I suck him until my cheeks go hollow.

With a roar he lifts me and pins me to the bed. "Taylor, what is this?" He peers into my eyes, desire and confusion warring inside him.

I spread my legs wide and rock against him. "I want you, my king. I need you deep inside me, mated and loved."

His low purr vibrates through me.

My fangs lengthen, and without a thought, I sink them deep into his shoulder. He roars and enters me, filling me as I cry against his warm skin, his blood flowing on my tongue. His hands grip mine, holding me down as I take everything he offers—his body, his blood, the bond between our souls.

I let go and lick my lips as he claims my mouth again, his body surging into mine and shaking the bed with each powerful stroke.

"Mine." He nips at my lips as he owns me again and again, his powerful body made for me and me alone. Releasing my hands, he grabs my hair and pulls, arching me so he can suck my throat.

Digging my nails into his back, I hold on as he pistons into me, my breasts tingling with pleasure as he dominates every bit of me, his hard chest rubbing me just right.

Gripping one breast, he runs his tongue along my nipple, then clamps down, his hips still working me as I gasp for breath and twist his hair in my fingers. I moan as he sucks the bud into his mouth, his tongue massaging the tip as my legs spread even wider. Every moment of contact between us is like a little spark of electricity, millions of them lighting me up from the inside.

He pulls away, his eyes dark, and grips my hips. With a rough yank, he turns me over and pulls me onto my knees. With a hard thrust, he enters me from behind. I cry out as he leans over me, his chest against my folded wings as he fills me with hard strokes.

My toes curl when he licks the back of my neck, then bites, breaking the skin with his fangs. He holds onto me like an animal, keeping me right where he wants me as he gives me everything I want. When he runs a hand beneath me and strokes my clit, I begin to shake, my pleasure winding around inside me like thread on a tight spool.

The sound of his skin hitting mine ricochets around the room, and the bed bangs against the wall to his impossible rhythm. I push back against him, driving him further inside me as his fingers strum my sensitive spot. He bites harder, the pain like gasoline on the fire that already burns between us. My hips seize, and I gasp as my release hits, the pleasure coursing through me, overflowing until I can barely breathe, barely feel anything except the tension unwinding in languid waves of pleasure.

Leander growls against my skin, then shoves hard and deep. His cock kicks inside me, and he spurts his seed with a roar. We pant together, our bodies joined and sharing in each other's pleasure. As my release fades, my knees spread, and I sink down into the bed, Leander on top of me, still inside me.

He releases the bite, then licks the wound. "We must go." He pulls out, and I breathe out a hard sigh.

Dressing quickly, he pulls my clothes from the floor and brings them to me.

"Hurry. We shouldn't have tarried."

"I enjoyed tarrying." I roll over and stretch my arms above my head.

His gaze goes to my breasts and then lower, the evidence of our love-making on my thighs. "Taylor," he growls. "You will drive me mad with lust." He searches around and finds a small towel. "Here." After cleaning me up, he hands me my clothes. "We have to get you out of here. It's not safe."

"I'm perfectly safe." I sit up and pull on my shirt. "You're the one who's iffy."

"What?"

I snap my fingers, and dozens of undead guards rush into the room, followed by my father, a cruel grin on his face. "*No!*" The voice inside me is louder. It's as if she grows stronger each moment we're in Leander's presence.

"It seems the traitor has come back to me." Shathinor motions for the guards to take Leander. "Foolish usurper. You should have burned my body and scattered the ashes across Arin."

"I'll get that taken care of this time around." Leander blasts the room with ice.

"Not so fast, lover." I call on my dark heart of death and send an orb of black to swirl around him like a shadowy prison. "Touch that and it's going to leave a mark."

"Taylor." He turns to me, his eyes wide. "What are you—"

"My daughter." Shathinor motions for me to come to him.

I shimmy my pants on and walk to his side, ever so obediently.

"This is your father?" Leander seems a bit less surprised than I'd expected.

"Did you know?" I ask.

He rolls his shoulders and keeps his gaze on me. Even now, caged by death, he's formidable and unfairly sexy. "I suspected you might have a necromancer in your lineage after what happened with Delantis and Vanara. But this ..." He shakes his head. "I never expected Shathinor, the evil of old."

"Your mate shares my blood. She is more mine than yours," Shathinor crows.

"*Not true.*" I silently send the words down the bond.

Leander's nostrils flare as if he heard me. "*Then why are you caging me?*"

"*All in good time.*" I wink.

"*What happened to you? Where did you go?*" He stares at me as if he can see through me. "*You're still you, but somehow not.*"

"I'm a better version of me," I say out loud. "Taylor the changeling was weak, pathetic. I'm strong, and nothing will stand between me and my destiny."

Leander's gaze never leaves me. "You speak of the prophecy?"

I shrug. "Guilty as charged. Destroying the summer and winter realms seems like a great start."

"They will fall and rise again under my banner." Shathinor puts his arm around my shoulders.

I groan inwardly.

"My daughter is the prophecy made flesh."

"She's my mate." Leander's gaze locks with mine, and my heart twists.

"That's unfortunate for you," Shathinor gloats. "But her heart is set on you. So, I will allow her to keep you as a pet."

"And if I decide to freeze you to death rather than be held prisoner?"

"Then I will kill your friends. One by one." He whistles.

Scuffling sounds in the hallway have Leander's glower deepening into thunderhead territory.

A host of guards yank Valen and Grayhail along, their bodies bound with iron.

"Release them." Leander steps forward, but when his elbow brushes my barrier, the skin blackens, and he steps back.

Something filters through me, something that has no place here—guilt. *"You **should** feel guilty. Let him go."* That voice, the one from inside is back like a bothersome gnat.

"Leander! I'm here. I'm here!" the voice screams, and I put my hands up to my ears. But it doesn't stop. Is she growing stronger?

"Taylor." His brows rise. *"I can hear you, little one."*

Another noise behind me catches my attention, and I turn to find the obsidian witch Selene leaning against the door frame.

She looks me up and down. "Your feral looks good on you, changeling."

"My feral?"

"The wings, the hair, the ruby lips." She shimmies, her hard breasts shaking. "Hubba hubba. I never knew the queen of darkness, the ender of worlds, the embodiment of death would be such a turn-on."

"Selene." Shathinor purses his lips. "One more word and I'll have you wrapped in iron like the other two."

"I'd like to see you try." She smiles, her black teeth glinting. "I let myself get caught, and I'll leave when I like." She splays her claws and examines them before returning her gaze to me. "Besides, I can smell doom, the first hint of the coming destruction. I want to taste it."

I walk to Leander and stand just beyond the orb. "You came for me."

"I will always come for you." He moves closer. "I promised you that, and I will keep that oath until I go to the Ancestors."

"And then?" My eyes water. Where is this weakness coming from?

"And then I will wait for you there."

He pushes his hand through the orb, the skin turning black, but he still caresses my cheek as his flesh withers. "You are mine, and I am yours. And nothing save death can part us. And even then, not for long."

"*Leander.*" The voice in my head—no, not just a voice. I know who it is. I've known all along. It's me. "*I love you.*" Both the Taylor inside and the one I've become say it together.

"I love you, too." He pulls his blackened hand back and turns his gaze to my father. "Mark this, I will be your end."

Shathinor laughs and pulls me back by his side. "Your threats are empty, *king*. Come now, Daughter. We have plans." He guides me out the door as the undead warriors advance on Leander.

As I lose sight of him, I can still feel him, the bond between us stronger than these stone walls.

"Well, this is cozy." Valen grabs the bars and immediately lets go. "Iron. All iron." He stands back from the side of the cage and looks up. "Up there, too."

"Settle down." Cenet stalks by the cage, his snakelike tongue darting out and tasting the air. "You aren't going anywhere." He points to the nearest changeling guard. "If they try anything, skewer one of them with your iron sword."

"Sir." The changeling guard steps forward, sword drawn, as Cenet leaves the throne room.

"Nice guy." Valen hitches his thumb in the direction Cenet went.

"Step back. You heard Lord Cenet. I'm free to skewer any of you if you rub me the wrong way."

"Skewer away." Gray—large enough that his ears almost graze the roof of the cage—grabs the bars, his hands sizzling. "But when I get out of here, we'll see which one of us dies on that thing."

The changeling steps back, the color draining from his face.

I peer around the throne room. We're caged along the side like prized trophies. No grim dungeon for us. Shathinor wants us displayed.

"How did you get captured?" I cross my arms over my chest.

Gray shoots Valen a glare. "Loverboy over here saw that blonde fae again, and she lured him into trouble. Of course, then I went to save him." He shakes his head. "And here we are. All because Valen can't keep cool around summer realm fae."

"I can." He shrugs. "But that one is particularly choice."

I should scold him, should reinforce the notions of discipline, restraint, and caution. But I find I can't say anything at all. Not after I made love to Taylor instead of making our escape. I rub my temples. Foolish.

"You were only just mated. It's normal for the instinct to take over sometimes." Gray, as always, seems to read my mind. "It was a trap either way. At least you got to be with Taylor."

"It was stupid." I give him a nod all the same.

"How did she change so much?" Valen plops down on the stone floor.

I've been asking myself the same question. "Selene said it was her feral fae."

"Whoa." Valen leans back on his elbows. "That's pretty much unheard of. Her feral fae manifesting like that, with her so young?"

"We don't know how old she is." Gray paces one side

of the cramped cage. "She could be older than Leander for all we know. And on top of that, she's a necromancer."

"A powerful one," Valen adds. "She's only just come into her magic, but she wields it like, like ..."

"Like her father." I grit my teeth.

"Pretty much." Valen points to my wasted hand. "That's not healing fast enough."

"Save your power for—"

He closes his eyes and summons healing magic, green energy swirling around my hand until it's repaired.

I flex my healed fingers. "Thanks."

He shrugs. "That's my job."

Gray continues to pace as Valen lies back and uses his interlaced fingers for a pillow. I keep scanning the room, looking for a way out of this. But I can't leave without Taylor. Will she come with me? Or stay here with Shathinor? The thought of her turning her back on me has me gripping the cage and yanking as hard as I can. The metal bends but doesn't break.

"Too strong for you, traitor." Shathinor strides in, his familiar smirk like a bad dream.

"I will get out." I release the bars and let my hands hang at my sides, the iron keeping bits of my sizzling skin.

"You will." He stops and peruses me with the same cold eyes that watched thousands of his own people fight and die, perish from starvation, and serve as nothing more than pawns in his war against the summer realm. "But only for your execution."

"You think Taylor will allow that?"

He laughs low and slimy. "I've given her plenty of leash, but it's almost time to yank it back. You think I don't know she plans on my overthrow? She's *my* daughter after all. It only makes sense that she wants the throne for herself. I don't mind that. I truly don't. And it will be easy enough to pull her into line."

"You don't know her."

"Neither do you." He cocks his head to the side. "You think she's the same foolish changeling who followed you through the Greenvelde and the Red Plains? One look at her tells you that's not the case. She has my wings, my darkness, my thirst for conquest. She is the greatest weapon in all of Arin, and I intend to use her until there's nothing left."

"You won't touch her." I pound the bars, the iron giving way but still not bursting free.

Shathinor doesn't move. "Your time is almost up. Prepare your betrayer's heart for the Spires. Tonight—" He turns toward a ruckus in the hallway. "What in the name of the Ancestors is—"

Thorn comes flying through the double doors and skids across the polished black floor. He flops onto his back, his face a bloody mess, as Shathinor gapes at him. "Shathinor. Long time, no see. How's that whole being dead thing treating you?"

"Thorn." Shathinor spits. "I think I'll have you change to a bear before I kill you. I'd like your hide on my bed."

Thorn nods appreciatively. "That is, by far, the creepiest invite to someone's bed I've ever gotten."

Shathinor kicks him in the stomach, and Thorn flies across the room, his back cracking against the rock wall. He coughs blood and heaves in a pained breath.

"I told you I'd bring you a gift, my king."

We all turn toward the door.

"Traitor!" Valen rushes the iron cage, but Gray holds him back.

"Ah, the apprentice has returned." Shathinor smiles as Brannon drops to his knee before him.

TAYLOR

*C*ecile knocks and enters, a new gown draped across her arms.

"What's this?" I've been lying on my bed, staring at nothing, and thinking about Leander. But the interruptions are nonstop. The other voice in my head grows louder, telling me that we are in this together, that I'm her feral form, that we both survive or neither of us do. That doesn't even make sense. I run this body. These are *my* wings. *My* magic.

"Taylor?" Cecile hesitates by the bed.

"What?"

She proffers the dress. "You asked what this was. I told you it's for tonight. But you ignored me and zoned out."

"How's your human?" Where did that come from? I don't care about her human.

"She's fine." Cecile lays the dress on the bed. "Mostly. Your death curse almost killed her, of course." She clamps her mouth closed.

There's that feeling again. The one that doesn't belong. *Guilt*. It's as if seeing Leander has unlocked the part of me that I keep trying to squelch.

The door opens, this time without a knock, and Selene glides in and drops onto my bed.

"Hey, watch the dress!" Cecile snatches it up. "I had to iron this myself."

I laugh. The Taylor inside me joins for a moment, then sobers.

Cecile raises a brow at me but doesn't respond.

"Afraid of you, this one is." Selene clacks her teeth at Cecile. "Meat always tastes better when it dies afraid."

Cecile shifts from one foot to the other, and part of me revels in her discomfort. The other part, the one I can't seem to get rid of, pities her.

"You spit out my pea." Selene lies back.

Cecile gags.

"P-e-a not p-e-e." I point to the chair at my dressing table. "Put it there and go." I wave her away. "It was time for me to shine, I suppose."

"Have you decided who you're going to be?" Selene rolls over to face me and rests her head on her hand, the obsidian crackling.

"I don't know what you mean."

"I'm personally rooting for death incarnate, the destroyer of Arin, the bringer of war, the—"

"I get it."

"That would be glorious. Just imagine all the bones." She sighs contentedly. "So many bits, parts lying around, pools of blood, guts, and ooohh, think of all the *teeth*!"

"I could skip the gore. But I will crush the summer

realm." I pull a small orb of death into my palm and play with it. "Killing only makes me stronger."

"You killed one in the Red Plains. How many have you killed here?" She turns those too-knowing eyes on me.

"Shathinor's had me using all my magic to reanimate." I roll my eyes. "He says that's the hard part, the most important part."

"He's right. More soldiers that way." She presses one finger into the black orb and pulls it back, staring at the pale skin revealed as the obsidian dies from the surface of her skin.

"Did you know that would happen?" I stare at her finger, the nail just like a regular fae's, no more claw, no more black obsidian.

"No." She shakes it, and the obsidian creeps back into place. "Interesting."

"Maybe I could—"

She harrumphs. "I am obsidian. I do not break."

"Okay then." I chew my lip. "You said this is my feral form. Is that true?"

"Yes. Your feral was locked away for so long by that soulstone, that once it was set free, it took over. You are feral."

"Right now? I'm feral right this second?"

"Don't you *feel* feral?" She raises her white brows. "You're power drunk, homicidal, and full of rage." Her tone turns dreamy. "A deadly treat you are, wearing your darkness on the outside."

"So, I can change back?"

"Can you?" She cackles, and I realize I'm not getting

any more straight answers from her. I glance at the dress and try another avenue. "What sort of stupid ceremony is he planning for tonight? Gloating over Leander and his pals?"

"You didn't answer my question. Who will you be? Death? Or, you could go back to being that little waif in the woods. The girl I met, the one who wanted to go home."

"*We can be whatever we want to be.*" Taylor's words float through me, melding with my own.

"I can hear her in there. But she's you." Selene taps my temple. "Confusing. But all will be one soon enough. Now answer my question. What shall you be?"

"I can't go home. I mean, back to earth." Leander's voice resonates in my heart. "*I am your home.*" I rub my eyes. "I don't want to." I realize that neither of us do. "I'm not a changeling. Maybe I don't know what I am or what I should be. But I *feel* this desire to destroy. It's so strong." I close the ball of death in my fist, and it disappears, then open my palm and watch it ignite again. "I want to take it all and rule."

"Your father. That's him in there." She taps my temple again. "It's you but not you. Locked away for so long by the soulstone, it came roaring out. Ready to tear the world to pieces and feast on its bones." She grins as if she likes the taste of her own words. "This feral form you're in is Shathinor's blood, his soul as black as night. The wings, the hair, the red lips." Her eyes dart to my mouth. "Makes me want to relive my college of magic days. Tempting feral."

I ignore her poor come-on. "Delantis said that the

feral is the same as the fae. She could call hers forth in the form of a gryphon, but its name was Delantis, and it was her. They worked together. I feel like I'm at war with whatever I was before the stone was removed. She wants to overtake me, to push me back down into darkness again and lock me away." I grit my teeth. "Never again."

"Delantis was correct. Very smart fae, that one." She picks at her teeth. "Who's Delantis?"

"Doesn't matter." I sigh and sit up. "None of this is getting me anywhere. Besides, I've chosen my path. War. I can't change what I am, whatever that is."

"I know what you are." She pats me on the head. "I've known since I tasted you in the Greenvelde."

"Then what am I?"

"A child of many worlds."

"You mean the prophecy." I toss the black sphere into the air and catch it. "That's not helpful."

"Not helpful? It tells you everything you need to know."

"It doesn't even make sense. 'She alone can start the war and be victorious, win or lose.' How can anyone be victorious if they lose?"

"Depends on what they lose and what victory means." She cackles. "Prophecies are always so tricky. Maybe the seer was hedging, eh? Not wanting to say one way or another, so she twisted it into a knot."

"One I can't untangle."

"No need. What will be is already set in motion. Choices have been made whether you know it or not." She rises and strides to the dress. "Nice. Perfect for tonight."

"Tell me what happens tonight." I itch to know where my father's keeping Leander. The bond between us is alive but dimmed.

"No, no, no. TMI, my dark beauty. T-M-I." She claps her hands, the slap of stone jarring. "Besides, I can't see the future." She lifts the dress and holds it up to her body, then dances around the room. "I can only taste the blood in the air, sense the hate that echoes along these stone walls, and covet the bones that are soon to be stripped from their owners."

A knock at the door draws my attention, and Cecile returns, her gaze down as Selene waltzes around her. "Your father summons you."

"Fine." I wave her away. "You can go."

She glances at Selene and shudders. "I-I'm to accompany you."

"Why?"

She shrugs.

"Whatever." I strip and grab the dress from Selene as she eyes my body.

Slipping it over my head, I roll my shoulders and let it fall in all the right places, my wings free through the open back. Before leaving, I take the obsidian blade, the haft always warm in my hand, reminding me of Delantis. She's still here—at least some part of her is—living inside the black sword.

Selene runs her fingers along the phylactery at my throat and licks her lips. "Blood."

"Not for you." I smack her hand, and she grins.

"Again?" She holds it out.

"You have issues."

"Assuredly." She turns to a terrified Cecile and takes her elbow. "Let's away to the throne room. While we walk, we shall discuss ripe meat and flesh, the kind that's rotted for weeks. Now, I like to strip the bones clean with my claws, then ..."

They stroll ahead of me down the long, dark hallway, Selene's voice growing quieter as Leander's begins to swell inside me. He's afraid. My steps quicken. But not for himself. For his friends. I break into a jog. Not just for his friends, for *Gareth.*

*B*rannon stalks into the throne room, Gareth in one hand and Beth in the other. "Your Phalanx needs a little work in the stealth department." Brannon smirks and gut punches Gareth, who doubles over.

"Stop!" Beth tries to claw him, but he shoves her into the waiting arms of a changeling guard.

The iron door swings open, and Gareth joins us while the guard chains Beth to the wall.

"I'm too good to go in the cage?" She wipes her busted lip on her arm.

"You aren't worth it." Brannon slams the cage shut, and the changeling jailor locks it and pockets the key.

"You shouldn't have come." I kneel beside Gareth, his face bloody and broken. "Why did you come?"

"You are my king. I owe you my allegiance." He spits blood as Valen goes to work on him. He can't do much, not now that he spent so much magic to heal Thorn.

Cenet strides in, a wide grin on his face. "We have almost all of them. This is easier than I ever imagined."

Beth runs at him, but her chains draw her up short. "You lying piece of—"

Cenet strides up and backhands her. "Shut your mouth, foul changeling."

Gareth growls. She falls to her knees but gives Cenet a look so venomous I suspect it could kill a small child.

I would scold Gareth for bringing Beth, but I have no doubt she insisted on coming. She's just as tenacious as Taylor.

Beth spits at Cenet, and he jumps back toward me. I reach through the bars and swipe for him, barely missing.

He darts away, his eyes going snakelike.

"You took my mate from me." I pin him with a glare. "And sealed your fate."

"I'm not the one in a cage." Cenet's smug face begs to be punched in. "And if you try anything, this changeling will be the first to suffer." He grabs Beth by the hair.

She shrieks and tries to pry herself loose.

"One hint of winter from you, and she dies." He darts his tongue out, licking her cheek.

"Don't touch her!" Gareth struggles to turn over and crawl to her.

"Lie still." I push him down. "You can't help her like this."

Cenet shoves her to the floor and re-takes his position across from the cage, his arms crossed and his gaze firmly on us.

Gareth grunts and closes his eyes. "I'm going to kill that bastard."

More soldiers flow into the room, lining the walls with undead, lesser fae, and changelings. Something big is happening. I try to send a warning to Taylor, but the bond is quiet. Too quiet. Is something blocking her?

The murmuring dead create a low hum around us as Cenet and Brannon stand watch. More soldiers trickle in, most of them looking at me with surprise, and a few with satisfaction.

Selene's cackle rattles around the throne room, and she walks in with Cecile on her arm, though the golden fae looks like she's on the verge of vomiting or fainting— maybe both.

My mind buzzes, the bond like a bolt of lightning linking me to my mate. She appears in a gown of midnight blue, and her eyes meet mine immediately.

"Taylor." I say her name like a prayer.

She walks up, her chin high as she peruses all of us. "This is the best the winter realm has to offer? All caught and imprisoned in iron like fireflies in a jar?"

"You rubbing it in, too?" Thorn tests his bruised jaw with tentative fingers. "We'll never live this down."

I put my hand through the cage. She takes it without hesitation, the bond snapping back into place.

"Something's blocking our connection." I squeeze her palm.

"I know. I think it's my father."

"He wants to use you." I lower my voice. "He intends to control you, to have you win his war for him and then—"

"Kill me?" She laughs, low and husky. "He has plans,

but so do I. I will take the realms, and you and I will rule them. We don't need him."

"Why do you want to run headfirst into bloodshed?" I move closer, peering down into her blue eyes. "Ruling the winter realm with me will have enough challenges. More than you know."

"I want it all." Her fangs lengthen. "It's mine to take."

"You will have to kill, Taylor—innocents, children, babes in their mothers' wombs. Are you prepared for that? Because that's what war is."

Her brows knit together. "I want—" She flinches. "Shhh. I didn't ask you."

"Taylor?"

She shakes her head. "Nothing. I will do what I must." Her voice is cold, and she pulls her hand free. "You'll see. When you're king of the realms, you'll thank me."

"Taylor, please, this isn't you."

"I am whoever I want to be."

"I thought you were my friend," Beth calls from where she's chained to the wall. "Or did you forget all about our chats and skinny dipping?"

"Don't speak to me, changeling." Taylor, menace rolling from her, cuts her eyes to Beth. "Keep to your own kind."

"I thought you were my kind," Beth persists.

"You thought wrong." Taylor turns her back and strides up the stairs to the throne.

I pull my hand back through the bars, my mate's warmth fading as quickly as a curl of smoke.

The crowd parts again as Shathinor strides by. He

doesn't even look at us, his head high. He's dressed in full silver battle regalia, his love of pomp still strong despite all these years.

Brannon turns to follow Shathinor up the wide stairs to the throne.

"This is how you repay me?" I yell through the bars.

Brannon turns, and the black runes pulse along his throat as he approaches through the crowd of warriors. "Repay you for what? Taking everything away from me? Your throne should have been mine."

"You would never have ruled the winter realm." I growl. "You don't have what it takes. Never have."

"Liar." He shoves the jailor changeling out of the way and rushes the cage, the impact rattling every bit of the iron. "I will enjoy watching your death." He presses his face against the metal and doesn't flinch at the sizzle of flesh.

"I told you." Thorn rubs his newly-mended arm. "He can't be trusted. The darkness in him is too great, too evil."

"Too unseelie for you, Thorn?" Brannon spits.

"Not at all. But too ugly? Definitely." He grins.

"You won't be laughing when Shathinor takes your head."

Thorn shrugs. "Guess not, but at least I'll still be handsome, even in pieces. Your ugly is permanent."

"Keep talking, fool. Your last words will be here soon enough." Brannon backs away. Cenet steps out of his way but gives him a long look. Perhaps he didn't know that Brannon had been Shathinor's chosen heir before the war began.

"Shouldn't have trusted him." Gareth winces. "I told you so many times that he was ruled by the darkness, too poisoned by Shathinor to ever serve as an honorable member of the Phalanx. I hate to say it, but there it is. I told you, Leander."

"You told me so, eh?" I grin and hold my fist over him.

"I did. I warned you. Thorn did, too. But you didn't listen, and now Brannon has gone and—"

I open my fist, and the key to the iron cage Brannon just slipped me dangles from my palm. "Now who's saying 'I told you so'?"

I stand next to the throne, the room filled with soldiers of all types, each of them bound by the desire for blood. Some of them think they're fighting for freedom. What they're really fighting for is *me*.

Shathinor climbs the stairs as the room goes silent. Once at the top, he turns and spreads his arms. "We are here to celebrate the capture of the traitor, the pretender to my throne, Leander Gladion."

The room erupts in a guttural shout, then quiets again.

Cenet stands on the other side of the throne. He glances at me, but I don't look at him. He's beneath my notice.

"Tonight, we cement our alliance, our shared goal of bringing fairness to the realms. War is not an easy choice, but this war is a righteous one. One that will give changelings and lesser fae the equality they deserve, and in the end, make the realms a far better place for all who dwell there."

Another roar from the crowd. The changelings and lesser fae watch Shathinor with devotion, their eyes alight.

Not Leander. I can feel him, his anger like ant bites on my heart.

But the soldiers believe every slimy word from Shathinor's mouth, devour the lies like they are starving for them.

"*They are*," Taylor says, her voice stronger than ever. It's as if the link to Leander pulls her forward, presses her consciousness into mine. "*They want freedom, and they deserve it. They shouldn't be slaves. Changelings and lesser fae should be equal with high fae. You know it's true. Their cause is just, and they want it so badly that they are blind to Shathinor's ev—*"

"Daughter?" Shathinor motions me forward, irritation gilding his tone as if he knows I wasn't paying attention.

I stand next to him, his cold arm around my waist.

"This perfect blade of death will lead us to victory. With her, we will be invincible. The realms will fall before us."

This is it. The moment when I embrace the prophecy and take my rightful place at the head of my father's army. My dark heart craves it. All of Arin is within my grasp. I have but to take it. "*Do not forget who you are,*" Delantis whispers to me. But she never told me who I am. No one can do that. No one except me. Am I death incarnate? Or am I something different?

The soldiers stare at me, all those upturned faces, but the only one I see is Leander's. He stands in the cage, his intense gaze like a touch, like his hand on my cheek and his lips brushing against mine. *"My love,"* he whispers. The bond is stronger than even Shathinor's attempt to block it. Leander's love infuses me, coating my heart with warmth.

The pure adoration in his stare, the emotion in his words, the feeling of being cherished—all of it breaks me in ways I didn't know were possible. My fury seems to melt away like a spring thaw, the need to destroy fading as I bask in his love. I try to fight it, to stand my ground. But what we have is too strong, a love that surmounted my father's curse, a bond too powerful to ever break. The wall between the old Taylor and what I am cracks, the distinction evaporating as she and I cross the barrier and circle each other around our shared soul. I am her, and she is me. The voice is gone. Because it's *my* voice.

My bond with Leander has tamed my feral heart, opened the locked door between the two sides of my nature. I blink away tears as he pours his love into me. *"We are one. We will always be one, no matter what form you take."*

I can't go back to the waif in the woods, but I can't become the destroyer of worlds. I'm somewhere in the middle, new but the same, old but different.

"You are perfect, little one." Leander's calming voice filters through my jumbled mind, calming me. Whatever I am, he loves me. And that has to be enough.

"I've been holding back, making sure she focused on honing her new skills, but neglecting her best." Shathinor turns to me, his eyes infinitely cold. "Death. But tonight, I will unleash her, set her free to deal as much destruction as she so chooses." He points to the cage. "The traitors—you will kill all of them. It's my gift to you."

I freeze, my heart storming in my chest as the crowd of soldiers roar their approval.

My voice barely makes a sound. "No."

Shathinor hears it and slashes his hand through the air, silencing the room. "What was that, my princess?"

"I already told you I won't kill my mate for you." I kick my chin up.

"I'm afraid you must, my dear heart." He pulls me tighter against him.

"No." I wrench myself free of his hold and back away. "That was not our agreement."

Cenet stands behind my father, his reptilian eyes slitted. "I told you, Father."

"Silence!" Shathinor thunders, and for the first time, lets his magic loose. Black tendrils flow from his eyes, fingertips, and mouth, the darkness swirling around him like a whirlwind. "Daughter, you will do as I ask."

"No." I call forth my own power, the blackness surging inside me. The well of magic is even deeper now that I've accepted myself, my mate, and the path we will walk together.

"I was afraid you'd turn on me, give in to that weak fool who lives inside you." He tsks as his magic grows.

"Leave her alone!" Leander roars from the cage.

"Don't push me." I summon black death into my palms and back away from my father.

"I'm afraid pushing you is my job as a loving parent," he sneers and matches me step for step.

"I'm leaving, and I'm taking them with me. All of

them. Including Cecile and the changeling Taylor. I was wrong to ever join with you. I don't want your throne. I don't want anything from you."

"Pathetic." Shathinor glowers.

"I will kill you if I have to." I pool my magic in front of me like a shield and keep the explosive orb in my palm. "But I don't want to."

"You will kill *for* me, my dear heart." He follows me, his rage growing as his magic spirals faster and faster. "You will do everything I ask. And that includes killing your traitorous mate and his friends, my darling princess."

"I am not your princess." My wings unfurl. "I am Leander's *queen*." I throw my deathly orb as a ruckus sends the room into a frenzy.

Shathinor screeches as my magic cuts through his whirlwind and strikes him in the gut. I draw the obsidian blade and brace myself for battle when a blast of ice freezes all the soldiers closest to me, clearing the way at the foot of the stairs. Leander surges forward, his face a mask of rage as he advances on Shathinor. His Phalanx have escaped their cage and engaged the crowd, fighting with a vengeance that doesn't bode well for Shathinor's troops.

Pumping my wings, I hover in the air and throw more deathly magic at my father.

Cenet jumps down the stairs, and Gareth rushes him.

"Don't look in his eyes!" I shout to Gareth.

They fall back into the fray, both of them fighting a vicious sword battle. Brannon takes out an entire row of soldiers with some dark tentacle monster he's summoned.

"My king." Valen throws Leander a sword. He catches it, then turns and hurls it into Shathinor.

My father yells as the blade slams into his chest and penetrates his armor. He looks down, his eyes wide.

Leander rushes toward him, but a blast of black magic bursts from my father, knocking Leander onto his back. Shathinor sheds the armor and the sword, black blood barely staining his shirt.

"He's already dead." I drop to the steps beside Leander, the obsidian blade in my grip. I can end my father, stop the war, and keep the realms safe.

Something tickles my throat, and I cough. I reach up and feel the phylactery, but it burns my hand, and suddenly, I can't move.

"There's no escape from the Spires this time." Leander summons a spike of ice as Shathinor's dark magic lifts him off his feet.

"You and your friends were fools to come here." Shathinor floats higher, the darkness oozing from his pores. "Getting captured was the last mistake you'll make."

"Mistake?" Leander climbs the stairs. "We *wanted* to be captured. You just brought the deadliest fighters in all of Arin into your throne room." He spares a glance to the melee behind us, the Phalanx a whirling dervish of death and ruin. Shathinor's soldiers are falling or running, only the undead attacking relentlessly.

Shathinor scowls and sends a rope of black magic to wrap around Leander's throat. The battle is a cacophony as I try to move, to yell.

"*Taylor.*" Shathinor's voice courses through me as if

he's in my head. As if, through the phylactery, he's somehow *part* of me. This damn necklace is cursed just like the old one.

I gasp as realization hits me. "Oh, shit. It's a horcrux!"

Shathinor speaks again. *"You will kill your mate. Now."*

"No." I try to back away, but I find I can't. I'm moving toward Leander, my sword up and my shield dissipating.

Shathinor laughs in my skull. *"You thought I trusted you? The child of that summer realm whore? You were pathetic until I found you. I've made you strong, and this is how you repay me?"*

"I was always strong." I fight against the pull, but I'm losing control, Shathinor's will replacing my own. Chaos reigns at my back, and Leander struggles to free himself from the dark magic that weaves around him like a spider's wrapping.

"This trinket is my insurance policy. I will always have you in the palm of my hand. You thought I cared about you? That I would ever let you sit on my throne?" He grins. *"You are a tool, a vessel. This body can no longer sustain me. But yours? I will take it as my own."*

"Not cool," I grit out and try to backpedal. I don't. I keep moving toward Leander, almost within striking distance.

"You will kill him. And then I will devour your soul and wear your skin."

"No!" I scream. To my horror, I can't stop, can't pull myself back. "Leander." My eyes water as I fight Shathinor's hold.

"Let her go!" Leander shoots a blast of raw ice at

Shathinor. It's enough to stagger him. The darkness around Leander abates, and he takes the opening and throws his ice spear at Shathinor, but the darkness swallows it up. He summons another and another, each of them destroyed by the magic. But Leander doesn't give up. He rushes my father, jumping at the last moment and tackling him onto his throne of bone. It shatters as they land and struggle, the heart of winter and the pit of death locked in battle. And me, powerless to do anything to help my mate.

They trade blows, their fight a blur of speed and ferocity. I can feel Leander's pain, but I can feel his resolve even more. He will die if it means he can take Shathinor with him. The mountain shakes with their cries and the strength of their hurled magic. Soldiers try to run past me to help their leader, but the Phalanx mows them down, dragging them back into the fray.

My father summons me closer, his voice pulling me toward him, commanding me to strike Leander with the obsidian blade, to run it through his heart.

"Leander, you have to stop me." I force the words out despite the burning in my throat that demands I stay silent. They don't go far, and Leander and Shathinor are too locked in battle to hear me. The mountain rumbles louder, rocks falling from the ceiling as Leander slams Shathinor to the ground. With fists of ice, Leander lands several hard blows to the necromancer.

Shathinor's wasted body is dying, but his laugh echoes in my mind. *"Let's show him what you can really do."*

Death seeps from my fingertips, filling the air around

me and circling the obsidian blade. If I strike Leander, there will be no coming back from it. I try to fight the pull, but I'm locked on my course, my feet climbing the stairs, shards of bone crunching beneath me.

Leander keeps fighting, using all his magic and his strength to slay Shathinor. My father's cursed life is dwindling. I can feel his wasted flesh tearing apart, his rotted heart beating out of rhythm. Soon, it will stop altogether.

"Lean—"

Shathinor silences my voice completely, constricting my throat with my own magic, blocking the bond that ties me to my mate. Tears roll down my cheeks as I raise the blade behind Leander's back.

"Now. Strike now!" My father's voice booms inside me.

With a scream, I slam the blade down.

*B*lood leaks into my eyes from a gash on my forehead, and I wrap my hands around Shathinor's throat, freezing it as I squeeze. His ruined face twists into a grin as he stares up at me.

Pain sears through me, ripping my heart in two. My mate. "Taylor." I let go and turn to find her on the stairs, her body limp and the obsidian blade rammed through her chest.

"Taylor!" I roar and rush to her, pulling her into my lap as her eyes flutter open. "No, no, no." I touch the blade as her hands fall from the hilt. Her precious blood spills onto her dark blue gown. It's warm on my fingers as the bond between us begins to shrink, to wither like a vine. "Taylor, no." I brush her hair back from her forehead. "Why?" My vision blurs as the battle rages on around us. It doesn't matter anymore. None of it does. "Why, little one?" I stroke her cheek.

Her blue eyes, still so bright, look into my soul, into my shattered heart. "Had to destroy Shathinor's horcrux.

The necklace. Controlling me. Wanted me to kill you. Wanted my body."

A smear of black blood from the destroyed phylactery mixes with hers, staining her fair skin with death.

"Don't go." I rock her. "Valen!" My yell carries on a winter wind.

"I'm sorry." Tears roll from the corners of her eyes, and I wipe them away. "Hurts." She tries to reach for the blade, but her hand drops.

I can feel her life draining away like water through my fingers, the stream flowing far too quickly for me to catch. It takes me down with it, my will ebbing as I hold her.

"Don't be sorry." I lean down and kiss her lips gently. They are too cool. "Never be sorry. You brought me to life."

"You are mine," she whispers. "And I am yours." Her eyes flutter closed.

"No." I yell for Valen again. "Stay. Valen can heal you. He can—"

"Delantis calls." Her brows furrow. "She calls, and I must go."

I gasp, agony wrapping around me like a fist as her breaths grow slower. "Taylor, please. Little one. Don't go to the Ancestors. I need you here. I *need* you. Please."

"Do you hear her?" A trickle of blood rolls from the corner of her mouth.

"Oh, no. My queen." Valen crashes to the stairs beside us, his face bloody. "She's—"

"Help her." I can't stop the helpless tears that escape, can't do anything to help my mate. Her suffering is mine, and I would do anything to take the pain from her.

"I'm drained, but I can try. But first—" He grips the obsidian blade and yanks it free.

Her scream shatters my consciousness as I hold her close, rocking her as Valen summons a weak green orb and presses it to her wound.

She gasps, her body going rigid, her heart struggling to beat.

I can only hold her and pray to the Ancestors for her life. My love. My everything. I only live for her, and I would happily give my life so that she can see another day.

"She's being pulled away." Valen collapses onto the stairs, his skin a sickly white. "The blade is too powerful. I can't stop it."

"Try again!" I howl. "Please, don't go." I'm being torn apart, the link between us dark as the grave as her blood continues to pour onto my hands, soaking my shirt with her waning life.

Valen gets onto his knees and summons another ball of healing and tries again, even though his eyes roll back. He presses it to her wound, the green glow entering her skin as he falls back, his magic spent.

She coughs, blood pouring onto her chin as a few more tears ease from her eyes. "Leander, it hurts." Her whisper rattles out on a breath, and then she doesn't take another one.

"Taylor." I clutch her to me. "Taylor, no. My light. Please stay. Please."

I feel the exact moment the bond severs, the link

between us disappearing like a wisp of smoke into a cold, dark night. There is nothing. Just an emptiness that can never be filled, a void of darkness that will never again touch the light. She is gone beyond my reach, clutched in Death's jealous embrace.

My roar of grief shakes the mountain to its roots.

"*W*ake up." Delantis pats my cheek.

My eyes fly open, and I reach for my chest. But there's nothing there.

"Am I dead?" I sit up and stare around at the black obsidian world.

"Yes." Delantis sits next to me, her eyes bright silver, and her body clad in a skimpy dress, her necklace glinting in the strange light.

"You're young."

She shrugs. "I can choose how I appear." She gestures toward my body. "You can, too."

My midnight wings are gone.

I'm back to my changeling form. "Huh." A creeping fear invades my confusion and bursts like a bubble. "Leander!" I jump to my feet. "He's in danger. They're all fighting for their lives. I have to go to him."

"He's not here." She rises and takes my arm. "Let's walk."

"Where?" I peer around at the obsidian world, ridges and peaks of black rock as far as the eye can see.

"Anywhere." She waves a hand and my dorm appears just as I remember it.

"How—"

"So, now you know what you are." She leads me up the front stairs. "Have you decided who you want to be?"

"I'm dead, so I guess it doesn't matter. Can we help Leander, please? He needs me."

"I'm afraid that's beyond my abilities." She seems truly sad about it.

I have to stop and lean against the visitor sign-in desk as the enormity of what happened rolls over me. "I've lost him." It feels like I've been stabbed through the heart all over. "I'll never see Leander again." My knees weaken, and I sink, the cold floor changing to the stone of Shathinor's throne room. Empty now, it looks as it first did—the white throne intact. My gaze strays to the stairs where I ... died.

"I'm really dead."

Delantis kneels next to me. "Take heart." She tilts my chin up until I meet her eyes. "All is not lost."

"It's not?" I press my palm to my chest. "I stabbed myself with the obsidian blade. I'm here. Leander is—" I look to where he held me, the stairs empty. A sob rocks me. "He's there."

"Here you are." A blue smoke materializes beside me and forms into a woman.

"You again." I cradle my head in my hands.

"Me again." It sits next to me. "I would have told you

about all this if you'd only come with me and stayed in the otherworld."

"I'm never supposed to follow the magic."

"Why not?" It leans back against the bone throne. "I'm not so bad. I've been trying to help. I even told Queen Aurentia about you."

"You mean you're the reason her soldiers attacked Leander at the border?"

It shrugs. "I told the queen what would happen if you reached the winter realm. She wisely tried to keep you from fulfilling the prophecy. But prophecies are funny things."

"What does it matter now?" My insides are cold, barren. I now realize how much I'd come to enjoy that link with Leander. Even when it was spread thin, it was always like a warm blanket, reminding me that he was in the world. But now, I'm empty.

"What does the prophecy matter? It matters." The magic inspects its fingernails. The form it's taken is almost familiar. "You underestimate me."

"Who do you look like?"

It blinks. "You like this look?"

"Just tell me who." I'm tired of its games, sorrow weighing me down as I struggle to keep my tears in check.

"Your mother." It shrugs.

"Callandra?"

"That's the one. She's with the Ancestors, but I thought this would be a nice touch."

"I met her once." Delantis smiles. "She was a beauty. That golden hair. But she was sad. I didn't know about you then. But I think keeping you secret and asleep weighed on her heavily. That's why she sent you to earth. To give you a chance to blossom out of your father's shadow. And it worked."

An idea strikes me, and I turn to the magic. "Can you go to the mountain and help Leander? Help all of them?"

"No." Magic shakes its head. "It's more fun in here. This blade is wild." It waves its hand and we're back in the expanse of obsidian, sparkling black sky and all.

"But they need help! Please, save them."

"Why would I save them when you can do it yourself?" The magic shrugs.

"Tell me how." I reach for its hand, then pull back.

It snaps its fingers. "I will for a price."

Delantis frowns. "You're just as bad as a high fae with the bargaining."

"I'll pay it. Whatever it takes. I have to go back. I have to make it right. The things I've done to Cecile, to the other Taylor. The things I've left unsaid with Leander. I can't leave it like this."

"You'll pay it, no matter what it is?" The magic grins like the Cheshire cat.

Delantis grabs my hand. "Taylor, you don't nee—"

"Done." The magic stands and stretches. "I'll be seeing you in the otherworld shortly."

"That's the price?" I rise.

"I want to dance beneath the dark moon and tell you my secrets." The magic starts to sway, its smoky dress moving to some silent music. "You're the child of prophecy, a changeling but not, a high fae but not. You are the legend. I want you for my own."

"For how long?" I swallow hard.

"Does it matter?" The magic pirouettes around me. "You already agreed to whatever I asked."

"I guess it doesn't." I take a deep breath and turn to Delantis. "I know who I am now. And I know what I have to do."

Delantis sighs. "You didn't have to make that deal."

"I can't leave Leander. Not like this and—"

"No." She shakes her head. "I mean you didn't have to make that deal."

She points as a silver wisp appears in the air, hanging down from the obsidian sky like a rope.

"What's that?"

"Your mate bond. Your own magic called it forth."

"My magic?"

"You have the power of death." She touches one of my hands and the black swirl of darkness appears above it. "But also life." She touches my other hand, and a green spell twirls up.

"I thought it could only reanimate the dead?" I lift the green magic and peer at it. "That's what Shathinor said."

"Because that was Shathinor's magic. Yours is something different. Something greater. You have the power of death *and* life."

"How?"

"It's an inherited talent from your mother. Your mate bond activated it." Delantis smiles. "I told you before. Don't reject the bond. It will save you. When your soul joined with Leander's—the love you share awakened your talent. Just as it made his winter powers stronger, it granted you the ability to give life instead of only death."

"Cecile." The connection clicks in my mind. "She has the same talent. Giving life."

"Also from your shared mother, yes."

I shake my head, then cut my eyes to the still-dancing magic. "You just made a deal with me *knowing* all the while that I didn't have to make it!"

It shrugs then shimmies.

"I tried to warn you." Delantis sighs. "Magic is wily." Her white light glows brighter, her fingertips almost translucent. "It's time for me to go and be with the Ancestors. Time for a rest."

I hug her hard. "Thank you for everything."

She strokes my hair. "I go to the Glowing Lands, but I'll see you again." Reaching behind her neck, she unfastens her soulstone and holds it out to me.

"I can't take that."

"It is mine to give." She fastens it around my neck. "Wear it well, and remember me." She presses her forehead to mine then backs away and begins to shine, her gryphon form emerging as she disappears in a bright flash of white.

I stroke the stone and swallow my tears for Delantis. She's right. I will see her again. I can feel it in my heart. But right now, I have work to do.

I square my shoulders and face the magic. "Tell me how to get back. Do I just climb the rope?"

It stops dancing and motions me closer. "Come here, winter queen, and I'll tell you a secret about the child of many worlds."

I lean toward it, and the magic cups its hands next to my ear and whispers.

I hold her.

The walls quake with the ice of my fury and loss.

I hold her.

The ceiling cracks and falls in chunks, obliterating soldiers as my Phalanx jumps out of the way.

I hold her.

"Leander." Beth rushes to my side, her wide eyes focused on my beloved. "She isn't ... Is she? Is she dead?" She takes Taylor's hand and moans, her eyes filling with tears.

"We have to get out of here." Valen wakes, his voice weak. "The mountain top is caving in." He casts a glance up the stairs. "Shathinor is dead. It's time to go."

"Go." I stroke Taylor's cheek, wiping away the last of her tears.

"Leander, come—"

"Go, I said." I don't raise my voice. I don't move to leave. I don't do anything, except ...

I hold her.

My love, my mate, my heart, my soul. Her end is also mine. I will go to the Ancestors with her. It's not a road she should walk alone.

Gareth runs up, bloodied and battered, but alive. "Leander, if we stay here, we die."

I look up at him, my hollow heart beating a funeral march. "Don't you see? I'm already dead."

"No." He holds his hand out for me.

I don't take it. "All of you go, leave this place now before it's too late."

Brannon and Thorn walk up the steps, both of them covered in gore with an injured Gray held between them. "We're not leaving—"

"I command you as your king to leave me here. Go back to the winter realm. Choose a new king."

"No." Gareth reaches for me again. "You are not going to die here."

"Did you not hear me, old friend?" I shake my head, and my loss is reflected in his barren face. "I'm already dead. Now, go. I command it. Your oath to me demands obedience."

Beth wails and hugs Taylor tight, her heaving sobs telling of a loss almost as great as my own. And I suppose losing the only friend you ever had can break you almost as badly as losing a mate.

Gareth struggles to my side and sits on the stair next to me. "Go, friends. I will see our king to the Ancestors."

"No, you won't." I jerk my chin at Beth. "This one needs your protection. Take her with you."

"What will you do?" Gray asks as a hunk of ceiling

shatters behind them, the mountain top shaking more violently.

I stroke Taylor's face. "I will hold her. Now go. I demand it as your king, and I call on your sacred oaths to obey me."

The tang of magic coats the air, and the oath takes hold. Gareth grits his teeth, but he rises, a trickle of blood flowing from his nose as he tries to fight his promise. But it's too strong. The old magic binds us, enforcing his vow no matter how he wants to disobey.

"Leander." His anguish should move me. It would have, before. But now? I can feel nothing but her loss, sense nothing but emptiness, and care for nothing but seeing her again in the Glowing Lands.

He takes a knee before me as do the others, all of them bowing their heads.

"My friends, it has been my honor to serve with you. No king has had a more loyal court." I pull Taylor closer as Beth releases her hold. "I will see you all again on the other side. Long may you live in this world."

"My king." Their voices meld into one as they rise.

"Beth." Gareth holds out his hand, and she takes it.

"When you see her, tell her I love her." Beth sniffs. "And that I'm still mad about not getting to watch the mating." Her small laugh turns to tears, and Gareth pulls her to his chest.

"Shhh, changeling." He kisses the crown of her head.

A landslide of rock takes out the right side of the throne room, burying our former cage in boulders and shards of sharp stone.

"Hurry," I urge.

They turn, their shoulders low, their hearts heavy. But again, I can't feel anything. She took my soul with her. I am empty.

Gareth gives me one more long look, and I know he wants to say more, to convince me to come with him. But the oath forces him to turn his back on me, because above all, Gareth is honorable. He and the others disappear into the corridor as more stone falls, crushing the bodies left behind, a few of the undead moaning.

I return my gaze to my beautiful mate. "I thought we would have more time." I kiss her forehead. "Centuries of learning each other. Children." I choke up at that, thinking of a babe with her wild blue eyes and my dark hair.

More stone falls revealing the night sky, the stars close enough to touch.

"I know so much about you but not enough." I rock her gently. "But I will see you soon, and we can be together. Just not here."

The mountain trembles and cracks as I send my ice deep into its core, breaking the stone and ending my suffering.

My chest hurts. Bad. The next time I stab myself, I'm definitely not doing it through the heart. Sheesh.

Leander's strong arms hold me close as my eyes open, and I inhale his winter scent. He's singing again, the same song he serenaded me with as I slept in his arms at the Vundi stronghold. I love the sound of his voice. But the sound of the throne room crumbling around us? Not so much.

"Leannnrr." I speak against his chest and push back.

He jumps, his song ending as he stares down at me with wide, haunted eyes.

"Taylor?" He says it so softly, as if afraid I might disappear if he speaks too loud.

"It's me."

"How?" He shakes his head.

"The bond. Just like Delantis said. Our bond saved me."

"I don't understand. But I don't care." With a yank,

he pulls me to his lips and crushes me in a kiss that sets my soul on fire, the bond surging to life. I hold onto it tight, determined to never let it go again.

I wrap my arms around him, tears coating my cheeks as I breathe him in. My love. My everything. He runs his hands down my wings, and I shiver. Then he pulls back and inspects my chest.

"Healed?" He runs his fingers along the spot where the obsidian blade pierced me. "Completely healed."

"Magic." I wiggle my fingers and green appears.

"You have healing magic?"

"A little gift straight from the otherworld."

The mountain rumbles, the back of the room collapsing and blocking the corridor.

"What happened?" I look around at the destruction, all of it coated with frost.

He cups my face in his palms. "You died."

I glance at the veins of ice that run through the floor, cracking the dark gray stone. "So you brought the mountain down?"

He shrugs and kisses me again, his need for me overwhelming and comforting all at once. I share the same desire. The same elation at being able to be with him again.

"What did you have to give for this?" He presses his palm to my heart to feel it beat and peers at the soulstone necklace.

"Doesn't matter." I try to get to my feet, but he stands and lifts me in his arms.

"It *does* matter, and you will tell me. But first, I have

to get you to safety. I'm not letting you out of my sight ever again."

"I'm grounded?"

"Yes." He kisses my forehead then frowns at the blocked corridor. "I need to find another way out."

"I think I have an idea." I kick my legs. "Put me down."

"No."

"Leander." I smack his chest. "Put me down."

He growls low but sets me on my feet.

I spread my wings. "I'm our escape plan."

"I'm far too heavy for you to carry."

"Maybe. But we fly together, or we die together. I'm never leaving you again."

He smiles, the worry draining from him bit by bit. "My mate." He cups the back of my neck and pulls my mouth to his.

I push him back. "Focus."

His eyes narrow. "Yes. To safety."

I spread my wings again. "Okay, if I can get enough of a running start, then I—" I scream as a bolt of darkness pierces my wing, and Shathinor rises from his spot next to the shattered throne.

I curl my injured wing inward.

Leander snatches the obsidian blade from the steps and turns, throwing the sword with vicious efficiency. It catches Shathinor in the chest, piercing his rotten heart.

He grabs it but can't wrench it free.

Leander takes my hand and keeps me behind him as he climbs the stairs, wrath tangible in each of his heavy steps.

Staggering back, Shathinor holds out a hand, as if it can ward off the fury of Leander, the vengeance of the heart of winter.

Leander surges forward and grabs the blade, twisting it and lifting Shathinor's ruined body off its feet.

Shathinor screams, the sound cloaked in death and darkness, and I cover my ears. Leander doesn't flinch as he slams my father to the ground, rips the blade free, and beheads him with one vicious stroke.

The mountain shudders.

He turns to me and inspects my wing.

"Wait." I step to my father's corpse, his black eyes still open. "I'm not letting his evil come back. Never again." I hold out my hand and black flames shoot from my palm. They envelope his body, burning him in the flames of death, destroying him so thoroughly that only a black outline of soot remains when the fire finally abates.

Leander spits on the ashes then takes me by the shoulders. "Fly, little one. Save yourself."

"No. We're not dying today." I hold my hand out and pull forth the healing magic. My wing heals, the skin knitting back together and the black feathers fluffing over the wound.

A huge chunk of stone falls and shatters so close that Leander grabs me and races away from the impact.

"Hold onto me." I reach down deep, dragging up every bit of magic I have left. Blackness infuses me, my wings spreading wide as a shadow encases them.

Leander grips my waist and presses his lips to my neck. "If you fly us out of here, the moment we land, I intend to worship this body as it deserves."

I shiver, my dark magic shimmering as I wrap my legs around him. "Shh. I need to concentrate."

He kisses his mark on my shoulder and holds on tighter.

I push my magic down, imagining the darkness working like jet thrusters. At first it simply pools beneath our feet.

"Hmm." I push it harder, trying to get some lift.

Leander kisses along my jaw. "Allow me."

With a swell of power, he creates a pedestal of ice that grows so fast it acts like a launcher, shooting us through one of the many openings in the crumbling mountaintop.

We surge into the night sky. It's exhilarating to see the ruined stone beneath us, my father's work caving in on itself.

But then the ice stops.

"Fly," he whispers, his mouth at my ear.

My wings stretch, the darkness still coating them with power, and I flap them hard. They ache, pain ripping down my back as I struggle to surge upward and away from the rock below.

I can feel what little magic Leander has left pushing through the bond, adding to my stores as I flap my wings, gaining a bit of distance between us and the mountain. The pain in my back is like razor blades skating down my flesh, but I power through it.

Leander peers down at the ruined cavern. "If you need to leave me—"

"Never." I push harder, every muscle in my body

straining as I finally get enough lift away from the peak that I can stretch out and glide. "But you weigh a ton."

The fires are still burning in the valley, so I bank hard away from them until I can see nothing but darkness below.

"We should land there." He points to a black area just like all the other black areas.

"What's there?" I aim toward the spot nestled at the base of the mountain. Rocks still slide down its sides, the top now fully collapsed.

"Friends." He peppers kisses along my chest, spending extra time on the spot where the obsidian blade pierced me.

"Distracting fae." I grit out as I let my wings catch the wind and float toward the ground.

He nibbles my ear lobe. "What did you promise the magic?"

"I can't hear you." I point to my ear and shake my head. "The wind is super loud."

He glares but doesn't ask again. Instead, he contents himself with running his hands along my sides and nipping at my throat as I glide lower, the stony ground beckoning and my back begging for relief.

When we're close, he lets go. I screech as he hits the ground and rolls, ending up on his feet as the pain in my back eases, though I land a little harder than intended.

He wraps his arms around me before I fall and pulls me against him. Our bond ignites, the light between us burning brighter than the stars. I feel his love, his fear, his need for me.

Turning, I wrap my arms around his neck, and he

kisses me with a fervor that sends heat to every extremity ... some more than others.

"I love you." He cups my face and kisses my nose, my forehead, my chin. "I love you so much, little one."

"I love you, too." I smile. "More than I ever thought possible."

He claims my mouth, his tongue expertly stroking mine as he grabs my ass and lifts me to his height. I run my fingers through his dark hair and relish his touch, his scent, the sparks that flow between us through the bond.

"I waited with the horses while you brought the mountain down."

Leander spins me to his back and draws the obsidian blade, then quickly stows it when Ravella appears from the darkness.

"And now you have wings?" She crosses her arms over her chest. "What else did I miss? Everything?" She glares. "I missed everything, didn't I?"

"You got to spend a little time with me. Worth it, right?" Phinellas appears from the gloom, his usual Catcher outfit gone, replaced with a simple black tunic and pants.

Ravella holds her hand up and closes it in a 'shut up' motion at him.

Someone grunts nearby, and all three of them draw their weapons and push me behind them.

"Guys." I snap my fingers and a black starburst appears in my palm. "I'm death incarnate. Remember? You should be behind *me*."

Ravella's eyes widen. "Whoa."

Another grunt, then Gareth's voice calling for Ravella.

"It's the Phalanx." Leander relaxes and takes my hand, leading me to the horses and his bloody, bruised, but still-alive Phalanx.

Gareth stills, his eyes on Leander. Then he whoops loudly and rushes to his friend. Their embrace almost bowls me over. Then, when Beth runs to me, I give in and let her tackle me to the ground.

"I thought you were dead!" She wraps her arms around my neck and squeezes so hard I see stars. "Wait, you *were* dead. What happened? Did Leander bring you back? Was there more mating? What in the Spires is going on?"

"I can explain." I laugh as she kisses me on the cheek. "Stop mauling me."

"No way." She kisses the other cheek then sobers a little, her eyebrows drawing together. "And you were a bitch, too. I'm glad you're back to the old Taylor."

"I'm not." We sit up. "I'm different. A little old. A little new. A lot to learn."

Valen limps up with Cecile and the other me, both of them scratched and dirty, but still alive.

I climb to my feet. "I also have a lot to make up for." When I step toward Cecile and the other me, they flinch. I can't blame them. "I'm sorry." I take a deep breath as Leander stands at my side. "I was out of control. My feral is sort of ..."

"Evil?" Cecile crosses her thin arms. "A lunatic? A homicidal maniac?"

I hold my hand up and waggle it in a "kind of" motion. "But I have it under control."

Neither of them look particularly convinced.

"Okay, I mean, not under control. It's a part of me, and we are one, and—" I pin my lips together, then try again. "I still have that darkness inside me. But I will never use it against my friends again. I'm sorry for what I've done to both of you, and I promise I will work to earn your forgiveness." The sizzle of magic reinforces my promise, and Cecile finally uncoils, then wraps her arm around the other me. "Come on, let's pick the best horse." They turn and walk past Brannon, Thorn, and Gray, all of them looking much the worse for wear.

When they gather in front of Leander and me, they all take a knee and bow their heads.

"Rise, my friends." Leander tucks me under his arm, and I lean into him. "It is time for us to return home."

"Wonderful. I'm way past due for some relaxation." Selene skitters into view, a makeshift bag thrown over her shoulder, human bones sticking out of the top. "Especially now that I'm the high witch of the winter realm."

"You survived." I would hug her. But, eww human bones.

"I'm obsidian." She grins. "I don't break."

"And wait, high witch of the winter realm?" I cock my head to the side.

"I made a bargain." She tweaks my nose. "Your king wanted to know where you were. I wanted all the gristle I can eat *and* a nice title."

"You aren't bringing that to High Mountain." Gareth grimaces at her pack of blood and bone.

"Try and stop me." She snaps her teeth at him.

The Phalanx rises, battle-worn but victorious.

"Hey." I turn to Leander. "The prophecy came true."

"How so?" He pulls me close.

"'*She alone can start the war, and be victorious, win or lose.*'" I press my cheek to his chest. "I struck the first blow against Shathinor. I started the war. And then I lost. I ... died. But here we are."

"Victorious." Leander rests his chin on my crown. "Because of you."

I snuggle against his chest. "I mean, I totally flew us out of danger. I'm kind of a big deal. Hey." I turn to look into his dark eyes. "If I remember correctly, you mentioned something about worshiping 'this body as it deserves' if I got us down to the ground safely?"

His low purr rumbles through me as he lifts me in his arms and stalks through the scrub brush and stone at the base of the still-crumbling mountain.

Gareth clears his throat. "Leander, we should go now before—"

"Wait for us." Leander's command leaves no question.

I press my lips to his throat. "I'm so sorry."

"Don't be."

"Don't be?" I grip him tighter as he jumps a ravine. "I betrayed you, had you locked in a cage, let your friends get captured and hurt. Of *course* I'm sorry."

He smirks. "I rather like the feral side of you."

"What?" I'm certain my eyes are wider than they've ever been in my life.

"The betrayal wasn't my favorite, I admit. But

treachery aside—" He shrugs. "I'm eager to learn every bit of you, no matter the form. And the wings?" He makes a whistling sound as he sits me on a rock ledge. "Undeniably sexy." He runs his hand down one, and a shiver courses through me. Pressing his forehead to mine, he says, "I'll take you however I can get you, little one."

A purr rolls through my chest. "Is that—"

He mauls me with a kiss that is as rough as it is welcome. I grip his shoulders as he spreads my thighs on either side of his hips. His hands go to my bottom and squeeze as his tongue does deliciously wicked things to mine. By the time he pulls back, I'm panting. And when he drops to his knees and presses his wide open mouth to my core, I moan and grip his hair. He thrusts his tongue inside me, and I strain to open my legs even farther. He doesn't need encouragement, his wide palms splaying me as his mouth owns every bit of my flesh.

Gripping his hair, I grind my hips against his face, unabashedly chasing my release as he licks my clit, grazing me with his fangs. He doesn't stop, and it's as if he knows just what I like.

"*I do.*" His voice is inside me, the bond bright and alive. As if to prove his point, he runs the broadside of his tongue along that nub of sensation, and my back arches.

"Leander," I moan his name.

But then the perfection of his mouth recedes. He stands and yanks down the top of my dress, his mouth going to one nipple as his cock presses against my entrance.

I run my hands down his back, my nails digging in and drawing blood. His purr escalates, and mine matches it. His cock rubs against my clit, up and down, coils of delicious arousal winding tight inside me.

"My mate." He growls and thrusts hard.

My toes curl as he pumps hard, his hands on my ass making sure I take every inch. I crane my head back and moan to the dark sky as he sucks my breasts, feasting on me as he makes me his again and again. I draw my knees up, spreading so that I get every bit of friction between us.

"My perfect mate." He kisses to my mouth, heightening the pleasure of his hard thrusting, his hands, and the feel of him against me.

I lean back and catch his gaze, then run my fingers down his throat. "I want to mark you."

His cock gets impossibly harder, his rough strokes verging on animal. "An honor." He pulls me close and grinds into me so perfectly I think I might pass out before I finish.

Some deep, dark instinct drives me, and I strike at his throat, burying my fangs in him as he roars to the top of the mountain. Our bond, already so strong, seems to go supernova, obliterating all that came before and promising love eternal.

He lifts me up and pounds harder as I hold on, the taste of his blood like wine on my tongue as my wet core tightens. When my release hits me, I cling to him, relishing each wave of bliss, each moment spent with him inside me. I cry against his throat, the pleasure overwhelming me and taking me deeper, melding me with him and letting me feel his fast-approaching release. When he lets go, I come again, my walls clamping down on him as he spends inside me with another primal yell that sends more rock crashing down the side of the mountain. Flashes of his feelings and love shoot down the bond, flickering like fairy lights. I bask in them, letting his soul envelop mine and hold it tight.

"Leander." I retract my fangs and rest my forehead on his chest.

"My love." He kisses my crown and wraps his arms around me.

"I never want to leave your side again."

"You'll never have to." His low purr resumes, comforting me like the softest blanket.

He holds me for a long time, the two of us linked on every level. I want to live in this moment.

All too soon, he rubs my back and pulls away. "If we don't return to camp, Gareth may explode from pure worry."

"You're not wrong."

He tips my chin up until I meet his gaze. "Do you feel worshipped, little one?"

I bat my lashes and run a finger down his chest. "I mean, I *do*, but maybe you should do a little more glorification, just to be sure."

He smirks, the sexiest fae I've ever seen, and pushes his hardening length deeper inside me. "As you wish, my goddess."

"*Y*ou're staring at me again." She casts me a glance.

"No." I shrug, but don't look away.

"You are." She laughs. "Do you want me to change back?"

"Definitely not." I kiss her little rounded ear. "I love you like this."

"Okay." She shrugs. "It's just that I've been in this form for so long, you know?" She looks down at her changeling body. "I feel more comfortable than in the feral. But if you prefer the feral, then I—"

I stop her words with a kiss and send my thoughts down the bond. "*I prefer you as you. Whatever makes you most comfortable. You taste the same either way. Honey on my tongue.*" I run a hand up her thigh.

"Hey!" She playfully smacks my hand.

Does she have any idea what that does to me? I want to put her on all fours and mount her.

"I heard that." She arches a brow at me.

"So, is that a yes?" I drag my fingers higher, almost to her panties.

"No." She grabs my hand and laces her fingers through mine, then casts a pointed glance at the soldiers surrounding us as we enter Cold Comfort.

"I'd tell them not to look."

"You're bad."

I kiss the back of her hand. "Yes."

The wide wooden doors swing inward as we enter on foot, and the entire town lines the main road for us. A roar goes up as we set foot onto the Ice Road, priceless petals from the greenhouse flowers strewn along our path.

"It's beautiful." She stares at the granite buildings with marble doors, each one decorated in ribbons of Gladion gray and white.

I can feel her wonder filtering through the bond, and I squeeze her hand.

Children run up and hand her flowers, bunches of frost tulips—the emblem of the winter realm. A light snow falls on her brown hair, and her fur cloak ripples in the cold breeze. So much pride wells inside me that I fear I might burst.

She kneels down and takes a bunch of tulips from a lesser fae girl with little white horns. "Thank you. What's your name?"

"Calendila." She smiles, her front teeth missing.

"What a beautiful name."

"Are you a princess?" She reaches up and touches Taylor's hair.

"Sort of?" Taylor laughs. "But really I'm just a regular person like you."

"Really?" The girl searches Taylor's face.

"Yes."

More children approach, each of them handing her flowers until she has an arm full. I motion for Gareth, and he takes them as we continue down the Ice Road, the peoples of the winter realm getting their first look at my chosen queen. She receives several bunches of blooms, the dark fae of Cold Comfort giving their best.

The wonder in their eyes matches the love in my heart, and the cheers of approval echo down the wyvern-stone streets as we finish our procession.

"Wow." She leans against me. "That was kind of intense."

"You're a natural." My soldiers surround us as a carriage approaches to take us up to High Mountain.

"You're pretty much a celebrity now." Beth prances past, a wide grin on her face. "Like Queen Aurentia but not as mean."

"Thanks, I think?" Taylor sighs. "I hope I did all right."

"You are the jewel of my crown, little one."

Her eyes lift to my actual crown. "That diamond is bigger than my fist. I'm still not over it."

"It's yours if you want it." I kiss her forehead. "Of course, we have a crown in the treasury for you, but you are welcome to choose whichever jewels you like."

"I'll leave that to you. Crowns are pretty much way beyond my area of expertise."

"Treasury?" Selene picks at her new dress, the

emerald green covering her odd angles far better than her tattered white funeral gown. "Anything for me in there? High witch should get something, yes?"

I'm on the verge of saying no when Taylor takes Selene's elbow. "Well of course. There has to be something in there for you. Right, Leander?" When she looks up at me with those sparkling blue eyes, there's only one answer that blooms on my lips: "Yes."

I would tell her yes if she asked me to go to the Spires for her.

When one side of her mouth quirks up, I suspect she knows it.

"This is ... This ... I ..." I give up and stare.

"To your liking?" Leander carries us on the winter wind as the carriages with our friends make their way up the steep mountain.

The castle is enormous, crouching on the snowy peak like a great, beautiful bird. It's made of the same shiny granite as the town below, but it rises in the winter sun, the turrets flying flags of gray and white as smoke floats from a dozen chimneys. A dark forest flows away from it on two sides, the rest of the peak a mix of sheer cliffs and stone, all of it covered in snow.

"It's so beautiful." I look up at Leander, his eyes on me. Always on me.

"It's yours."

"I can't believe you live here."

"*We* live here," he chides.

"Yes." I hug him closer. "We do."

"Branala has been arranging the mating ceremony while we've been traveling."

"Is it going to be big?" I still can't take my eyes from the massive castle, soldiers dotted along the battlements at intervals atop the high outer wall. Inside, a courtyard is filled with people dressed in furs and thick cloaks, their dark hair and pointed ears marking them as winter realm high fae.

"The biggest mating this realm has ever seen."

"That sounds ... intimidating. And what if the nobles aren't into having me as their queen? But maybe they'll get used to me during the engagement and—"

"Engagement?" He arches a dark brow.

"Yeah, we're engaged, right?"

"Engaged?"

"You know, when people are going to get married, they are engaged for a while first and plan it all and then get married."

"This isn't a marriage." He presses a sweet kiss to my lips. "This is a celebration of our unbreakable bond."

That doesn't sound so official. "Okay." My nerves settle a bit.

And it happens tomorrow."

My brain seems to freeze. "Tomorrow?"

"I won't wait to crown my queen. They will love you as I do." His confidence in me brings tears to my eyes, and the time frame creates panic in my mind.

"Did you say tomorrow?"

"At sunset."

"That's so ... so sudden." I press my palms to my cheeks.

"You would prefer to wait?" A hint of hurt colors his question.

"No." I shake my head. "No. It's just a lot. But—" I rest my hand over his heart. "I'm ready. I'm yours."

"As I am yours." He tightens his hold. "Don't worry about the nobles. They will accept you."

"Even in this changeling body?"

"In any body you choose." His never-ending faith in me still strikes a note of wonder in my heart.

I glance back at the waiting nobles as Leander drops us slowly to the courtyard. "I don't think they're going to like my ideas."

"They don't have to like them." He laughs low in his throat. "I get the feeling that if they don't accept the equality you seek, your feral side may take matters into her own hands."

The tips of my ears prickle, and my back starts to itch. "Your feeling is dead on."

"Control it, little one." He nuzzles my hair. "Don't let her control you."

I relax in his arms, my feral heart calming under his soothing touch. "I want to be me." I shake my head, and when I stop, my ears are pointed. "But I also kind of like the ears. Is that weird?"

"Not at all." He kisses the tips. "They're quite sensitive, no?"

A tingle rushes through me, and I have to pull away from him. "Stop. You're going to have me all, you know, excited. And then the scent thing will happen. And, oh my god. I can't have other fae smelling me."

"If you insist." But he kisses my ear when he sets us down in the courtyard.

We approach the nobles, many of them staring at me in open shock.

Leander's voice booms over the crowd, power soaking every word. "I have returned from battle with the evil of old, Shathinor. With my mate, we defeated him. He is no more, his soul sent to the Spires."

A murmur ripples through the crowd.

"He lured many unsuspecting lesser fae and changelings to his cause with promises of equality in the realms."

I squeeze Leander's hand.

"Shathinor lied, of course. He never intended for changelings and lesser fae to be treated as equal to the high fae."

A few nods of approval in the crowd has me grinding my teeth.

"But that changes now." He holds up our joined hands. "Bow before your new queen. You owe her your allegiance as the ruler of the winter realm."

Some of them gasp, but none of them dare disobey Leander. I can see why. Fierceness emanates from him in waves of command, his demeanor one of controlled power. If I thought he was alpha before, this is a whole new level of badassery. I bite my lip as the entire court-yard kneels before me.

He leans to my ear, his voice soft for me. "I can scent you, little one. Power excites you."

My cheeks heat. "*You* excite me," I whisper back.

"Rise," he commands, then wraps his arm around my waist and leads me into the castle as his stunned nobles gain their feet and stare.

"This place is amazing." I catch sight of a silver throne bathed in light from stained glass windows, but Leander pulls me away.

"Where are we going?" I hurry along with him as each soldier we pass stands at attention.

"Taking too long," he growls and picks me up, slinging me over his shoulder.

"Hey!" I cry, but he takes off, sprinting through several rooms—some grand, some rustic, each of them with a roaring fire and cozy-looking furs. "Where are we going?"

He enters a long corridor, the soldiers there straightening and giving Leander deferential nods as he races past.

I push up on his back and see the hall receding behind us. "What in the hell are you—"

He bursts through a set of doors and before I can blink, he tosses his crown aside and has me pinned to a huge bed, his mouth on mine and his hips settling between my thighs.

"The way the males looked at you," he growls and yanks up my dress. "I wanted to gut them, to destroy them, to freeze their hearts, shatter them, and burn the shards."

I whimper, my arousal hitting me like a bolt of pure heat.

Ripping my panties to shreds, he grinds his cock against me and fastens his mouth to my throat.

"I need you." I rock my hips up to him.

He frees himself and plunges inside me, my cry swallowed by his mouth as he masters me, body and soul.

I squeal when he pulls my dress down, exposing my hard nipples, and drags his fang across one.

Sucking it into his mouth, he pumps his hips as I meet him, each impact shaking the massive bed and stoking my arousal.

"More," he growls and rolls to his back.

I slide down onto him, my heart pounding as I savor the feel of him. He pulls my dress down my shoulders and cups my breasts as I rock on top of him.

His eyes linger on my mouth, my breasts, and then lower. "Show me, my beautiful mate. I want to see what's mine."

I moan and pull my dress up, and his eyes go to where we're joined. A blast of cold hardens my nipples even more as he grips my hips.

With a hard pull, I strip off my dress and toss it to the floor.

His purr of approval resonates down the bond, and I ride him slow and sultry, learning this new position and letting my pleasure lead me. He locks gazes with me, both of us here, relishing the moment together. My hips move faster, the pleasure demanding I chase it in earnest, so I do. I grab the wooden headboard and grind on him as he leans up and licks my breasts, his hands kneading my ass.

When he moves one hand around to my front and massages my clit, I explode, a keening sound rising from me as my hips seize and my body gives itself to pleasure. He surges inside me and groans low and masculine, his cock kicking inside me as I collapse onto his chest, my body so alive it almost hurts.

He kisses my sweaty forehead and runs his hands up and down my back.

"Do you think they heard?" I whisper.

He laughs, the sound decadent. "If they didn't hear it all the way down in Cold Comfort, then we need to do it again."

*T*his is ridiculous. I cradle my face in my hands as the seamstress parades another set of fabrics, this one in a brocade with some sort of pretty sparkles along the pattern.

"That's nice." Beth munches on a plum.

"You've said that about every piece of fabric she's shown us," I mumble through my hands. "And I still haven't even picked a design."

"Can we get it in black?" Selene asks for the third time.

"No!" Ravella and Branala chime in together.

Nadian, the seamstress, sighs and lays the fabric on the pile of discards, then pulls a few more from her enormous case. "These colors are a bit more night realm." Her slight cough tells me that she doesn't care for them, but she displays them nonetheless. "Darker jewel tones with silver stitching is classic for their endless evenings, but uncommon here in winter. It would work if you want to be untraditional but could also cause a stir."

"A stir?" I shake my head and rest it in my palms again. "This is impossible. Hopeless."

"Let's go back to the white." Ravella pats me on the back. "She seemed to favor those."

I chew my bottom lip. "I don't know if I do. That's a human world thing. But you said white isn't customary for mating ceremonies here."

Ravella glances at the door again.

"You can go." I sigh.

"No, I don't mind helping out with the dress stuff. It's, um, it's fun."

I give her a wry look. "I've spent enough time with you in the Wasted Lands to know you want to be out checking security with Gareth and Brannon instead of picking fabrics with me. Go ahead."

She takes my hands. "Thank you, my queen."

"And knock that off. You know it's Taylor."

"Yes, right." She hurries past the seamstress, grateful for her reprieve from dress duty.

"How about this one?" Nadian pulls a dark magenta fabric to the fore.

I peer at it. "Is this a normal color to choose?"

"You can choose whatever you like. You're going to be queen." Branala rises as a knock sounds on the door. After a quick convo, she turns and says, "Flowers," with an excited smile, then disappears.

"Anything else in black?" Selene flops onto the bed, her chin resting on her hands and her feet kicked up behind her.

"You're relentless."

"I am obsidian. I do not break." She grins.

"I'm going to get some more food." Beth lifts the empty tray.

"Didn't I say we need to get you checked for a tapeworm?"

"What?" She picks the last crumb from the tray and downs it. "I'm just storing up food for the winter. That's what the animals in the winter realm do, right?"

"I know you're just trying to escape dress duty."

"Me? Never." She winks and disappears out the door.

"At least I've still got you." I give Selene a hopeful look.

"I think black. Black and shiny." She nods.

I tamp down my frustration and turn back to Nadian. "Maybe I should do like a light pink? With a poof skirt?" I try to think about what would look good on me, but the problem is that I never had a real sense of style and having to develop one on my wedding day seems more than a little bit daunting. "Poof skirt says queen, right?"

"Of course you'd go amateur princess wannabe." Cecile strides in, my doppelganger by her side.

I jump from my spot on the bed. "Cecile. Taylor. Welcome."

"You didn't invite us, but I heard you're having style trouble." Cecile's upturned nose and haughty tone warm my heart. She's back to her old self. Did I hate her old self? Well, yes, most of the time. But that's neither here nor there.

She strides to Nadian who sizes her up with an arrogant stare of her own. "You're showing her fabrics that are far too heavy for her frame."

Nadian's pointed ears twitch. "The winter realm favors thicker—"

Cecile waves a hand at her. "If you want her to look like a frumpy spinster, you're on the right track. Otherwise, show me what you have in lace, tulle, and spidersilk. And don't show me a thing unless it's in Gladion gray or white." She settles onto my bed, her back straight and her eyes alight.

Nadian looks at me questioningly.

I shrug. "You heard her."

She turns on her heel, her simple black dress fanning out, and rummages through her wardrobe again.

I would thank Cecile, but I'm too fragile for the tongue-lashing she'd give me in response.

"Taylor?" I approach the other me.

She recoils a little, and I stop.

I hold my hands out, palms toward her. "I don't blame you. I actually meant to come talk to you, but this whole mating ceremony thing sort of took me by surprise, and then Leander kept me busy all night and ... Okay, just pretend I didn't say that last part."

She smiles a little, and I realize I'm kind of cute with my heart-shaped face and plump lips.

"No. No. No." Cecile shoots down fabric after fabric with frightening efficiency.

I focus on the other Taylor. "But, anyway, I am so, so sorry for what I did to you."

"Thank you." She drops her chin a little, then meets my gaze. "I would be lying if I said I'm over it."

My heart sinks.

Then she reaches out and takes my hand. "But I will be. I think it'll just take some time."

"Can you ever forgive me?" I hold my breath.

"I do *if* you forgive Cecile and me for sending you to Arin and landing you in the dungeon."

"Done." I squeeze her hand a little. "And to be honest, you sending me here is the best thing that could've happened to me."

"You're going to be a queen. That's definitely an improvement on our dorm room."

"You aren't kidding." I step closer, and she lets me embrace her. "I'm so glad that you're here for my mating ceremony."

"It's the first one I've ever been invited to. Changelings generally don't get to attend family events like this in the summer realm." She starts to say something. Then stops.

"What is it?"

"It's just something I've been wondering about for a long time. Could you tell me ... about my mother and father?"

Cecile stands and inspects the fabrics more closely. "This white lace and this gray spidersilk. Yes. Taylor is a bit dumpy in the waist, so—"

"Hey!" The other Taylor and I both turn and glare at her.

She shrugs a thin shoulder. "I'm sorry, but it's true. Don't worry. You're going to look like the perfect hourglass when I'm done." She ignores us and begins outlining the silhouette she prefers.

I pull Taylor to the bed and we sit on the edge, our hands still clasped. "That's a difficult topic."

"Oh." Her shoulders hunch a little. "I kind of suspected, I guess, when your mom—I mean, *my* mom—didn't call you at all during the time I was living with Cecile at your college."

"Yeah. Mom is ..." I sigh and start off with our history. At first, it comes haltingly—the death of my father, the emotional distance, the neglect. And then it speeds up, the more painful parts pouring out of me as she listens to every word.

When I'm finally spent, the ugly truth laid out for both of us to see, she says quietly, "She let your stepfather hurt you."

I hate hearing it, even if I know in my heart that it's true. "She didn't believe me. Steve was convincing, and she really wanted it to work out with him. She was lonely, I guess?"

"She sold you out." Her shoulders straighten. "I know what that feels like. Being a changeling slave is full of betrayals."

"Oh, no." I shake my head. "What I went through is nothing like your life. I can't even imagine what you've had to endure."

"It could be bad sometimes." She nods, then looks at Cecile with such adoration in her eyes that I look, too, to make sure we're seeing the same person. "But Cecile saved me from the worst of it. She was older than me, but we pretty much grew up together. I was like her little sister. She defied her father by taking care of me. I think at first I was like a baby doll for her to play with, but then she grew to care for me, and as I got older, I couldn't imagine being without her."

"She loves you. I could tell that from the first moment I saw you two in that horrible cave. And, to be honest, it took me totally by surprise. I had this one view of Cecile, but then there was this whole other side I never guessed at."

"Sort of like being a fae and having an evil feral inside you, but appearing human on the outside?" She gives me a pointed look.

"Oh, come on. I'm not evil ... That side was just, sort of, you know, locked away for a long time so when I got free I was—"

"Murderous and cruel?"

Okay, so minimizing it isn't an option. I shrug. "It's like I'm half Gryffindor, half Slytherin."

Her eyes light with recognition. "I read your books. I want to be a Hufflepuff."

"Oh, no, honey." I pat her hand. "No one *wants* to be a Hufflepuff."

"Stop rubbing your nerd off on her." Cecile snaps her fingers. "Now come over here and try this on. I need Nadian to pin it until I'm satisfied. Then she only has a few hours to sew it. And I'm going to need every second of that time to fix your uneven complexion, lackluster hair, and slouchy posture."

Taylor and I both straighten our shoulders.

"Harsh." I frown.

"You get used to it." The other Taylor shoos me toward Cecile. "I'm excited to see it all come together."

Beth traipses in with another tray of food and a pitcher of wine. "The party is back on."

"I think you may have cleaned out the pantry."

"Not a chance. This place is stocked. Did you know they have a room just for jam?"

"I've heard."

Beth sets the food down next to a snoring Selene as Nadian wraps lace around my torso and spidersilk along my bottom half, her hands moving so fast with pins that I can barely see them. It takes a while, and about a hundred modifications from Cecile, before the dress is up to her standards.

Beth's eyes grow misty when it's all finished. "You are a queen."

Cecile circles me, her eyes running over every inch of the fabric. Finally, after a few more pins, she says, "This will do. Sew it."

Nadian carefully removes it and whisks it away for finishing.

I sit on the bed as Cecile goes through every bit of makeup and toiletries in the vanity.

"Are you ready?" Beth pops a grape into my mouth.

I chew it slowly and contemplate the enormity of her question. Was I ready to be sent to Arin? No. Was I ready to meet Leander? No. Was I ready to learn who my true father was? No. Was I ready to learn who I was? No.

But being ready didn't make a hill of beans when the time came. Things happen. They never stop happening. And I've realized that I have to grab happiness wherever I can find it, because I don't know when things will change, when destinies will be revealed, or when I might be sent to a strange new world to meet my eternal mate.

It's enough that I know what I want.

Leander. Forever. Just the thought of it makes a smile take hold, joy surging from deep inside me.

With a deep breath, I speak the truth of my heart. "I'm ready."

"*S*he's here." Gareth adjusts his fur cloak for the hundredth time.

"Who?" I twist my crown a little to the right. "Is this straight?"

"Let me." He reaches up and turns it back to the left. "Queen Aurentia. Her doves arrived early this morning, half frozen, with word that she would be attending the mating ceremony. I granted her and a small contingent of guards permission to enter the realm in the hopes that she will explain the incursion. Being that she is coming here in person, I can only assume those hostilities are ended. But she owes us an explanation. We already have a handful of nobles clamoring for war."

"Oh." My thoughts stray to Taylor. How will she look? What colors will she choose? Is she nervous?

"Leander." Gareth's voice is tinged with exasperation. "Are you listening?"

"Yes." *No.* "Go on."

"She waits for you in your study."

"Right now?" I turn to him.

"She wants a word before the ceremony."

I twist my crown back to the right. "I will not keep my mate waiting for anyone, not even the summer queen."

"Well, you're in luck, because Taylor isn't ready yet. That roommate of hers has taken over, bossing everyone about like a—"

"I'll meet with the queen." I run a hand down my black attire, the gray thread along my collar catching the light. "Do you think Taylor would have preferred the silver thread?"

"No." He gestures to the door. "Queen Aurentia."

I follow him out and down the hall, every guard in the castle lining the corridors as guests arrive for the ceremony. I catch Taylor's scent as I pass our bedroom, and it takes an intense force of will not to burst in and get a pre-ceremony taste.

"Focus." Gareth strides next to me.

I grunt in response.

A small contingent of summer realm soldiers cluster outside my study door, their eyes wary as they part for us to pass.

Queen Aurentia's back is to us as we enter, her gaze on the snowy courtyard. "It's been so long since I've visited winter." She presses a palm to the glass. "I'd almost forgotten what it is to be cold." Turning, she walks to us, her lilac coat pulled tight around her.

"Would you care to explain Tavaran's incursion now or later?" I put the bite of winter into my tone.

"Now." She folds her hands in front of her. "I sent Tavaran through the border—thank you for returning him unharmed, by the way."

"We aren't needlessly cruel in the winter realm, no matter what the summer realm propaganda says," Gareth bites out.

I cut to the heart of the matter. "Why did you break the truce?"

Her silver eyes lower, and a tired sigh flows from her. "I felt I had to. But we do not seek war." Her gaze meets mine again. "I sent Tavaran to capture your changeling—"

"My mate, you mean."

She nods. "Forgive me. Yes, your mate. After you had left Byrn Varyndr, I began having strange dreams. At first, I believed they were memories of the last war resurfacing. I ignored them, and they seemed to fade. But the night before the incursion, I had one so vivid, so real, that I realized the dreams weren't memories. They were new. Your mate appeared in them, but she was ... different. It was then I understood the dreams were prophetic. They were of the *coming* war. The disappearances, your mate, the king beyond the mountain—all of it was linked. And my dreams foretold that if the king beyond the mountain was able to capture your mate, then it would set all of the death and destruction that I saw—" She touches her temple. "In here, in motion. So, I attempted to stop it by bringing Taylor back to Byrn Varyndr where she would be safe, and I ordered Tavaran to use any means necessary."

Gareth crosses his arms over his chest. "You expect us to believe you violated a hard-won treaty over a *dream*?"

"It is the truth. Make of it what you will. I have no intentions to break the treaty or start a war with your realm. I only wanted to keep her safe and away from the king beyond the mountain." She turns back to the window. "But my spies tell me I was too late, and that perhaps our incursion served as the distraction Shathinor needed to take Taylor."

"You knew it was Shathinor and didn't tell me?" I don't bother hiding my contempt.

"Of course not." Her golden-crowned head lowers, her voice softening even more. "I only learned that after his destruction. I fear my sight has not been clear over the last few decades. The dreams were the only harbinger of knowledge, and they came too late."

I rub the bridge of my nose. "This can be remedied. My nobles will demand a formal apology from the summer realm for the incursion."

"Granted." She waves a hand.

"And we should collaborate on the equality decrees that Taylor seeks. If both the summer and the winter realms work toward banishing the old ways of division and strife, then the changelings and lesser fae wouldn't feel the need to follow a false leader like Shathinor. There would be no more threat of war."

She shakes her still-bowed head. "I'm afraid it's too late for that."

"What?" Gareth paces to the fireplace. "How is it too late? Shathinor has been defeated."

"His evil lives on." She turns, and her mouth is set in

a sad line. "The war is unavoidable. I have seen it, and it will come to pass."

"That doesn't make sense." Gareth shakes his head.

"How?" I bristle, foreboding creeping along my spine. "How does his evil live on?"

"In his heir." That's when I realize her sadness is for me.

"You mean my mate?" I growl.

She nods. "My dreams speak of Shathinor's bloodline, and I see a dark-winged warrior casting death onto a battlefield. It is her, your mate."

I keep my voice even, though my feral side demands I bare my fangs. "Taylor is not the same as her father."

"Perhaps not, but it doesn't change what I have seen, what I still see." She looks through me, her silver eyes haunted.

A knock at the door is followed by Brannon's voice. "Taylor is ready."

"We will discuss this later." I roll my shoulders. "But nothing you can say will stop me from crowning Taylor as queen of the winter realm. She is my mate. I know her. I know the good that lives in her along with her father's bloodline. She will never commit his evil, no matter what you may have seen."

Queen Aurentia doesn't respond, just stares with those sad eyes.

I turn and leave, Gareth at my back, and stalk past the summer realm soldiers. We stop outside the great hall, the room full of winter realm nobles, foreign dignitaries who could make it on such short notice, and plenty of winter realm citizens.

Gareth turns my crown back slightly to the left and smooths my black fur cloak. "Just a dream. She doesn't know Taylor. Not like we do."

"I put my life, my faith, my realm in her hands with no reservations." Nothing can change my bond with her. I will cherish Taylor until the end of Arin, and I know her heart is a shining thing, one that gives love to all who need it.

Gareth steps back and gives me a final once-over, but trouble creases his brow. "What is it?"

"Nothing." He shakes his head and glowers as if he's scolding himself on the inside.

"I can read you, Gareth. So you may as well get it off your chest before we enter the great hall."

"I don't want to spoil your ceremony."

I stare at him and cross my arms over my chest.

"Don't do that." He pulls my arms down and straightens my tunic. "Wrinkles."

I laugh, half at him and half at the joy welling up in me as I contemplate seeing Taylor in her mating dress. "Quick now, I can't keep her waiting. Spit it out."

He curses himself, then says apologetically, "I just had a thought about the mate bond. About how it hasn't happened for anyone else in the realm."

I sober. "I've thought about it, too. I intend to consult with Branala on it as soon as possible after the ceremony." I put a hand on his shoulder. "We will find your mate. I swear it."

"Don't intend to get on it too soon after the ceremony." He smiles, the gloom fading away. "I think you'll be quite busy for a few days with your mate."

Just the thought of the filthy things I intend to do to her sends a jolt of need through me. "Let's go." I nod at the soldiers to open the doors.

The entire room stands as I enter, a sea of faces turning to look as I stride toward the throne. The crowd murmurs, nobles and commoners sharing their excitement for the royal mating. This, above all, is the thing that can bring my realm into an even more stable existence. More than that, I want everyone to know that my mate is without equal and totally, unequivocally *mine*.

Branala stands at the top step, just aside from the silver throne, her hair plaited in a rope and the Book of Ancients laid out before her. The Phalanx lines the stairs on each side, my most trusted warriors dressed in silver armor or simple black.

When I reach my place at the front, I turn and face the crowd. They all bow or curtsy, but I'm not interested in them. My gaze is firmly fixed on the doors at the back of the great hall. Thousands turn and wait for my mate, their curiosity coloring the air. Gareth takes position beside me, and I know he's scouring the crowd for threats and to ensure our most important invitees are in attendance.

Queen Aurentia enters through a side door and, after a quick nod of deference, she takes a seat to the side.

"Ready?" Gareth asks.

"Eager." I clasp my hands in front of me. She's almost here. I can feel her nerves through the bond. "*I can't wait,*" I whisper to her.

"*Shhh!*" she shoots back. "*Trying to concentrate here.*"

I laugh even though it gains several stares.

Gareth clears his throat. "Looks like every diplomat who could make it here in time did. I see plenty of good alliances out there."

I can't tell if he's chattering about politics because he wants to or because he's trying to keep me calm. Either way, he doesn't stop until the doors finally begin to open.

I straighten and stare.

When she appears, I send every bit of my excitement down the bond, skittering along our connection like a wildfire.

She meets my gaze, her sparkling eyes the most beautiful blue in all of Arin. My heart seems to beat triple time as she walks toward me, her gown like a winter's dream of white lace and gray spidersilk with a white fur cloak trailing behind.

It's as if the entire room draws in a breath, shocked by the gorgeous queen who must surely be straight from the Glowing Lands. Her hair is loose and wavy, perfect for my fingers. It's a shame her dress is so beautiful, because I intend to rip it off the moment I get her alone after the ceremony.

She climbs the steps, her eyes locked with mine.

With her at my side, I am the most blessed king Arin has ever known.

She stops beside me, and I can't help but take her hand and kiss it.

Branala clears her throat. "My lord."

We both turn to face her as the guests take their seats.

Taylor's hand shakes as I hold it, and Branala begins reciting the ancient liturgy, the words of binding. Magic begins to sparkle in the air around us, blue and white flickers that dance as our bond becomes visible.

"You put all other queens to shame."

Her cheeks redden, and she sneaks a look at me from the corner of her eye. *"You murdered my panties the second I saw you."*

My low growl stops Branala, who gives me a scolding glare. I force myself to calm and nod for her to go on.

She shakes her head but continues reading.

"You are going to get a spanking for that, little one."

Her eyes widen, but I can sense her interest tickling down the bond.

"My queen is far naughtier than I ever imagined." I squeeze her hand. *"Thank the Ancestors."*

Her cheeks brighten even further as the magic intensifies, Branala's words sealing our bond for all to see.

When she finishes, we turn to face the crowd, and Gareth brings forth Taylor's crown.

"That's for me?" She puts one hand to her mouth. "Delantis." Her eyes water. "It's perfect."

"Fit for a queen." I take the silver circlet with the soulstone diadem and place it on her head.

"More to the right," Gareth whispers.

I smile and adjust it as the magic swirling around us intensifies.

When Taylor looks up, her eyes sparkling and her mating mark practically glowing, my heart feels like it could burst.

I raise her hand. "Your queen, Taylor Gladion."

A roar goes up and applause breaks out.

She smiles, but then it fades.

"What?" I face her, blocking her from the crowd and cupping her cheek. "What's wrong?"

The guests quiet.

"The curse." She squints at the magic. "Don't you see it?"

I turn and stare at the blue and white sparks, the wisps of bond magic. "No."

"The dark is there, staining it. I can *feel* it, like oil on water." She reaches toward it. "Look." A tendril of her dark magic flows from her fingertip.

The guests gasp, and Gareth yells for calm.

A thicker wisp of darkness appears from the maelstrom, one I didn't see until Taylor pulled it forth.

I tense. "Be careful."

"It can't hurt me. It's part of me." She opens her palm, and the darkness thickens, flowing into her from the shimmery circle. It grows lighter and lighter, the sparks turning into stars, the hues growing even more vibrant, our bond in its full glory.

When she pulls the last tendril inside herself, the magic bursts in an explosion of light, and a ripple cascades outward with a boom.

She falls back into my arms, her eyelashes fluttering.

"Taylor." I pick her up. "Are you all right? Taylor!"

She opens her eyes, and her lips turn up into a luscious smile. "That was kind of wild."

I kiss her, sealing our mate bond and anointing her as queen of the winter realm.

Branala's voice rises, silencing the chatter in the room. "The ceremony is now concluded. All hail the king and queen!"

A cheer goes up, but confusion still reigns in the hall.

"Handle it," I bark to Gareth as I hurry past with my queen in my arms.

"But you must attend the feast and the—"

"I said handle it," I call back as I dodge well wishers and dash down the center aisle. Once free of the great hall, I waste no time getting to our bedroom and slam the door behind us.

"What was that?" I lay her on the bed.

"I don't know. I just saw all that dark power there for the taking, and I wanted it." She covers her face with her hands. "Does this mean I really am evil?"

"No." I grab the front of her beautiful dress and rip it in half.

She yelps. "You're going to be in so much trouble with Cecile and Nadian for that!"

"I'll take whatever trouble comes as long as you are mine." I shred her panties and free myself from my black pants. With a hard thrust, I'm inside her, and she claws at my chest.

"More," I demand and grab her shoulder, holding her in place as I spread her legs even wider, claiming what's mine.

She arches for me, her pink nipples ripe for the taking. I suck one hard peak into my mouth as she grabs my hair, yanking the strands as she moans and writhes beneath me like the goddess she is.

I can't be gentle, can't take my time with her. I need to soak her with me, to let everyone know that we are bound body and soul.

Licking my thumb, I press it to her clit, and her heady

scent of arousal grows. I run a hand through her hair and pull, watching as she lets herself go, her soft body perfect against my hard one.

My control is gone, and I can't resist biting her. When I sink my fangs into her mating mark, she comes wildly, her legs shaking as I bury myself deep inside her warmth and coat her with my seed.

I roar to the tops of the granite turrets, my soul forever bound to hers, my heart in her hands, and my kingdom at her feet.

EPILOGUE I

"Take it all off." The magic pulls at my dress as Selene dances around a roaring blue fire, her naked body reflecting the flames.

"This is ..." I gape as Delantis sways into view, her nudity putting her (frankly amazing) rack on full display. "What are you *doing*?"

"Just go with it." Delantis howls at the moon and dances away, her hips in tune to a distant drumbeat as her gryphon prances along behind her.

The magic twirls around me, shimmying and sparkling under the full moon. "No one will see."

"This is insane."

"Take it off!" Selene cries from the other side of the wide bonfire.

"Peer pressure." I pull my tunic over my head and drop my skirt but keep my panties in place.

"Prude." The magic frowns but leaves me alone to swirl around the fire.

Delantis grabs my hand and pulls me along with her,

the drumbeat seducing me as the moon glows high above, the otherworld dark all around us. I dance, swaying as we trample the grass underfoot and raise our arms to the sky, howling like wild animals as the music grows louder.

I let my wings out, my back aching as they unfurl.

"Yes," the magic hisses and holds out its hand, blowing onto its palm as if sending me a kiss. A sparkling wind lifts me into the air, and I soar around the fire, wheeling and shooting up into the night sky. Delantis's gryphon joins me, the two of us racing and chasing each other as the others laugh around the fire below. My heart expands, the dark chambers working together with the light.

"*Having fun?*" Leander's voice ripples down the bond.

I flap harder and pinch Delantis's tail before dropping toward the ground. The eagle head caws, and she chases me as I giggle.

"*A little,*" I tell him.

"*Just a little? What, exactly, are you females doing in the otherworld?*"

Delantis's gryphon soars past, its tail whipping out and yanking my panties away. We're wild and free, naked and a little crazed.

"*We're just doing girl stuff, you know.*" I pull my wings close and plummet downward, Delantis chasing me and nipping at my heels with her beak.

"*Mmhmm.*" He doesn't sound convinced.

I open my wings and the wind catches me and drops me to the emerald grass. "*Don't worry.*"

"*I have to worry. The bed is cold. I'm snapping at*

everyone. *I pondered removing one of my noble's heads earlier, simply because he spoke out of turn. I need my mate.*"

"*I'll be back soon.*"

"*When?*"

"*Soooooon,*" the magic croons down the bond.

I shiver. "*That's creepy. Like someone listening to my phone calls.*"

"*Stop worrying, winter king. She will return when she is ready.*"

He growls, his feral coming through loud and clear. "*Wily magic. She better be back here in my bed, safe, within the week, or I will come there myself and rip out your—*"

His voice cuts off as the magic titters with laughter. "Wrong number."

"Naughty." I fall to the grass and splay my arms over my head as I stare at the swirling sky above. "*I love you. I'll be home soon, promise.*"

"*Fine,*" he grumbles. "*I will wait. Impatiently.*"

Selene collapses beside me, then Delantis falls on my other side, her gryphon curling up next to her.

The magic turns into a faun, its deer-like ears twitching as it pulls out a lute and begins to play softly.

"Secrets," the faun whispers. "Tell me yours, my queen, and I shall tell you mine."

"I don't have any." I yawn.

"You have plenty."

"I want to know about the royal mating. Is Leander as kingly as he looks, eh?" Selene elbows me.

I blush down to my toes.

"It's just us girls." The magic morphs into a female faun, bare-breasted and beautiful.

"I can't talk about that."

"Sure you can!" Delantis grins. "My mate could barely keep up with my appetite. I think he went to the Ancestors simply to escape my lusty desires."

"Oh, I've had my share of males." Selene cackles. "I've sat on so many faces that I can only remember a few."

"TMI." I cover my face.

"TMI." Selene's voice sobers. "Is that why you brought Taylor here, magic? The true reason? To give her TMI?"

The lute stops. "Too soon for such conversation." She starts playing again, louder this time. "First, let us make merry."

I turn to the magic. "Is it about the future? About the war?"

She stops on an off note. "You know of the war?"

I sigh and lie back on the grass. "I don't know for sure, but I can feel it."

"Feel what?" Delantis rises on her elbow.

I tell the truth that has been haunting me, the one that wakes me in the night and has Leander comforting me with soothing touches. "Death. It seems like it waits with bated breath, ready to pounce." I flex my hand and call forth a black flame. "I can feel it, like a deep inhale before diving beneath the surface. I've sensed it ever since the Gray Mountains."

Selene clacks her teeth together. "Taste it, I can. Dark things know of what you speak."

The magic sighs as if it's tired, the exhaustion bone-deep, but continues its song. "First, make merry. Then, secrets and darkness and prophecy."

"And bones?" Selene asks hopefully.

"And bones." The magic nods.

"Do not fear." Delantis grabs my hand. "You have allies, more by the day. Whatever comes, keep them close."

I let out a breath and push the worries to the back of my mind. The magic is right. We must grab our pleasures while we can. Tomorrow is not promised, and each day with my mate is a singular joy. "As long as I have Leander, I can weather any storm."

"Yes, Leander." Selene grins. "Let's get back to him. Does he mate like a beast or a gentlefae? Does he ride you like a dragon? Stroke you like the kindest breeze? Rage inside you like a monster? Whisper sweetness into your ear? Pull your hair? Tell, tell, *tell!*"

The lute plays, the sky glitters, and I let myself sink into the emerald grass of the otherworld. I turn to Selene, mischief in the air between us, and ask, "How much time do you have?"

EPILOGUE II

A pile of stone shifts, the rock crumbling as a figure rises from the destruction. Under the moonless night, he creeps along the ruins of the mountaintop cavern, bones crunching beneath his feet as he struggles to find a way out of the debris of rock and death.

It takes time, but eventually he climbs from the pit and stands atop the cold, dark mountain, the valley spreading out below. Some soldiers still dwell there, campfires burning in the night. They didn't go back to their realms. Not all of them, anyway. Enough remain. Enough to start again.

But he can't lead them. Not as he is.

His snakelike tongue darts out, tasting the air. The winter king has gone, returned to his realm, assured that the war was thwarted.

He turns and looks down at the throne room, at the exact spot where his father was turned to nothing more than ash. Though he never loved Shathinor, never cared for him at all, he knows that he cannot lead without him.

But he's gone, his physical form utterly destroyed by that bitch of a sister.

Cenet reaches inside his tunic, past the brand of the twisted tree, and snags the golden chain that hangs around his neck. Pulling it free, he peers at the phylactery. It emits a crimson glow in the dark night, a promise of things to come.

Carefully, he unscrews the top. Even more carefully, he lifts the vial to his lips. Closing his eyes, he drinks his father's blood.

And when he opens his eyes ...

ABOUT THE AUTHOR

Lily Archer believes in fairies, mermaids, and fierce fae warriors. Armed with nothing more than her imagination and a well-worn MacBook, she intends to slay the darkest beasts of the fantasy worlds and create true love where none seemed possible.

Please sign up for my newsletter to receive alerts when I have a new release.

www.lilyarcherauthor.com

Printed in Great Britain
by Amazon

18553303R00330